THE SPIRITS OF
SRON DUBH

The Fifth Book
of Dubious Magic

In loving memory of my Mum & Dad, and May.

For my Ileach family and friends,

and, as always,

for my darling Muse Meredith.

Published by *Meredian Pictures & Words 2018*
Ballina, Australia

CONTENTS

CONTENTS (Continued)

1 CUTS OF THE CANE

"Aiden McCrory! Come to the front of the class!"

"Why Miss? I havenae done anything wrong."

"You're willful and disobedient! Come to the front of the class, I said!"

"Yes, Miss," he said quietly.

As the boy shuffled forward, he felt the faces of the others in the room turned toward him. Some, he sensed, were nodding in approval. Others radiated their own fear. Their features were vague and indistinct – the only person who mattered was the white-haired schoolmistress.

"Hold out your hands. Both of them!" she demanded.

Aiden knew his hands were shaking as he obeyed. He could see his soft white palms trembling.

"Let this be a lesson to all of you," said the teacher as she flexed her cane.

As young McCrory got to the front of the room he heard a female voice he didn't recognise from somewhere behind him murmur, "No..."

Another voice, male and also unfamiliar, came from the back of the room saying, "This isn't right."

"To all of you, I said, and I meant it!" snapped the schoolmistress.

She slashed the cane down from behind her shoulder. The arc of the rattan was a white blur. There was a sharp crack. The thin cane sliced through the boy's hands, severing them both completely, just past the wrists. The gory spray spattered the blackboard, but not a drop sullied her starched blouse or grey woolen skirt.

The ten-year-old Aiden McCrory fell to his knees screaming, watching his blood pouring from the stumps of his hands. It formed a pool on the

*timber floor of the classroom. Young Aiden watched, horrified, as the pool
spread rapidly, seeping down through the cracks between the floorboards.
The blood spread to, but didn't touch, the teacher's high-buttoned boots.
He felt his heart fluttering in his chest.*

In his hotel bed, the sixty-three year old Aiden McCrory clenched his fists
in his sleep. His heart stopped beating – his brain convinced there was no
blood left in his body to pump.

A few miles away, Jacinta Parrish (better known as 'Jazz') sat up sharply.
"No…" she said softly into the darkness of her room.

The pretty blonde engineer got out of bed and pulled a thick gown around
the shoulders that she realised were trembling. It wasn't just from the cold
Scottish island air, she knew.

Jazz pulled the curtain aside slightly and looked out. Moonlight illuminated the nearby distillery where she was currently employed. The dreams
had started since just before she came to the island, and there was a distressing sameness to them.

There were two recurring themes. Some were about being somehow
trapped, and threatened with fire. Many others, like this latest nightmare,
involved a school that she sensed was on or near the site of the distillery.
But the distillery had been there for years – she'd been told that when she
first arrived to redesign the building's water reticulation system. Was the
school in her dreams something from the past, or something else?

She hadn't remembered a lot of the dreams upon waking, but this one was
vivid enough for more details than usual to stick. She didn't recognise the
boy, but as she gazed out into the night the blonde knew that the image of
his severed hands spinning through the air would stay with her for a long
time to come.

On the other side of the planet, John B. Stewart's afternoon nap had ended
abruptly. He gripped the arms of his overstuffed chair and looked around.
The Waramanga cottage he called home was empty. "I'm really getting
to hate this. That was the worst yet," he said. "I wish I knew what was
behind these bloody bad dreams."

He stretched uncomfortably and stood up. He ran a tired hand through his shaggy curls. In the months since a blow to the head had triggered a peculiar magical power – his wishes came true, albeit often in unpredictable ways – he'd become used to strange dreams. Recently though, they were different.

He couldn't say that they were darker. Many of the dreams he'd had since his collision with a poker machine had been of smoke on the water and fire in the sky. But these new ones were more threatening – almost like they were deliberately intimidating. Fire that wasn't distant, but close and dangerous and somehow personal.

And the school. The damned school. With that governess, or teacher or whatever she was. He could remember no details about her beyond the striking white hair and the air of absolute authority. This latest nightmare underscored the ruthlessness of that authority.

John B. Stewart wasn't a man intimidated by authority. Or ruthlessness, and he'd seen a bit of that in recent months. What he'd seen in his sleep – what he'd seen happen to that boy he didn't recognise – that made John B. angry. When he wished he knew what was behind the dreams, the wizard had the steely conviction that he would find out and that somebody would be called to account.

Back in the U.K. '*Scottish Member of Parliament Mr. Aiden McCrory died in his sleep*,' the newspaper said. It didn't mention that he died screaming.

.o0o.

2 WHAT'S TO BE SEEN

Effie Lindsay sat on a wicker chair at the door of her cottage, looking out to sea. Her late husband had built the little porch so that she could watch in two directions. One way lay the bay sometimes called Loch a'Chnuic that was edged by the gloomy promontory Sron Dubh. Gaelic for 'dark point', the name was apt for the short finger of black rock that jutted out, pointing the way to the Irish coast. A turn of the head away was a view over the village that shared the name of the point. Her cottage sat on one edge of the little hamlet.

Little happened in the village of Sron Dubh that Effie didn't notice. She often didn't like what she saw, though, and for her own peace of mind would frequently spend her time watching for seals, otters and various sea birds. It was a clear morning, and with the aid of her trusty binoculars she could see right across the bay to the Ardmore islands.

Today she was particularly watching the distant Eilean Craobhach. The name translated into English meant 'tree-covered island' but it was obviously a very old name for what was now a very bare outcrop. Or perhaps it had been meant ironically a long time ago. As usual the island was well populated with birds, on the rocks and in the air above.

The squeak of her garden gate alerted Effie to the arrival of visitors. She gave no sign of even glancing momentarily away from her binoculars, but nodded in off-hand greeting to her sister April.

"Morning Effie," said April.

"Morning April. Good morning Auld Wullie."

An odd quirk of Sron Dubh was that many, indeed most of the men of the village were christened William after their father (and grandfathers, and great-grandfathers and… well, you get the idea). In order to distinguish them and avoid confusion, every 'Wullie' had his own nickname. April's husband was Auld Wullie Bromleigh. Presumably that hadn't been his nickname as a boy, but that was so long ago that nobody could remember.

"Effie," replied Auld Wullie with a nod as he closed the gate. He was a man who was noted for saying little, and was presumed to think much.

At the sound of the gate closing, Effie finally deigned to put her field glasses down and turned to talk to her visitors. "I'd ask ye in for a cup o' tea and a biscuit, but I've no' been tae the shop and I've no' enough tae go around, ye ken."

Auld Wullie had many years experience of his sister-in-law's hospitality. "We ken, aye," he said levelly.

If April was in any way bothered, she didn't show it either. She was more generous in nature than her older sister – the middle one of three – but in truth that wasn't hard. "Never ye mind, Effie. We're just passin' and I thought tae say 'hello'. Have ye seen the paper?"

The youngest sister knew perfectly well the answer to that question. All three of the women were voracious readers and all would immerse themselves in the local newspaper from cover to cover on the morning it was issued. Their fields of particular interest varied, but every article was at least scanned.

"Of course I have," replied Effie. "We'll be having tae vote for a new Member of Parliament."

"Shame about auld McCrory. He was a decent man," said April. She sounded genuine, if not particularly upset.

"Och, he was bloody useless."

April smiled at her sister's blunt assessment. "He was a politician. They're all useless."

A thoughtful look crossed Effie's face. "Paper didnae say owt about why he was here. What was he doing, coming tae the island? We only ever see him nigh on election time and that's over a year away."

April replied, "Jessie at the Bingo says he'd come tae see the Reverend's lass. Party business so Jess says. She's in the local branch, ye ken. Only there tae keep up wi' gossip of course."

Studiously keeping out of the conversation, Auld Wullie looked out to sea while the sisters spoke. He didn't seem to need the binoculars to become absorbed in the view.

"Terrible gossip, that woman," said Effie.

"Aye, true," agreed April.

"Can't abide her, myself."

"No a bad source o' information, I've found."

"Oh, aye." The three sisters valued any such sources, however reluctantly they'd admit it.

April continued. "Seems the lass is likely tae take auld McCrory's place, assuming she can get herself elected."

There was a long silence as all three looked out to sea.

"Storm brewing, ye ken," said Effie quietly.

Auld Wullie folded his arms. "Aye."

There was scarcely a cloud to be seen.

Effie picked up her binoculars and peered out into the bay.

"Yon Sith Dubh's out. I wonder what he's up tae," she said.

A small dark figure could be seen paddling a tiny currach in the direction of the Ardmores. The little boat, made of canvas stretched over a wooden frame, was barely big enough to hold even its diminutive occupant, but it made remarkably good speed.

"Never know, wi' the wee fella," observed April.

"It willnae be anythin' guid," said Effie balefully.

"Hard tae say, wi' that yin," was April's much milder response. She was clearly less distrustful of the man known as the Black Elf.

If Auld Wullie had an opinion on the matter he kept it to himself (as usual) but there was a look of concern in his eyes as he watched the progress of the currach.

After a minute or two of silent contemplation April turned to her sister and said, "We'll be off then. Mind how ye go, Effie."

"Aye, and you too," her sister replied. It was probably as close to an affectionate exchange as the two had been known to share in over sixty years, and perhaps a measure of the vague sense of foreboding both felt.

Auld Wullie Bromleigh took his leave of his sister-in-law with a polite nod, which was answered by a small wave of the hand. Effie's attention was once again focused on the view through her field glasses.

As the old couple wandered back into the village April spoke to her husband. "I know ye see things most people dinna."

"Aye, as do ye, in yuir own way," he replied.

"There *is* trouble comin', ye think?" she asked, seeking confirmation of her own misgivings.

"Trouble's already wi' us. What's coming is something different."

April looked at the man she'd spent the last fifty-something years of her life with. "Different better, or different worse?" she asked.

"Things have a way o' getting worse before they get better," said Auld Wullie. He quietly took his wife's hand and held it gently as they walked on towards another cottage, out on another edge of the village.

.oOo.

3 SOMETHING STIRRING IN THE NIGHT

Wilko glanced at the clock beside his bed. Nearly seven o'clock. The golf game had finished later than anticipated, but he'd managed a win so he didn't really mind. The experience of playing in Hawaii had boosted his confidence. That was reflected in the standard of his play, and in turn, in his results.

It probably wouldn't last, he mused, that being the nature of golf. Thereby of course he set himself up to hasten the inevitable dip in form. The power of positive thinking was an unknown science to the Tasmanian, except when he was positive something would go wrong.

He folded the bright orange shirt he'd been wearing and laid it neatly in the laundry hamper to wash tomorrow. Sunday was washing day. Time for a quick shower, then catch a cab over to the Daramalan Devastators' Club.

Tonight was the night of John B. Stewart's 'Farewell To Work' drinks. Having recently come into money – quite a bit of it, apparently – Stewart had at last decided or perhaps recognised that he was not best suited to a career in the Public Service. A small circle of friends had been invited to the Club to raise a glass or seven to mark the occasion.

Wilko (Robert Wilkes according to his passport but few people addressed him as such) had been a good friend of Stewart's since they'd both arrived in Canberra to work in the same office some years earlier. They'd worked together and travelled together. Wilko had been present on the night that John B. ran his head into a poker machine at the Devastators' Club.

He steadfastly repudiated Stewart's claims of magical ability though, despite the fact that he'd been closely involved in the series of adventures that had befallen the self-proclaimed wizard since that night. Too closely, in his opinion, having been shot at and threatened on numerous occasions, and been otherwise too close to a series of weird, un-natural and downright dangerous events.

Still, the travel had been interesting, and he'd met some interesting people, he mused as he stepped out of his golf pants.

Right on cue, his mobile phone rang. Despite being the only person in the room, innate modesty compelled him to pull his trousers up before answering the call.

It was Jazz – coincidentally the very person who'd been at the forefront of Wilko's mind as he contemplated the interesting people he'd met while travelling with John B. Stewart. Of course, John B. would have said that it was no coincidence.

"Hello mate!" said the Tasmanian warmly. He was very fond of the English girl, more so than he let on, even to himself. "How's sunny Scotland?"

"Actually, it is pretty sunny here this morning, which is nice. Hello to you, too. How are you going, mate?"

Jazz had travelled the world extensively working as an engineer, and had a talent for 'fitting in' wherever she went. She slipped into Aussie vernacular seamlessly when talking to Wilko.

It took only a few moments of small talk for Wilko to look at the phone in some concern and say, "I know I can't see you, but you sound tired."

"I am, to tell the truth. It's barely eight in the morning and I've been awake for hours. I'm not sleeping very well. Listen, this is going to sound a bit strange, and I'm sorry, but when you see John B. next, can you ask him to get in touch with me please? Just a quick call, and I'll ring him back on your phone so it shouldn't cost you so much."

While he appreciated her concern for his finances, a small part of the Tasmanian was a little put out by the feeling that it was Stewart she really wanted to talk to.

"I can give you John's number, if you like. You can call him direct."

"John B. has a mobile phone now? That's a surprise."

"I think that things are changing for him. Hang on while I get you his number…"

"I'd really much rather talk to you, mate, but thanks."

"Really?" he asked, and then mentally kicked himself, unfairly thinking he sounded rather pathetic.

"Yes, really. I love talking to you, you dill. But I know there's stuff you don't like talking about."

 Wilko smiled, reassured although he wouldn't admit it. "Could I just pass on a message?"

"I thought about that, but it's to do with a dream. It's weird and I know you don't like weird."

"I'm getting more used to it than I'd like," was his wry response.

"Hawaii wasn't what you'd hoped, eh?"

"Some of the golf was good, the scenery was beautiful, and some of the people were nice."

"And you got to put the pedal to the floor in a Mustang!"

"Well, yeah. That was good. But people being killed because of politics – I don't like reading about it, far less being so close to it."

"I'm sorry, mate. If I were there I'd give you a hug. Might not make it better but it might cheer you up," Jazz said with genuine feeling.

 Wilko smiled. "I'm sure it would, thanks." He realised he truly meant it.

"To tell you the truth, mate, it'd cheer us both up."

"Are you okay?" He'd caught a very disturbing edge to Jazz' voice.

"Ye… well, truthfully no. Not really. These dreams are really getting to me. Nasty, and getting nastier."

"Nightmares, you mean?"

"I guess you'd have to call them that. Being trapped in burning buildings, or being in this really awful school. I watched someone be killed in one dream the other night."

The smile had gone from Wilko's face. He'd seen death at close range a couple of times recently, and didn't like being reminded of the experiences, even by Jazz. But his own discomfort only added to his sympathy for the clearly distressed engineer.

"Grab a pen, and I'll give you John's number…"

*

It was true that John B. Stewart now owned a mobile phone, in defiance of his long-standing declared aversion to "the wretched bloody things". That didn't mean he was particularly ept at using it though. Not willfully inept, but perhaps unconsciously.

That explains why it wasn't until quite late in the evening, when Wilko asked whether he'd heard from Jazz, that Stewart realised his phone was on 'silent'.

"Oh bugger! I've missed two calls from her!" the wizard exclaimed. He turned to his Tasmanian buddy and asked, "What was she calling about, do you know?"

Wilko sighed, put his beer down on the bar, and did his best to explain what Jazz had said about her bad dreams. He knew better than to think that John B. might dismiss her concerns, but was surprised by how disturbed Stewart seemed to be.

The look on John B.'s face was also noticed from across the room by Elizabeth McKew. The relationship between the recently divorced Elizabeth and John B. was a matter of considerable conjecture among their friends and workmates. They'd worked together for a few years, and had a history of cheerful flirting that nobody had ever taken seriously. Then her marriage to Sonny Dance had fallen apart to the surprise of most (who hadn't seen the carefully hidden tensions). Ostensibly Stewart and Elizabeth were still Just Good Friends, but those closest to them, like Wilko, could see what was developing. Even if neither of the two admitted it.

 Elizabeth excused herself from the conversation she'd been in and went to the bar.

"Are you okay, babe?" she asked, laying a hand on John B.'s arm.

"Mm? Yeah. Yeah, thanks Q," he said quietly, using the nickname only he was allowed to call her by. "Wilko's just been telling me some news about a friend of ours."

"Anyone I know?"

"Jazz Parrish. English girl we met in Central Australia," Stewart replied.

 Q nodded. "You've both told me a bit about her. What's happened?"

 Wilko looked uncomfortable as he answered, "She's working in Scotland. She rang to say she's been having some really bad dreams."

"Well, that's certainly not nice…" she began.

 John B. cut her off, not rudely but deep in thought. "The disconcerting thing for me is that, from what Wilko's just told me, it sounds like I've been having the same dreams."

 Elizabeth and Wilko looked at each other in concern.

 The wizard continued. "I've got a really bad feeling that there's something nasty going on. Not just weird, but nasty. Excuse me for a bit, folks – I'm going to go out into one of the clubrooms where it's quiet and give Jazz a call."

With that, he walked out of the main bar, looking at his phone with a creased brow.

"Now I know he's worried," said Wilko.

Elizabeth gave him a puzzled look.

"He didn't take his Scotch with him," the Tasmanian pointed out.

Fifteen minutes or so had passed before John B. rejoined his party. A glass of good single malt firmly in hand, he was full of chat and bonhomie. Q and Wilko's quiet questions were met with a quick low, "Later."

Accepting this, a bit reluctantly, the two joined in the general cheerfulness of the occasion. John B. was well liked in the office. He took neither himself nor the job too seriously, which was a refreshing change from some of the Career Public Servants who made up a good percentage of Canberra's population. Those who'd come to the Devastators' this evening mostly shared his attitude, and would genuinely miss the unkempt figure with the wardrobe-full of purple t-shirts.

Drinks, jokes and stories continued to flow freely for another hour or two before people started to drift out to seek taxis or buses. As is often the way with these things, when the first few departed it triggered a general exodus. It wasn't long before only Wilko and Q were left to keep company with John B.

Elizabeth returned from the bar with a round of drinks. She handed Wilko his beer, then clinked her wine glass against the whisky she'd just handed to John B.

"To your Great Escape," she said, smiling.

"Thank you, ma'am," replied the guest of honour.

"Now, tell us about the phone call," said Elizabeth, letting the cheeriness slip and the concern be revealed.

John B. was silent for a moment, gazing into his whisky as if envisaging its country of origin.

Finally he answered. "Jazz is pretty worked up. She can't explain why, but it feels like the nightmares are personal."

"All dreams are personal. They come from what's lurking inside our own head, good or bad," replied Q.

"These don't feel like they do. They feel like they're coming from… I don't know… outside, somehow. Like personal attacks. And what's really strange is that we're both copping the same stuff."

"What have you and Jazz got in common?" asked Q, applying her analytical mind to the matter.

After a moment's thought John B. replied, "Wilko."

"Thanks very much mate! You're not saying this is my fault, are you?"

"No, no. But that's the most honest answer I could think of. I mean, we both went through some of the same drama in the Outback that time, but so did you and Darren and as far as I know neither of you have been dreaming of fires in locked rooms or sociopath schoolteachers."

Wilko shrugged. "Certainly not that I can remember, but I sleep pretty deeply."

"Soundly, I'd say," observed John B.

"I do *not* snore!"

The Tasmanian was adamant that, as he'd never heard himself, he must sleep quietly. The truth was very different, as both of his companions could attest having tried to sleep in the same room or an adjoining one. Wilko asleep produced a remarkable range of sound effects, varying wildly in pitch, volume and character. The only person known to sleep peacefully through his nocturnal concert was Jazz, who'd been in an adjoining cell in an Alice Springs watch-house. It was to Jazz their collective thoughts returned.

"She's getting to the point where she's afraid to go to sleep, and that's not healthy, in a lot of ways," said Stewart. "Mate, I really think you need to get over there for her."

That provoked the soundless mouth movement known to his friends as 'Wilko's goldfish impression'. Eventually he got out the words, "Don't be ridiculous! How am I supposed to do that?"

"She's seriously upset. It's you she's called. How the hell can you *not* want to go to her?" said John B. sharply.

"It's not that I don't want to! For cryin' out loud, there's nothing I want to do more! But to just jump on the next plane to the UK, that takes the sort of money I can't just pluck out of thin air!"

"Q, you're brilliant at arranging travel deals at work. Do you reckon you could find a decent deal?"

"If I can't, nobody can," promised Elizabeth. John B. wasn't understating her administrative skills, and she was confident enough to acknowledge it.

Wilko shook his head. "You're probably right, but what with getting over to the UK, then getting over to this island Jazz is on, it's still going to cost a grand or two. I spent most of the reserves I had in Hawaii. I'd figured on keeping my financial head down for six months or so, and letting it build up again."

John B. sighed deeply. "So what you're saying is, if she's still in trouble in six months or so, then you'll go to her."

Wilko echoed the sigh, his frustration evident. "Well, yeah," he said awk- wardly.

"Right then. I've got the money – you know I had that little windfall…"

That was the term John B. had taken to using for his gaining possession of the substantial Swiss bank account formerly owned by the mad Russian scientist who'd kidnapped him months earlier.

He continued before Wilko could give voice to the inevitable protest. "Jazz is in strife. You want to help. So do I. I'll spring for your travel and you can pay me back in six months."

"I don't like borrowing…"

"And I don't especially like lending. Next to sex, money is potentially one of the worst things that can happen to a friendship. But I've got the very definite feeling that this is important. It's not a loan, it's an investment."

The Tasmanian sighed again. "I can't fault your logic. But I can't… I just don't…"

"Look mate, I know we don't talk about emotions much. We're blokes. It's part of the contract. But I'm not dense. Blind Freddy could see that Jazz means a bit to you, and that the feeling's mutual. For that matter, I got to be pretty fond of her myself when we were all out in the Centre together. Darling Elizabeth, can you please see what you can arrange to get both Wilko and I over there? If I can't use the money to help out a couple of mates when they need it, then what use is it to me, or anyone else?"

Q showed no reaction to 'darling Elizabeth' – she'd gone straight into organizational mode. If she had any thoughts about the merits or otherwise of John B.'s proposal she gave no sign of them. "I'll take care of it in the morning, okay? Wilko, be ready to leave on Monday or Tuesday. You might even find you've got some sort of paid leave still available. I did the forms before you went to Hawaii and I reckon there'll be something there for you."

"Why am I not surprised you know my personnel details better than I do? Okay, okay. Borrowing the money will probably keep me awake at night, but worrying about Jazz will already be doing that."

"Keeping *you* awake? That's a sure sign there's something wrong, mate," said the wizard with a smile.

'Given the dreams I've been having lately, and that Jazz has too apparently, you're not missing much,' was what John B. thought but didn't say.

.oOo.

4 SCENES FROM A VILLAGE

The mid-morning news crackled through the speaker of the Bakelite radio on the table beside Rose Ellison's chair.

The old woman sat patiently listening. Well, that may not be strictly true as 'patient' was a word seldom, if ever, used in connection with Rose Ellison. She grumbled, muttered, and generally passed editorial comment throughout the entire news bulletin.

As the announcer began to detail the day's weather forecast for Glasgow Rose reached over and switched the radio off. She looked down at the local newspaper on her lap.

"Well, Mister McCrory, ye wernae interestin' enough for yuir passin' tae make the news in Glasga, it seems."

April and Auld Wullie had not long departed after a 'casual visit' to the eldest of the three sisters. The gist of the conversation had been much the same as it had with Effie, right down to the disparaging comments and grudging acknowledgement of the value of Jessie at the Bingo as a source of information.

It seemed that all three of the sisters shared an uneasiness about the demise of their local MP, even if none could be sure why.

Rose picked up a magazine from her table, a 'true crime' detective magazine with a typically lurid and sensational cover. She read maybe a paragraph or two before her chin fell forward onto her chest and she began to gently snore.

She did a lot of her best thinking while asleep.

*

Less than a mile away, the Reverend Gordon Dotterel frowned over a heavy cloth-bound ledger. He was reviewing his service of the Sunday just past. More accurately, he was reviewing the data pertaining to the service: attendance, the contents of the collection plate, even who had sat where and been seen to speak to whom.

He tapped the tip of his ballpoint pen on the open page and studied what he'd just written. Lips pursed, he laid the pen down on the page he'd been working on and leafed back to a point a thumb-width earlier in the book.

There was a list of names. It was quite a long list. The reverend scanned the seventy-odd names. Then he turned back to the page where he'd left the pen and wrote down a dozen names. It was something that he did every week, and he was pleased to note that the list he wrote was getting shorter.

Faster progress would be better of course, but his faith was unwavering. He hummed an old hymn. A burly blonde man standing on the opposite side of the room grinned.

"Going well, Reverend?" he asked.

"The work of the Lord always goes well, DS, as you should know."

"How many left?"

"With the new arrivals in the village since Victoria's list, well, the list that my daughter *obtained*, I think seventeen."

The man addressed as DS smirked. "What about these new folks? The girl engineer and that manager fella. Should I deal with 'em?"

The reverend again tapped his pen. "The distillery – that vile instrument of Satan – that's what drawn them here. It will give me great pleasure to see it closed!"

"Yeah!" DS looked like the sort of man who'd be deeply unhappy at the prospect of closing a distillery, which only goes to show how misleading appearances can sometimes be. Instead he said, "Is there anything I can do to help?"

"Perhaps, my friend, perhaps. We'll give it another night or two."

*

The Manager's Office in the Sron Dubh distillery wasn't large. Very little connected with Sron Dubh was large, except perhaps the local inhabitants' sense of history. The office now occupied by Robbie Keith reflected both history and modesty of scale. The woodwork and paneling of the room were made of good Scots pine that age and the occupation of several heavy smokers had deepened to a rich dark honey colour.

There was enough room for three people to sit comfortably. Just. Blue-suited Robbie Keith sat behind his desk, tense in his leather chair. In two classic old tub chairs on the other side of the desk were the Office Manager Moraig McConnell and the recently hired consultant engineer Jacinta Parrish, known already to everyone as Jazz.

None of the three looked well. More specifically, none of the three looked like they'd had enough sleep for a while.

Jazz was a new arrival to the village, having arrived only a few weeks earlier to design and arrange installation of a new system to make efficient and creative use of the copious amount of steam the distillery's process- es produced. She was planning ways to provide comfortable year-round warmth in all of the workplaces in the small complex, and in time, she hoped, some of the workers' accommodation.

The 'big bosses' had brought in Robbie Keith after the sudden and unex- pected death of the long-time manager, who'd apparently succumbed to a heart attack in his sleep. Originally a Gloucester boy, he'd worked in some of the Highland distilleries and was good with both his product and his people.

The genuine local was Moraig McConnell. Her father had been a malt- man at Sron Dubh for years, like his father before him, turning the grains as they slowly opened on the malting floor heated by the fire of burning peat. Traipsing the malt room, they'd wielded the broad flat shovels until both men had carried the awkward deformity called 'monkey shoulder'

that was as much a badge of honour to their trade as a missing finger was
to a butcher.

But all of them were struggling. The loss of Keith's predecessor had hit
Moraig hard, not because she was especially close to him, but because it
meant she had a greater responsibility to assist the new boss in running
things as smoothly as possible. That had been difficult. She'd been cop-
ing with her own restless nights, but adding bad days to the equation was
tough.

And the days were bad. Increasingly so. Production was starting to slip,
and at an alarming rate. Staff were leaving. Staff who'd been loyal and
hard working. Some who, like Moraig, had family histories in the business. It wasn't that they were going to work for any of the other distilleries on Islay, or moving to the mainland. They were just… staying home.

Take Cranky Wullie McCaulkin, as placid a man as you'd want to meet
(hence his ironic nickname) – who'd manned the pot stills for fifteen of
his thirty-odd years. Cranky Wullie had walked into the office last Friday
morning shaking his head sadly.

"I'm sorry. I cannae do this any mair," he'd said.

"What do you mean, you can't do this any more?" Robbie had asked.
"What's the matter? Are you not well – can we do anything…?"

McCaulkin had shaken his big head slowly. "Sorry Mister Keith. I've
just got this… I cannae… it's… well, it's just not *right* any mair," he'd
said, and walked out.

The three figures in the office all sighed at once, almost in harmony.

"It's the dreams," said Moraig in a flat voice. "Night after night. Sometimes it's the fires o' Hell awaitin' tae claim me for bein' a part o' the Devil's work here. Other times it's tha' damned schoolteacher, over and over.
'Do what you're told, or you'll be punished!' she'll say, again and again.
It's maddening, right enough."

"Literally, I think," agreed Jazz. "No wonder people are quitting. I've only had it for the couple of weeks since I got here, but if you've all been suffering it for longer – well, like I said, I'm not bloody surprised at how things are going!"

"They started months ago. Been getting' slowly worse. More frequent, and just… worse." There was something chilling about the office manager's toneless voice, as though the life had been ground out of her.

"I don't understand," said Robbie Keith plaintively. "I'm not getting these dreams that everyone's talking about! I just can't sleep because I'm so worried about the business. The Board sent me over here to get things working properly again after… after poor Mister McIvor's passing, and all that's happened is the situation is getting steadily worse. I think I may have had one night where I dreamed about being back in school, but I don't remember anything. If I did, it was probably just a result of hearing everyone else talking about it. I don't know why…"

 Moraig interrupted the General Manager's nervous chatter. "You're not from around here, are you? Maybe whatever – *this* is, it only affects locals."

"What about me, though?" asked Jazz. "I'm from Stratford originally. I've been all over the world, sure, but this is my first time on Islay. And I'm getting these bloody nightmares, sure as hell. Sorry, Moraig – pardon the expression."

"I don't know," said McConnell with a shrug. "I wish I knew what it was, and how to make it stop." She meant what she said, but there was no enthusiasm in the words.

 A smile played across the engineer's face. "That reminds me," she said. "I've been in touch with a mate of mine. He's good with weird stuff. He's a wizard, kind of. I reckon his magic might be able to help."

"Magic?" said Moraig in surprise. Her voice became vague and distant. "I'm not sure… that would be *approved* of…"

.oOo.

5 DEPARTURES

The morning after the farewell party was a typical Sunday morning in Canberra suburbia. As lunchtime approached the sound of lawnmowers filled the air in the leafy precincts of Waramanga.

The one bedroom cottage owned by John B. Stewart was the venue for a hastily convened gathering of friends.

John B. sat his favourite comfortable overstuffed armchair. One hand held a cup of coffee, the other idly stroked the upholstery, echoing the movements he would have employed on the fur of his still much-missed Kat. There was still a veneer of the late Persian's white fur in parts of the cottage that Stewart had never had the heart to remove.

The wizard's housemate, Darren James Bond, sat cross-legged on the floor. He'd folded his long frame into the lotus position after furnishing their guests with coffee and shortbread. He'd been working at the *Mojo Tojo* (a hippie-themed Japanese restaurant) the previous night so had missed the event at the Devastators, but Stewart had quietly brought him up to speed on events in Islay, such as they were known.

The tall young man had gallantly offered his usual armchair to Elizabeth McKew. The recently divorced Elizabeth had been an infrequent visitor to the cottage prior to John B. and Wilko's Hawaiian excursion, but she knew enough to be unfazed by the peculiar living arrangements.

Whenever John B. was at home Darren slept in a makeshift bedroom under the big dining table. The draping of large tablecloths and quilts afforded him some privacy, reinforced by piles of books and boxes of antique weaponry surrounding the table.

On any occasion when Stewart was away for more than a few days at a time: work trips or holidays – the young man was welcome to move himself into the "real" bedroom. Darren was remarkably comfortable with the situation, and had made no effort to find a 'place of his own' since arriving at Waramanga months earlier.

John B., for his part, had come to accept his tenant gracefully. They had been friends since Darren's early teens, were both domestically undemanding, and importantly respected each other's privacy. Their friendship had deepened, rather than suffering from the friction which some observers expected.

One of those initially surprised had been Wilko. Then he had travelled with both of the housemates and realised the extent to which they shared a relaxed attitude to many things. Sometimes he wished he could adopt the same approach, but knew he just wasn't wired that way.

Now he sat on a kitchen chair he'd brought into the lounge, looking and feeling tense as plans were made – well, not so much 'made' as 'announced' by Elizabeth.

"There's a flight out on Tuesday evening. Canberra direct to Singapore, then to London, Glasgow and a little hop over to the airport on Islay. Glenegedale, it's called. All a bit messy, I'm afraid, but I thought quickest seemed the best option and any other route involved at least eight hours stay in Dubai or somewhere."

"Makes sense," agreed John B. "Darren, are you okay to mind the fort while I'm away?"

"Sure. I've got to work on my application to get into Uni, so having the place to myself will let me spread my stuff around while I get organized."

Wilko looked surprised. "Uni?" he asked.

"Yeah, I'm going to try to learn more about computers. I really found I was enjoying that research stuff I was doing in Alice Springs, and especially when you were stuck on that place down in Bass Strait."

That elicited a grin from John B. "Well, I'm glad you enjoyed it old friend, 'cos it certainly helped these two get me out of a very bad spot. Speaking of bad spots on small islands, that commute over to Islay sounds like it should work. Thanks, pretty lady."

"Mah pleasure, kind sir," replied Q in the Southern Belle voice she some-times affected. "Wilko, we'll have to go into the office tomorrow and do some paperwork before we go."

The Tasmanian nodded. "I've got some work I'd like to finish if I can – it'll probably take Monday and Tuesday. No bad thing – it might take my mind off whatever's happening with Jazz."

"Uh-huh," John B. acknowledged before steepling his fingers and address-ing Elizabeth. "I distinctly heard the word 'we' in there."

Q grinned. "You're not flying off without me this time, boys!"

*

Wilko might have been determined to put in a busy couple of days in the office to clear out his In tray, but Elizabeth McKew had a very different intention when she signed in on Monday morning.

First came the phone calls and paperwork to finalise the arrangements for the trip to Scotland. John B. was going to be entrusted with contacting Jazz while the other two were working, but the Tasmanian was quietly insistent that he would take care of that.

At the regular Monday 'team building' morning tea, Q made her big announcement. Not just that she was taking off on an overseas trip – she was quitting. Jaws dropped, and it took some moments before anyone could assemble a coherent sentence to ask, "Why?" No answer was forth-coming, just a demure and pretty smile. Even Wilko was caught com-pletely off-guard.

Elizabeth knew her leave entitlements. She would walk out the door at exactly sixteen minutes past three, take fifty-four days of accrued leave, and then officially cease to be employed by the Department. By 10 a.m. she had already packed her desk and handed in her official resignation letter.

At three o'clock she started to do the rounds of the office, saying her fare-wells to various members of the team. Tinkerbell in particular received a long and affectionate hug, which the big guy enjoyed, albeit a little awk-wardly. He knew Elizabeth was very recently divorced, wasn't sure how much that had to do with her announcement, and was (just quietly) a lot more shy with attractive brunette women than he ever let on.

The last stop on Elizabeth's final tour of the office was to see the boss, Ron Kaiser (more usually known as Kaiser Ron) and hand over the pass card that allowed her access to the building.

The Kaiser looked genuinely downcast. He'd meant what he said in his formal speech at Elizabeth's hastily arranged farewell lunch. He knew he was losing one of his best workers. He quietly acknowledged to himself that her administrative skills had kept his own office running smoothly. It was in appreciation of that fact that he'd restrained his normal impulse to gossip.

He turned her building pass over in his hand and said, "So let me get this straight. You've left Sonny to be with John Stewart?"

"No Ron, that's not straight. Not that it's really your business but I'll try to make it simple. Item 1 – I left Sonny. I'm sick of being intimidated and treated like a possession. Item 2 – I want to make my own decisions. Move on and work out what I want to do with my life. Item 3 – one of those decisions is that I want to be with John B. Stewart."

Kaiser Ron shook his head. His coiffure – a much-lacquered confection devised by his wife the creative hairdresser - wobbled slightly. "Whatever you say. Seems like a strange choice."

"To you maybe. Not to me. He treats me with respect. Courtesy. Care."

With a small chuckle Ron jokingly replied, "Is this the same John Stewart we're talking about?"

Elizabeth didn't laugh at the jest.

"Yes, it is. The man who cares about me. The man I care about. Goodbye Ron. I'm going to Scotland. Wherever I go next, it won't be here."

.o0o.

6 ANYTHING TO DECLARE?

It was late Tuesday afternoon.

Wilko was still in the office, busily finishing the last of the reports he'd wanted to complete before taking "leave of unspecified duration". He would have finished earlier, but for his 'quick phone call with Jazz'. She'd called after lunch (about a quarter to four in the morning in Scotland – another sleepless night) to finalise arrangements for the arrival on Islay of "her cavalry" as she called the trio "dashing to her aid".

The engineer had a hire car, and she'd be collecting them at the airport when they arrived. It should be at 9:45 in the morning, if everything went according to timetable. Wilko was privately sure that it wouldn't, but then he couldn't help his pessimism. Jazz was blithely confident that every-thing would work out because John B.'s magic would keep everything working smoothly.

The Tasmanian had shaken his head, bemused and vaguely irritated at the attitude. "You shouldn't encourage him!" he'd admonished.

"But it works. You know that – you've been there," she replied.

"It's coincidence. That's all. A lot of it, I'll concede that. You ought to be careful about how much faith you put in him."

Despite her extreme tiredness, Jazz chuckled down the phone. "You know mate – you sound jealous."

That left Wilko nonplussed. His mouth moved for a moment with no words coming out. Tinkerbell glanced over from his desk and wondered why 'the little guy' was doing his goldfish impression, but thought better of calling out to ask.

Jealous? Surely not! That was… that was…

Jazz responded to the silence down the phone.

"Hey, I was kidding," she said jovially, then quietly added, "I might want John B.'s magic to help, but it's you I want to have here with me."

"Oh…" was the best that Wilko could manage at first. Eventually he added, "Thank you."

"Thank *you*, for dropping everything and coming over." She giggled a little. "I'll try to make it worth your while, hey?"

Tinkerbell could see the deep blush, and really had to bite down hard on his curiosity, and the urge to eavesdrop.

If he hadn't resisted, he would have only heard Wilko say, "Um… ah… thanks. That'll be… um… great. But I just want to be sure you're alright."

"I will be, when you guys get here. Especially you."

It really had taken some time before Wilko could properly concentrate on finishing his report.

*

John B. and Q were sitting at a small table in the airport lounge bar. With Elizabeth doing the arranging, they'd arrived with plenty of time to spare. They were checked in, their luggage was entrusted to the hopefully tender care of the baggage handling staff, and now they could relax over a couple of drinks while they waited for the third member of the party to arrive.

Elizabeth put down her wine glass and leaned close to the wizard. In a quiet voice she said, "Listen – you don't, er, mind that I sort of invited myself along on this trip with you and Wilko, do you?"

John B. looked at her, genuinely surprised enough at the question to put down his own glass of good single malt. "Mind? Q, seriously, there is nobody in the world that I'd rather go see the world with!"

She smiled and took both of his hands in hers. "Why thank ya, kind sir," she said, affecting the Southern drawl they'd long jokingly used with each other. Then, much more seriously she looked him in the eyes and said, "You do know that I love you, don't you?"

John B.'s smile in response was broad, warm and gentle all at once. It started at his eyes and spread all over his face.

"Yeah, I'd kind of worked that out. You do know the feeling's mutual, don't you?"

Elizabeth's smile mirrored his. "I was kind of hoping…"

The rest of the sentence was cut off as he leaned even closer and kissed her.

"I've wanted to do that for a while," he admitted.

"Worth the wait?" she asked.

The best reply was to repeat the exercise, for long enough to make one older couple at a nearby table squirm uncomfortably, while another even older couple smiled a little wistfully.

Wilko could take his time arriving, as far as his travelling companions were concerned.

*

Of course, it wasn't long before he *did* arrive. By the time the Tasmanian strode into the lounge bar Q and John B. had gently ended the clinch they'd fallen into, and were sitting almost demurely sipping another round of drinks. Wilko did notice, though, that they were holding hands in a far more conspicuous manner than they had before.

He didn't notice the looks that the pair was getting from people at other tables.

There was just time for the new arrival to have a beer before they were called to board their flight.

A good percentage of their travel was to take place in darkness, which is a good way to spend a long aeroplane journey.

On the way from Singapore to London Q settled into a window seat, where she could watch either the night sky or the in-flight entertainment as the mood took her. John B. was less interested in the view outside. He listened to music, read a thick book on the history of Islay whiskies, and enjoyed the company of the green-eyed brunette beside him.

As the hours of darkness wore on, from the seat behind came the not-so-gentle sounds of Wilko sleeping. Worried flight attendants had been reassured that "it's alright – he always sounds like this". They'd walked away shaking their heads. The unhappy businesswoman in the seat beside him jammed her ear buds in as hard as possible, wrapped a scarf around her head, and pulled a wooly cap down over her ears. All of that helped less than the series of vodkas a sympathetic flight attendant kept delivering.

After several hours Elizabeth glanced at the wizard as he sat with head bowed and eyes closed. What sort of a man had she fallen for? Kind? Yes. Gentle? Yes. Eccentric. Yes. A wizard? Well, he thought so, and certainly things happened around him that weren't easily explained, however hard Wilko tried.

She gently stroked the back of John B.'s hand as she quietly said, "I wanted to know all about Sonny. And I did. But I realized that the more I learned the less there was to know about him. Does that make sense? You understand? There was nothing *to* him."

"Why do you assume I'm different?"

"Oh! JB… I didn't think you were awake…"

He smiled without raising his head or opening his eyes. "About as much as you are. Like I said – why figure I'm so different to Sonny? I'm just a simple bloke."

"Hardly! But more importantly, you're *not* like him. There's a big difference between 'simple' and shallow."

"Go to sleep, pretty lady," Stewart whispered, raising her hand to his lips.

She smiled and closed her eyes. "Mmm – I've always loved it when you call me that…"

As she drifted back to sleep the wizard leaned over and kissed her. "More than pretty. You're beautiful."

*

The Customs queue at Heathrow was pretty much as it usually was. There was a fair chance, John B. reflected, that this was where Lennon and McCartney had first written *The Long And Winding Road.*

"This is like that bloody line-up in Hawaii," grumbled Wilko, who was often not at his best soon after waking up.

"You're not wrong," agreed John B. "I wish we could get through a lot quicker."

Wilko rolled his eyes, while Elizabeth smiled indulgently and a little expectantly. John B. looked around innocently. There was a commotion at the entrance to the Customs Hall. A flight had just landed from New York. A girl in the queue ahead of Wilko looked back over her shoulder, and her eyes went as wide as saucers.

"OMG!" she shouted, possibly even knowing what the letters stood for. "It's *her*!!!!"

The girl's friends turned in response to her exclamation. Immediately they echoed her excitement. The effect was like a carelessly dropped match in a field of dry grass. By chance, a large proportion of the queue happened to be aged under twenty, and celebrity recognition spread through the throng like a wildfire. Obliged to keep the family 'together' to get through Customs, parents and younger siblings were towed along as a mass assembled around the poor unfortunate singer who was barely waking up from her own long flight. Her 'minders' had been similarly dozy and failed miserably in their appointed task of ensuring a low-key arrival.

As many of the arrivals charged toward the badly rattled pop star, another Customs officer happened to arrive to open her counter. Less than five minutes later, John B., Q and Wilko were standing on the other side of the Customs desks, working out where to go to catch their connecting flight to Glasgow.

"Not a bloody word, okay?" asked Wilko tersely.

Stewart shrugged. No comment seemed necessary. Q just smiled and put an arm around his waist.

.o0o.

7 SOMETHING ON THE HORIZON

Robbie Keith ran his hand through what was still quite thick brown hair. He wasn't a young man any more, but he certainly didn't feel *old*. Well, not until very recently, when he'd caught himself saying, increasingly often, "I'm too old for this…"

He was muttering those very words as he pushed open the door of the little room that had been given over to the distillery's new consultant engineer.

Robbie stood in the doorway, watching in surprise. Jazz had her back to him, leaning over the table she'd placed in the middle of the room. It was covered with sketch paper, and the pretty young blonde woman – she did *not* look like the stereotype image of her profession he mused to himself yet again – was ruling lines and scribbling notes on a particular sheet. She was whistling – *whistling* – as she worked.

Keith stood straighter and tried to smooth some creases out of his rumpled blue suit coat. There was something delightfully contagious about the cheerfulness in that whistle.

"You sound happy, Jazz," said the General Manager.

"Too bloody right, boss. For one thing, I reckon I've got this design worked out. *And* - my cavalry arrives tomorrow morning. I'm picking them up at the airport around ten."

"Ah, yes – I found your note on my desk about not coming in. Er… cavalry?"

Jazz grinned. "Yep. John B. is… um…"

She stopped, pondering for a moment. Was the General Manager someone who would believe, far less understand, that she had watched Stewart face down a demented professor who'd used human sacrifice to turn himself into an ancient sea god? Or, as she'd been reliably informed, that he'd survived kidnapping by a mad Russian scientist and defeated a crazy Hawaiian terrorist who'd tried to blow up a volcano?

She settled for, "He's got a knack for sorting out unusual problems."

Robbie nodded uncertainly.

The engineer continued, "I haven't met the girl with him, but I gather they're pretty close. And the other bloke, well, he's a bit special too. To me, anyway, so I'm looking forward to him being here."

"Do you really think they can make a difference?"

"Yep," Jazz repeated.

"I hope you're right. We're haemorrhaging staff and I just got a letter this morning from some woman on the regional Chamber of Commerce telling me they've had complaints that our business is 'behaving in a manner contrary to the moral well-being of the community'. Whatever that means."

"It means that somebody wants to cause trouble for us, hey? I'll tell you what, boss, it just adds to my conviction that this whole bad dreams business isn't just freaky, it's somehow deliberate. Someone's bloody controlling it!"

That brought another puzzled frown from Robbie Keith. "I'm not sure that's even possible, is it?"

Jazz grinned broadly. "I don't know, but if it is, I know just the blokes to stop it."

*

Muttering and cursing all the way, Rose Ellison hobbled from her armchair to the front door of her cottage. As she neared the threshold she shouted, "Wha' the hell is it noo?"

There was no immediate answer. Rose opened the door to find her youngest sister standing with hands on hips and an affronted expression on her

37

face. Auld Wullie stood a little behind her, wearing his usual carefully neutral look.

"That's a nice greetin' I must say! Wha's rattled yuir cage this afternoon?" asked April.

"Och, sorry April," said Rose, thus proving how out of sorts she felt. 'Sorry' wasn't a word she used often, especially when conversing with either of her sisters. "I've just had a visit frae that bloody old biddy Ishbell Mac-Neill an' her pal Skinny Mary."

"Right pair o' miseries, them," said April sympathetically. "What did they want?"

 Ushering her visitors in, Rose growled her reply. "Ah, the usual. Tryin' tae drag me oot tae their kirk on Sunday. Doin' the biddin' o' that so-and-so Dotterel.   Man should mind his own business."

"He is," said Auld Wullie placidly.

"Eh?" said Rose in a voice of outrage.

 Even April looked at her husband in surprise for a moment before understanding dawned.

"It *is* his business," she explained to her older sister. "Dotterel's business is tae get his kirk and his collection plate as full as he can. If Ishbell and Skinny Mary are daft enough tae help him then that's their lookout."

"Aye, well…" Rose grumbled as she dropped heavily back into her chair.

 April lowered herself only slightly more gracefully into another armchair. Auld Wullie ignored the couch and brought a wooden chair in from the kitchen.

 Before he could sit Rose called to him, "Help yoursel' tae a drink, man. You know where it is."

This was a little less generous than it sounded, as Auld Wullie actually provided most of the bottles that made up the contents of his sister-in-law's modest drinks cabinet.

While he poured himself a small whisky – he knew it was still too early in the afternoon for either of the women – the sisters got down to the business of information exchange.

"So, what is it ye've got tae say?" asked Rose.

"Well, I was talkin' tae Jessie at this morning's Jazzercise class in the Hall…"

"Jazzercise?! Ye arnae doin' Jazzercise are ye? What a sight that'd be! Ye cannae even see yuir toes, far less touch them!"

"Och, I only go for the music. But it wouldnae do you any harm tae get oot of yon chair a bit more often. Anyway, Jess said there was an 'Extraordinary Meeting' o' the Party last night. It's no' public knowledge yet, but it's been confirmed that the Reverend's lass is tae stand in the vote tae replace poor old McCrory."

"That bloody Victoria Dotterel – hell mend anybody that'd bloody vote for her!"

"Oh aye. But then, we wouldnae have thought she'd be popular enough tae even get the candidacy. There's something a bit… not right aboot that lassie."

"What can ye expect, April? That's a family tree wi' tangled roots and twisted branches."

Auld Wullie said nothing, but looked thoughtful as he stared into his whisky glass. They were funny things, families, he mused.

.oOo.

8 FOR PEAT'S SAKE

For all its size, or lack thereof, there has been air traffic to Islay since the early days of flight. Originally planes landed on the long flat coastal area called The Strand, but in the early 1930's a proper grass landing strip was established at Glenegedale.

The strip was expanded and tarmac laid in World War 2, when the island was a base for RAF patrols over the Irish Sea and elsewhere. The Glenegedale Airport wasn't large, but the folks there knew their history and were proud of it.

As their small plane approached the runway the three Australians gazed down at their destination.

"That's an impressive looking golf course," said John B.

"A proper links course," observed Wilko. "Some of those holes look like fun."

He was being slightly ironic. Wilko had a genuine love/hate relationship with golf, often describing it as more like an addiction than a passion.

The only other passenger – a lawyer with an office in Bowmore – offered the three companions a lift if they were going that way.

"Thanks, that's kind of you," said Elizabeth. "But we should have someone waiting to pick us up to take us to Sron Dubh."

"Ah, that's an odd wee spot for a holiday. Not much there. Nice enough wee distillery, but there are a number o' those on the island," replied the big man.

"We're visiting a friend," the pretty brunette explained.

The man nodded. It wasn't 'peak season' for visitors, so that explained it.

"There is still plenty to see and do here, so I hope you enjoy your stay. If you're in Bowmore in the next few days please do call in for a wee dram." He held out a hand across the small aisle and introduced himself. "Aaron Craig. Most people just call me Craig."

"Craig it is, then," said John B. shaking the offered hand, immediately won over by the offer of whisky.

 The lawyer leaned back in his chair, looking out as the little plane made a smooth landing. "I do hope everything's alright," he said a little distantly.

"Is there any reason it wouldn't be?" asked Elizabeth, whose radar for trouble was good.

"Eh? Oh, sorry," said Craig. "Idle musing. I've been away from the island for quite some months. I gather from my staff that there's – well, a bit of an odd wee tone about the place. That's why I'm here. An unusual number of property transfers, Will changes, that sort of thing. The workload is getting on top of my small staff. Ah well – it'll all resolve itself, I'm sure," he said, getting up from his seat.

 Gallantly he allowed Elizabeth the opportunity to exit first.

 John B. returned the gesture, remarking as he did, "So you *are* a local then?"

"An *Ileach* by origin – that's the word for a person from Islay - but not for a very long time, I'm afraid. My main office is in London now. I maintain a presence here out of loyalty more than anything else."

"That's admirable," said John B. as he stepped out of the plane after the lawyer.

 Once in the small terminal building handshakes were exchanged all round, and a promise to get together soon. As Craig went to leave, he stopped suddenly and stood back. His large frame would fill the doorway, and he was chivalrous enough to step aside to allow entry of the young blonde woman who was arriving at a run.

Jazz didn't break stride, calling a quick "Thanks" as she passed before literally jumping into a hug with Wilko. Fortunately the Tasmanian had his feet firmly planted. He was the same height as the engineer but rather more solidly built, and didn't flinch as he caught her. His two travelling companions were aware of his embarrassment – Wilko was a very private man noted for disliking public displays of emotion. They'd been standing with an arm around each other's waist, so turned to share a passionate kiss. Purely to give Wilko some privacy for a moment, of course.

Releasing her embrace but keeping a firm grip on Wilko's hand, Jazz beamed at the other two arrivals as they unlocked lips.

"Hey, John B.! Good to see you, mate! Thank you *so* much for coming! And you must be Elizabeth," she said approvingly, and extended a welcoming hand.

Stewart waited politely while the blonde and brunette shook hands, then took Jazz in a hug of his own.

"Good to see you, too," he said quietly.

The blonde's delight at their arrival was obvious, and she chattered almost constantly as they gathered their luggage.

"Did you want a cuppa?" she asked. "The Drome Café here has a good reputation." When the others declined the offer she led the way to the car park.

"This is my chariot – I call her Anastasia. No special reason, I just like the name," she said, patting a silver sedan as she opened the boot for their bags.

The two men checked it out. "Rover 75," said John B. with obvious approval.

Both he and the Tasmanian had a deep fondness for British vehicles.

"Yep. Last one they made," observed Wilko. "She'd be over ten years old now. How does she run?"

"Beautifully. Smooth as silk. Two and a half litre V6 engine, five-speed auto that still works a treat. It's a bloody shame they went bust, if you ask me," said Jazz who knew quite a bit about cars herself.

Wilko nodded as he settled himself on the front seat that was offered to him. "Bad management, not bad product," he opined.

Jazz was still talking rapidly. "I figured the first thing we'd do is head for the cottage and unload. There wasn't much option for digs when I got here, especially since I'd rather walk to work than drive. All I could get was a little two-bedroom place in the village – it's neat and tidy enough, and I've stayed in a lot worse around the world! It's cozy but I figure we'll all fit."

"Two bedrooms?" said Wilko in surprise, doing the math.

"Yep," grinned Jazz. She reached across and playfully squeezed his leg. "Hey, we've shared a jail together in Alice Springs. This should be more comfortable than that!"

The Tasmanian managed an awkward smile to replace the goldfish impression he was perilously close to commencing. Clearly he hadn't expected quite such a reception from Jazz. The couple in the back seat watched his reaction with a mix of sympathy and amusement.

Elizabeth turned her gaze out the back window as the car rolled along the A846, the main road that ran down the south of the island.

"It's flat out here, isn't it?" she said.

"A lot of this area is old peat bogs," explained Jazz.

"Which give Islay single malts their distinctive character," added John B., the Scotch enthusiast.

"Correct," said Jazz. "Our little distillery is one of the few left who cut and burn our own peat for the malt kiln. Hey – while we're out this way do you want to meet a couple of our peat cutters in action?"

"That'd be great," enthused the wizard. "Um… assuming it suits every-one else."

Elizabeth squeezed his hand and said, "Fine by me, babe."

Wilko shrugged and said to Jazz, "We're here for you, mate. We've got all day to unpack, so whatever you say, goes."

Grinning, the engineer soon swung the car off the road and drove a short way out to where a couple of much older vehicles were parked. Three men were hard at work around a small embankment cut into the peat.

One was using a large flat spade to strip the coarse sedge grass from the surface. He did this by cutting squares of turf the width of the blade, first making deep vertical incisions. Then with the help of the leverage created by the long curved wooden handle he sliced under the turf and lifted each thick slab, tossing them into a heap.

That exposed the black mass of the peat – richly organic material large-ly composed of decomposed moss and lichens heavy with the tang of years of salt sea air. The second member of the team stood at the edge of the embankment, equipped with his own unique implement. It might be described as a rectangular flat blade, about the length of a man's forearm and the width of his hand. At the bottom of the blade a corner was formed by a sharp piece of slightly greater width. Like the spade, this blade was attached to a long wooden handle. The man wielding it drove the blade into the edge of the peat, gave a little twist of the handle, and pulled.

The damp peat clung to the blade, and he lifted a neat rectangular block of the substance clear of the bank. A deft turn of the handle rolled the slab onto the ground behind him.

That was the cue for the third member of the team to carefully gather up the cut peat and carry it a little way distant. He was building a series of small conical structures, made from rings of the peat blocks standing on the edge of one end, propping each other up at the top. That construction allowed air to circulate, drying the peat slabs out over a period of weeks so that they could be taken away and stacked in shelter to dry completely over months.

The dried slabs were burned in the distillery in a kiln that heated the barley that came off the malting floor, the distinctive smell of the peat smoke infusing the grains as their germination was halted. That distinctive aroma made its way into the mash that became Sron Dubh's whisky – a characteristic smell and taste typical of the Islay style.

After watching from the car for a few moments, Jazz got out and led her friends over to make introductions. The three workers looked up and greeted her with grins. They were sweating, even in the brisk wind that blew across the peat.

"Mornin', Miss Parrish!" cried one – the tall thin man who held the angled cutting tool.

The other two, similar as peas in a pod except for a few inches difference in height, touched their flat caps in greeting. At a signal from the engineer the three men stopped their work and walked over to where the cars were parked.

Jazz introduced the new arrivals, and then the members of the peat cutting team: Lanky Wullie McPhee and the two brothers, Duncan and Gordon Macintosh.

"They're all *Ileachs* – everyone at the distillery is except for me and the Manager, Robbie Keith. But they all put up with us! Lanky's a good Sron Dubh native, and the boys drive down from Bowmore every day," she explained.

Glad of the break from their labours, the three locals explained their jobs to the visitors. John B. willingly had a go with Lanky Wullie's *tairsgear* – the cutting blade with the right-angled wing, producing a couple of peat slabs judged to be of "aye fair quality".

Offered a turn, Wilko threw up his hands. "No thanks, fellas, I'm an office boy. That looks like too much hard yakka!"

Duncan looked blank. "Yakka?" he repeated.

"Bloody hard work!" explained Wilko with a grin.

"Ah! Aye, 'tis that right enough. 'Tis why we swap the jobs around twixt us every half hour or so," said Duncan.

"Course, 'twere easier when there was six o' us. Quicker too," added his brother.

 Ever the efficient administrator, Elizabeth asked, "What happened to the other half of the workforce?"

"One by one they just stopped turning up, didn't they lads?" said Jazz.

"Really? Why?" persisted Elizabeth.

 The three workers looked uncomfortable.

"Ehh… wouldnae like tae say." Gordon looked very intently at a patch of sedge grass near his feet.

"It was the dreams, wasn't it?" said John B. bluntly, leaning on the *tairs-gear.*

 The three peat cutters looked up sharply.

"How d'ye…? Miss Parrish, have ye…?" Duncan struggled to find the words.

 Jazz shook her head. "No Duncan. John B.'s just arrived. But he's good with - *unusual* stuff and I reckon he can help us."

 Prompted by a discreet nudge from Elizabeth, Wilko kept his mouth shut. The cynical response he'd had in mind wouldn't help these men anyway, he realised.

"Horace was the first," Duncan explained. "He fronted up one mornin', put his hand on his heart an' said, 'I cannae in all conscience continue tae do work tae the benefit o' the devil himsel' – or words tae that effect."

 Lanky Wullie snorted derisively, "Och, Horace was aye soft in the head. Too much book learnin' I say!"

"This wasnae comin' fra his usual books, ye ken. He was quotin' Scripture an' Horace was aye readin' books o' science an' philosophy and what have ye," admonished Duncan.

Gordon nodded, supporting his twin, and said, "Then Donald Campbell passed away in his sleep."

The tall man from Sron Dubh wagged a bony finger and said, "Donald Campbell was sixty-odd years old, at least. He shouldnae have still been cuttin' turves at his age."

"Donald Campbell wasnae sick a day in his life!" snapped Duncan. "I hope I'm as hale as he was when I'm in ma sixties!"

The shorter brother interrupted, cutting off any argument, "Then two weeks ago, Black Graham didnae turn up. Duncan an' I went tae see him after a couple o' days when he hadnae come back – he lives in Bowmore, ye ken. 'What's yuir problem, Black Graham?' I asked. He jus' shook his head an' mumbled somethin' aboot his wife wouldnae let him work for the distillery any mair. Sinful, she said it was. And this after it's been puttin' a roof over her head an' food on her table for ten years! She couldnae sleep wi' herself she said, and so neither could Black Graham."

"He never could say 'no' tae her," observed Duncan quietly.

"And what about you three?" asked John B. "How well are you sleeping?"

Lanky Wullie tilted a defiant chin. "I sleep deep and sound, me. Most nights. If I'm dreamin' I dinna remember it."

"That'd be the half dozen drams ye're havin' ere ye get tae bed," observed Duncan sagely.

"Nowt wrong wi' that!" said the tall man defensively.

"I never said there was, pal. I never said there was. 'Twere a fine thing if it'd work for me. I dinna dream every night like some do, but when I do I wake up sweatin' and that's the fair truth, Mister Stewart."

The wizard listened thoughtfully. "Fire in your dreams, Duncan?" he asked.

"Nae, it's… well, I'm in school, and I never liked school, ye ken?"

"We wernae the best scholars, neither o' us," explained Gordon. "Going back there, even in wer sleep, isnae verra nice. Especially wi' that… *woman* there."

Stewart nodded. "White hair, very old-fashioned?"

"Aye, that's the one. Ye know her?" asked Gordon in surprise.

"Not *know*, but I know the dreams. Same as Ja… Miss Parrish," John B. answered, remembering to respect Jazz' apparent position of authority.

The lady in question was puzzled. "But Gordon, Duncan – you don't get the fire dreams?"

The twins looked at her blankly. Lanky Wullie rubbed his weathered hands uncomfortably.

"Ah, well… I… er… now that ye mention it, there might ha' been once or twice when I… er… woke up sweatin' a bit more than usual," he said.

John B. scratched at his chin thoughtfully. The usual scruffy stubble was on the verge of becoming a scruffy beard. "There's a pattern to this, I'm sure. I just can't see it yet. Gentlemen, thanks for being honest with us. I'm not stupid enough to promise I'll sort this all out, but I will do my best. Be nice to catch up over a drink. Not when you're working," he added quickly as he saw Lanky Wullie start to pull a hip flask from a pocket. "Anywhere you'd recommend?"

Jazz was about to say something when it dawned on her that the wizard was working on forging a link with the men, whose local knowledge and experience may help resolve the mystery of the recurring nightmares.

"There used tae be a nice wee snug in Sron Dubh," said Lanky Wullie,

"But that scunner o' a Reverend made such a carry on that it had tae close down."

"Aye. Damn shame that," said Duncan. "The *Lost Goose* in Port Ellen is where ye'll find us on a Friday night. On Saturday ye might just find Gordon an' myself at the *Dockside* in Bowmore."

"Oh aye!" said Gordon brightly. "There's a ceilidh on this Saturday at the *Dock*. Ye all should come!"

"Well, they call it a ceilidh," said Duncan, "I dinna reckon it's much more than a disco mahself, wi' a few old style things played in between by a braw young couple fra up Port Askaig way."

"So a 'kay-lee' is a dance?" asked Wilko.

"Part dance, part concert, mostly party," explained John B., whose adoptive father had been a musician in Glasgow in his younger days.

"Sounds like fun! We should be around on Saturday night – let's go!" enthused Elizabeth.

 Neither John B. nor Wilko were enthusiastic (nor particularly adept) dancers, but the idea of a party appealed so the suggestion was well received.

 Hands were shaken all round, and the peat cutters were left to get back to their tasks. Gordon took over the *tairsgear* while his brother cut the sedge away and Lanky Wullie bent his tall frame to stacking the peat blocks to dry.

 With a cheery wave Jazz headed back towards the A846. Anastasia's wheels slipped and skidded on the damp sedge, and threw up small sprays of damp peat.

"You get used to it," said the driver lightly as the Rover bounced onto the sealed road. "I don't come out here much – what the boys do out here isn't really part of my job, but I like the countryside and the company. And it helps to know as much as I can about the whole operation."

"That makes sense," agreed Elizabeth, who would have adopted the same approach.

 The wizard was gazing out the window. "Is it just the distillery, I wonder?" he mused. "I think we need to do some discreet asking around."

"You'll find some in the village will talk more than others," warned Jazz. "And even among the chatty ones you might not always like what you hear."

.o0o.

9 LESS THAN WELCOME

The four of them had climbed out of the Rover and were examining the peat still clinging in dark festoons to the side panels.

Wilko looked particularly rueful. "We'd better wash that off pretty quick. It's going to eat into the duco otherwise, and the rental company'll sting you for the cost. And sting real hard if I know what they're like."

"Not to worry, a bucket and some soapy water and we can have it clean in no time," said Elizabeth breezily.

"Mm. If the weather was a bit warmer that job could look especially appealing," said John B. with a slightly lascivious wink.

"Cheeky!" laughed the woman he called Q, who knew quite well what picture the wizard's imagination was displaying.

Jazz did too, and shared the laugh. It took Wilko a moment to catch on, but then he too grinned broadly.

"But sadly mate, it's *not* a bit warmer, so you'll just have to leave any idea of bikinis and wet t-shirts parked firmly inside your head," said Elizabeth with a playful wave of an admonishing finger.

John B. mustered his best look of injured innocence. As usual it fooled no one.

He was about to open the boot to extract the luggage when the door of the cottage next door was opened with a bang.

"Uh-oh. Here comes trouble," muttered Jazz. In response to the others' quizzical looks she explained, "My landlady. Ishbell McNeill. Bit of a dragon, I'm afraid, but this was the only place available when I arrived."

"I quite like dragons," observed John B.

"Not this one you won't, I'd say."

The landlady strode quickly across the short distance between the two cottages and up the path to Jazz's temporary home.

Ishbell McNeill was a rather pudgy woman, wearing a dark grey shift and cardigan. Both of these items were only saved from shapelessness by being a size too small for her and thus taking on her own dumpy form. On her feet were battered black boots that might have been used for kicking nails into hardwood.

She was short – looking up belligerently through steel-rimmed spectacles at Wilko's chin. Her hair had been roughly cut in a severe pageboy style.

"Miss Parrish," she said sharply. It was intended as a greeting, but the words landed like rocks on plate glass so it came out more like a call to attention.

"Afternoon, Mrs. McNeill," said Jazz as brightly as she could. "These are my friends: Wilko, John B. and Elizabeth. They've come up from Australia. They'll be…"

"Ah trust ye'll no' be imagining that they'll all be staying here," the landlady interrupted. "I run a guid Christian establishment. There'll be no hanky panky under a roof o' mine. The Reverend Dotterel himself has recommended me tae his visitors from – overseas."

She said the word 'overseas' as if it had been dipped in something particularly unpleasant. Clearly 'overseas' was a place she'd heard about and didn't approve of.

Jazz took a half step towards Wilko. She had some idea of grasping his arm and telling this high-handed, high-minded busybody just how high she could stick her cottage.

Ishbell was oblivious to the aggravation the English girl was radiating. Perhaps her own irritation field was set so permanently high that nobody else's had a chance to register. She'd already cast a critical eye over each of the newcomers.

"Ah note by the absence o' rings none o' ye are decently married," she sternly pronounced.

 Elizabeth stepped forward, making a placating gesture towards the landlady.

"Mrs. McNeill, please don't concern yourself," she said. "I quite understand – we wouldn't dream of jeopardising your reputation. I'm sure Jazz and Robert will conduct themselves properly." She held John B.'s hand demurely. "The two of us will of course be staying elsewhere."

 Jazz looked momentarily nonplussed, but Wilko and John B. had seen Elizabeth play the diplomatic role in the office plenty of times before. They knew how good she could be at it.

"Absolutely no panky, quite right. And I don't carry a hanky, just a couple of tissues."

 Ignoring John B.'s input, Ishbell was in any case slightly mollified. She didn't look at the others but bobbed her head a little at Elizabeth.

"Aye, well, ye seem a decently brought up lass. So where is it ye'll be staying? Ye'd best mind out, ye ken. There are some folks in the village that dinna run so respectable an establishment as ah insist on."

"Thank you for your concern, Mrs. McNeill, but I really can't talk about where we'll be staying."

There was a suspicious glint in the eyes behind the short woman's glasses.

The brunette continued. "After all, you'd be not best pleased if *your* guests were to be discussing *your* business. True?"

"Mm, aye… that's… certainly true." She sensed she'd been maneuvered, but wasn't sure where to or how. She turned her steely gaze on Jazz. "So ye two *will* be behavin' yuirselves."

 The blonde folded her hands pristinely in front of her and in her best guileless voice replied, "Oh of course, Mrs. McNeill."

Jazz knew how to fake sincerity. In her head were the words, "There's more than one way to behave" – but she managed to not say them aloud.

"Right then, ah'd best be about ma business." The landlady looked to be leaving but then half turned back and waved a stubby finger at the group. "Ah'll be watchin' oot, mind!"

 Satisfied that she'd gotten in the last word she stormed away. Her steps were short, rapid and loud. It was as if she was expressing her general outrage at the world by slamming her brogues into the floor with every footfall.

"She doesn't walk. She stomps," observed John B. He looked to the brunette holding his arm and asked mildly, "So where is this 'elsewhere' that we're staying?"

"Don't worry babe, there's bound to be some cozy little somewhere – some kind soul will take us in."

 The wizard smiled at her. "Uh-huh. I wish it'll be so."

"There you are. See, nothing to worry about!" laughed Q.

 Jazz chuckled along, then Wilko gruffly said, "I wish you two wouldn't encourage him."

"Come on," said Jazz, much happier after Ishbell McNeill's departure. "We'll put Wilko's stuff in the cottage, give the car a quick clean, then I'll drive us into the village proper and we'll see what we can find for you two."

.oOo.

10 VILLAGE PEOPLE

The best place for a visitor to find information in any British village is the local post office, or whatever passes for it. In Sron Dubh it was *McMurtrie's Hardware and General Store (And Branch Post Office)*.

The woman behind the counter was willowy - not as thin as Ishbell Mc-Neill's friend Skinny Mary. She would have been striking in her youth, but the responsibilities of running the 'economic hub of the village' as her late husband had called it, had prematurely aged her. The iron-coloured hair was distinguished, but in quiet moments she remembered looking rather better than distinguished. The dear departed Donald McMurtrie had stood by the mantra: "The key to success in business is to be good with people." He wasn't especially good at it himself (widely known as a grumpy old sod, actually) but his wife Mary had proved to be a natural. So much so that when Donald's heart had given out unexpectedly early, she had kept the business and improved turnover considerably.

 Mind you, the '*Hardware*' part of the enterprise had been reduced to a small shelf of hand tools (two hammers, a chisel, pliers and a limited range of screwdrivers), some rolls of tape and four jars of assorted screws and nails.

Jazz and her visitors chatted amiably as they waited in line to speak to the shopkeeper. When it came to their turn she smiled at the unfamiliar faces.

"Hello, and welcome tae Sron Dubh. I'm Postie Mary," she said. Jazz had already explained the village's tradition of 'Wullies' – the same practice held to distinguish the various Marys.

The consultant engineer, already a known figure in the store, introduced the others. Elizabeth explained that they were looking for accommodation in the village. The postmistress looked thoughtful.

"I'm afraid you may have tae look over in Port Ellen. There's no' much in the village at best, and I don't know that there's any vacancies in those," she mused. "Miss Parrish, you've got Ishbell McNeill's cottage, haven't you?"

"Yeah…" Jazz replied grimly.

There was a poorly suppressed chuckle from behind them and a quiet, "Och, ye poor lassie…"

The foursome turned to see an elderly stocky woman in a floral shift and red cardigan. Her short hair was almost the same colour as Postie Mary's but that was where the resemblance ended. April Bromleigh was considerably older, stood barely Wilko's height and her girth would probably have matched Wilko and John B. standing back-to-back. She supported herself with a gaudy rainbow-coloured walking stick.

"Och, I am sorry," she said. "I didnae mean tae say that out loud."

Jazz grinned. "No offence taken. I mean, you are absolutely right."

April returned the smile.

Postie Mary, whilst feeling obliged to be diplomatic about the widow Mc-Neill, had a small grin of her own as she carried out introductions. "April Bromleigh, I don't know that you've met Jazz Parrish? Miss Parrish is working at the distillery."

"Aye, ye're the lass that's doing clever things wi' steam. I've heard of ye – nice tae meet ye at last," said April, offering a handshake. Just for a moment the old woman squinted at Jazz, "Hang on – are ye no'…? Nae, cannae be – sorry, dinna mind a daft old woman."

They shook hands and the English girl introduced her companions.

April addressed Postie Mary, asking, "D'ye ken whether Rhona Hine has anybody in at the moment?"

"I don't think she's taking guests any more, April. You know, wi' Hamish being unwell and havin' tae fly back tae Glasga so often. She's over at the Hall noo if ye want tae ask her – it's her turn tae do the cleanin' this week."

The old woman gave John B. and Elizabeth a long searching look and announced, "I dinna think that these two would need a lot o' lookin' after."

"Oh – JB and I quite self-sufficient, aren't we babe?" Q said with an arm around her boyfriend.

"Well, except for not having our own transport around the island, like say between here and Port Ellen. We're reliant on Jazz's car for that. But otherwise, aye, we are," John B. replied.

'Oh spare me – he's going native already!' thought Wilko.

"Right then! I'll just pay Postie Mary for these biscuits and I'll walk ye tae see Rhona. I'll put in a word for ye and I'm quite sure she'll be able tae gi' ye a cozy wee place tae stay."

The four friends politely stepped away to let their new benefactor finish her business.

"She's a nice old stick, isn't she?" whispered Elizabeth.

"Stick? She's more like a whole forest! But nice enough, yeah," Jazz agreed.

April carefully placed her biscuits in her handbag, a capacious red leather antique that looked large enough to also hold six bottles of wine, a frozen chicken and three tins of soup (which Postie Mary had seen it do).

"Will you be at the lapidary group tomorrow night, April?" asked the shopkeeper.

"Oh aye. I havenae quite got the hang o' the rock tumblin' yet - I seem tae be best at makin' gravel – but I do enjoy lookin' at what ye're all makin', ye ken," was the reply. There were very few community activities in Sron Dubh that weren't visited by the inquisitive, enthusiastic and substantial figure of April Bromleigh.

With a cheery wave and a call of "Good luck tae you!" from the postmistress, the little group set out for the hall to book Rhona's guesthouse.

Their progress along the high street of Sron Dubh was necessarily slow, keeping pace with April's arthritic gait. As they went, she pointed out people and places that she thought might be interesting to her young companions. The Laundromat (*Suds Central*) – "Ye'll need that. I'm sure Ishbell would only have an old copper out the back, and charge ye extra for the use o' it." There was a dress shop that also sold "the loveliest wee cakes in town, but ye have tae ask fer 'em special – Dottie doesnae have them on display". There was a recently opened *Curry House* that got a glowing recommendation.

"Noo, comin' up on the corner here is the chemist's. Truth tae tell, I don't think that'll be here much longer. They dinna make their own medicine any more. They bring it in frae Port Ellen and frankly it's quicker for most folks tae drive doon the road fer themselves. Doc Wullie – his rooms are just around the corner, lovely lad, he does his best tae put business their way but honestly it's no' much more than a glorified gift shop wi' a few shelves o' headache powders an' wintergreen rubs an' such…"

The garrulous local's commentary stopped abruptly at the sound of raised voices from the little corner pharmacy. The door flew open and a man strode out onto the street. Dressed all in black, he wore about him an air of affected dignity that could easily be read as arrogance. His white collar revealed him as a Man Of The Cloth, and an old-fashioned cut of cloth it was.

Before the door could swing shut it was pushed open again by the formidable figure following him. The resemblance to April Bromleigh was obvious – a similar figure if a little shorter, a wilder shock of curly silver hair, a brightly coloured floral shift but teamed with a green cardigan and a walking stick of plain utilitarian grey. Clearly furious, the woman limped painfully at the man in black. She wasn't quite shouting, but she had a voice that carried clearly without apparent effort.

"How bloody dare ye come in there and bloody hector me in public about ma 'sins and shortcomings'? If I wanted ma own affairs talked about in public I'd stand on the street corner and do it ma bloody self! And I'm damned sure that if I wanted anything tae do wi' you an' yer cronies I'd ha' been the one tae come tae you. And since I havenae it should be bloody obvious that I'm no' interested! Are ye stubborn, or just stupid, mon?"

 By now a third figure had emerged from the shop – a brawny blonde man who stepped defensively in front of the Reverend. "You can't talk to the…"

 The woman poked the younger man in the belly with her walking stick. "Quiet, you! I'm talkin' tae the butcher, no' tae his block!"

 The Reverend Dotterel visibly suppressed a laugh behind his companion's back. His would-be defender on the other hand reddened with anger. He didn't always know when he was being insulted, but on this occasion there was no mistaking the woman's tone of voice. The man in black laid a restraining hand on the larger fellow's shoulder.

"Take a deep breath, DS. Remember the Lord's injunction against being quick tae wrath. And you, Mrs. Ellison. I'm truly at a loss tae understand you. You're a respectable woman, held in high regard around the village…"

"Dinna crawl tae me, mon!"

 His voice continued smooth and unperturbed. "I merely observe that you're highly thought of as a woman of good character, and yet you steadfastly refuse tae come tae kirk on Sunday. I'd have thought you'd be one tae support the good old-fashioned values."

 Mrs. Ellison glared at the Reverend. "There's nowt tae value mair than freedom!"

"But of course! Freedom is a central tenet of what I teach. Our country and our religion are predicated on that freedom – my daughter Victoria is a fine testament tae – "

"And dinna blather tae me aboot yuir bloody daughter, either. There's a lot mair tae freedom than the freedom tae agree wi' you!"

 John B. couldn't resist the urge to applaud.

The Reverend and his burly off-sider turned and glared at the sound of clapping. They stared at all four unfamiliar faces. The man in black stared particularly intently at the shaggy fellow in the purple t-shirt, before saying, "Mrs. Bromleigh, I might make the same observations tae you as I have tae your sister. You are not without respect in the village, you and your husband. You might not choose tae join the kirk community, but I'd ask you to prevail upon your friends tae show due respect tae those o' us who do the good Lord's work."

Before April could reply Stewart took a pace forward, returning the preacher's steady gaze. "I've just met this charming lady, and I'm absolutely sure she's as respectable as you reckon, so if you want to talk to me leave her out of it and have the decency, and the guts, to talk to me direct."

The big blonde man growled and went to advance on Stewart, but the older man again put a restraining hand on his shoulder.

"Not now, DS, not now. Young man, you are new to this village so I'll forgive your impertinence. You are invited tae join us in the presence of the Lord on Sunday." His gaze shifted to the others. "The invitation extends tae all of you."

He turned and walked briskly up the street before anyone could reply.

The man addressed as DS shoved his hands into the deep pockets of his coat, but struck a menacing pose. "I ain't as forgiving as the Reverend. You disrespect him again and I'll beat your head in. Or worse even, got it?" His accent was rough and English – a seamy part of Manchester perhaps, certainly not local.

"Worse than beating me to death? Now I'm intrigued," said John B. casually.

The big man lifted one side of his coat back slightly. The little group could see the handle of a gun tucked into the waistband of his trousers.

In a quiet, menacing voice he said, "I can shoot you so you die real slow an' nasty like, see? Don't cross the Reverend or me again."

He was just turning to follow the preacher when Elizabeth, shaking her head, remarked, "Wow – you're a real ignoramus, aren't you?"

The man looked at her blankly for a moment, then jutted his jaw and replied, "Yeah – and don't you forget it, girlie."

With that, he swaggered away to catch up with his mentor.

She opened her mouth to call something after him, but John B. laid a hand on her arm and said, "Don't waste your breath."

Q blinked once or twice. "Well, that was an experience."

Mrs. Ellison limped over to them. Arthritis badly affected one hip, so she stood some inches taller on one leg than the other. Thus she could be either taller or shorter than Wilko. Before she could introduce herself though April pounced. Well, metaphorically pounced – a cat-like leap was clearly beyond her.

"Rose Ellison, have ye no shame? Arguin' in the street like a fishwife! What'll people think?"

"I wasnae arguin'. I was standin' up for maself is all. And I don't give a bugger what a'body else thinks. I'll nae have that bloody old misery Dotterel and his idiot tryin' tae tell me what tae do. On Sunday or any other day!"

"That sounds fair," said John B. Stewart, unlikely diplomat.

"Aye, right enough, I suppose," said April, more grudgingly than she felt. "He is a bloody old rogue, I think. Rose, these yins are new pals o' mine, come over frae Australia. This is ma sister Rose."

The visitors introduced themselves, Wilko with polite reserve and the others with more warmth. They'd all taken an immediate dislike to the preacher and his companion, so by extension took the side of the feisty old lady.

"So who were those two charmers?" asked Elizabeth.

April replied, "The old yin's the Reverend Gordon Dotterel." (Everyone politely avoided reacting to her description of the preacher as 'old' when she clearly had a couple of decades start on him. Even Rose didn't take the opportunity to comment, probably because she was the eldest of the three sisters.) "He's in charge o' the kirk at the end o' the village. All hell-fire an' brimstone, full o' tellin' folk their sins an' the damnation they're tae rightfully receive in his not-so-humble opinion."

Her sister nodded. "The other yin's his… I don't know what ye'd call him. Follower maybe. Bodyguard mair like it. DS Mills."

Wilko looked troubled. "D. S.? Detective Sergeant? That man's a policeman?"

The sisters both laughed.

"Och no," said April. "Tha's his initials. Nob'dy knows what they really stand for."

Rose gave a contemptuous snort and said, "When the Reverend's no' in earshot he'll tell folk it stands for 'Dark Satanic' Mills, but that's a lot o' nonsense."

"He doesn't seem the type for poetry," observed Jazz.

"Aye, ye're right there," agreed April. "Somethin' he heard at school and decided he liked, I'd say. The man's a fool. If brains were dynamite he couldnae blow his own hat off."

"A penny for his thoughts and ye'd get change," added Rose.

"I wonder if the Reverend has to water him twice a week?" mused John B.

The two sisters looked at him. April smiled. That expression didn't seem to come readily to Rose but she gave an approving nod and said, "Be a waste o' water if he does." She drew herself up to her taller height and squared her shoulders. "Bloody old ratbag distracted me fra' ma shopping. I only came oot fer a packet a' headache powders, a' noo I've got a bigger headache than I had tae start wi'! I should ha' just ignored him."

Her younger sister nodded. "Aye, ye should. But ye willnae, I know. No' that I blame ye mind. He's as aggravatin' as a boil on yer bum. Noo, I'm awa' tae take these yins tae see young Rhona about puttin' a roof over their heads."

"Is Hamish well, then? I hadnae heard."

"Probably no' – he hasnae been for a wee while. But he's still wi' us, an' this *fechter* an' his bonny lass need a bed."

Rose nodded approval and said, "Aye, well, recommend them from me."

"As if ma say-so wasnae enough!" said her sister indignantly.

"All testimonials gratefully received, thank you ladies!" said Elizabeth, quickly.

Rose gave a wave of acknowledgement and hobbled back into the chemist's store. If any of the staff there had any opinions about her exchange with the Reverend they were smart enough to not let her know them.

As they continued on their way to meet the guesthouse owner Elizabeth asked, "What did Mrs. Ellison call John B.?"

"A *fechter* – a fighter. Rose is aye capable o' standin' up for hersel' but I dinna think it hurt tae have some support. Especially wi' that lump Mills there. He's a bad yin. I'm quite sure he'd no' hesitate tae lay hands on anybody, no matter their age or their sex – if he thought nobody other than the Reverend was watchin'."

Wilko was taken aback. "Surely the preacher wouldn't stand for that? I mean, I'm no fan of the church, but…"

April laughed wryly. "Mills is auld Dotterel's pet attack dog. If he tugs his leash it's for his ain purposes, no' any sense o' decency. Noo, the Hall's just round this corner. I'm sure Rhona willnae mind a wee distraction frae sweepin'…"

Rhona & Hamish Hine owned a neat little two-storey house in Port Ellen.

They lived upstairs, and had run a thriving bed and breakfast from the downstairs room until Hamish's unspecified "unwellness" had come to occupy too much of Rhona's attention for her to manage the business as she wanted. Small outings like this day's 'civic duty' had become rare treats for her, she explained.

After the initial introductions Jazz and Wilko diplomatically waited outside the hall, sitting close together on a stone fence. There were clouds building and they wanted to enjoy each other's company in whatever sunshine was available as much as they could.

At first it seemed April's optimism might be misplaced. The guesthouse was officially closed, after all. The endorsement of the two sisters clearly had an effect though. It was clearly something out of the ordinary and not to be ignored, noted Q. A deal – a very good deal – was quickly struck. Hamish was asleep at home. No phone call was necessary, as it was clear he'd go along with whatever his good lady wife decided.

"I cannae guarantee a hot breakfast every morning," Rhona warned. "There's a wee galley kitchen downstairs that you're welcome to use if I'm no' available."

"No problem. We'll do some shopping and look after ourselves, Mrs. Hine," said John B.

"Och, no shopping required – there's plenty o' makings in the kitchen for you to use. And call me Rhona." The landlady looked slightly sheepish. "I should tell you – the room's a bit on the small side. Since we've no' been takin' in guests I'm afraid I've taken tae using the bigger room for storage. If you'd like, I suppose I could –"

"No, seriously, it's not a problem," John B. repeated. "Small is good. I'm sure we'll be fine, won't we sweetheart?"

"Cozy is just what we asked for," agreed Elizabeth, giving him an affectionate hug. "Please don't worry, Rhona. We've got our bags in the car, at the other end of the village - and we can be over in a while. Do you need a lift home when you're done here?"

The offer was smilingly refused, and the deal was sealed with a hand-shake, as the best deals are.

As they walked back outside John B. asked, "Can we see you home, April?"

"Don't be daft, lad. Ma place is just up and over yon, at the edge o' the woods there. I toddle up and doon here all the time. But it's good o' ye tae offer, mind. Here – the four o' ye must come for tea. Auld Wullie will be glad tae meet ye." She patted first John B. then Wilko on the arm. "He doesnae complain, bless 'im, but I think he'd enjoy a wee bit o' new male company."

Elizabeth smiled broadly. "That'd be lovely! Tomorrow night, maybe?"

Having missed the puzzled look on April's face she got a gentle tap on the arm from Jazz. "The word 'tea' here doesn't mean 'dinner' like in Oz. More like afternoon tea," the English girl explained softly. "I can finish up early at the distillery I reckon. We could pop round after that?" she suggested.

"Och, I cannae. I've just promised Postie Mary I'd see her at the lapidary back here in the village hall. But dinner is a fine idea. Could ye come around on Wednesday? It'll no' be anythin' fancy, mind, but I'm sure I can whip up some stovies."

"Ooh, if you do a good stovie, that would be brilliant!" said John B., gen-uinely. The other two Australians looked at him blankly, forgetting for a moment he'd been raised by a couple of expatriate Scots.

Grinning at his enthusiasm, and at least familiar with the meat-pota-to-and-onion mix that was a 'stovie', Jazz agreed. "Wednesday night – about six? At your place, next to the woods, right?"

"Sounds grand," agreed April. "Auld Wullie will probably want tae talk yer ear off aboot yer work, mind ye. He's got a bit of a passion for whis-ky, ye ken."

"I can relate to that," said John B., returning April's cheery wave as she turned to totter off toward her cottage.

 Wilko, also waving, looked sidelong at his old friend. "No argument
about that."

.oOo.

11 FIRST NIGHT DOES NOT ALWAYS GO TO PLAN

Jazz parked Anastasia outside the Hine's house. John B. pulled his kitbag and Q's suitcase from the boot of the Rover.

"What do we want to do about dinner?" asked the wizard.

"I try to avoid eating in, even on my own," said Jazz. "I can just imagine bloody Ishbell listening to see that I chew my food the correct number of times!"

"Does she really eavesdrop on you?" asked Elizabeth, aghast.

"Oh, not that I know of," admitted the engineer with a smile. "But I wouldn't put it past her."

Still in the passenger seat, Wilko looked unhappy. "Now I'm really glad there are two rooms. That biddy as an audience – stone the crows," he said.

Jazz said kindly, "Poor Wilko. You're a bit conservative, aren't you mate?"

"Afraid so," he replied. "Most Tasmanians are like that." (That may not have been quite true, but it had certainly been his experience growing up.)

The girl who waited so enthusiastically for his arrival playfully fondled his leg and teased, "It's all right, I'll help you get over it."

His answering smile was a bit nervous, but sincere.

From the footpath John B. said to Jazz, "Be gentle."

That prompted an expression of some irritation from his old friend, and quizzical looks from the women.

"Don't rush him is all I mean. Give the world time to adapt to a racy new Wilko. Now – about dinner?"

The driver replied, "There are two pubs in Port Ellen. The *Lost Goose* is more fun, but we're going there on Friday anyway. The food at the *Ferryhouse* is okay. We could go there. Pick you up sevenish?"

"Maybe earlier. Six or six-thirty?" suggested Elizabeth. "I don't know about anyone else, but I don't want a late night out."

There were signs of agreement all round. Sleep deprivation, whether by long-distance travel or bad dreams, was taking its toll on all of them. With that plan agreed, Jazz and Wilko headed back to their cottage.

John B. fished the keys Rhona had given him from his pocket. The front door of the house was already unlocked, but he had to fumble with the lock on the door to their room.

"I suppose I could put down the luggage, sweep you up and carry you over the threshold," he said, finally getting the key to turn the right way. He stepped back, pushing the door open for his beloved.

"No you don't!" laughed Q. "Not until we have our own… oh! Oh… my."

Stewart realised she was looking over his shoulder into the room. "What's wrong?" he asked as he turned. "Oh. I see…"

He let Elizabeth enter ahead of him, then followed carrying his bag on his shoulder.

"Well, I did say 'cozy', didn't I?" said the brunette.

At the far end of the room a small television was mounted on the wall above a little table. To use the table it would be necessary to sit on the end of either of the single beds. There was space for the luggage – just – at the foot of each bed, on either side of the table. The space between the beds was less than one of the single mattresses. As the door swung shut they realised that there was a bar fridge behind it, at the head of one bed. There was a narrow coatrack opposite the fridge, behind the other bedhead to the right of the doorway.

"Mm, yes. Rhona did mention that the bathroom was across the hall," observed John B. in a carefully even tone.

"Good. You wouldn't want to try to fit one in here," Q replied in a similar voice.

John B. adopted the Southern drawl they flirted with. "Would ma'am like the bed with the view?" There was a curtained window above the right hand bed.

"Why thank ya, kind sir," she replied in kind, carefully slipping her case into the gap by the table.

Finally, unable to restrain herself any longer, Q sat on the bed, her face in her hands, giggling helplessly, or was it sobbing? Dropping his kitbag on his own bed, Stewart sat beside her and wrapped an arm around her shoulders.

"I'm so sorry, sweetheart. This bloody magic, I can't control it. I've got to watch what I say. 'Some cozy little somewhere' I wished for…"

"Sorry babe," Q said through what the wizard sincerely hoped were tears of laughter. "That was what I said, and you were kind enough to go along with me. Look, it's small, but it's really quite a pretty room. It's just… I've been so looking forward to our first night alone together, and… hee hee…"

She really was giggling, John B. realised with relief.

"And… I never imagined single beds! I feel like Doris Day!"

"Rock and Doris shared a bed on screen you know, and quite demurely. They each slept with one foot on the floor on opposite sides of the bed."

"Oh, trust you to know that!" Q cried, and laughing, hit him on the shoulder.

He responded by grabbing her in an embrace. Her arms went around him and they toppled sideways onto the bed.

It's surprising how roomy a single mattress can be if you're creative.

*

By the time Jazz and Wilko arrived at six-fifteen, the other two had showered, changed clothes, and were sitting very contentedly in the little front parlour.

Elizabeth wore woolen tights and an aquamarine cashmere sweater that John B. thought fitted her absolutely perfectly. The wizard had also donned a clean outfit, but it was hard to tell by looking. Q had glanced into his kitbag and been more surprised than she should have been to realise that his wardrobe really was mostly comprised of jeans and purple t-shirts. A purple polo shirt and similarly hued Hawaiian shirt lurked at the bottom of the bag in case of situations where a collar was an unavoidable requirement.

"Do you not feel the cold, babe?" she asked in some concern as they got into the car.

"Not so far," Stewart replied casually. "I suppose I'll pick up a jacket or something somewhere, if I need it."

"No sense, no feeling," observed Wilko from the front of the car. He was well rugged up against the prospect of wind and rain, as was Jazz.

The *Ferryhouse* hotel turned out to be much as the engineer had described it. Not sombre, but not rich in character or charm either. But the food was satisfying. Wilko had a plate of mutton chops that were far tastier than he'd expected, while the others all enjoyed the House Special. It was *Cullen Skink* – a thick soup of smoked haddock, onions and potatoes.

As much as the four friends enjoyed their meal and each other's company, it wasn't long before the level of energy around the table fell away. The jet lag that had been temporarily overcome reasserted itself on Elizabeth and John B., while Jazz' recent run of dream-provoked sleep interruption had her yawning too.

"We'd better head off soon. I won't be able to drive if we wait much longer. I'm probably bloody pushing it already," admitted the Englishwoman.

Wilko reached and took her hand. "Maybe I'd better drive," he said. "I got plenty of sleep on the trip over."

It was true. The ability to sleep through the labyrinthine sound catalogue of his own snoring also meant that the Tasmanian seemed impervious to outside noises, lights or incidents that would jar less fortunate mortals into wakefulness.

The bill was paid. The foursome made their way out to the car, the three exhausted ones scarcely aware of the rain that was now falling. Fortunately it wasn't heavy. Wilko carefully piloted the silver sedan along the coast road back to Sron Dubh. He looked forward to the opportunity to 'open her up' and give the Rover a good workout along what seemed to him an interesting stretch, but this wasn't the time.

At Rhona's house her new guests almost tumbled from the car. If the rain bothered them, it didn't show. After fond but brief goodnights the tenacity with which they held each other as they opened doors and made their way to their little room wasn't entirely a product of romance. Just keeping each other upright was part of it.

It was a good thing Wilko drove. Jazz' head was on her chest by the time the Rover got back to their cottage. He gently roused her, then came round to the passenger side of the car and held his jacket over her as he shepherded her to the door.

Peeking furtively through a gap in her own heavy curtain, Ishbell McNeill nodded in grudging approval.

She sipped at a cup of cold weak tea. Eventually the rain eased off. The drumming noise from her roof now stilled, Ishbell was able to press an ear to the thin wall nearest her guests' cottage. Only a narrow gap separated the two buildings.

The widow McNeill stood close to the wall, listening intently. What *was* that strange sound? A series of rumbles, groans, snorts, squeaks – whistles even… Then suddenly she recognised the rhythm, from the long-ago days of her marriage to Grey Wullie. It was snoring.

She stayed listening a wee while longer. Surely nobody else could sleep alongside that noise, so they *must* be in separate bedrooms. Good! No sinful carryings-on there, then.

Satisfied, she clumped off to her bed to read a chapter or two of Leviticus before she fell asleep. She liked the book of Leviticus. It gave some interesting explanations of the sorts of sins that the neighbours might get up to. And offered some excellent instructions on how they should be punished.

.o0o.

12 OBSERVATIONS

Robbie Keith wasn't entirely sure what to make of the man that his engineer was pinning such hopes on. He looked scruffy – exactly the antithesis of Robbie's own neat blue suit, morning shave and fortnightly-trimmed hair. He'd been self-effacing about his experience and 'abilities' – yes, he had an unusual talent and had been through some strange stuff but no, he could make no promises beyond doing his best to help.

In truth, that was some relief to the General Manager. If Stewart had come in with all guns blazing and vowing that he'd fix everything, Robbie would have been suspicious. He didn't trust carnival barkers.

And the man certainly knew his whisky. As he led Stewart and his two politely quiet friends on a tour around the facilities he was struck by just how much the purple-shirted fellow knew about the production process.

At one point though, it dawned on him that it wasn't just whisky making in general that he knew – it was this distillery he seemed to know. Presumably Miss Parrish had already explained much to him, although neither she nor Stewart had mentioned it.

The point where surprise gave way to incredulity was when the visitor had pointed to the car park beside the little tenement row that housed several members of staff and their families on-site.

"There used to be another row of houses there, didn't there?" he'd asked.

Now, that was a reasonable inference to draw from the layout of the building and car park. The kicker had been his next sentence.

"That was where the maltmen lived. They worked all hours, so it was easier if they all lived apart and could come and go at whatever time without disturbing anyone else's sleep," Stewart had explained.

Keith had nodded. "So I believe. That was many years ago, of course. I… wait a minute. How did you know that?"

The man in purple had blinked and looked puzzled. "I have no idea. It just… came to me while I was looking over there."

"I'd like to say you get used to it, but you never do," remarked the shorter chap with them – Wilkes his name was, Robbie recalled.

Moraig McConnell had later confirmed Stewart's observation. Her grandparents had lived in the old building – demolished soon after the War when the whisky business all over the island had gone into drastic decline. She now occupied one of the half dozen surviving tenements. All the residents, like Moraig, had long family histories at the distillery.

As they wandered, John B. had quietly spoken to everyone he met, being careful to avoid interrupting their work. No detailed probing. Just polite conversation about the job, 'how are you keeping?', 'how long have you been here?' type of questions.

And yet, at the end of the tour, back in Robbie's office Stewart was able to say, "I see your problem. A whisky distillery without spirit is just wrong. If there were any more bags under the eyes out there you'd be better off going into the luggage business."

Robbie and Wilko both winced. Jazz and Moraig were in their respective offices and Elizabeth was trying to will herself to love John B.'s puns. It wasn't easy.

"I don't reckon that it's coincidence. Hard to see how it could be deliberate, though. How do you get on with the competition?" the wizard asked.

"The other distilleries on the island? Oh, well enough," answered Robbie. "The workers all know each other to some extent of course. There are only 3000 or so people on the whole island so there's never more than a degree or two of separation. At the management level we're all quite sociable. Collectively we produce a big slice of Scotland's biggest export so while technically we compete, if we all cooperate in making the market as big as possible and the product as good as possible, we all get a share."

"That's a good healthy attitude," observed Elizabeth.

"Oh, it doesn't always work," the manager admitted. "But for the most part we rub along quietly. Certainly there's been nothing aggressive since I've been here, and Moraig hasn't mentioned anything of the sort."

John B. scratched at his chin. The stubble had definitely reached bristle length. "Maybe it's the place itself. Something dark in its history, and now something has – disturbed things? Unquiet spirits?"

Not unexpectedly, Wilko gave a skeptical snort. "Bloody ghosts, you reckon, mate?"

"I know you don't believe in 'em old pal. Or magic either. But you've seen your share of strange stuff."

"More than my share!"

The wizard continued. "But I'm not convinced it's just here. Concentrated maybe, but not exclusively. Nobody in the village mentioned anything yesterday, but we weren't really asking."

"Bad dreams aren't the sort of thing that come up in casual conversation when you first meet someone," said Elizabeth.

"Fair call," agreed her lover. "I've a feeling the lovely Mrs. Bromleigh might be a help. I don't think she misses much in the village."

"You're right there!" interrupted Robbie. "Sorry. Her husband has had a bit to do with this place over the years. I don't think he was ever actually on the staff – more like a consultant, before the term was invented. He still turns up now and then if there's a problem with a batch that our lads are struggling with. Mrs. B. though – bundle of energy. Into everything."

"Slow moving energy," said Wilko.

"Slow moving, but bloody hard to stop, I'd reckon," smiled Elizabeth.

"Indeed," agreed the manager.

John B. grinned. "I wouldn't like to get in the way of her sister, either."

"Which one? There are two," said Robbie.

"We've met Rose. She's a character!" replied Stewart.

"Ah. Yes. So I believe. I'm surprised you met her – apparently she doesn't get out much. The other sister, Effie, is much the same in that regard I gather. Mrs. Bromleigh is the sociable one."

The wizard nodded. "Okay. I'll try asking around a bit for myself, but we're seeing April soon anyway. Thanks for your time, Mr. Keith. Like I said before, no promises, but I'll do whatever I can."

John B. and Robbie shook hands, the manager still a little bemused at what this man might be able to achieve. But then, he honestly had no idea of what the trouble actually was, only that it was all too real. If a shaggy Australian who seemed to know things he couldn't might help, well, good. Jazz Parrish trusted him, and she was excellent at her job.

"We'll pop in on Jazz before we go," Stewart said, just as Robbie had thought about her. "We can walk back to the village rather than have her drive. Get a bit of lunch and see who we bump into."

*

Given the frequency with which coincidences happened around John B. Stewart ("You're a bloody walking improbability field!" Wilko would complain) it was no surprise that as the three friends walked into the village's only tea room they almost collided with April Bromleigh. The old woman had been distracted by bickering with one of her own companions about the price of a cup of tea.

On one side of April was a lean man whose thatch of wavy brown hair belied his lined face. It was impossible to pick his age, but surely it couldn't be less than late 70s?

At her other side was another woman – the one who'd been contending about prices. She was the same height as Rose stood on her 'bad' side, and shared the same build – apple shaped. A very solid apple. She wore a floral shift in more muted pastels than April's, with a cardigan in blue that was either faded or dully pale. Two black walking sticks helped her stand.

"You must be Effie! A pleasure to meet you, ma'am," exclaimed John B.

Someone else may have been surprised to be recognised by a total stranger from the far side of the planet. This woman wasn't. She transferred one stick to free a hand that she extended.

"Effie Lindsay. Ma wee sister here's been tellin' me about ye all."

"Mrs. Lindsay. Sorry," the wizard said, taking the proffered hand and bowing.

"Och, no, Effie will do fine."

The three Australians introduced themselves. April in turn introduced her husband, Auld Wullie. He gave a polite nod of greeting to Elizabeth and Wilko.

To the wizard in purple he nodded and quietly said, "Guid tae see ye." There was a glint of recognition in his eye that John B. neither recognised nor returned.

"I'd love tae stay and chat," said April, "I'm afraid we have tae get Effie home, but."

"Aye," agreed the middle sister. "I'm sorry, but ma legs arnae so good any more. I'm better off in ma own chairs at home ye ken, but Auld Wullie's car's no' so bad."

"Quite okay. I do want to have a talk with you, April, but it can wait," said Stewart.

After the three senior citizens departed and sandwiches had been ordered the Australians sat at a table watching the activities on the main street of the village.

"Auld Wullie doesn't say much, does he?" said Elizabeth.

“Probably out of practice. Can’t imagine he gets much of a word in edge-ways with his wife.”

“You’re a harsh man, Wilko,” observed John B. “But April does certainly stand out in the village. Look out there – what do you see?”

“Shops. A few people. It is a small place you know,” said the Tasmanian.

 Elizabeth gazed out the window, trying to pick what had caught Stewart’s eye. “The people I can see are just walking, shopping, minding their own business…”

“Aye. That’s the odd thing. All with heads down, no one chatting or greeting each other. Like you said mate, it’s a small place. Everyone knows each other. You’d expect a bit of polite chat at least. Even Rhona this morning – we only saw her for two minutes at most. Nice enough, sure, checking there were enough eggs and bacon for us to make breakfast, but without April there to chivvy things along conversation just didn’t hap-pen.”

“Well, she does have a sick husband to worry about,” said Wilko.

“Sure. But she didn’t even think to ask anything like how we found the room. I was just a bit… surprised, that’s all.”

 They watched the streetscape for a while. When their tea and sandwiches were served John B. tried to engage their young waitress – another Mary according to her nametag – in conversation.

“And which Mary are you?” he asked her genially.

“Eh? Oh – ye know aboot how we’re called around here? I’m er… well… they call me Giddy Mary. It’s a bit embarrassing. I’ve loved tae dance since I were a bairn. I’m no’ very good at it, but.”

“So you’ll be going to the ceilidh on Saturday night?” asked Elizabeth.

 The waitress brightened. “Oh aye, miss! I think there’ll be quite a lot fra’ the village going. Well… but… the Reverend prob'ly willnae approve and that might stop some. A bit o' fun would be a nice change…"

Her voice dropped. "I prob'ly shouldnae say that…"

"It's okay Mary. We won't tell anyone," said John B. sympathetically. "A lot of people here do seem a bit withdrawn. Like they're very… tired?"

The expression on Giddy Mary's face told him he'd hit a mark. But before she could say any more a voice came from behind the shop counter.

"Giddy Mary! Leave the customers in peace and get aboot yer work! If everyb'dy has been served there's dishes need washin'!"

"Right, Miz Chisholm! Sorry, Miz Chisholm! I'll get right tae it! Sorry, folks," she added in a whisper as she turned away.

"No worries. See you at the dance," Elizabeth called softly after her. One look at the stern-faced redhead behind the counter was enough for her to be sure that Miz Chisholm was likely to be one of those not attending the ceilidh.

*

The afternoon brought little more success to their investigations. Even the politest of shopkeepers and locals were hardly talkative. Some were downright taciturn, though none quite crossed the boundary of rudeness.

Even a return visit to Postie Mary brought only the observation that "people wernae as cheerful as they used tae be, right enough." The widow McMurtrie wasn't one to reveal any confidences she may have heard (unlike many of April Bromleigh's network). Of herself she said only that "runnin' a shop is wearyin' business, ye ken, and I'm no' as young as I was."

As he dropped Elizabeth and John B. back at their accommodation Wilko grumpily said, "I was reading a magazine on the flight over from Glasgow. Said the people on Islay have an 'air of pride and contentment that keep visitors returning for more'. The woman who wrote it hadn't been to Sron Dubh, I reckon."

Stewart sighed. "Not much fun this avo, no. Sorry mate. We can try Port Ellen tomorrow? It's not far, but we might get an idea of how localized this thing is."

"Whatever it is," replied the Tasmanian. "Indian tonight?" he suggested.

It was Elizabeth who demurred. She knew Wilko's fondness for food so fiery it could take layers of skin off another person's mouth. "I think I'd like something less spicy. Simple pub food was good last night – we could try that other hotel tonight, and do curry on Thursday."

"Sure. Can't imagine Jazz objecting. Pick you up about six thirty again?"

Stewart patted Anastasia's roof and said, "Sounds good. Hey, we might all be awake enough to make a bit more of a night of it, eh?"

.oOo.

13 MEETING THE LOST GOOSE

When they first arrived at the *Lost Goose* the four friends settled at one end of the front bar for the first rounds of drinks.

"It's a funny name for a pub," said Elizabeth.

"Ah, I did a bit of reading while I was waiting for Jazz to come home. Islay's famous for a flock of geese that stop here in winter as they migrate," said Wilko, pleased that for once he had a bit of the inside knowledge that John B. so often produced and credited to 'something he'd read'.

"A verra big flock," agreed the barman as he placed a pint of ale in front of Wilko. The others had single malts, watered for Elizabeth and Jazz ("They're allowed, bein' lassies," the barman had said.) "We get upwards o' *seasgad mile* o' them ontae the island. More every year. They're startin' tae come in noo – ye'll see a great *neul* o' the buggers any day, mark me."

"Um… thanks," said the Tasmanian with a blank look. Between the accent and the scattered Gaelic he'd understood very little, but knew enough to be polite. "Miles of geese?" he said to Stewart quietly when the man had gone to serve another customer at the far end of the bar.

John B. smiled. "*Seasgad mile* – sixty thousand. Upwards of that's a bloody big flock alright. And our friend reckons we can expect a big cloud of them to fly over soon."

"You speak Gaelic?" asked Jazz in surprise. "Not many people outside Scotland do! Jeez – you're handy to have around. There are some blokes at work who I need bloody subtitles for!"

"He speaks all sorts of stuff. On rare occasions some of it even makes sense," said Wilko. Only someone who knew them well would have recognised it as good-natured banter.

"A *bideag* – a bit," said Stewart ignoring the jibe as usual. "My parents were Scots, and my mother's family still spoke the language. I learned a little from her."

Only Elizabeth caught the momentary pause in his voice before the word 'parents'. Unlike Wilko she didn't yet know John B. had been adopted. She realised there was still a lot she didn't know about the man she loved. What she didn't realise was how much he didn't know either. Such conversations would come later.

At the next round the barman, by then identified as Bruce, explained further the origin of the hotel's name. Diplomatically waiting until after he'd moved on John B. translated for his companions.

"Normally the geese settle on a big loch at the other end of Islay. Years ago one of them didn't go with the rest, and spent the winter in the courtyard out back of the pub. Early on it frightened off someone trying to break in – they can be aggressive as well as loud. The landlord reckoned it was good luck, and fed it well enough that it stayed instead of taking off after the other geese. So he wound up changing the name of the hotel."

Laughing, Elizabeth raised her glass. "Good story! Here's to the goose!"

They shared the toast.

Bourbon or chardonnay had long been Elizabeth's regular preferred options, but JB was winning her over, she explained. "To whisky, I mean."

Soon after, Bruce chanced to be standing nearby with no other customers requiring his services. John B. got his attention.

"Mate, this might seem an odd thing to say, but thanks for making us feel welcome. I know it's your job, but, well, not everyone we've met round here has been quite so… friendly."

The barman looked slightly embarrassed, not on his own behalf as it turned out.

"Och, I'm sorry aboot that, pal. Dinna think too harsh o' folks. There's a lot havenae been themsel's of late. *Aisling dona*, I'm hearin', though naebody's talkin' o'er much aboot it."

"Bad dreams? That's nasty. You're not getting them too, are you?" The concern in Stewart's voice was genuine.

"No' at all, funnily enough. Mind ye, I work nights and sleep days maself. It's hard tae have a nightmare when the *grian* is up, eh?"

"That must be it," agreed the Australian and raised his glass. "Here's to the sun, mate, and thanks again."

Bruce grinned. "Ye're welcome sir. And welcome tae Port Ellen, all o' ye." With that, he went to pour a round of beers further along the bar.

"That was interesting," observed Elizabeth who'd managed to follow most of Bruce's heavily accented speech.

"The mystery deepens," said Jazz, finishing her drink at a gulp, after which she announced she'd drive everyone home that night so would be switching to water for a while.

"I think better on a full stomach. Why don't we go investigate our dinner options in the lounge?" suggested Wilko, who'd drained his ale and was feeling quite peckish by this time.

"Good idea, mate. I'll come with you while these guys finish their drinks," said Jazz, taking his hand and leading him off.

Stewart grinned. "She knows perfectly well I'm long finished. No, don't hurry, sweetheart. I'm happy to let them have a bit more time together. If you're okay on your own for a bit I might – ah, go and make room for dinner."

Q returned the grin. "You do that, babe. Be comfortable. I'll be fine on my own for a bit till you get back. Nobody's going to bother me."

That turned out to be a slightly optimistic assessment. Only recently divorced from an especially insensitive husband, Elizabeth didn't really appreciate how attractive she was. While John B. was Occupied (that's what the sign on the door said) his vacant bar stool was suddenly taken over by a fellow who'd clearly been investing heavily in the liquid assets of Islay for a while.

"Good evenin' young lady. Is thish seat taken?" he asked, landing on the stool before she could answer.

"Actually, it is," she said, but was ignored.

"Ye're no' from round here, are ye? I'd recon… recon… recon'ize ye. Ma name's Wullie Barclay. They call me Lush Wullie."

"Oh, that *is* a surprise," his intended target answered drily.

"Naw, naw, ye dinna understand. 'Lush' as in comfortable. I'm a bit… a bit… well off. An' a bit luscious too, I'm told," he said, leaning forward to giving a conspiratorial wink that almost toppled him to the floor.

 Elizabeth raised her eyebrows. Perhaps the word had a different meaning around here.

 Barclay tried to sidle closer to her, a move that threatened his precarious balance on the stool. "I'd like tae share wi' ye the besht bits o' Port Ellen," he offered.

"Oh yes?"

"Aye. Aye. I keep 'em right here," he said with a leer, patting his crotch.

'Well, that's a line I haven't heard before,' she thought, rolling her eyes.

"Don' ye worry, lashie," Lush Wullie said as he tried to drape an arm around Elizabeth – an arm she firmly pushed away. "I'll still respect you in the morning."

"Really? That's a surprise. There's no sign you respect me now."

Barclay blinked, puzzled. "Huh?" was the best he could manage.

"You're not my type. I prefer a man who can hold onto me without holding on. I think that girl over there is more what you're looking for."

"Ah, orright…" Clearly no stranger to rejection the drunk slid off the stool and staggered in the direction she'd indicated, as yet unaware that the buxom girl he was aiming for was adorning an advertising poster.

John B. arrived back just in time to see Lush Wullie's wobbly departure.

"Sorry sweetheart. Was he bothering you?" he asked in concern.

Q replied casually, "Nah, I outwitted him."

"Well done."

"Thanks babe, but it was no big effort. A ping pong ball could have done the same."

"Ah. A battle of wits with a one-armed man."

"Unarmed, more like it," she replied with a smile. With a final sip to finish her drink the brunette indicated the lounge. "Should we join the others before they come looking for us?"

"Do you think that's likely?"

"Hmm. I think Wilko is still getting used to his new world."

They linked arms and strolled off.

*

The food was good. More extravagant than the *Ferryhouse*, and a cut above what the Australian contingent expected from a small town pub. Seared scallops with pork belly. Venison meatballs with fettuccine. And from the menu selection headed 'Traditional Scottish Favourites' – macaroni cheese with bacon.

"It's in the pronunciation," John B. theorized. "Put the emphasis on the 'mac' syllable."

After dinner Wilko patted his stomach contentedly. It had been a generous serving of fettuccine.

"A round of post-prandial drinks?" offered the wizard.

"Port, if they've got it," said his Tasmanian mate.

"That sounds good!" agreed Elizabeth.

The driver bit her lip. "I reckon I can manage another half nip of a good single malt. Pick something nice, John B."

"Trust me!" he replied as he stood.

"On this one, I reckon you can," admitted Wilko as Stewart ambled toward the lounge bar.

Jazz laughed, and then leaned towards Q. "I didn't tell you! I heard that bloody dragon Mrs. McNeill clomping around in her seven league boots after we'd gone to bed last night. I'm sure she was listening through the bloody wall! Checking we were in separate rooms!"

"And of course you were," said Elizabeth grinning.

"Some of the time," the Englishwoman replied with an answering grin.

Both women laughed. Wilko looked uncomfortable, not least because he hadn't known about Ishbell's nocturnal nosiness.

"I'll go see what's keeping John," he said brusquely and took off for the bar where he found his friend spoilt for choice of single malts and inveigling sample whiffs from the bartender. He offered to help.

From the table Elizabeth watched the shorter man's back. She was fonder of Wilko than most people knew. They'd faced death together in Bass

Strait, and that does create a bond.

"Take it easy on him. He's not the most worldly of blokes," she counseled.

Jazz waved airily and said, "Oh, I'll work on him."

"Seriously. Like JB said, be gentle. He's a good man."

There was a pause as the two women looked into each other's eyes. (It's something men seldom do, even in significant moments. Shoulder to shoulder is more comfortable.)

Finally Jazz said, "I know. It's a lot of what attracted me to him. I've known too many blokes who were all style and no substance."

"Mm. I was married to a bloke that turned out to have neither."

That elicited a laugh. "Oh, I've had them too! No, Wilko's a bit difficult, but he's… lovable. Not like a cuddly toy, I mean, but under that grumpy exterior there's something really sweet."

The brunette smiled. "You're right, I think. But be careful cracking through that shell, hey? He's spent a long time building it – for whatever good reason. Don't hurt him is all I'm asking."

"I don't aim to," answered the blonde sincerely. "You really think I'm rushing him?"

Elizabeth shrugged. "It doesn't matter what I think. How does he feel? Push too hard and I reckon you'll soon know."

"Let him do the pushing? Not really my style. And I reckon I might have gotten old waiting for him to make the first bloody move. But I get your point. The ball's rolling now, I don't need to kick it along."

"Quite right. There's a time and a place for kicking balls."

Both women were still laughing when Wilko and Stewart got back bearing glasses of excellent port and superb vintage whisky. The Tasmanian had winced at the prices but John B. could afford it, and was sure the company was worth the investment.

"To good friends and lovers," the wizard said as he raised his glass.

"I'll drink to that," agreed Q.

"That is *my* line, ma'am!"

Even Wilko laughed at that.

It was a good night.

.oOo.

14 STILL WATERS

Sadly the good night had not continued once they'd all gone to sleep.

 That much was obvious by the drawn faces when they gathered for break-fast at the tearoom before Jazz went to work. John B. was at the counter, placing the order with Ms. Chisholm.

"If that's what everyone here has been going through, no wonder they're going mad," was Elizabeth's blunt assessment. "God, she was horrible! But kind of… irresistible."

"You got the schoolroom too?" asked Jazz.

"Hell, yeah. That woman in the old-fashioned outfit. Making every-one recite lines – 'thou shalt be obedient', over and over. It's still going around in my head! Even after that shocker that came later."

 Wilko shook his head. "You've lost me with the school stuff. All I remember is what sounded like screaming, and a lot of heat. I woke up sweating, I can tell you!"

 Stewart had just arrived at the table. He nodded. "No visuals with it. Same here, this time anyway. Pity I can't say the same about that damned classroom."

 His old friend looked at him and said, "You've been getting these since Hawaii? No wonder you wanted to look into it, mate. And you've had it even worse here, haven't you?" he said to Jazz, taking her hand.

"Afraid so, honey. At least now I've got you here to wake up to. That helps, thanks. Say, I wonder if Ishbell McNeill gets the same dreams?"

 The wizard yawned. "I reckon she might, but I reckon she's one of those kids at the back of the classroom. You know – the ones you can't see? It feels like they approve somehow. Maybe even enjoying themselves."

"Mm. It wasn't that clear for me. I'm sort of dimly aware of what you mean," said Elizabeth. "This could be another one of that same bunch though," she said indicating Ms. Chisholm who was approaching with a tray of their breakfasts.

The meals, such as they were, were delivered wordlessly. Meagre portions, accompanied by tepid tea, no coffee. It was as though their presence, or at least their desire to break their fast, was disapproved of.

"At least she's not looking for a tip," said John B., trying to inject some levity that no one rose to.

"Can you drop me at the distillery before you go into Port Ellen, please?" asked Jazz.

"Sure. Whenever you're ready." Wilko pushed a limp rasher around his plate unenthusiastically as he spoke.

"Right, let's be off then," said Stewart, standing suddenly. "We can't do worse looking for some tucker there, surely."

Nobody disagreed. Four plates and cups, scarcely touched, were left for Ms. Chisholm to collect. She'd no doubt leave them for Giddy Mary to wash when the girl came in.

*

The *Ferryhouse* in Port Ellen turned out to offer breakfast – a pleasant surprise for the three Australians who were in need of something to lift their spirits. It was nothing flash, but well cooked and with decent coffee to wash it down, the meal was worth lingering over.

They did notice though that the young man serving them didn't say much. It might have been a hangover, or he might be naturally sullen, but John B. and Elizabeth fancied that the dark circles under his eyes told a familiar story. They were kind enough to not press him.

When they left the hotel it was still relatively early. Not many of the shops had opened yet, not that there were a lot anyway. Port Ellen was bigger than the village they were living in, but it barely ranked as a small town. The police station had long ago shut down and services were scanty. The ferry terminal and the hotels gave it life but a tourist seeking a bustling hive of activity would have been sorely disappointed, especially before ten in the morning.

As the trio ambled along the main street window-shopping they spied a strange figure approaching.

He was a little dark man, in a brown suit that had been awkwardly cut to fit him. He wasn't quite a midget, but Wilko, who sometimes privately fretted about his own lack of height, was more than a head taller. Tucked under his arm was a leather satchel, almost the same shade of brown as his suit. He walked with a purposeful stride.

Before their paths crossed, the little man stopped at a doorway between two shops and knocked loudly. He waited patiently for a moment and then the door opened. A haggard man in striped pyjamas peered out, puzzled, then looked down and spotted his visitor.

"Aah! Sith! I…" he cried in some shock.

The small man was unperturbed and spoke politely. "Good morning, Mr. Buchanan. Ma apologies for waking ye, but ye did tell Mr. Craig ye want- ed these documents as soon as possible."

"Oh! Yes. I… um… sorry, I havenae slept well…"

That got a sympathetic clicking sound from his visitor. "Aye, there's a lot o' that aboot at the moment. Shall I wait while ye sign these, or shall I come back tae collect them later?"

"No! I… er… the wife's still abed. She's taken a draught tae try tae get some rest, ye ken? I'll… er… I'll get the bus tae Bowmore later and drop them intae Mr. Craig's office maself."

"As ye like, Mr. Buchanan." The dark man was a pint-sized model of professional courtesy as he took a small sheaf of papers from his satchel and held them out. "It's clearly marked where ye and Mrs. Buchanan are tae sign."

The man in pyjamas went to take the forms, but the small man held them for a moment more, saying in a stern voice, "I hope ye really have given this serious thought, sir. Tis a significant step ye're taking, and not tae be taken lightly if I may say so."

Buchanan was visibly sweating as he answered, "Aye… aye, I know. We're no' happy aboot it, but… well… it's like we have tae, ye ken?"

"No, Mr. Buchanan, I don't. But tis your decision, for ye and your wife tae take. So long as ye're sure in yourselves." He released his grip on the papers so Buchanan inadvertently almost snatched them.

"Sorry! No… no, but nae choice…" he mumbled, closing the door, the very picture of a defeated man.

Shaking his head sadly, the little man continued on his way, stopping by the three Australians who were standing by a shopfront, trying unsuccessfully to look like they hadn't witnessed the exchange.

"Far too much o' it happening, in ma opinion," the fellow in the suit sighed. He held out a hand. "Arsaidh MacAdam. Welcome tae Islay."

John B. was first to shake the proffered hand, and was impressed by the firmness of the grip. As the others repeated the greeting and introduced themselves, the wizard asked cautiously, "Did I hear that bloke call you 'Sith'?"

"Aye, I get that a lot. *Sith Dubh* – the Black Elf. Heard it all ma life. It disnae bother me. Use it if ye wish."

"I think not, Mr. MacAdam," said Elizabeth firmly. "You've a given name, and unless you prefer otherwise that's what we should use, out of common courtesy."

MacAdam smiled. It was a good look, his teeth almost radiant against his dark features. He wasn't negroid, but his skin was a deep brown that might have been Mediterranean or Middle Eastern – it was impossible to be sure of his origins.

"It's no' such a common thing, this common courtesy. I thank ye, lass."

She returned the smile. There was an old-fashioned charm about Arsaidh MacAdam that she immediately warmed to. "So you work for Mr. Craig? We met him on the plane the other day," she said.

"Aye, I help him oot, part-time as it were. I have other things tae do."

There was a definite sense that the Black Elf was not a man who worked *for* anybody. He seemed very much his own man.

"Pardon my asking, Mr. MacAdam," said John B., "But far too much of *what* happening?"

Arsaidh appeared to weigh his answer carefully. "People making business decisions that don't appear tae be in their best interests."

"Why is that, do you reckon?"

"Fear, Mr. Stewart," the small man said simply. "Noo, I should be aboot ma work. I've much tae do today, like every other day. Good tae meet ye all – I'm sure it'll no' be the last time," he said, looking squarely at John B.

With a courteous bow MacAdam walked on up the street.

When he was a safe distance away Wilko remarked, "When Craig said he had a small staff, he wasn't kidding."

John B. laughed softly. "Mate, that was worthy of me!"

"Jeez, don't tell me that! Hey listen, why is it so many people here seem like they know you somehow?"

Elizabeth nodded and squeezed her boyfriend's arm a little tighter to her side. "I've noticed that too, babe. Nothing said, just a… look you get from some people."

"No idea. I've noticed it too, but honestly folks – it's a mystery to me too," John B. admitted. But then, quite a bit of John B. Stewart's life was a mystery, even to him.

As they continued along the street they came upon a parked car that caught the eye of both men.

"Now there's a funny thing," remarked John B. "We're driving about in the last Rover 75, and here's the first model with that name. Made in 1951." He beckoned for Elizabeth to look at the front of the car with him. "Single fog light mounted in the middle, see? Gave the car the nickname of Cyclops."

"And still a verra useful item on this island, many a time," said a voice behind him.

They turned to see Auld Wullie standing with his hands in the pockets of his fawn vest, and a smile creasing his face.

"Yours?" asked Wilko.

"Aye lad, since she were shiny an' new. Still hums along like she did then, too." The old man took a step forward. "I was wantin' tae meet wi' ye, John B. Stewart. We've aye much tae talk aboot, you and I."

"Really?" the wizard said in surprise. "Well, here I am."

"A wee blether somewhere mair private?" suggested Bromleigh, gesturing towards his car.

"Well, we were going to try to pick some brains around town…" Stewart began.

Elizabeth gently propelled him towards the old man. "Wilko and I can take care of that, babe. I think it's important that you go and blether with him."

"I fear yer pickin's may be slim lass, but thank ye fer that," said Auld Wullie graciously as he opened the passenger door for John B.

Stewart slid onto the red leather bench seat, and couldn't resist sliding a hand across the cedar dashboard. "They don't make 'em like this any more," he said admiringly.

"Aye. That's progress, I'm told," replied Auld Wullie evenly as he got behind the wheel.

John B. leaned out the window and kissed Q's hand. "Will I see you back here at um…"

"I'll deliver ye back tae Hamish and Rhona's," said his aged chauffeur.

"That's a good idea," agreed Elizabeth. "Take your time, gentlemen. I'll see you whenever, babe," she concluded in a softer tone.

Wilko gave an uncertain wave as the old Rover glided away, its sixty-something year old motor purring. "What's that all about, do you reckon?" he asked.

"I know as much as you do, mate," the brunette replied. "But instinct tells me Auld Wullie's on our side.

The Tasmanian nodded. He'd learned to trust Elizabeth's instincts.

*

Considering Auld Wullie's remark about having much to talk about there was very little conversation as the antique Rover made its way along the coast road. John B. thought about initiating a chat, but decided to wait for his host to open up any discussion.

They drove through Sron Dubh. Auld Wullie indicated a small cottage behind a stone fence and high iron gate that looked like it had rusted open decades earlier.

"Our hoose," he said. "Mind, dinner at six. April fixes a fair stovie."

"I'm looking forward to it," came the honest reply.

They continued in silence through the woods. Auld Wullie suddenly turned off onto a track that couldn't possibly be found by chance. Some minutes driving later they emerged from the trees onto a grassy hillside. A few more minutes saw the old car negotiate something like a goat track with surprising ease before the driver stopped on a convenient flat area.

Wordlessly he got out of the car and started to stroll up the gentle slope. The wizard shrugged and followed him. Near the top of the small hill the old man stopped. The ground was cleft, as if struck by a massive axe. Water bubbled up from the dark rock and ran in a small steady stream down the far side of the hill, seeping into the soft ground at the edge of a paddock.

There were two impressive large standing stones at the fringe of the paddock. Numerous such stones littered Islay, some thought to be Norse, many thought to be much older. A few other stones lay dotted about the paddock.

Auld Wullie pulled two small glasses from the pocket of his jacket. Holding them both in one large hand he knelt and dipped them into the running water, then offered one to John B.

Both men sipped at the brilliantly clear cold liquid.

"The true *uisge badh* – water of life," observed the wizard.

Bromleigh nodded and smiled as he added, "And the secret tae a truly fine whisky."

He pointed down at the stones. "If ye were tae stand down in yon paddock, tae the right o' the stones, and look back at them at just the right angle…"

"Which is?"

"So the edges look tae be aligned, front left tae back right, then ye'd see one particular stone in the face o' the hill itself, lookin' like the third in the row."

"The hill's not as solid as it looks, right?"

"Take the wee wedgin' stone out frae the base at right, and the big stone'll pivot like a kirk door. A time ago there was a braw wee still in the cave."

"Not now though. Not for… quite a few years." John B.'s voice was thoughtful as he gazed down at the paddock. He turned to Auld Wullie. "Why do I have the sense that I know you? That I know *here*? It's not just the dreams that are stuck in my head. There's a feeling of familiarity that I can't explain, and you're a part of that."

Bromleigh stared out over the paddock towards the ocean. "It's been a long time," he said softly. He drew several heavy breaths, and then continued without shifting his seaward gaze. "There was a lad, when I was a lad. Wullie MacEwen. Braw Wullie he was called."

'Lad', John B. realised, could mean anything from five to thirty-five in local parlance. Perhaps more to Auld Wullie.

"He was a 'homer', ye ken?" John B. looked blank.

Auld Wullie explained. "They were orphan wains – children, fra' the mainland. They got sent oot tae the islands, mostly by the papist kirk. Nae background checks, they'd arrive on the ferry wi' the name of who-ever'd put their hand up tae be the 'keeper' family on a card around the wain's neck."

The old man's eyes looked distant. It was the longest speech John B. had ever heard him make, and even the fairly simple explanation was clearly resonating somewhere deep within. 'Was Auld Wullie a 'homer' too?' the wizard wondered.

"Braw Wullie wasnae wi' us long. Just long enough, as is rightly the way o' things." Bromleigh sighed. "Perhaps I've let masel' get too settled."

John B. said nothing, respecting his companion's privacy as Auld Wullie appeared to slip into a reverie. The man in purple looked up and watched clouds gathering, and several sizeable skeins of geese flying over.

Suddenly a noise came from by Stewart's feet. It was somewhere between a howl and a meow. A cat had emerged from some long sedge and was rubbing itself against the Australian's ankles. It was a dark tabby, stocky but powerfully built. There was something almost like a short mane, and a long tail covered with long thick bristles of dark fur. The noise had changed to something like a rapid drumbeat.

"Now tha's somethin' I've no' seen before!" exclaimed Auld Wullie. "I mean, I've seen the cat around often enough, but he's aye kept a respectable distance."

"It's a heckuva looking feral!" said John B., cautiously bending to stroke the cat's head and back. The volume of the purr increased.

"No' feral – that yin's a proper Scottish wildcat. There arnae a great number o' them left any more, here or over in the Highlands. They're no' noted fer approachin' people, certainly no' like that yin is!"

The wizard spoke quietly to the animal. "This is your place, isn't it, mate? Thanks for sharing it with us."

He knelt and the wildcat almost climbed onto his lap in its efforts to be close to him. The beast was heavy, even heavier than his late lamented white Persian Kat had been. The wildcat was all muscle.

Auld Wullie shook his head as he watched the wizard and the strange behaviour of what was supposed to be a dangerous predator, to be approached with caution or better yet, not at all.

"What do ye remember o' the history of the distiller's art?" he asked.

Stewart had been a prodigious reader of history since childhood. He numbered items from his mental catalogue on his fingers. "The Egyptians called it 'the gift of Osiris'. The Chinese were distilling rice and sugar into arrack nearly three thousand years ago. The Indians were doing something similar before the time of the pyramids. James Cook found stills being used by Pacific Islanders who'd never seen a white man. The early… Thracians, I think, had a god of distilling named *Dionysos Bromios*. It's about as old as civilization. Maybe one of the things that defines 'civilization', eh?"

The old man chuckled and patted a purple shoulder. "Verra good, young man! By the latter days o' the Romans they spoke o' *Demetrios Bromos*. *Bromos* – oat-born, not *bromios*, born of fire from the sky."

"*Demetrios*, son of Demeter the earth-mother, or grain-mother, right?"

"Aye! Well done! It comes back tae ye?"

"Well, I must have read it somewhere. I couldn't tell you where or when…"

Bromleigh's face clouded again with something that might have been disappointment. He quickly composed himself, though.

"The Roman writers' told o' a 'dangerous intoxicant made fra' grain' that came fra the northern tribes. Might be this, heh?" he asked, producing a silver flask from an inside pocket of his vest.

He poured a small nip into each glass. The liquid was a pale gold. Rapunzel could only have wished for hair of the same colour. Stewart sniffed. A strong scent of the sea, but also hints of wildflowers and even honey. He sipped, and eyes closed in delight.

"Your own, I assume. You do magnificent work, Auld Wullie. Thank you."

The old distiller smiled in acknowledgement. "I've had plenty o' practice. But ye're welcome."

John B. savoured the spirit in his mouth. It evaporated more than was swallowed before he said, "So tell me, Auld Wullie, why *did* you bring me up here?"

Bromleigh gazed into his glass a while before replying. "I'd hoped ye might… Nae. I'm realizin' – it's no' the time. Ye'll know. Perhaps we both will…"

"You're speaking in riddles, my friend."

"Eh? Och… forgive an old man's maunderin's. There's a dark *geas* on all o' us the noo. It's been buildin' fer a bit an' I fear it's comin' tae a head. I'll gie such help as I can, but it'll take a *draoidh* tae defeat such a spell."

"I'm no druid, Wullie."

The old man's face creased into another grin. "Och, the word's much older than that. 'Druid' is a poor translation o' the sort o' wizard I'm referrin' tae." He raised his glass, the last dregs of its contents sparkling in the sunlight that was rapidly being lost behind clouds. "Tae yer good health, lad, and tae that o' those who stand wi' ye."

"*Slainte*," replied John B. returning the salute. Both men stood silently for a while, treasuring the clear cool air and the warmth of the last few golden drops of liquor.

Stewart gazed down at the paddock, fixing in his head the details Bromleigh had explained. Such knowledge was presumably part of the promise of help. Somehow.

He scratched the wildcat's broad head. "You'll stand guard, won't you my friend?" he said softly. The beast pushed its skull up into the palm of his hand, and then with a final short howl bounded back into the cover of the sedge.

The Australian stood and lightly touched his companion's arm. "Wullie? There's a young lady waiting for me. As patient as she is, I…"

"Och, sure lad. I understand, she's a bonny lass an' I dinna blame ye fer wantin' tae get back tae her."

 The journey back to Sron Dubh was made in a thoughtful but more companionable silence.

.oOo.

15 PAST AND PRESENT

An afternoon nap turned out to be a considerably better source of rest than the haunted sleep of nighttime. It seemed to support the experience of Bruce the barman. So much so that on their way to dinner John B. seriously suggested to Jazz that she propose to Robbie Keith a siesta be officially worked into all of the day shifts.

"The hour or so you'd lose would be made up in the time people felt better afterwards," he explained.

Certainly the engineer couldn't help noticing (and envying) how refreshed all three seemed to be after an hour or two of deep slumber.

Widow McNeill had heard the sound of snoring from the rental cottage. She was surprised, as at lunchtime she'd let herself in to check that both beds were showing signs of being slept in. Nobody this side of a hospital matron made up a bed with the millimetric precision of Ishbell McNeill. She felt she should disapprove of sleeping in the daytime, and considered rapping loudly on the door or wall. To her dismay though, she couldn't find any admonishment against afternoon naps in her Bible, not even in Leviticus. She would ask the Reverend about it later.

It was a pleasant evening, so after Wilko had collected Stewart and Elizabeth from their guesthouse it was decided that they'd walk to dinner. It was a bit of a distance but that would only enhance appetite on the way there, and aid digestion on the way back.

John B. navigated the way to the Bromleighs' cottage. The old gate and dry stone fence gave an indication of a much larger property than would be expected of such a modest building.

After a characteristically hearty greeting April explained that the cottage was one of the last surviving structures on the old Ramsay estate. "I'll tell ye a bit o' history over dinner," she promised.

While April busied herself preparing food, Auld Wullie led the way along a good track into the woods. Neither he nor John B. mentioned any details of their earlier expedition and the others had so far suppressed their curiosity.

 The path led upwards and brought them into a small clearing. A gap in the trees gave a splendid view out over the sea. The vista was a little different to the one Effie had. The more northerly islands like Eilean Craobhach couldn't be seen, but Eilean Bhride – Bridget's Island – stood out from the water shining in the evening light.

"What's the sailing like out there?" asked Wilko. After Bass Strait he'd realised he was interested in exploring his long-held interest. That it turned out to be shared with Jazz was a very happy bonus.

"Depends on the winds," Bromleigh replied. "There's inclined tae be a heavy swell, but if the wind's frae the east ye've nae chance o' moorin' in the bay."

"Pity – it might have been nice to get out to some of the islands and do some wildlife spotting," said Elizabeth, also a keen sailor. "Once all this weirdness is sorted," she added quietly.

 Auld Wullie didn't react to the last comment, suggesting that rather than sail a small rowboat of some sort was often a better option for visiting the little outcrops.

"Ye have tae be fit, mind. An' it helps if ye know the wee currents that can gie ye a bit o' a boost. There's no' a lot tae see – most o' them are barely mair than a few rocks pokin' up frae the water. Nobody's lived on any o' them for years."

"They were inhabited once then?" asked the brunette.

"A couple o' them. A verra verra long time ago." Auld Wullie's voice suggested he was talking of centuries or more. "Awa' then. April should be right ready tae serve."

 Mrs. Bromleigh's stovies were simple, homely fare, but thoroughly satisfying.

"The trick's in fryin' the onions an' tatties in a wee bit o' bacon fat first, 'fore ye add the beef shavin's," she explained.

Wilko and Elizabeth had been canny enough to buy a bottle of wine in Port Ellen earlier. It was a Uruguayan red that the Tasmanian would ordinarily have never considered, but the range in the little store had been thin. The offerings in the two hotels were even less inspiring – takeaway wine was not a priority in either obviously.

To Wilko's surprise it turned out to be a good choice. A little lightweight but good fruit flavour and a long finish made it a nice accompaniment to the meal. April polished off her glass enthusiastically. Her husband smilingly handed her his and poured himself a whisky.

"I do enjoy wine, but ma wee lassie seldom gets tae indulge," he said.

April just giggled at the 'wee lassie' line.

The visitors insisted on doing the washing up, but in the small kitchen that proved a job for only two. Wilko was determined to be one, and Jazz was equally determined to be at his side.

They were quite able to hear the conversation in the front room anyway, as April delivered her promised explanation of the history of the estate.

"It was aye large. Took in the woodlands an' a fair part o' what's noo the village, near as far as the distillery, an' all the way up tae just afore the standin' stones. Twas held by the Ramsay family for generations. There was a big manor hoose, an' muckle cottages an' crofts for his tenants."

"What's muckle?" called Wilko from the kitchen sink.

"It means 'lots' – many a mickle makes a muckle: lots of little things add up to a big thing," explained his girlfriend quietly as she dried a plate.

As April continued Auld Wullie quietly moved around the room pouring whisky for anyone who wanted some i.e. everyone.

"Then came the Clearances. Are ye familiar wi' them?" asked the old woman.

Not surprisingly it was Stewart who answered. "Lots of people, all over Scotland were pushed off the land their families had lived on for generations, to make way for sheep mostly. Some were killed, some got pushed out onto land no one could possibly scratch a living from, and some were shipped off to all corners of the world. A few did alright out of it in places like Canada or even Australia, but a lot more starved or died on nightmare journeys."

"Sounds dreadful! The government allowed this to go on?" asked Elizabeth.

"Q darling, they encouraged it! Aided and abetted, even. The more money the landowners could make, the more they could be taxed. Sheep generated a lot more income than anything the poor crofters could scratch together, no matter how hard *they* were fleeced!"

"Aye, bloody shameful it was. Or it would ha' been if they'd had any shame. John Ramsay was holder here in the 1860's as well as bein' the local MP. He was one tha' deported all his tenants off tae America, whether they wanted tae go or not. The stubborn ones were dragged oot. One o' the last tae be hauled oot was an old woman who lived in this verra cottage. As Ramsay's men dragged her off she cursed him an' his family."

Wilko leaned towards Jazz and whispered, "I bet I know where this is going."

She flicked him with the tea towel and held a finger to her lips.

"Both Ramsay an' his wife died soon after, right enough. The estate fell intae ruin. Those left o' Ramsay's household scattered for the most part. A few o' the servants stayed on in wha' became the village. A few descendants are still around. Yon bloody Reverend's one o' them."

Auld Wullie sipped his whisky. "Odd story, that yin. Ramsay served for a while in India afore he came back tae the island, bringin' wi' him a Hindu as a servant. Some sort o' holy man accordin' tae old tales. Different religion, same family."

 The washing and drying done, the pair from the kitchen entered the front room.

"The bloke we saw in the village doesn't look very Indian," said Wilko.

 April waved a finger. "It's been a few generations noo, an' it's no' like there were others o' tha' type tae mix wi'."

"The blood's run thin, eh?" suggested Jazz.

"The colour, anyway," replied April. She was looking at the Englishwoman, a strange expression on her face.

 Auld Wullie stepped between them before the others noticed anything. He and his wife exchanged looks, both brows momentarily creased.

 April hoisted herself up from her chair. "Pardon me fer a bit – yon wine's goin' straight through me, I think. I'll put the kettle on when I come back."

 She hobbled out. The others fell to quiet conversation between themselves. Auld Wullie motioned John B. into the corner and spoke quietly.

"They've all got the Sight, all three sisters. There's more than a touch of the old blood in them, ye ken."

"No, I don't ken. Not yet, but I think I'm getting there slowly. These Dotterels – have the Reverend and this charming daughter I've heard about got a touch of the old blood in them too?"

 Bromleigh looked thoughtful as he poured another wee dram for each of them.

"Maybe," he replied. "There's more than one kind of old blood."

"Kettle's on. Who's fer tea?" came his wife's voice from the kitchen.

*

The rest of the visit passed without significant comment. April asked plenty of questions about life in Australia, a country she only knew by reputation as Australian visitors to Sron Dubh were "rare as hen's teeth" she said. She also mentioned a lecture to be given the following night, "if ye're up tae a bit mair history, wi' supper thrown in."

As predicted, Auld Wullie and Jazz chatted about the latest goings on at the distillery. Jazz did most of the talking, but it was clear the man approved of her plans as she detailed them. It was also clear he shared her misgivings about the declining workforce. When the engineer expressed her confidence that John B. would be able to help she was sure she sure she saw the old man's eyes twinkle for a moment before he said somberly, "I certainly hope so."

Eventually it was Elizabeth who said, "It's after ten. We must let these good people go to bed."

"Is tha' really the hour? Nae wonder I'm yawnin' – it's long past ma bedtime!" exclaimed April.

"I'm so sorry we've kept you up," said the brunette in concern.

"Och, dinna fash yersel' lass. I've had a braw night. I cannae recall the last time Auld Wullie an' I had a wee dinner party."

Even Wilko could work out that Elizabeth wasn't to fuss and their hostess had had a very good night. But he was also aware of Jazz' tiredness and as much as he'd enjoyed himself was quietly pleased to be leaving.

Farewells made, the four visitors went out into the night to walk home. Auld Wullie had offered them a lift in the spacious Cyclops but they'd demurred, realising that he was probably as far past his usual bedtime as his wife.

It was still fine, but cloud cover made for serious darkness – the few streetlights in the village were by the shops and the distillery. Elizabeth pulled a small but effective torch from her clutch purse and played the light on the roadway for them to walk safely.

"Always prepared, hey pretty lady?"

"Weren't you ever a Boy Scout, JB?" she asked.

That got a laugh from Wilko, as Stewart replied evenly, "I've never been keen on uniforms."

"Hmm. I'll bet. Snuggle closer will you? The air's cold and this top isn't as warm as I'd hoped."

In a t-shirt John B. wasn't well equipped to provide more than a bit of body heat, but he didn't have to be asked twice. Walking on the other side of the circle of torchlight, Jazz and Wilko had already settled into a comfortable closeness, even if they were both more sensibly dressed.

As they neared the *Hardware and General Store* they heard a sudden commotion from the laneway beside the store and realised a light had been flicked off. They stopped at the mouth of the lane and Elizabeth raised the torch.

It illuminated a little gaggle of young men in their middle to late teens. Their faces registered a range of emotions from defiance to embarrassment to fear. The defiance mostly came from the three who moved quickly to stand at the front of the group.

One was tall and broad-shouldered, another small and wiry, and the one in front was scruffy enough to make John B. look almost dapper.

"Whatcha up to, gentlemen?" asked Stewart casually, a small pace away from Q.

Wilko pulled Jazz back a step. He didn't think his friend would be spoiling for a fight, but he'd seen him wade into a brawl with a group of G.I.s once, and it stuck in the memory.

"Nothin'," said the scruffy youth, evidently considering himself the spokesman.

"Ah. Nice night for it," John B. replied and folded his arms. "No spray cans, tins of paint, petrol – nothing daft like that, then?"

His voice was mild. Elizabeth held the light unwaveringly in the boys' faces so they could see little, but it dawned on a couple that the man talking to them was wearing a t-shirt. But it was bloody cold tonight!

"No, nothin' like any o' that," said the big guy near the front.

"So what if there was, anyway?" demanded the self-styled leader.

John B. didn't move. "I'd be annoyed. I happen to like the woman who owns this place."

"So wha…" began the surly one, who was surprised to be interrupted by one of the gang at the back.

"Er… ah… she's ma auntie, actually." The speaker was a pale, very skinny boy. In daylight it would be obvious that his arms and legs looked like white twine with knots at the elbows and knees. In the night air his hoodie billowed like a sail around ribs Q suspected resembled an ivory toast rack.

"Quiet, Thin Wullie!" snapped the scruffy front man.

The name was no surprise, but Stewart didn't react. "Do you like your auntie, Thin Wullie?" he asked.

"Oh aye! She's…"

"Ah said quiet, ye bampot!"

"Sorry, Scuzzy Wullie."

"It's Scuzz. I've told ye time an' time again…"

Clearly, trying to break local tradition by crafting his own nickname hadn't quite worked out.

John B. tried humouring him a little though. "Now now, Scuzz. Relax. Your pal's just a wee bit nervous, eh?"

Suddenly the small youth at the front of the group yelped – his resemblance to a fox terrier at that moment was striking – and flicked the hand he'd kept behind his back.

Scuzzy Wullie rounded on him. "Och ye bampot, Wee Chrissy! Dinna drop the bloody thing!"

"Hey, it's ma fingers were burned! Dinna call me a bampot, ye bampot! Gerroff me, Kev!"

The last was addressed to the big lad who'd gently pulled him back from Scuzz.

John B. carefully hid the grin he felt coming on. He'd passed around a joint or two in younger days, although never with the relish of some of his mates.

"Now then lads, don't fight amongst yourselves," he said. "No harm done. I'm sure you've more to share, haven't you? Just have a care you don't burn down your auntie's shop, eh Thin Wullie."

A little bloke near the back of the group, obviously one of the youngest, gave a nervous giggle.

"Shouldn't you be in bed?" asked Elizabeth.

Her stern voice provoked a reaction. Several of the boys paled, although with some it was hard to tell.

'Interesting,' thought Stewart.

"Crivens! Who can sleep? Who wants tae?" exclaimed Kev.

The wizard nodded almost imperceptibly. 'Ah. Much is made clear,' he thought, and pointing to the tiny ember dying in the laneway said, "Helps you sleep better, eh?"

"If we're lucky," admitted Wee Chrissy (who really wished he'd been born a Wullie like his older brother Wee Wullie who'd gone off to Motherwell to play football).

"Will you lot shut up?" cried Scuzzy Wullie in exasperation. "We dinna even know who this guy is!"

For the first time John B. allowed his expression to change. The clearer eyed boys could make out a smile.

"A friend. Maybe. But you want to be careful. I think there's some bad buggers about," he said.

It was Kev who nodded, but Scuzz who snarled, "We can take care o' werselves, pal."

"See that you do, then."

At a surreptitious gesture from the wizard Elizabeth swung the torch quickly away, plunging the boys into blind darkness. By the time Scuzzy Wullie had thought to fumble the cigarette lighter from his pocket the four friends had briskly but quietly walked on.

Nothing was said until they were approaching Jazz' cottage. Not so near as to risk being heard by Ishbell they huddled together.

"I recognised a few of them!" said Jazz softly. "The scrawny one – Wee Chrissy – his Mum does some office work in the distillery. His Dad passed away a few years ago. The big bloke is Kevin Macalpine. His father's a storeman for us. He'd like Kevin to join him but the kid wants to be a basketball player of all things."

"He's got the build for it," said Wilko.

"But not the reflexes, according to his Dad. Not slow in the head, but slow off the mark apparently," the engineer said, sounding honestly sympathetic. She'd have liked to be an athlete once.

Elizabeth shivered. "Interesting as this is, and as the whole night has been, can we talk about it tomorrow please? I think I'm turning the same colour as JB's t-shirt." She thumped his arm. "Could you at least try to look cold?"

"Sorry sweetheart. Umm… brrr?" he offered, utterly unconvincingly, eliciting only a sigh from his beloved.

"Would you two mind driving yourselves back to Port Ellen, and bringing Anastasia back first thing?" asked Jazz, an arm tightly around her beau.

 Elizabeth grinned. She understood the English girl's plan for generating some body heat. Approvingly she said in a quiet voice, "That's a good idea. Come on you two. I'll light your way in."

 Hugs and almost inaudible 'goodnights' were exchanged. Jazz and Wilko were huddled conspicuously close together - for warmth, obviously - but there was no sign of observation from the landlady who in fact was already asleep. Q drove away as inconspicuously as possible, no revving of the Rover's engine or turning on the lights until well away from the cottage.

 Soon after, John B. and Q were back in their own small cozy room. She hugged him tightly.

"Your skin's not even particularly cold. How do you manage it?"

"Naturally hot blooded maybe? Not that I've ever noticed."

"Hmph. Let's squeeze under this quilt and test that theory."

"Yes ma'am."

'A whole lot better than trying to sleep,' he thought.

.oOo.

16 CAKES AND CONFLICT

Another night. Another restless one, although what with one thing and another, perhaps not as bad as the one before.

Jazz did wonder whether the boys they'd encountered may be onto something. Where to find a supplier in Sron Dubh? There was no way she'd look for Scuzzy Wullie and ask him! How would Wilko react to the idea? Probably not well.

The man in question prepared her breakfast in the Spartan kitchen of their cottage – tea and toast with marmalade. He'd have something more substantial when he got to Bowmore. Before they left, they pulled back the sheets and playfully rolled around on the bed in the second room, so both would look slept in.

Stewart arrived with Anastasia at an appropriate moment, then diplomatically sat in the back seat as his old friend drove to the distillery with his arm clasped by the pretty blonde.

Wilko even dared a public kiss goodbye in the car park before heading for the Hine's guesthouse to collect Q who'd still been showering when John B. (a little reluctantly) left. Jazz smiled as the silver Rover departed. 'Yeah, we're getting there,' she mused. 'Not sure where, but getting there.'

If the Tasmanian had any deep emotional thoughts he wasn't sharing them yet, even with himself.

Bowmore is as close to an administrative capital as Islay gets. As such, it has slightly more shopping and dining options as well as more 'professionals' doing business, although it still didn't take them long to do the rounds.

A real coffee shop provided real pancakes and pastries. A modest supermarket provided the makings of meals of their own, even with the limited kitchen facilities Wilko had to work with. The meat on display at the town butcher's shop looked especially appetizing, and they promised them-selves that would be the last stop before they left. They even took the time to visit a couple of gift shops, one of which had some excellent little souvenirs for friends and Wilko's family 'down under'.

As they went, John B. and Elizabeth in particular made casual conversation with shop staff and other locals, discreetly drawing out snippets of information.

The atmosphere was less testy than Sron Dubh, or even Port Ellen, but there was still a troublesome undercurrent.

Politics is never an easy subject for chat in a strange town, but here there was no need to try to broach the topic. It was clearly on the minds of many, and yet it was talked around, not about. There seemed a vague if somehow reluctant agreement that everyone must support "her". Nobody mentioned "her" by name, but John B. especially was willing to take a good guess.

What was absent was much reference to dreams of smoke and fire, or strong reaction to dropping those particular words. To mention 'flames' in Sron Dubh was almost guaranteed to elicit a startled glance over the shoulder.

"Definitely a pattern," observed Elizabeth. "While we're here we should stop in on Mr. Craig, even if only to be sociable. But he might know something useful."

"We did say we'd drop by," agreed Stewart.

"And he did offer a wee dram," added Wilko wryly.

They soon found the lawyer's shingle beside a doorway that opened onto a narrow staircase.

'A bit squeezy for the big fella,' Wilko mused as they climbed the steps.

Suddenly Arsaidh MacAdam appeared, clutching his satchel on his way down the stairs.

"Good mornin', sirs and madam," he said as pleasantly as if he'd expected to encounter them there. "If ye're seeking Craig, he's in his office."

"Thank you, Mr. MacAdam," said John B., pressing against the wall to allow the Black Elf to pass. Even for someone of his stature it was a tricky maneuver. The dark man gave a genial wave as he departed.

At the top of the stairs was a small unattended reception area, behind which the door to the office itself was open.

Sitting at his desk, Craig looked up from a pile of papers he was sorting. He'd heard MacAdam's voice and smiled in recognition.

"Hello there! Do come in! How lovely to see you all again." His orator's voice was warm and welcoming.

As the Australians entered what was a good sized, if cluttered room the lawyer frowned for a moment. "Oh – a slight insufficiency of chairs, I fear." He addressed a sandy-haired man who stood at a large bookshelf in a corner. "Lachlan, would you bring a chair in from the waiting room please?"

The man looked affronted at being asked to do a menial task, but quickly hid his reaction as Craig introduced him. "Lachlan Maclean. Qualified accountant with a law degree – an absolute boon to my business. Takes care of the financial jobs. Lachlan, these are visitors from Australia. John Stewart, Robert Wilkes and the charming Elizabeth McKew."

Maclean made a polite greeting and then went to fetch a chair.

"I do apologise," said Craig. "My receptionist and all-round office whizz Anne has left me, I'm very sorry to say. You haven't encountered a girl good with paperwork on your travels, have you?"

"Does it have to be a girl?' asked Elizabeth with a hint of frost in her voice.

"Eh? Oh, I suppose not," said the lawyer with a smile. "It's just I've found women in general to be better organized than we mere males."

"Can't argue with that, sweetheart," said John B. as he pulled the best visitors chair out from the desk for her. "Kaiser Ron would have been lost without you. Will be, by now."

Mollified, the brunette took the offered chair. Wilko accepted the one beside it while Stewart stood.

"Actually, we have met a young lady who could do with a better situation," admitted Elizabeth. "I've no idea if she has the skills you need, but she seems good with people."

"An excellent start. If she's literate and reasonably bright we can soon teach her the ropes. Would you mind having a word on my behalf?"

It had taken Wilko a moment to catch up with Elizabeth's train of thought. "You mean Giddy Mary?" he said. "I don't reckon she'll get much of a reference from that miserable boss of hers."

Craig laughed. "*Giddy* Mary? Ah, Sron Dubh's a funny place. Not the most prepossessing of names, but if she has your recommendation that compensates for the word of a miserable employer. My judgement is that I rather trust your judgement, Miss McKew."

"Smart man," said John B. as Maclean handed him a stiff plastic chair. The accountant gave a miniscule twitch before wordlessly moving to sit at his own desk and seeming to lose himself in a register.

"So, my friends, how have you found Islay thus far?"

The wizard gave a wry smile. "Some good people, a few less so. It's been a bit challenging."

The big man looked concerned. "Oh dear – how so?"

"Trying to get a good night's sleep, for one thing," said Wilko with some bitterness. He wasn't enjoying waking up in a sweat, even alongside his pretty blonde girlfriend.

Maclean glanced up furtively as his boss' face clouded.

116

"You too. Already. Oh dear." The lawyer's voice was distant, before he pulled himself together. "I fear I've suffered the same problem since my return, so you have my sympathy. I have wondered… no one has indicated it, as such, but I begin to suspect there may be a connection with the upsurge in business that has brought me back."

If anyone had noticed, Lachlan had lost all interest in his register and wasn't very adept at disguising the fact.

"How so, Craig?" Stewart asked.

"There is only so much I can say, of course. Client confidentiality, you understand. But there has been a spate of Will changes, transfers of property and quite substantial assets and the like."

"You mentioned that on the plane," said Elizabeth.

"Mm, so I recall. It's rather more prevalent than I'd realised. Lachlan has been doing a remarkable job staying on top of so much, but with so many cases I've had to call on Mr. MacAdam's assistance and shoulder a share of the workload myself. And what I'm finding disturbs me."

The accountant suddenly got up and left his desk. "Excuse me. Bathroom," he said as he hurried out of the office.

Curious, the wizard watched him go. "Praise affects some blokes in a funny way, eh?"

"Disturbs you how, Craig?" asked Elizabeth.

"Hmm. It seems to me that in many cases the traffic, as it were, flows in one or two quite specific directions."

The brunette had been casually casting her eye across the lawyer's desk. The name on file near his hand caught her attention.

"W. Barclay – Port Ellen? Would that be Lush Wullie? We've met," said Elizabeth as tactfully as she could. "He mentioned something about being a bit well off."

"In fact he is. He used to be a good investment advisor before too many whiskies got the better of him."

 Wilko nudged his purple-shirted companion and quietly said, "There but for the grace of God, mate."

"Yeah, alright. I tried saying 'no' to alcohol but it didn't listen. I have cut down, and I don't need Jiminy Cricket in my ear," came the equally quiet reply. The Tasmanian had been known to take on the role of Stewart's conscience in times past when it seemed required.

 The lawyer either missed or politely ignored the exchange. "I can't reveal details, obviously, but Mr. Barclay called me only this morning. He has suddenly decided to transfer a substantial percentage of his asset base to an – *unexpected* recipient."

 Just as the three Australians were exchanging puzzled looks, Lachlan Maclean came back into the room wearing his own expression of annoyance.

"Everything alright, Lachlan?" asked the senior lawyer.

"Eh? Oh – yes, Craig. Sorry. A wee bit distracted today."

"Have you been sleeping okay, Mr. Maclean?" asked Elizabeth politely.

 The money man blinked. "Pardon? Why – yes. I sleep quite contentedly."

'Half your luck' was a thought that went around the room, but nobody said it out loud.

 What the big lawyer did say was, "Where are my manners? I've not offered anyone a drink yet. It's perhaps too early for a dram…?"

"It's never too early for a good Scotch. Somewhere in the world it's past five o'clock," announced Stewart, who'd been nettled by Wilko's earlier remark and was determined to have a drink out of defiance.

Craig smiled. "Quite so. Anyone else? No? Coffee perhaps? Ah, no…
the powdered substance we rely on in this office is not to be inflicted on
friends. Allow me to invite you all to be my guests at the *Harbourside
Café* across the street."

The suggestion got an approving smile from Elizabeth. "We've been
there. It's a nice place."

"Excellent!" Craig beamed. "Mr. Stewart, I shall join you in a small
sampling of an excellent single malt from an establishment in the west of
our island, and we shall join you at the Café shortly. Lachlan, would you
please lead the way for our guests? Let the staff know that the order is to
go on my account, please. I'll put the 'Back ASAP' sign up when I leave."

Evidently content to share in Aaron Craig's hospitality, Maclean ushered
the woman and the shorter man out.

"See you soon," Stewart called.

As they went downstairs Wilko leaned forward to whisper to Elizabeth,
"Sorry – I think that might be my fault. Poke and he'll poke back."

"Don't worry, mate. He's a big boy, and we're not joined at the hip. He *is*
drinking less."

The Tasmanian was relieved. "Yeah, well, I reckon you've got a lot to do
with that."

On the stairs behind her, Wilko couldn't see the smile that brought to the
brunette's face.

They'd just emerged onto the footpath when Maclean suddenly turned
and almost ran several paces up the street. He fell into step alongside a
smartly dressed woman striding towards the 'Aaron Craig' shingle.

The other two heard him exclaim, "Victoria! I just tried tae call you…"

"Ah, yes, Lachlan. I recognised your number. I didn't bother to answer as I was just on my way up to see you. I want to go over some figures in the Trust Account.”

Immediately it was as if the visitors he’d been asked to look after had vanished from the face of the Earth.

“I’m sorry Victoria. Craig’s up in the office, and he has company.”

She looked at the two Australians with the air of someone inspecting a disappointing exhibit at the zoo. At the same time, they studied her.

Victoria’s hair was the almost shocking white blonde you see on some children. But that usually changes around the age of ten. She was considerably older than that, although it was tricky to guess which side of thirty she was, and by how far.

Neither party seemed impressed by what they saw. Maclean was oblivious.

“I can bring whatever papers you want tae your office shortly,” he offered.

“No, not to the Chamber’s rooms. Just call me when the… lard bucket is gone and we can have some privacy.”

“Not a nice expression,” observed Elizabeth through tight lips.

Victoria looked at her as if surprised to find she still existed. “You think so? I think it’s an accurate description, if a little more colourful than he deserves.”

“He’s being… difficult. I think you might have tae give him more attention,” said Maclean. It really was almost as though he’d forgotten the Australians were standing beside him.

“Thank you for the suggestion,” Victoria replied, with no hint of actual gratitude.

The accountant, obviously smitten, was blissfully unaware. “You know,

120

just this morning that Sith told me tae be wary o' you. Vexing wee devil –
I told him tae mind his own damn business."

"Well done," she said, patting his arm. It was a gesture suitable for a
small lapdog.

Wilko tapped Maclean's shoulder. "Tell you what, mate. You two have a
nice chat and we'll find our own way over to the coffee shop. I'd hate to
think we were distracting you."

"Eh? What?"

Without waiting for a reply, and with only the barest of nods to the object
of Lachlan's affections the two Australians crossed the street and went into
the café.

They sat at a booth to wait for John B. and Craig.

"Victoria. The famous Victoria Dotterel you reckon?" said Wilko.

"No doubt," agreed Elizabeth. "She's quite something, isn't she?"

"Yeah. But what, I'm not sure."

It turned out to not be a long wait before Stewart and Craig arrived.
Having made his point, in his own head at least, the wizard was content
to make short work of what was a very tasty single malt. He did take the
opportunity to probe a little further with Craig. As he'd hoped, in Lachlan
Maclean's absence the lawyer was slightly more forthcoming about the
'traffic flow' he'd alluded to.

"I really can't give details, you understand, but quite a number of these –
redirections – have a political bent."

"Really? That surprises me. To be honest, I expected it to be a religious
thing."

The big man's eyebrows raised and he asked, "How did you...?" He paused, and then said quietly, "There's been a significant amount of that too, for some reason."

"You haven't had the hellfire and brimstone dreams, have you mate? Which in itself is interesting. Not that I'm wishing them on you!"

"I have no idea what you're talking about, John," the lawyer admitted.

"Well let's hope it stays that way, my friend," replied Stewart, finishing his dram.

 They went straight to the café, Craig pausing only to close the door and hang up his sign. Victoria and Lachlan were nowhere to be seen.

 The lawyer was surprised to find only the two visitors waiting for them, but less surprised when told of the encounter with Ms. Dotterel.

"I must apologise. I'm afraid Lachlan's become quite… keen on her," he said.

"No accounting for taste!" said Wilko.

 John B. was recalling April's off-hand mention of Victoria's political aspirations, and Craig's recent remark about the direction money was flowing in. "There's not a conflict of interest happening here, is there?"

"Oh! I don't think so!" was the startled reply, followed by a thoughtful pause. "I've always trusted Lachlan to be professional. The cases I've looked at all seem to be, let's say, legitimate, albeit sometimes surprising. Perhaps I should look again…"

 At that moment Maclean turned up at the door to the office. The accountant looked over to the café, waving to catch the eye of his senior. He pointed at his watch and performed a complicated charade that managed to convey that he was expecting a phone call at his desk.

 Craig waved acknowledgement and apologised again to his guests – Maclean was normally more sociable, or at least polite, he assured them.

Elizabeth smiled at him and replied, "It's not your responsibility to apologise for him, but thank you."

They turned the conversation to lighter matters over coffee and a plate of fresh oatcakes topped with slices of unsalted butter. Craig recommended places worth visiting when not 'investigating' – an activity he preferred to distance himself from for the sake of his clients' privacy.

Respectful of that, and grateful for his generosity, the three friends were genuinely sorry when the big man finally announced that he must get back to work.

After settling their bill he declared, "I hope I'll see you again soon," as he left them to finish another round of good coffees.

"I'm sure you will, mate – and thanks again!" called Stewart to the departing figure.

It was several minutes before the threesome made a leisurely move out onto the street.

"Where to now?" asked Wilko.

"The Bowmore distillery's just up the way. We could check their tasting room and gift shop," suggested John B. Before the others could comment he continued, "Let's see if there's any sign of the same troubles that Sron Dubh is having."

Agreeing that this was a good idea, Wilko was leading the way when he was almost bowled over by a burly figure coming around the corner of the town's main intersection.

DS Mills glanced at the person who'd bounced off him and stopped.

"You lot again? What are you doin' 'ere?" he snapped.

"Minding our own business, mate. You should try it sometime," Stewart suggested casually.

"I'm on business for the Reverend. I always am. Keep me eyes an' ears out for 'im I do. So if I hear you've been saying anything about 'im you shouldn't oughta, well, remember – I warned you before."

There was a note of wonder in Elizabeth's voice as she said, "You're a gross ignoramus, Mills."

"Damn right - I'm like one of 'em big ones in the movie what bite the roofs off and tear people in 'alf. So you just better be'ave!"

So saying, the bullyboy stalked away, fists bunched and swinging at his sides.

"Yep, he's 144 times more ignorant than the usual…" she said quietly.

Wilko couldn't help chuckling at that as he dusted himself off and reassured the others he was barely shaken, not bruised.

Looking the other way, happy to not be watching him, they didn't notice the thug encounter Victoria Dotterel outside the Chamber of Commerce. They didn't see the conversation, Mills' furtive thumb jerked over his shoulder toward them, or the frown on the woman's face as she glanced up at the window by Lachlan Maclean's desk.

Walking in the opposite direction the Australians realised that meeting the Englishman had put them off more pursuit of bad dreams and depression. Rather than going to the distillery they followed the scent of sea air to a quiet spot near the wharf. All of them smiling, they quietly took in the scene. Some of the migrating geese flew over. A few fishing boats bobbed by the dock. Perhaps they'd go out at night. Or perhaps fishermen had debilitating nightmares too.

Each in their own idyll, they didn't notice the sound of running feet behind them until a second or two before Mills' elbow crashed into the small of John B.'s back. Luckily the target had turned fractionally in that second so the blow just missed the spine – it was hard enough to have done permanent damage, which was the obvious intention.

As it was, Stewart pitched forward and a flailing arm that caught a bollard was all that saved him from plunging into the water. Wincing, he quickly pulled himself upright to see Mills grabbing Wilko's jacket with the evident intent of flinging him off the dock.

"Can't fight someone your own size face to face?" barked the man in purple.

Mills shoved his smaller victim away. Q lunged to catch an arm and save the Tasmanian from a nasty drop over the edge.

DS wore a broad but evil smile as he advanced on John B. He was bigger than his opponent, and was confident in his own strength and brutality. He looped a big right hand at the Australian's head.

Crouching low to avoid the roundhouse blow, Stewart wrapped his arms around Mills' legs and gripped the calves in a bear hug. He stood up quickly, lifting the startled thug into the air, and then bent forward sharply and released his opponent.

Mills landed hard on the flat of his back, momentarily stunned.

John B. grabbed the fallen man's ankles. He spread Mills' legs and held his own heel threateningly over the bully's crotch.

"If you even *try* to reach for that equalizer I know you carry, you're going to be singing in a different section of the church choir for the rest of your life."

Mills' hand stopped moving immediately.

"Wilko, check his pockets and get his gun. Remember DS - you so much as twitch and any dreams you had of fathering children will be shattered."

The Tasmanian found the pistol jammed in a coat pocket. He removed it gingerly and exchanged glances with Elizabeth. John B. was staring fixedly at Mills, who couldn't tear his gaze off the looming heel. Following the direction of her blazing green eyes Wilko hurled the gun out into the water.

DS flinched at the sound of the splash. John B. smiled at him.

"Lost your toy? Aww. Hey sweetheart," he called to Q. "There's a length of rope hanging from that bollard. You and Wilko both know how to sail – how about one of you practices some knot tying?"

"Mister Wilkes, would you mind?" the brunette said formally. "I'm more of a power boat girl."

Wilko took the end of the rope and cautiously approached.

"Thanks mate. Round this leg here please," Stewart indicated with a nod. "Good and tight, like you were tethering a mad dog."

Satisfied that Mills wouldn't be able to free himself quickly, the wizard released his hold and walked away without a word. His back hurt but he wouldn't let it show. Flanked by his friends he strode back to the main street where there would be, if not a crowd, witnesses. They walked at a steady pace but didn't run.

The English thug cursed and fumed as he tugged at the knotted rope, his erstwhile victims turning a corner out of his sight without a backward glance.

Safely settled in Anastasia and back on the A846 Elizabeth at last allowed herself to relax.

"I can't decide if I want a drink on the way home, or just a good quiet lie down," she said.

From the back seat came John B.'s weary voice. "I'm for option B."

That's when the others knew he was hurting.

.oOo.

17 A HISTORY LESSON

A bit of whiplash, perhaps. Certainly a substantial bruise was already showing over one kidney. Rest however did help John B.'s back. So too did the 'wintergreen oil' that Elizabeth had obtained from Rhona, explaining that her boyfriend "had a bit of a fall".

The most effective treatment though was the gentle way that Q had massaged the menthol-scented oil into his skin. She wasn't at all upset when he'd fallen asleep under her ministrations. After thoroughly washing her hands she'd followed his lead.

Wilko had also taken the opportunity for a dreamless afternoon snooze. The peaceful couple of hours stood them in good stead for the evening. Unfortunately Jazz hadn't had a similar opportunity.

She was more than keen for a drink at the *Lost Goose* after finishing work, and her refreshed companions were happy to agree.

"Not a good day in the office, mate?" Elizabeth had asked when they sat lined up at Bruce's bar.

"Bloody hell, no. Another bloke quit – a good handyman who knew the stills. That only leaves Kevin Macalpine to deal with any problems, which is a lot to ask of one bloke. Then I got a message 'requiring' me to forward money through to a bloody bank in bloody Africa."

"One of those scams, eh?" said Wilko sympathetically. Jazz hadn't mentioned this bit of the day's travails when she'd come home.

"Nah, this is legit. Well, as legit as these things can be – it's all part of lining up a job there when I'm finished at the distillery."

"How so?" asked the puzzled John B.

The engineer shrugged and swigged at the lager she'd ordered – it had been *that* sort of day. "It's how the system works if I want the job. Graft and corruption. It's a cultural thing."

"Really?" said Stewart.

 The blonde shrugged again and replied, "Well, it has been since the days of European colonization."

"The Europeans being the ones who actually built the whole administrative structure that's in place now," said Elizabeth drily.

"Exactly," agreed Jazz.

 John B.'s voice was mild as he asked her, "And you think that it's a good thing, this system?"

"Well no – obviously not."

"Then don't play that game. You're good enough to get the job or you're not."

 Wilko was perturbed at the whole 'job in Africa' thing, but he defended the woman he was at least sharing a cottage with for now.

"You don't quite connect with the real world, do you John?" he said with some asperity.

 The reply was mild. "I think the real world can be whatever we choose to make it."

Jazz shook her head and persisted, saying, "The system in most African countries simply doesn't work that way. Honestly, I mean."

 Stewart was just as persistent. "And it never will if nobody ever tries to break the cycle."

 The weary blonde snorted and said, "Nice idea, but why should it be me?"

"Why not? Why not be the better one?"

"Oh, don't get all preachy on me," the English girl moaned.

128

"I'm sorry - I don't mean to. I just think you've got the ability, more to the point the character, to be better than that."

Wilko took Jazz' hand and admitted, "For what it's worth I agree with John about that, at least. I reckon you really are better than that."

Jazz looked at him. "Actually, that's worth a lot. Let me... think about it for a bit."

They drank in companionable silence for a little while, looking at but not watching a news broadcast about another war in another country.

Finally it was Q who said, "Let's do dinner. We were going to try the Indian place in the village."

Wilko drove them back to Sron Dubh, but they were disappointed to find a 'Closed" sign on the *Curry House* door.

"Funny," said Jazz. "He's usually open on a Thursday." She sighed. "It's just the way my bloody day's gone, really. Back down to the pub, I guess."

"Um... do we have to? I mean, I'll go along if it's the will of the majority, but are there any other options?" asked Q.

They pondered. Neither household could offer much from their own kitchen.

John B. then suggested the lecture in the village hall that April had mentioned.

"I know you guys haven't quite got my interest in history, but you might enjoy it. And she did say supper was included."

"You're right, history's not my thing unless it's military history. But I can't imagine April recommending something where the food wasn't decent. Or plentiful," observed Wilko.

No one had any better suggestion, so they drove over to the village hall. It wasn't a full house, but a respectable crowd for a village of its size. Ileachs like to be entertained, even when they're below their best as so many in attendance clearly were.

"This many drawn faces should be in a comic book," quipped John B. quietly.

Several of those faces were already familiar, including the surprising presence of Wee Chrissy. The young man, upon recognizing Stewart's purple t-shirt, gave a silent and somewhat embarrassed gesture of acknowledgement and tried hard to blend into the background.

"I bet his buddies don't know he's here," said Jazz with a grin.

The most familiar of the faces was of course April Bromleigh, accompanied not by Auld Wullie, but her sister Rose making a rare foray into the Sron Dubh night. Stewart suspected (rightly) that the widow Ellison had it in mind to correct any errors she believed the lecturer to make.

"Ye'll keep a civil tongue in yer head tonight, please Rose," they heard the youngest sister say as they approached.

"Och, as if I wouldnae! Ah – hello you lot!" the oldest sister said as she spotted the four friends.

Jazz was introduced to Rose who, to nobody's surprise, had heard of her. "Ye look familiar…" the old woman had said thoughtfully, mystifying the blonde. "Ne'er mind, it'll come tae me."

April admitted that she was glad of the good numbers as she'd helped organize the evening. "I'm in the local Historical Society, ye ken."

"Is there any bloody club or society here ye arnae a part of?" asked her sister.

"I don't play bowls an' I'm no' in the darts club," replied April calmly.

Keeping a resolutely straight face, Elizabeth asked, "I have to say, Mrs. Ellison, I wouldn't have thought there was much about ancient Islay that you and your sister didn't already know."

"The day ye stop learnin' is the day ye die, lassie," Rose replied. "This fella just might tell me somethin' I've no' heard before."

Their speaker was introduced as Cecil, a teacher "frae o'er on the Eastern island". This description of the British mainland tickled Wilko, who'd grown up in Tasmania with Australia being referred to as 'the north island'.

Cecil was a rather intense middle-aged man, with thick black hair that had receded from his forehead like a very low tide. He had large, rather yellow teeth so his frequent wide smile looked like a wedge of Edam – a proper cheesy grin.

He certainly knew his material, as even Rose later conceded.

After touching briefly on the Stone Age settlement of the island, known from numerous archaeological finds of tools, middens, and even chambered cairns from the late Neolithic period, Cecil warmed to his main topic – the time leading up to and including the Vikings.

The island was known to have been settled since at least the 3rd or early 4th century A.D. From about the 6th century it was part of the Scots kingdom of Dalriada.

Dalriada warred with and finally seems to have absorbed the local population of Picts.

Cecil explained that despite the common misunderstanding these Picts ought not be confused with the ancient *Pechts* – the small dark race legend recounts as the earliest inhabitants.

The religious history of the area stretched back to those days with records and remains of small monasteries, churches and hermitages dotted across Islay and the little rocky offshore islands.

The Norse came to the main island in the first half of the 9th century. They didn't call themselves 'Vikings'. That word was more of a descriptive term for what they did – take to the seas to acquire things, by trade or by force.

That was one of the many misapprehensions about that race, Cecil said. Another was the unpleasant form of execution called 'the blood eagle', whereby the lungs and other organs were ripped out and splayed from the back of a living victim. Legend held that this had been the fate of a venerable priest at the church at Kildalton, a couple of miles to the north. But, the teacher explained, there was no actual evidence that the grisly practice was ever carried out.

Cecil explained that this had been a saga writer's misunderstanding of twelve words in a verse from the 11th Century, and the sensationalizing of subsequent writers keen to play up the savagery of the invaders. The rather more conventional, accurate, but less thrilling translation was that a carrion bird slashed the back of the slain.

It was suggested that the Scandinavians were responsible for the island's name - Islay perhaps derived from 'Yula's Isle'. Yula was a Norse princess reputed to be buried under a single standing stone that could still be seen on the east side of Port Ellen. Respectful tradition or perhaps superstition had prevented any archaeological digging under the site.

"Tis shameful tae gie such regard tae a heathen!" was the none-too-quiet opinion of a woman sitting in the row in front of John B.

She got a clip on the shoulder with a rolled-up paper from April, and a low growl of "Mind yer manners, Nell Crowdie," from Rose.

On the small stage at the front of the hall Cecil continued, oblivious to Nell's editorial. The Norse, he said, were in charge of Islay for some three hundred years. Evidence of their presence was all about. Archaeological, structural and linguistic evidence. Place names were significant clues. The word 'dun' referred to the Iron Age forts that the Norse occupied, and the name lingered even where the walls had not.

"And I've always thought it was just an Aussie joke name for a house. Y'know, like Dunroamin or Dunboozin," whispered Wilko to Jazz, who'd travelled enough to get it.

John B. noticed that Q was scribbling notes in the little book she routinely carried with her. Evidently Cecil's talk was striking a chord. The wizard smiled and stroked her leg. In wordless reply she leaned over and kissed him. Watching from the corner of her eye (more discreetly than usual) April smiled in approval.

The teacher wrapped up his presentation by describing how in 1156 Somerled, Lord of Argyll, himself a descendent of the northern raiders, defeated the Norsemen of his day in sea battle off Islay, using small maneuverable vessels that improved on the Scandinavians' own design. These compact galleys were ideal for the waters around the islands, and were anchored at Dunyvaig, three miles southwest of this very hall.

With his war galleys and a defensive castle at Dunyvaig, and a highly defensible administrative centre at Finlaggan in the north of the island Somerled made Islay his base as he took over the Southern Hebrides. His offspring founded Clan Donald, with his descendant Good John of Islay the first to take the title 'Lord of the Isles' in 1329.

Cecil had rattled through this last section as though confident that it was all well known to his audience, as it was for most of them. He took a bow to polite applause and then supper was served. 'Supper' comprised plates of sandwiches, cakes and buns prepared by the ladies and gentlemen of the Historical Society. The baked goods were typically filling Scottish fare, much to the delight of the hungry Australians. John B. and Elizabeth would have liked to chat with Cecil, but the teacher slipped away early. He preferred to be in front of a crowd not in it – or perhaps talk *to* them rather than *with* them.

After warm farewells to Rose and April the four friends headed home with brains and bellies satisfied. No tense encounters, no threat of inclement weather – just a drive and a stroll on the arm of a loved one. All of them would go on to sleep deeply and well. It was a good night for them.

.o0o.

18 TOO HOT FOR CURRY

Seribreyong Phunket Goom was a decent hard-working man. He hadn't been in the village long. He was keen to fit in as best he could. The difficult accents didn't help – neither his nor those of the folks in his new community – but he did his best.

He smiled and nodded a lot. He put photographs of the food in the menu of his little restaurant, simply named the *Curry House*. Then he added little symbols beside them, outlines of a chicken or a cow or a carrot, because his customers mostly couldn't tell a chicken tikka from a beef rendang from a vegetarian vindaloo just by looking at the pictures.

He would go to the *Lost Goose* once per week on Monday - the only night that his own restaurant was closed. He would sit at the bar and drink water, and take small cautious sips from a glass of single malt whisky that would last him nearly an hour. He enjoyed watching football with the men. He understood only a little of the commentary, and less of the banter in the bar, but he soon worked out the appropriate moments to cheer, and when to look disappointed, disapproving, indignant or outraged.

The little restaurant was becoming well known and well liked – probably more than Seribreyong Phunket Goom realised. He was steadily putting money aside. If things continued as they had, he hoped to soon bring his family to Sron Dubh to join him. There were many reasons he looked forward fondly to that day, among the least of which was the prospect of having someone to share the workload.

Most days and nights he did everything: the shopping, cleaning, cooking, taking orders, answering the phone, serving meals, pouring the wine or beer that people brought (he really must get a licence one day), working the till, locking up – all smiling, always smiling.

Saturday nights were his busiest – he'd actually hired a girl named Mary from the village to help him on those nights, and on other occasions when he knew he needed some help. A 'wee lass' Mary was called, although with his accent the words came out as 'Willis'.

So the nickname of Willis was promptly applied around the village to Mary. She bore it with good grace – it was an improvement on 'Mousey Mary' as it had applied to her hair. Work was hardly plentiful for a girl in Sron Dubh. Mr. Goom paid well and treated her respectfully, and she could see the *Curry House* getting busier, which meant the prospect of more work.

His Asian specialties were even starting to be recognised as a genuine alternative to the deep fried delights of the mobile fish-and-chip van that visited the village every Friday night.

The *Flying Fry-up* had become something of a local institution over a decade or more, but at last it faced some healthy competition. That couldn't hurt, admitted even the most dedicated consumers of "deep-fried black puddin' wi' a side of chips".

The little restaurateur was working his way into the fabric of Sron Dubh. One day perhaps he would be known as Indian Wullie. Not that he was from India, but the actual details of the sub-continent and south-east Asia beyond were of little interest to most of the villagers. Curry equaled India. Everyone knew that, and the cook was wise enough not to argue.

The one concession that Seribreyong Phunket Goom would not make was his faith. He was not an especially devout Hindu. He certainly had no desire to convert anyone else, nor to criticize their own choices – but his religion had been part of his upbringing and was simply a part of his life. He had no wish to change it, thank you very much. The only outward sign of that upbringing was a modest framed photograph of the 10th century Lawkananda Temple standing in the ancient Burmese city of Bagan. The photograph hung discreetly on the wall of the *Curry House* behind the little front desk.

So when two ladies from the local congregation came to invite him "tae the kirk" he smiled politely but declined. Although he was careful to give them more than a token donation for "the poor of the parish". It had all been very civil, the ladies had seemed quite courteous and had gone away apparently pleased with the donation.

Thus, he was surprised to receive a visit from the preacher himself soon after. He was even more surprised by the man's attitude. Gordon Dotterel's accent was far less heavy than many in the village, so the restaurateur was in no doubt about the sheer hostility being expressed.

"I know your kind!" the man in black had said over and over, amongst other hurtful things.

 Smiling politely hadn't helped. Seribreyong Phunket Goom spread his arms, trying to be open and conciliatory.

"I do not understand, sir," he said. "What is it that you would have me do?"

"Ye Godless cur! I would have ye…"

"No, no, no sir!" the little man interrupted quickly. "I am not godless. It may be a different God to yours, but I assure you that –"

"Silence, ye heathen! There is but one righteous God, who commands us tae smite the unbeliever! You ask what I would have ye do?" Dotterel's voice lowered, and he leaned into the man framed by the restaurant doorway. "I would have ye die."

 Seribreyong Phunket Goom may actually have been less frightened if the preacher had shouted at him, but that last word had been low, quiet, and dripping with malice.

 Dotterel had turned and quickly departed. He didn't look back at all as he walked away, taking such long strides that he seemed to be avoiding touching any ground the little Hindu may have trodden on.

 Seribreyong Phunket Goom scarcely slept that night, nor the night after. The hate-filled eyes and voice of the reverend haunted him at all hours. Regulars among his customers on both of those evenings noticed that his fare was not of it's usual standard.

"Oh aye, not bad right enough, but no' so good as last week," was the considered opinion of Lanky Wullie, who was beginning to consider himself an authority on Butter Chicken.

After two nights and days though, sheer tiredness caught up with the restaurateur. When no customers had appeared by seven o'clock he hung up the CLOSED sign – any would-be late diners would have to bear the disappointment – and wearily trudged to his bed in the flat above the *Curry House*.

The familiar scents of the kitchen below wrapped him like an extra blanket, just as they always did. This night however, even they couldn't comfort him. Exhausted, he fell into a deep but difficult slumber.

He was standing before the Lawkananda Temple. But something wasn't right. It was flat. Two-dimensional. He stepped towards it. He didn't want to, but he was drawn. Pulled. Or was it pushed?

Then he saw what was wrong with the Temple. It wasn't real. It was a photograph. It was the picture that he had on the wall of his restaurant, but it was life-sized. Or he was photograph-sized.

Still he was impelled towards it.

There was smoke. He could smell it.

There! He could see it! The edges of the photograph were charring. The blackening crept inwards and the picture started to curl. Inwards. Towards him. And still he was walking forward.

He wanted to stop. To run away. To wake up. But he could do none of that. He could only put one foot in front of the other, again and again, inexorably stepping into the embrace of the smouldering image.

He saw and felt the paper curling completely around him. Even if he could have retreated now there was nowhere to retreat to. The Temple was all around him. The smoke was getting thicker. Now the photograph wasn't just smouldering, it had started to burn. Really burn. Flames licked around his feet and danced across the printed image. Still he couldn't stop walking forward. The smoke and the heat hurt his eyes.

Closing them didn't help – he was still too, too aware of what was hap-
pening. The Temple was gone. There was only the inferno. The flames.
They were part of him. He was part of them.

He would have screamed, but when he opened his mouth only smoke
poured out.

In a room not far away, Gordon Dotterel ceased his quiet chanting. He
blew out the candle he'd been staring into, and smiled.

.o0o.

19 SINKING IN

Wilko was holding open the passenger door of the Rover for Jazz when a voice from behind made them both jump.

"Old fashioned chivalry! I'm surprised tae see that! Sadly lackin' in today's world if ye ask me."

They hadn't noticed the landlady lurking at her door. To her disappointment they hadn't indulged in any amorous horseplay on their way to the car. Wilko's reticence about public displays of affection had spared them her intended chastisement about defiling the reputation of her establishment.

Jazz suddenly decided to take some advantage of the moment. It was as close to positive as she'd ever seen her landlady.

She approached Ishbell and using the respectful tone she'd found worked well for Elizabeth, said, "Mrs. McNeill, I was wondering… You've been around a while…"

The small woman bristled. "Eh?"

Quickly her tenant made an apologetic gesture. "I'm sorry. What I mean is, you've got a keen understanding of everything that goes on in the village, don't you?"

Her vanity suitably stroked, Ishbell replied, "Oh. Och, aye. I see everything that goes on around here. And I see it clearer than that old biddy Effie Lindsay."

'Not surprised there's no love lost there,' thought Wilko, a fascinated but shrewdly silent observer.

"Um, right," Jazz continued. "So. I was wondering – there's Reverend Dotterel, and his daughter, but never a mention of a *Mrs.* Dotterel. What happened to her?"

"Och, *her*! Dreadful creature. Went mad. Although I always thought there was something wrong wi' her to begin with." The opportunity to pronounce moral judgements, to any audience, was clearly irresistible to Mrs. McNeill. "And the way the sinful Jezebel carried on towards the end – as if her husband was the very devil himself. And him one o' the noblest, grandest men on God's Earth! Och, there's some as say it was the loss of the daughter that pushed her over the edge…"

McNeill paused for a moment, as if somehow struck by her own choice of words, but continued before Jazz could think of a word to get in edgeways. "But I believe that it was nowt more nor less than a Divine judgement."

"Loss of the daughter?" said Jazz, puzzled. "But Victoria's very much alive."

"Och, no' her. The other yin. Brazen she was, even as a wee lass. A disgrace. Took after her mother. I'll thank ye not tae mention they two to me again. I feel unclean talking about them."

"I'm so sorry. I hadn't meant to distress you. Thank you so much for explaining it to me. Well, I must be off to work now."

"Away tae that den of iniquity! Nae place for a young lassie tae be employed. Of course, I've long said that a woman's place is in the home…"

"And I'm sure that one day mine will be, Mrs. McNeill. Must dash. Thanks again," Jazz called as she dashed back to the car and shut the door Wilko still held.

Giving a little wave to the harridan next door the Tasmanian rushed round to the driver's seat and got Anastasia going with something just short of unseemly haste.

"Do you reckon any of that was relevant?" he asked as they approached the distillery car park.

"Who knows, mate? But tell the others anyway. You never know what's useful."

There was nobody else in the car park when they arrived. Their lingering farewell kiss steamed up the Rover's windows, but it *was* a cold morning.

*

It was still chilly later when Anastasia was parked by Kilnaughton Bay.

Over breakfast in the *Ferryhouse* Wilko had expressed frustration at their not yet achieving anything to help Jazz or anyone else. He wasn't suggesting giving up, but questions were getting them nowhere. Could a day of doing something else hurt? He'd been surprised when the others readily agreed.

A brain break, Elizabeth called it. Do something different but relaxing, let the subconscious mull things over and see what popped into anyone's head.

Wilko had his camera in the car. Auld Wullie's suggested spots to visit had included a famously picturesque lighthouse built in the 1830's. It wasn't far from Port Ellen, so that's where they agreed to go.

Elizabeth and John B. turned out to be quite content to admire the *Carraig Fhada* Lighthouse from a distance, but Wilko saw photographic opportunities in the building's angular geometry. Appropriately dressed in heavy pants and a waterproof jacket he walked off towards the far end of the bay where a causeway led out to the lighthouse.

The Rover was near the sizeable cemetery that serviced Port Ellen and much of the southern part of the island. Stewart declared his interest in pottering about there, "to see who he found, and if they'd give him any clues". He spoke lightly, but wasn't entirely joking.

"Not my cup of tea I'm afraid, babe," Q said, and decided to take a stroll along the beach. The view across the bay was pretty, she was well rugged up against the cold, and she'd heard mention after the lecture of a derelict old chapel at the far end of the sand from the lighthouse.

She'd strolled for a little while before realising that a jumble of stones some distance away wasn't part of the cliff face – she could make out the rough shape of an arched window.

Quickening her stride, the brunette peered intently at the ruins, trying to make out detail. Distracted, she failed to notice at first that her boots were making an unpleasant sucking noise as she walked. It took a minute or two for her to realise how much her progress had slowed, and how much effort was being required to lift her feet.

Stopping was the wrong thing to do. Almost immediately she'd sunk to her calves in wet sand. With a startled look around Elizabeth realised she'd wandered into a large patch of the stuff. She cursed as she tried to tug her legs free. The good hiking boots would be ruined! And her woolen leggings…

With a start she realised that the woolen leggings were soaked, as now was the lower part of her wool skirt. Their wet weight was rapidly pulling her deeper into the sinkhole. There was nothing to grab for purchase to haul herself out – how deep was this damned thing? She was up to her hips…

Elizabeth screamed. "Help! JB – help me!"

The wizard had been crouched by an old headstone, trying to read the inscription. He looked up like a meerkat. It was the first time he'd ever heard panic in Q's voice.

It was unlikely that anyone had ever witnessed John B. Stewart move faster. He vaulted the low stone wall of the graveyard and leapt down the rocky embankment to the beach. Instinct or something guided his feet to the right spots to avoid shattering an ankle or worse, and then he was on the sand. At a run he took off in the direction of the cries.

As he neared he realised that only half of his beloved was visible. What was happening?

Q heard him running. She shouted, "Wait JB, be careful! It's quicksand or something!"

The wizard skidded to a halt just as he reached the edge of the boggy patch. Trying to combine caution and speed he skirted its edge, looking for a way to get to Elizabeth. He managed to get within a few yards of her, but could step no closer without sinking into the same predicament. Already he was up to his ankles. He lost both canvas deck shoes hauling his feet out of the mire.

He backed up slightly. "Don't struggle, sweetheart! Keep as still as you can!"

Q watched, astonished, as he quickly took off his jeans. He threw himself full length towards her, gripping the end of one leg of the jeans and flinging out the trousers like a denim rope. Somehow she caught the other cuff and gripped it like a life preserver.

Spread-eagled on the sand he called, "I've got no leverage to pull you up. You're going to have to drag yourself out – I'll counterweight you."

"But you'll sink too!"

"Not as fast. I've got myself spread out as much as I can, and I'm not wearing wool!"

That was certainly true. A t-shirt and underpants was the entire inventory.

Elizabeth took a deep breath. No more panic, just determination. Her ribs were wet. Tough. She pulled hard on the trouser leg. For a moment it slipped towards her but Stewart dug an arm into the beach and stopped his movement. Hand over hand she hauled herself gradually out of the sand. It didn't release its sucking grip readily, but it did release. It was like dragging herself through sloppy brown treacle, she thought, and almost cried with relief when she grasped John B.'s hand, her legs bent painfully but almost free.

"Keep going, pretty lady – use my arm as a rope now."

His voice was muffled, and Q was shocked to see he had his head turned like a freestyle swimmer as he tried to keep his mouth out of the sand.

Frantically she hauled herself along faster, terrified that her weight would force her rescuer under to drown, or suffocate… what was it you did in quicksand? 'Neither, damn it!' she told herself as she slithered across his back.

Free of her weight, Stewart wrenched himself over in a roll that put him face up. As Elizabeth scrambled across the shallower muck to dry sand, he rolled again. Once, twice more and he was at a spot shallow enough to get to his hands and knees. The sound that the sand made as it gave up his body was like wallpaper being torn from a wall. He half dived, half fell beside Q, and both shaking, they got to the security of a boulder big enough to accommodate them as they sat.

Elizabeth's face was filthy as she pressed it into John B.'s chest. She didn't care. She took huge wracking breaths, determined not to cry, unaware that tears were already streaming down her face. She was equally oblivious to the wizard's tears running into her hair. For a little while all they did was hold each other.

Eventually they both realised that their breathing was something like normal again. They released their embrace and stood on shaky legs. Looking at each other, they both started to giggle, then to laugh out loud.

"I'm sorry, darling," John B. finally said. "You're the most beautiful drowned rat I've ever seen."

"Hah! You should see yourself! You look like a wax model that's been left in the sun and started to melt."

"Oh. Not Adonis, then?"

"You're *my* hero, lover!"

They made their way back along the beach, arms around each other.

They were almost at the car when Wilko turned up coming from the other direction. He stared at them, open-mouthed.

"What the hell have you two been doing?" he managed to ask.

"Um, had a run-in with some muddy sand, or is it sandy mud, d'you reck-on?" Stewart replied.

"I don't care what it is! You can't get in Jazz' car like that! The uphol-stery'll be ruined! What the hell were you thinking?"

More calmly than she felt, Elizabeth answered, "Well, I was thinking of not dying."

Wilko's complaints stopped short as he tried to process that statement.

"I'll explain soon," the brunette promised, and then asked, "Isn't there a picnic blanket in the boot of the car?"

"Er – yeah. And an old towel, I think. But they'll never be enough to cope with all that muck, sand, whatever it is…"

John B. grinned as inspiration struck him. "They won't have to for me, old mate," he said, then turned and ran across the beach into the sea.

The others looked at him, astonished. "You'll freeze, you idiot!" shouted Elizabeth.

"Nope. It's cold, but not that bad. We're near the Gulf Stream, I think," came the answering call.

Elizabeth looked down at her ruined clothes and then at Wilko. "Mr. Wilkes, would you be so kind as to fetch a blanket, and if possible a towel from the vehicle please? And bring them down to the waters edge mo-mentarily? Thank you so much."

Without waiting for a reply she ran after John B. and laughing, plunged into the water. In seconds she'd shed the heavy wool and the boots.

"You're right, it's cold - but I've stayed in hotels where the shower was worse."

Stewart grabbed her hands, serious for a moment. "I've faced death, and some really bad, bad stuff before, but that scared the hell out of me. I love you, pretty lady."

Q grabbed him and tumbled them both into the water, fearing that if the tears started again they wouldn't stop.

They both frolicked for a bit, just to wash the sand from faces and hair and other places where sand was especially uncomfortable.

At one point Q winced at the dark bruise on her lover's back – legacy of Mills' vicious elbow. But Stewart didn't react at all when she tentatively touched it.

"Whenever you're ready," called Wilko from the water's edge, holding up the blanket and a threadbare towel.

As his friends emerged from the bay he tried very hard to look in any direction but at Elizabeth's very wet, very lacy underwear and almost succeeded.   He'd put his camera back in the car, but the image would live in his memory. John B. Stewart was a lucky man.

The smiling lady took the blanket and very formally said, "Thank you, good sir," as she swaddled herself in it.

John B. contentedly took the towel, dried off as best he could, and wrapped it around his waist. That pair of jeans would not be seeing service again any time soon. They were jammed into a shopping bag together with Elizabeth's former attire, and tossed into the boot of the Rover.

"It's bloody cold when you get out of the water!" exclaimed Q, shivering in her blanket.

"You two better both get in the back seat. I'll crank up the heater and get you home. Definitely to your place. Whatever your story is, it won't be good enough for Ishbell McNeill!"

*

Auld Wullie had chosen to stay outside and tinker with the Cyclops' engine while his wife was in with her eldest sister. He wasn't avoiding Rose, but he wasn't inclined towards their verbal sparring today. More and more he found himself craving peace and quiet. A happy thought…

April lowered herself carefully into the chair opposite her sister. Rose had the courtesy to reach over and turn down the volume of the radio she was listening to. It was the middle-sized one – the one permanently set to pick up the news coming out of Glasgow.

The little portable transistor was for the closest there came to local news – a community station in Oban on the mainland that broadcast across the Southern Hebrides. Sitting on its own table in the bedroom was the 'big yin' – a powerful receiver that Rose's late husband Black Wullie had built for her. It could pick up stations from across Europe, and possibly further in really clear conditions, but Rose "couldnae be bothered wi' all that messin' around" so had it almost exclusively tuned to the BBC World Service.

"What's on?" asked April.

"Just the news," replied the older woman.

"Owt worth knowin'?"

"No' really. Same as usual."

"Och aye." April nodded. She knew Rose had a finely developed filter, and anything genuinely significant would stick in her head and be duly reported. Run-of-the-mill politics, sport, and the radio equivalent of the social pages didn't register a blip.

"Sad news about the *Curry House*," April observed. She'd guessed Rose hadn't been out of the house yet and was satisfied to see an eyebrow raised in curiosity.

But her sister would never admit to it. "Never been there. Curry gives me wind."

"Och, everything gives you wind. Ye're like the barber's cat – full o' wind and water."

"Curry's too hot for ma mouth."

"Ye've nae sense o' adventure, that's yuir trouble. I'll bet you've never even tried a curry. Me, I'll try anythin' once."

"You'll try it more than once."

"Aye, I will, if it's any good. But I'll no' be havin' it frae there any more, more's the pity."

"Och aye?" Rose's curiosity was genuinely piqued.

"Aye. Young Willis – ye know, that lassie that works there on Friday nights – called by the kitchen early this mornin'. She does that tae check if Mister Goom needs any shopping frae the greengrocer…"

"Tryin' tae get in the boss's good books."

"Ye cannae blame her for wantin' mair work. There's precious little of it aboot."

"True enough," agreed Rose sadly. "All the young yins will be leavin' before long. Especially if the distillery does close, ye ken. Ah blame bloody old Dotterel. Interferin' old so-and-so."

 April frowned – not her usual expression. "Aye, ye're right there." With a sharp shake of her head she got back onto her topic. "So, there wasnae anyone in the kitchen, and Willis says that's never the case. Bein' worried that somethin' was wrong, Mr. Goom were sick or somesuch, she went up the stairs and knocked on the door of the flat. Nae answer. Well, by this time, she says, she was a bit worried. Had a feelin' that something wasnae right."

"This Willis – she's one o' Reet Cameron's grand-daughters, aye? Auld Reet had a touch o' the Sight, I recall," said Rose thoughtfully.

"Aye, ye're right. Anyway, the door o' the flat wasnae locked, no' unusual apparently, so she let herself in tae check. Poor lass, she found Mr. Goom lyin' dead on the floor aside his bed."

"Poor lassie." There was a pause. "Nae… signs o' violence, were there?"

"Nae. It were as though he'd fallen oot o' bed and died on his way doon, she said. But she did reckon his mouth was open an' his skin was very red."

"Well, he was an Indian."

"No' a Red Indian, ye daft besom! I don't think he was even Indian in truth. Frae one o' they little countries further along. I never thought tae ask him the times I had lunch there. Thing called a massaman I had – very nice. Like a beef stew, only mair interestin'."

"Beef stew doesnae need tae be mair interestin'. A good beef stew is right enough as it is. So, ye'll no be havin' any more o' Mister Goom's curries then."

"Sadly no."

The two sisters lapsed into a thoughtful silence for a minute or two.

"How've you been sleepin'?" asked April eventually.

"Och, same as ever. Barely at all."

This wasn't actually true. Rose got a very full complement of sleep. It was just that it came in short blocks of ten minutes to an hour, right across the day and night. Very often she didn't even notice her naps – she could doze off with a cup of tea in her hand and wake up a quarter of an hour later without having spilled a drop. She'd complain that "the tea ye get these days doesnae stay hot like it used tae", mind you.

"And yerself April? You sleepin' okay?"

"Och aye, always do. Ma head hits the pillow at nine an' I'm oot like a light till six."

That was true. Auld Wullie could have set his clock by his wife's sleeping patterns. In their courting days and the early nights of their marriage he'd learned that any dalliance they might fancy (and there was quite a bit of that, he happily recalled) had to be done before nine o'clock. If April did manage to stay awake past then she was, well, not good to be around next morning. No matter how much she'd enjoyed the night before. The night of the 'wee dinner party' was a good example.

"Aye," continued the younger sister, "Dead tae the world, that's me."

Rose looked at her sister sharply. She rapped her knuckles on the little wooden table beside her.

"Sorry," said April in genuine contrition. "No' the best choice o' words these days."

The eyes of both sisters lost focus as they slipped into their own deep thoughts.

.oOo.

20 SMALL FRY AND THE BIGGER PICTURE

It didn't take long for word to get around in Sron Dubh. By the evening there were few who hadn't heard of Willis' unhappy discovery that morning, so there was a rather more sombre than usual air in the little crowd around the *Flying Fry-up* that Friday night.

The Asian newcomer had been a popular, if puzzling figure and his passing was felt more acutely than the recent loss of the MP McCrory (though his death had also left a definite sense of unease).

The owners and staff of the mobile fish-and-chip van were appropriately sensitive to the mood. The *Curry House* may have been their only competition in the village, but that was no reason to be disrespectful.

Refreshed and recovered after a long soak in a scented bath, Elizabeth and John B. had told Jazz of their 'adventure' on the beach.

"Ooh – nasty! Oh, now I think of it, Moraig told me when I first arrived to be careful of soggy patches in the middle of dry sand. I'm no beach bunny, so it slipped my mind – I never thought to warn you! I'm so sorry!"

"No need," said the brunette with a smile. "Who'd have thought we'd be on the beach in this weather?" Both women looked meaningfully at the wizard, blithely standing in the queue in his usual clothing.

"How many of those t-shirts does he have?" asked the blonde, and got a laugh and a shrug in reply.

Wilko had made it to the counter. He naively asked if they sold anything that wasn't deep fried, and was looked at as though he'd asked for a pork sausage at a Jewish wedding.

"Good thing Scarlet's not here, hey?" said Stewart, beside him.

Scarlet Burke was an old travelling companion, formerly inclined to be a rather fastidious vegetarian. Her new life in Central Australia, nominally as an Assistant Librarian but really the unlikely girlfriend of a local bike gang leader, was effecting some changes her friends would be surprised by.

With a wry nod, the Tasmanian settled for a "Deluxe Chip Buttie" (potato wedges on a soft white bread roll) and risked a crumbed sausage. Not his regular fare, but 'when in Rome', he thought. A serve of fish and chips for Jazz, and two large mugs of tea completed his order.

John B. requested an order of fish, "Crumbed, not battered please," for his lady love, a serve of deep fried black pudding and a deep fried chocolate bar for himself. A mug of tea and a bottle of soft drink were chosen to finish.

As they stepped away waiting for their meals to be cooked, Wilko said to his friend, "What's that sound? Wait, I know – it's your arteries hardening in anticipation."

"Mum did a lot of deep frying when I was young. It was quick, and harder to get wrong for someone who didn't like cooking anyway," he explained.

"But, deep fried chocolate?"

"A Scottish invention, I think. A good batter actually offsets the sweetness really nicely. You should try it."

"Thanks, but no thanks," said the Tasmanian as they collected the dinners, wrapped as tradition dictated in newspaper.

"Just bring they mugs back when ye're finished, aye?" said the matronly woman who served them.

"Will do!" promised the wizard.

The four friends perched on a convenient stone fence and tucked into their meals.

"It's nice to take part in a regular local institution," said Elizabeth cheer-fully.

Even Wilko found himself agreeing. He looked at the rather luminous orange soft drink that Stewart was happily consuming, and peered at the bottle.

"Weird name," he said. "It's not really brewed with iron, is it?"

"Oddly enough, it is, according to tradition." John B. looked closely at the ingredients listed on the label. "Here it is. Ammonium ferric citrate 0.002 per cent. Supposed to be good for the health, way back when. My Dad was fond of it, but bloody hard to find in Australia."

The Tasmanian shook his head. "Scottish cuisine is just strange."

The women laughed as Stewart said mildly, "You think so? Never occurred to me. Evening, lads. Keeping out of strife?"

This last was directed at a coterie of boys who were slouching past – the group they'd encountered in the laneway.

The first response was a set of blank looks, and Scuzzy Wullie's typically belligerent, "None o' yer business!"

It was Wee Chrissy who was sharp-eyed enough to recognise the t-shirt – everyone else in Sron Dubh was dressed to keep out the chill wind – and say, "Ye're the guy frae the other night!"

"Yep, that's me. So you guys do the Friday night fry, too?"

No one in the little gang knew quite what to make of him: the accent, the lightweight clothing, the attitude shown the night before last, the casual conversation now. Most adults in the village ignored them, avoided them, or hectored them.

The other three on the fence stayed out of the exchange but watched with interest.

Big Kev Macalpine managed to reply, "Actually, a takeaway curry would ha' been good…"

"But that isnae gonna happen noo, is it?" interrupted Scuzz.

"Aye, that's a shame," said Kev, ignoring the scruffy youth's sneering tone. "I s'pose at least the Reverend'll be happy. He reckoned Mr. Goom was a filthy heathen an' it was sinful we'd ever allowed 'im in town."

"Ma Mum reckons tha' old gowk doesnae approve o' anyb'dy. Well, she doesnae call 'im that but I do!" said Wee Chrissy.

"Hey – Kev. How d'ye know what ol' Dottery reckons anyway?" asked Scuzzy Wullie.

The big youth looked uncomfortable, but he was an honest bloke and answered, "I, er, go tae kirk on Sunday morning."

That got a snigger from Scuzz. A couple of the others uncertainly followed suit.

"Hey, it makes ma Pa happy," said Kev defensively.

Wee Chrissy responded with unexpected wistfulness, "If I still had a Pa I guess I'd wanna make him happy too."

Their self-styled leader curled a lip and said, "Och, yer all a bunch o wet nancies!"

John B. had been barely listening. He was pondering the Reverend's reported vitriol, and thinking of the man's own pedigree as reported by Auld Wullie.

Distracted and irritated by the young man's tone he off handedly said, "I wish you'd learn a bit about feelings, Scuzzy Wullie!"

The remark provoked an elbow in the ribs from Elizabeth.

"Ow! What...? Oh." The penny dropped. "Well, it doesn't look like he was listening anyway."

The deliberately rough-looking character was leading the pack away without a backward glance, although Kev and a couple of others managed an uncertain wave. The group would come back when the disconcerting man in the purple t-shirt had gone.

"Does it matter if he's listened?" asked Elizabeth.

"Um… maybe," John B. replied, convincing neither his lover nor himself. He changed the subject. "I'd like to see the stats on people dying in their sleep. I bet the figures around here are a damn sight higher than the national average."

"A combination of bad dreams and weak hearts?" suggested Jazz. "I'm glad my ticker is okay!"

The wizard thoughtfully chewed the last of his deep fried chocolate before replying, "Maybe. Maybe someone's actually exploiting that combination."

"You can't *make* someone dream something. That's impossible," protested Wilko.

"I dunno, that's like how hypnosis works," the engineer pointed out.

Elizabeth said, "Not very long ago I'd have said it was impossible for dozens of people, or more, to all have the same dream at the same time. Yet now I'm one of them."

"Mass hypnosis?" Jazz replied.

"It's hard to see any opportunity for it," said John B. "I've a very strong hunch the holy terror Dotterel is in this up to his dog collar, but I can't work out how. Or just as importantly, why. I reckon we need to know that to stop him."

Q put an arm around his waist and hugged him. "Hey babe, you broke the grip the beach had on me. You can break the grip of the 'preach' too."

Wilko glared at them in mock seriousness. "Puns from you now, Miss McKew? You, sir, are corrupting this young woman."

"Oh, I hope so!" It was Elizabeth who replied.

Laughing, they handed back the mugs, binned the old newspapers, and all strolled off into the night together.

.o0o.

21 THE TEMPEST

Saturday morning seemed a good time to visit the launderette. The previous morning's outfit might be beyond salvation for Elizabeth, but there were other clothes to be cleaned. The others were also running low on wardrobe options.

As April had assumed, there was only an old copper at the McNeill cottage: old technology that Jazz and Wilko might have mastered had they been so inclined. They weren't. Over at the Hines', Rhona had apologised that'd she had only just put the sheets on in her washing machine. She did provide a large thermos of coffee and some freshly baked fruit-cake, however.

Her generosity was much appreciated all round when the four friends gathered at *Suds Central*. The last of the cake was just being polished off when a familiar figure hobbled in, awkwardly dragging a tartan shopping trolley.

"Rose! Here, let me help you with that!" cried John B., rushing to take the trolley. It was full of damp clothes and bed linen.

The others helped the old woman to one of the thinly padded chairs, which she gratefully dropped herself onto.

"In the dryer, if ye would, please," she said, rummaging for coins in her purse.

Politely waving away the money, Jazz scurried to help John B. sort the laundry. She rightly guessed he'd have no idea about different fabrics needing different settings. Wilko rinsed a cup in the sink and poured coffee for the new arrival.

Meanwhile Elizabeth stayed by Rose and made conversation.

"I take it your dryer isn't working," she said.

"I dinna have one. I've got a line tae hang things oot on. It was fine when I put the washing on, ye ken, but I wasnae expectin' the weather tae turn so quick!"

 The Australian girl looked outside for the first time in a little while, and was shocked at how dark it was. Heavy dark clouds had blown in and hung threateningly low.

"Looks like we're in for a storm," she said with some concern.

"Aye, we do get some good yins here. Och, thanks laddie," said Rose as Wilko delivered her coffee before pulling up a chair for himself. "So, tell me wha' ye've all been up to?"

 While the other two finished loading three dryers and wandered back over, Elizabeth recounted the story of what had happened on the beach at Kilnaughton Bay in fairly graphic detail, figuring that this was how Rose liked to hear things. She was quite shocked then to realise how disturbed the old woman looked by the narrative's end.

"Oh – I'm sorry, I didn't mean to upset you! We're both fine now."

"Tisnae that, lass – tho' I'm glad ye're both safe o' course… But I must tell ye - exactly the same fate almost befell me as a wee lass. I couldnae ha' been much more than five at the time. I wandered intae just such a sinkhole on the verra same beach, in a thick woolly outfit tha' was like lead when it got wet… It was Braw Wullie that saved me."

 Wilko rolled his eyes and muttered, "The human improbability field…"

 Ignoring him, Stewart asked, "Was that Braw Wullie MacEwen?"

"Aye, he was a fine young man that yin. He was…"

 The old woman stopped and looked at John B. Q almost fancied that she could see a light going on over Rose's head, then realised it was the flick-ering of a fluorescent tube.

"He looked like John B.?" asked Elizabeth.

"No – no quite – much tidier he was, for one thing. But there's something aye familiar. A resemblance tae be felt more than seen."

"Reincarnation? A past life?" wondered Jazz aloud.

"Wha's tae say? Auld Wullie would be the man tae talk tae about that."

The wizard looked thoughtful. "Mm. I think possibly we did. Whatever happened to Braw Wullie?"

"He went off tae war. He was one o' they poor buggers had tae be picked up frae Dunkirk. After the Evacuation he came back tae the island for a visit – that's when he saved me on the beach. It wasnae long after that he went back on active duty. Gibraltar, I think, maybe back tae France. All I know is that he wasnae seen on Islay again."

Wilko did some mental arithmetic. If Rose was 5 or 6 in 1940 by now she'd be in her eighties. He discreetly examined her – that'd be about right, he guessed. She turned and almost caught him looking her over.

"It's a funny old world," he quickly said.

"Why dae ye think folk who say that dinna laugh aboot it?"

It was Elizabeth who rescued his awkwardness by asking Rose, "What did you think of Cecil's lecture?"

The resulting discussion of theories, especially around Picts and Pechts, kept them occupied until everyone's washing was dry. The weather outside by then, however, was not. The rain was heavy and judging by the clouds, likely to get heavier.

"Och, bugger! I was hopin' tae beat that home," said Rose.

John B. shook his head. "No problem. The car's parked nearby – we can give you a lift home, right gang?"

Only the old woman looked uncertain. "Will we all fit?" she wondered.

"Sure. Washing in the boot. You sit in the front, Wilko drives, and I'll squeeze in the back with the girls."

"Ye dinna mind that?" the widow Ellison asked drily.

Stewart grinned. "I'll make the sacrifice."

"And *I* will sit in the middle," said Q firmly.

The arrangement worked. An umbrella Jazz had left in the boot even allowed the ladies, John B. and the laundry to get to the Rover mostly dry, while Wilko had managed to not get soaked in fetching the car.

They'd pulled up outside Rose's cottage and John B. was just getting out with the umbrella when the sky was lit by a forked bolt of lightning and a loud crack of thunder hurt their ears.

"Ye cannae drive in this!" stated Rose emphatically.

"Not keen to sit out here in it!" was Wilko's equally sincere reply.

"Right – inside, the lot o' ye!"

John B. held the umbrella over Rose with one hand and with the other helped as she hauled herself up out of the car. From the driver's seat Wilko bit his tongue as the heavy-set woman pushed off against his shoulder. Elizabeth had taken the proffered key and dashed to open the front door.

Stewart called into the back of the Rover, "Wait there – I'll come back with the umb…"

"Fat chance!" exclaimed Jazz, jumping from the car and following Elizabeth as another bolt of lightning struck a tree over in the woodlands.

Wilko more prudently waited until John B. had gotten Rose to her door relatively dry and then come back to give him some shelter. They opened the boot a little and, as carefully as possible, extracted Rose's laundry. As much as possible they protected it with the umbrella and Wilko's body as they ran for the cottage.

"Wow! It's a corker!" said Jazz, gazing out the window as more lightning split the sky.

"It's a damned nuisance is wha' it is," Rose said with feeling. "Still, there's nowt fer it. Best make yersel's comfortable," she said as she settled herself in her chair.

Elizabeth got the other lounge chair, while Jazz and Wilko sank into the old couch, feeling a little as though the upholstery was swallowing them. Waving away the suggestion of a chair from the kitchen, John B. sat comfortably cross legged on the floor.

Something caught his attention over by the door they'd just come in. The wizard smiled. "Beautiful dog," he said.

"Too right. Looks just like 'Lassie' on the old TV show," agreed Jazz. "Collie, isn't she?"

"Where did it go? I just saw it out of the corner of my eye," said Elizabeth.

Wilko looked baffled. "What are you lot talking about? What dog? I'm looking right at the door."

From her chair Rose was looking nowhere but at the blonde engineer. "Aye," she said. "Tha's Gem. A braw watchdog she was."

"Was?" repeated Elizabeth, but Rose wasn't paying attention.

The old woman had changed her expression while no one was watching her.

"So tell me aboot yersel', young Jazz. Engineer's an odd profession fer a lass, even today, is it no'?"

"Eh? Oh, I guess so still. A bit. I guess I just really liked drafting at college, and figured machinery's more interesting than buildings. Buildings don't *do* anything except stand there."

"Aye, I see. And where was college?"

"Stratford-upon-Avon. I'm from Shakespeare country," was the proud reply.

"If anyb'dy would like tea feel free tae make a pot. Or there's a bottle o' Auld Wullie's whisky on the sideboard if ye'd like a dram. Stratford, eh? Family fra' there, were they? I'm nae bein' nosey, just… interested," she said reassuringly.

'If she's offering hospitality, then from what her sister's said before, she really must be interested,' thought Elizabeth. 'I wonder why?'

"Dad's lot has been there for hundreds of years! His great-great-great something was one of two brothers that owned the *White Horse Hotel* back in the 1560's. The family name was Perrott back then – it got changed somewhere along the way. Dad's Jarrod Parrish."

"I think spelling was a bit random in record keeping for a while. Or it could have been as simple as someone's dodgy handwriting," said John B., student of history.

 His Tasmanian buddy wore a bemused smile. "I'm just getting over the idea of a pub two hundred years older than the country I'm from."

 He got an affectionate squeeze of the knee from Jazz who said, "The *White Horse* is older than that mate. It opened in about 1450."

 Wilko whistled.

"So is the hotel still in the family?" he asked.

"No such luck, mate! We just drink there sometimes! It used to be owned by a brewer named Robert Perrott and run by his brother William. William and nearly all his family were killed in the Great Plague of 1564.

That was really sad – William had commissioned this beautiful big painting on one wall of the big lounge for his wife. It was of a story from some obscure book of the Bible - *Tobias & The Angel*. She must have been pretty religious."

"Didn't do them a lot of good, eh?" said Wilko drily.

"I don't think anyone was safe from the Plague, old buddy, believers or not, rich or poor," observed John B.

"The funny thing is," Jazz continued, "When the pub was being renovated in 1927 they knocked a bunch of wooden panels off the wall and found some big oak beams, and old William's painting. My Pop must have told me that story a dozen times over a beer. His Dad, or maybe his Pop, was there when they found it."

 Impressed, Elizabeth asked, "Is it still there, or did it go to a museum or gallery or something?"

"No, it's part of the wall. It's a bit faded but you can still sit in the lounge and admire it while you have dinner – if you like religious art with your pie, chips and ale."

"Rules me out, then," admitted her boyfriend.

"What aboot yer mother? Is she a Stratford lass?"

 Jazz' smile dropped slightly. "She wasn't. She died not long after I was born."

"Och, I'm sorry, pet!"

"It's okay Rose. I never knew her to miss her. I've always been real happy with how Dad raised me on his own. I didn't mind not having to share him – he was happy with only one kid. I was probably enough of a handful for a bloke on his own. Probably still am, hey?" she teased Wilko.

"I'm learning to cope," he answered straight-faced.

She blew him a kiss. "Anyway, Dad's never talked much about her. Jeannie, her name was. She was Scottish, I know that much, but I don't think she was a very happy woman. I don't reckon even Dad knows a lot about her to tell the truth. Bit of a whirlwind romance that probably wouldn't have worked out if she'd lived."

Abruptly changing subject Rose said, "I hear ye've been sufferin' badly wi' these awful dreams, ye poor lass."

It didn't click with the English girl to wonder where this might have been heard, as she hadn't talked about how badly she'd been affected with any-one but her Australian friends. But she felt strangely relieved to talk about it now.

"You know, it started before I even got to Islay! Nowhere near as bad, but when the really uncomfortable ones started I realised… I felt I'd been in that bloody classroom before."

John B. knew exactly what she meant. He'd been seeing the school, and the flames, long before he'd gotten off the little plane days earlier. The wizard suspected it was another strange twist to the magic that lived in him – an unwelcome one. He said nothing.

They were all startled by a knock at the door, and realised that the storm was no longer raging. Even the rain had stopped during Jazz' story but they'd all been too engrossed to notice.

The door opened. April and Auld Wullie walked in, hanging wet mackin-toshes on a hook as they did.

"Afternoon, all! I saw yer car outside when we arrived. Just came tae check on ye, Rose. That were a stoater o' a storm!"

"Och, I'm fine. Why wouldnae I be?"

The youngest sister looked at Rose sternly. "Cos at oor age we know tae be careful o' wild weather. Thunder, lightnin', rain – aye?"

In response the oldest sister looked a little contrite, then explained, "This lot were kind enough tae bring me home frae the laundry hoose. Damned storm surprised me. We've been havin' a nice wee blether." She gestured at Jazz who was vacating her chair for April. "Yon lassie's frae Stratford-on-Avon, ye ken?"

"Really? Tha's nice. Interestin' town. I went there on a bus trip wi' the Historical Society a few years back," she replied.

Auld Wullie waved away Elizabeth's offer of a chair. He stood by the sideboard, and poured whisky for himself and John B. who'd courteously stood when they came in. Jazz accepted one too as she motioned Wilko to stay in his seat. The small man wordlessly but politely declined a drink.

Rose gave her sister a suspicious look, saying, "Ye didnae go tae see *Mac...* the Scottish play, did ye? Pack o' bloody lies tha' is..."

"Hush yer whisht. No, I didnae. It was *Hamlet* we saw there."

With a satisfied nod Rose replied, "Now there's a story o' revenge that doesnae come fast but comes aye certain."

"Did you visit the *White Horse* by any chance?" asked Jazz.

"The one wi' the bonny auld mural? Aye. Funny tae think the Bard himsel' sat under that picture, eh? Who would he ha' seen, an' what would he ha' heard?"

Elizabeth suddenly clicked her fingers and said, "Oh, April, while I think of it – Wilko and I finally met the lovely Miss Dotterel. I forgot to mention it at the lecture."

"And what did ye think o' oor likely new Member o' Parliament? Impressed?" asked Rose.

"Not in any positive way!" was the blunt reply.

"Her, an MP? From a little spot like Sron Dubh? No offence," said Wilko, much surprised.

"She visits her auld yin a lot but she doesnae live in the village noo, ye ken," explained April. "Grander ambitions. She'll be awa' oot o' Bowmore an' the Chamber o' Commerce soon enough."

The words 'Chamber of Commerce' rang a bell for Jazz, but for the moment she couldn't think why.

In a quiet voice Auld Wullie explained, "The electorate is aye bigger than this island, but tha' young woman is becomin' an influential figure one way or another."

"Wait a minute," said John B. "There's no General Election due this year, is there?"

Rose looked sour. "We need a new local member since the last yin died. In his sleep."

There was a pause while the visitors digested that piece of news.

With obvious skepticism April said, "O' course she claims tae not be ruled by the Party but by the will o' the community. Grass roots support she calls it."

"As long as the will o' the community conveniently reflects her own will o' course," added her sister grimly.

"A grass roots politician is one who doesn't aspire to grow to any great heights," was John B.'s contribution to political discussion.

April gripped the arms of her chair. "Well, noo I know yer safe and soond we'd best be on wer way. Nice tae see you young yins – look after yersel's mind. Come on, Auld Wullie," she said hauling herself upright before anyone could offer to assist.

Bromleigh put his empty glass on the sideboard and exchanged nods with Jazz and John B.

"Cheerio, April!" the wizard called as he went to rinse the three glasses in the kitchen.

Elizabeth stood up and discreetly helped the Bromleighs take their raincoats off the hooks, sparing arthritic shoulders. "We should be going too, while the weather holds," she said as the old couple left.

"I think yon storm's blown past us noo, but aye – I wouldnae mind a wee nap," admitted their hostess. "I did enjoy the natter, mind. Thank ye all."

Her chin was on her chest that rose and fell in gentle slumber only minutes after her guests' goodbyes.

"You got the Inquisition, didn't you? Not that I minded hearing your life story," said Wilko as he drove.

"Really? It never occurred to me. I don't mind – who doesn't really like talking about themselves, eh?" replied Jazz.

Elizabeth looked at John B. He was looking out the window.

.oOo.

22 EVERYONE LOVES A PARTY, DON'T THEY?

"We've got to take her home and get her into the Weather Bureau. She was right on the money about the storm."

 Wilko was talking to John B. on the footpath outside the Hines' guesthouse. He was quite correct about Rose's prediction, it had turned into a beautifully clear, if still brisk evening. They were waiting for the girls to emerge to go to the ceilidh in Bowmore.

 Elizabeth had prevailed upon Jazz to take her into Bowmore early, almost as soon as they'd unloaded the washing from Anastasia's boot.

"Secret women's business!" she'd told the boys in no uncertain terms.

 With a shrug Wilko had walked back into the cottage, while Stewart was similarly comfortable with putting his feet up in the parlour. Both men, in fact, enjoyed quite long afternoon naps.

 They expected no clues about the shopping expedition when the ladies returned, and were almost right. Each man was surprised to receive a new shirt from his beloved.

 The Tasmanian was delighted with a black and grey Western style shirt, even appreciating the tiny roses discreetly embroidered across the shoulders and pockets.

 On the other side of the village, Stewart's jaw had frankly dropped when he opened his parcel. It was purple, yes. That's where the resemblance to his usual garb ended. The shirt was long sleeved, with gold buttons on the cuffs and all the way down the front. The purple was a two-toned paisley pattern. And it was made of silk.

"Oh my…" he breathed. "I don't think I've ever worn anything like this in my life."

"But do you like it, babe?" Elizabeth asked nervously.

"It's… stunning. You better believe I like it!"

"Oh, I so wanted you to say that! I love the feel of silk against my skin, and I hoped you would too. No peeking at my parcels! The others are coming here in a bit so Jazz can change here for the dance."

"Oh, fabulous! A collective Great Unveiling!" John B. had said sincerely.

Now the men stood in their new finery, waiting patiently to see what their partners had chosen for themselves.

Jazz emerged first. It was a classical little black dress to match her beau's new shirt. Little flecks of silver glistened in the porch light. Shiny flat black shoes, sheer black stockings and a cropped black velvet jacket for warmth completed the ensemble.

"You look bloody fantastic!" was exactly the response she'd hoped for from Wilko. She wrapped her arms around him as John B. stood by, smiling broadly his approval.

Then Q came out. Her outfit didn't match the colour of John B.'s new shirt, but it was silk. A shimmering sea-green halter neck top was attached to a fluted skirt in a darker shade of the same colour. The hem of the skirt flared slightly just above her knees. Strappy silver sandals on her feet, pale tights were her only concession to the climate. 'It better be warm in this place,' she'd thought as she dressed.

With a calculatedly casual air she greeted John B. "Hey babe."

Making an effort to match her reserve the wizard smiled. "I love it when you say that. Makes me think of Lou Reed."

"You can take a walk on the wild side with me any time."

That ended the restraint. Their embrace would have had Ishbell McNeill running for a bucket of cold water – for them or herself.

Wilko rolled his eyes. 'Honeymoon period', he thought to himself before realising he was probably no better.

The atmosphere in Anastasia on the way to Bowmore was joyous. Whatever drama still surrounded them, tonight was about putting that aside for a while and having fun.

That attitude pervaded the *Dockside*, as though everyone at the ceilidh needed the same sort of release. It was a sizeable crowd. Some wore plain casual clothes, but many had made an effort to dress up, which meant that the overseas visitors didn't feel conspicuous. Both women attracted plenty of admiring looks, mind you, to the pride of their partners.

It was an event of a type not quite familiar to the Australians. At times it resembled a folk dance, at others a discotheque. Much of the music was provided by a sparrow-like woman named (according to the hand-painted sign on her mixing desk) "Disco Daisy".

Her playlist comprised some traditional Scottish reels and a lot of 70s pop hits.

One of the first tracks played was the Rocky Horror Show's *Time Warp*. Quite apt, thought John B.

Sometimes Disco Daisy turned off her equipment, and a young couple in matching blue pantsuits occupied the small stage. They belied their Osmond-esque outfits. He played a steady reliable rhythm guitar. She was a skilled multi-instrumentalist, moving easily between accordion, flute, mandolin and even pan pipes. The Australians didn't recognise anything they played, but the rest of the crowd knew at least some, and loudly approved of all.

The management of the *Dockside* kept up a steady supply of platters of finger food throughout the night, which in turn kept a steady stream of customers at the bar. The beer, wine and of course whisky kept the dancers enthusiastic and active, whatever song Daisy played.

At one point *My Sharona* came over the speakers.

"I've never understood why this song was so popular," said Wilko.

In response Jazz pointed over to their right. There was Giddy Mary, her strange loose-limbed dancing ideally suited to the song. Certainly young Kev Macalpine, dancing just out of range of her flailing arms, seemed to approve.

He seemed to be the only one of the little Sron Dubh 'gang' in attendance. Most of the others were probably too young, and the rest probably fancied themselves as too tough or too cool to go to a dance. Their loss, as far as Kev was concerned.

Neither Wilko nor John B. was a much better dancer than Giddy Mary. Less frenetic, but not much more coordinated. The Tasmanian lacked any sense of rhythm ("You'd be a terrible Catholic!" Jazz joked) and his friend suffered from what he called 'terpsichorean dyslexia'. On a dance floor he couldn't tell right from left.

Elizabeth had seen the way he moved when he fought, and in more intimate moments. She was puzzled. Evidently it took a certain sort of adrenalin to get his body moving smoothly and quickly. 'Never mind – at least he's having a go,' she thought, twirling under his hand in a jive move her new skirt was perfectly designed for.

To her and John B.'s delight, one of the last tunes of the night was *Walk On The Wild Side*. They sang along while they embraced and somehow managed to fit awkward waltz steps to the tempo. Really it was just an excuse to hold each other close. Q had been serious about how much she loved the feel of silk on her skin. It hadn't happened with her ex-husband, and the new dress gave her ample opportunity to enjoy the feel of his sleeves on her bare back.

The Blues Brothers' *Peter Gunn* turned out to be the unlikely tune that got Wilko swaying and moving in close step with Jazz. The blonde laughed, kissed him and hugged him tightly as they danced.

At exactly thirty minutes past midnight the music stopped. The bar had closed half an hour earlier. It was a happy, if not entirely sober crowd that drifted out of the *Dockside*. Some like Wilko had remembered that they were supposed to be driving home and had been careful what they drunk. Others had been less careful and walked or found other means of getting home. Some weren't careful at all and lurched to their vehicles to drive home regardless.

It was to let those particular hazards get well away that the four friends waited on the footpath by the door of the *Dockside* for a while before departing. Diligent cuddling was required to keep the girls warm. Most of the vehicles had gone by the time they decided to set off.

With the size of the crowd, Wilko had been obliged to park the Rover on a street a few blocks away, but it wasn't an onerous walk.

As John B. and Q stepped out to cross a side street there was the sudden roar of an engine. Headlights flashed on and a big glossy black Range Rover bore down on them at speed.

Blinded by the light (a song that had played barely an hour earlier) Stewart grabbed his girlfriend and almost threw her into the arms of the startled Wilko, still on the footpath with Jazz. The three flattened themselves against a wall as the 4WD swerved so one set of wheels mounted the kerb.

The wizard dived headlong for the gutter and hit it hard. Fortunately it was wide and deep – enough to hold him while the black machine passed above.

The Range Rover crunched back down onto the street, the back wheel landing just in front of Stewart's outstretched arm, screeched around the corner and accelerated away.

Elizabeth rushed to John B.'s side as he picked himself up, cursing bitterly.

"Are you alright, babe?" she asked fearfully.

"Yeah, I am, but my new shirt isn't!" The gutter had still been running with water from the earlier storm.

"Oh, baby, if that's the worst of it I'm happy. A shirt can always be washed or even replaced. I can't replace you!" she said throwing her arms around him.

"It seems daft to speak ill of an inanimate object, but I really hate those bloody things!" said Jazz. "Especially that one! Sorry – I know you guys have a soft spot for British cars…"

"No apology necessary, mate. I'm not sure those things count as British cars any more," said John B. "Anyway, it's the nut behind the wheel that's the dangerous component. Damn fool must have been hammered from the dance."

 Wilko had stared after the retreating vehicle, trying to make out the number plate.

"Yeah…" he said. "Come on buddy – let's get home before any other lunatics appear."

.oOo.

23 FOR GOD'S SAKE

Q had already learned to expect the unexpected from John B., but even so, his announcement that he wanted to 'toddle along to the morning service with Rhona' came as a surprise.

Mrs. Hine was delighted. She routinely attended the morning service, but more as a social outing than a show of commitment to the church.

"I'm a believer, ye ken," she said as she handed a plate of fresh toast to her guests. "Just no' necessarily a believer in the Reverend Dotterel."

Elizabeth had no interest in joining them. She asked Rhona if there were any books in the house that might help her research some family history. She knew her father hailed from the Scottish islands somewhere, but knew little else about him. He'd 'skipped out' on her mother when she was an infant and not been spoken of (except in occasional bursts of abuse) since.

"Och, tha's a terrible thing some men do. Cowardice, I call it," the landlady had said sympathetically.

Her seldom-seen husband turned out to have taken up the study of genealogy as a hobby when he'd retired, and the young woman was assured that he'd be more than willing to assist.

Coffee and toast finished, Elizabeth stood in the hallway watching the oddly assorted pair prepare to stroll off to the service. He hadn't said as much, but she'd decided JB was going on a 'know your enemy' reconnaissance.

At the doorway Rhona turned and brightly said, "Hamish will be doon tae join you in the parlour shortly. He's just getting' a few books together for ye both tae go through."

"Thanks! Um… JB darling, are jeans and t-shirt appropriate for church?" Q asked cautiously as they were about to leave.

"They are on me," he said with a grin.

Rhona smiled too. "It's my belief that the Lord looks at the inside, dear, no' the outside."

'I wonder how many others in the congregation will think that way?' thought Elizabeth, waving as the door closed.

And yes, there were several who looked at his outfit in shock and/or horror as they walked into the churchyard. Stewart was utterly unconcerned, admiring the view. The little kirk was situated at the top of a small hill overlooking the village but more importantly in his opinion, the woods in one direction and the bay in another.

*

Jazz and Wilko also stayed home on Sunday morning.

The English girl was determined to 'take advantage' of Ishbell's absence - i.e. not feel they had to speak in undertones and creep about the place like mice.

Gazing out the window at the dumpy figure stomping away in the distance, she said, "Bloody dragon'll be at church till lunchtime." There was more than a trace of bitterness in her voice as she continued, "I've been here long enough to know the routine. Y'know, I've played along 'cos I need a roof over my head, but…"

After a deep breath her voice rose and she shouted out the window. "I hate this bloody furtive stuff! I'm not bloody ashamed of you, or me. Or how I bloody feel about you!"

With that off her chest, she turned expecting to see Wilko cringing and was ready to apologise for embarrassing him. Instead he was standing there smiling at her.

"Thank you," he said and opened wide his arms.

She ran into them. They didn't bother trying to be quiet.

*

At the church it soon became clear that numbers were well down on what the Reverend wanted. Not everyone had pulled up well after the ceilidh, it seemed.

Dotterel wasn't hiding his irritation well as he greeted his parishioners on arrival.

He did manage a restrained reaction on meeting Stewart.

"Thank ye for coming. I hope ye'll learn something tae yer advantage."

"I hope so too," replied John B., returning a smile so thin it could have sliced bread.

Rhona demurely shook the Reverend's hand (which hadn't been offered to her houseguest) and as usual gave Hamish's apologies on the grounds of poor health.

"And as ever, we will pray for him," Dotterel replied.

As they entered the church John B. whispered to her, "Not helping a lot do you think?"

Equally softly she answered, "Prayer has tae be sincere tae be effective."

"Good point."

They sat down in a pew near the back, a tactful and wary distance from the pulpit. Several familiar faces filed past, or were already inside. Ishbell McNeill was in the front row of course, beside the well-named Skinny Mary. The red locks of Miz Chisholm were visible a row behind her.

The wizard recognised young Kev Macalpine seated a little in front of Rhona. Clearly he'd managed to recover from the ceilidh and Giddy Mary's dancing. The man beside Kev must be his Pa. He was a half head shorter, but the resemblance otherwise was obvious.

Rhona nudged him and indicated a thirty-something year old man on the far side of the kirk. He was well-proportioned, with a tousle of shoulder

176

length reddish blonde hair. "Tha's Doc Wullie. A good man ye should get tae know," the landlady said quietly. "And th' bonny lass is young Tegan McKechnie. She wants tae be a writer."

John B. admired the attractive dark haired girl in the pew behind the doctor. "She looks like an actress," he said. "Must be a 'creative look', eh?"

DS Mills walked in and was startled to see the now familiar purple t-shirt.

He slid onto the pew beside Stewart, leaned close and in a low murmur said, "I swear I'm gonna kill you yet."

The Australian turned to him and casually replied, "On hallowed ground, DS? What would your master think?"

The angry thug raised his voice. "I'm gonna…"

Rhona looked over. At that moment Gordon Dotterel walked past on his way to the pulpit. He tapped the Englishman's shoulder.

"Ah, Mr. Mills, could you assist me please?" he said, and continued his progress.

"Off you go, Fido," said John B. as the growling minder left.

Dotterel's fire and brimstone sermon was much as Stewart had expected, exhorting piety and chastity, but mostly obedience. The preacher painted a lurid picture of the torments of Hell, and vowed that only he could show the congregation the way to salvation.

He laid emphatic claim to the tradition and the heritage of the early Saints who first brought honour and glory to the island. Notably he invoked Findlugan, who in the 6th Century after Christ had saved the life of holy Columba on the neighbouring isle of Jura, and founded an Ileach monastery on the site that still bore a more modern spelling of his name.

"As heir tae the legacy of Saint Findlugan, tis I who shall lead the ways o' the righteous!"

John B. found the historical allusions intriguing, but the repeated dire threats of damnation wearisome. He wasn't sorry when the show was over at the end of an hour, and after the passing of the plate (he contributed some Australian coins whose local value didn't amount to much) the parishioners started to file out.

"No tea and cake?" he asked Rhona with a grin.

"Frae this lot? Hardly!" was her laughing but diplomatically quiet answer.

As the congregation departed, Dotterel again stood at the door, dispensing homilies or chastisements as he saw fit.

Rhona had gone on ahead while her guest stopped to offer the fair Tegan some encouragement, and briefly exchange pleasantries with Lanky Wullie. The peat cutter wasn't at his best but came to kirk because he "had tae, ye ken?"

When John B. exited the Reverend piously said, "I expect we shall see you here in the presence of the Lord again this evening and next Sunday."

Stewart stopped, and looking the preacher in the eye observed, "That's funny, I'd have thought you'd reckon us to be in the presence of the Lord every day."

"In this, His House!"

The wizard looked around and spread his arms. "Surrounded by His Creation, in all its glory? What do you need a house for? The man made walls and roof just separate you from the daily miracle."

John B. wasn't shouting, but neither was he taking care to keep his voice down. A few of the parishioners who hadn't yet left the churchyard had stopped to listen. Some looked outraged, simply that anyone would have the temerity to debate with the Reverend. It was as well for Jazz' lease that neither Ishbell MacNeill nor the faithful Skinny Mary were within earshot.

There were others, though, who looked more thoughtful.

After Stewart had walked away from the preacher with a smile and an insincere bow, he was approached by the father and son Macalpines.

Cautiously the older man asked, "Isnae the kirk the body o' Christ? It's no' really just stone an' mortar, surely."

"You've got to decide that for yourself," said the Australian. "You're a man who works with your hands. You look at the building. You look at the world around you, look at your Scripture with open eyes and open mind, and you decide. Don't let anyone else tell you what to think."

A youngish woman with a striking bob of radiantly white hair suddenly appeared beside him. "Don't you dare undermine my father, whoever you are. Mr. Macalpine – you will ignore this *person*."

Kev Junior looked for a moment like he may argue, although his father didn't. John B. shook his head, and the Macalpines went on their way.

John B. realised that this was his first meeting with Victoria Dotterel. After hearing so much about her he wasn't surprised by his first impression.

She proceeded to reinforce his opinion, snarling, "God will *get* you for that!"

"Pardon?" The Australian's impulsive smile faded. "Wow, you're actually serious, aren't you?"

"Of course I am! My father and I are leaders of a God-fearing community."

"And there's my problem," Stewart said with an effort at patience. "You see, I'm more about God-loving than God-fearing. That's what my God is all about. Love."

Victoria snapped, "The Lord my God is a jealous God!"

"Very Old Testament, yes. I lean more towards *the greatest commandment is this – to love…*"

The younger Dotterel interrupted him brusquely. "The Devil may quote Scripture to suit his own purpose!"

John B. turned away from her and looking out at the view said, "You know, the more I see of this planet the more comfortable I am with God as a creator and sustainer of life. And the more I distrust organized religions that claim God's authority to have authority over ordinary people."

He sighed, and saw Rhona Hine out on the footpath heading for her car to take them home. "Miss Dotterel, you might reckon I'm a bad influence, but in that particular game I don't reckon I'm even in your league."

He walked away, leaving her to fume as she watched him go.

It was only when he was nearly home that it dawned on him where he'd seen Victoria before. The realization alarmed him.

.oOo.

24 I'VE JUST SEEN A FACE...

"I'm amazed you didn't recognise her when you met her!" he said to Elizabeth in their little bedroom.

"The hair is the right colour, sure, but JB, the schoolmistress in my dreams isn't… she doesn't have… well, there's no face. She's just this glowing figure – shining even - who just sort of radiates authority."

The wizard looked frustrated. "I guess it's the same for Jazz and Wilko or they'd have said something."

Q held his hands. "I think it's the same for everybody, or surely someone would have mentioned it."

"That makes sense, but why do I see her face? What makes me different?"

"Oh, lots of things, babe!"

Her kiss cleared some of the clouds.

"Whether I'm right or wrong, this morning's given me no more answers. Just more questions. Keep cheering me up, sweetheart. Tell me about your morning."

Happy to oblige, Q explained that Hamish had helped her trace the McKew name. It was a convoluted line, in the normal way of clan histories, but she proudly declared that her bloodline went all the way back to the father of Somerled.

With the little information she knew about her father she was pretty confident that he'd been from the Shetland Islands, and there was a definite long-standing Celtic/Norse connection there.

"When this is all over, I'd like us to go there, please," she said, having got the genealogy bit between her teeth.

"Whatever you want, my love. Before that, I think we might go visit Finlaggan. You've got a link there. The island hangs a lot of its history of the place. And Gordon Dotterel has a particular fascination for it."

"Can we not think about the Dotterels for a while? I've got other things I'd like to do with the afternoon, if you're interested," she said mischievously.

John B. was happy to play along.

*

The Reverend Gordon Dotterel was not a happy man. He took the drop in attendance (not to mention contributions) as a personal insult, and was further affronted to have been openly challenged by the scruffy visitor.

"Who is the wretch?" he asked his daughter. "He arrived wi' Rhona Hine, who I'd thought harmless enough, and I first encountered him wi' yon scurrilous Mrs. Bromleigh and her rancorous sister. He's incurred the dislike of young Mills."

"Hunh – that's not a difficult achievement. Lachlan Maclean told me there were strangers asking around at the law office. I'd say he's one of them."

"Asking about what, child?"

Victoria folded her arms and scowled. "My business, father. Mine and yours."

*

The dark mood in the Dotterel family only deepened when the congregation at the evening service was even smaller than that of the morning. Perhaps some folks were still nursing hangovers, or embarrassment at having had one. But the preacher indignantly realised that a number of people from the morning meeting hadn't returned as they normally did.

His daughter angrily suggested that they were people who had been within earshot of the man in purple when he'd disputed with her or her father.

182

The Dotterels were locking the front door of the church while Mills attended to the back door and windows.

The Reverend said angrily, "The devil takes up arms against us, daughter, and we must take up arms against him. I will seek guidance in…"

Suddenly a bottle smashed behind them. A little cluster of youths loitered at the churchyard gate. The most disreputable looking of them – the one who'd evidently thrown the bottle, taunted the preacher.

"Closin' up early? Wha's the matter, auld man? Ye gave a sermon an' naebody came?" laughed Scuzzy Wullie.

At the back of the group Kev winced. He'd come along to try to make sure things didn't get out of hand. "Come on, Scuzz. Ye've had yer fun. Let's get outta here," he urged.

Emboldened by Scuzzy Wullie's bravado, Wee Chrissy joined in the taunt, calling, "It's sad, innit Mister? Naeb'dy wants tae see ye! Or be seen wi' ye, mair like it!"

Victoria took a step forward but her father laid a restraining hand on her shoulder.

"No dear, don't soil your hands. Mills!" he shouted.

At the sound of the well-known thug's name the boys took off. Teasing the Reverend and his daughter was one thing, facing Mills' brutality, even when they outnumbered him, was a different proposition.

The minder ran around the corner of the church. "What is it, boss?" he puffed.

"A gang of disrespectful youths," Dotterel replied, pointing down the street at the running boys. "Deal wi' them for me, please." He gripped Mills' sleeve for a moment. "Discipline, DS, not death, thank you. I want a point tae be made and a lesson tae be learned." As his 'enforcer' gave chase the Reverend observed, "He's willing enough, but I doubt he can catch them all."

Victoria sneered, "It doesn't matter. I know who the ringleaders are."

Her father nodded slowly. "I believe I do, too."

*

Mills wasn't especially fast, but he was persistent. Although the boys had promptly scattered the Englishman was a hunter and had picked his target: the slowest of his prey.

Neither pursued nor pursuer could aspire to the steeplechase. Fences and gates were struggled over, not vaulted as would have been preferred. Kev couldn't lead Mills to his home, the man might do anything to his parents! So he headed for the outskirts of the village, hoping to disappear into the darkness.

Instead, the gloom was his undoing. He misjudged the height of a dry stone wall, tripped and fell heavily. Mills had been closer than he'd realised and now loomed, a threatening shadow against the night sky.

Panting, the Englishman remembered his orders. No death. Pity. He took a gun from his coat pocket and knelt.

"Dinna…" began Kev, before DS from close range fired a shot that tore through the terrified boy's ankle.

The lad moaned, shock already setting in. Mills calmly examined his handiwork. No, a bit too neat. He picked one of the stones from the wall, and with careful aim hurled it onto the spot where the bullet had passed through. The projectile finished the job of shattering the ankle bones.

The pain brought the relief of unconsciousness, and Kev was spared the sound of Mills' jaunty whistling as he walked away.

.oOo.

25 SCUZZY WULLIE'S DREAM

"May I please leave the room, Miss?"

"No, you most certainly may not!"

"Pleeease, Miss – I really have tae go!"

"You are not going anywhere, young man."

"But I have tae…"

"Stand up. Come to the front of the class. Now stand there, facing me."

The boy squirmed, his distress obvious. Someone behind him sniggered. A girl giggled.

"Please, Miss…" he tried again.

"Silence! You are to stand there. Just stand there. Do not move."

Tears of embarrassment and now pain started to streak his face. The lower reaches of his stomach gave a protesting grumble, which only drew more mirth from some of those behind him.

"I said silence, boy," snapped the schoolmistress, as if his guts' noise was deliberate.

A violent cramp tore through his insides, buckling his knees and almost doubling him over.

Almost in his ear she shouted, "I told you to stand still!"

Despairingly he tried to pull himself upright. It was too much for him. His bowels emptied.

"Stand still I said!"

The boy's legs trembled. Pain. Shock. Humiliation. The sound of voices behind him, some gasps of shock, some snickers of malicious delight. And the dreadful warm feeling that was all over his buttocks, now running down his thighs.

He couldn't stop the flow. Couldn't imagine how he could have ever eaten enough to produce so much of this…

"You're making quite a mess there, boy."

It was true, he knew. He knew there was a terrible puddle forming around his feet.

His intestine was finally empty. With terrible speed the warmth in his short pants and down his legs was turning into an even more awful clamminess. He felt his thighs sticking together.

"That is a terrible mess, isn't it class?"

"Yes, Miss," chorused a few.

"And this is the boy some of you have foolishly chosen to follow the example of."

The teacher reached out and made as if to slap him as she would a fly. A girl's voice at the back of the class shrieked in protest. The hand stopped in the middle of its sweep.

The schoolmistress appeared to seek the source of the cry, but without success. However, her hand lowered. She made it obvious that she would not sully herself on the quivering boy.

"There is only one authority in this room. One person for you to follow and obey. Let this be a lesson to you all."

At the front of the room, his loathsome back to the class, one boy's spirit was broken.

 .oOo.

26 DOCTOR DOCTOR

There were few on Islay that slept well that night. A researcher would have noticed the unease was especially high in the southeast of the island, with a statistically significant concentration around a little village that adjoined a distillery.

Many woke with an uncomfortable feeling in their lower intestines that needed urgent purging. Many remembered another sensation, too – that of being too close to something terribly hot. Exactly what it had been wasn't clear upon waking. It may not have been clear when sleeping, but nobody wanted to talk about it to compare notes.

Jazz had suffered particularly badly, at one point waking with a shriek that even startled Ishbell McNeill next door. Rather less than it startled Wilko, though.

After spending the next few hours fretting, watching her toss and turn and whimper, by morning he was determined that something had to be done.

Handing her a cup of tea he said, "Look, let's try something conventional. A strong sedative. If you sleep deeply enough maybe you won't get these damned dreams. There's a doctor in the village, isn't there?"

The girl nodded, too exhausted and dispirited to argue.

Robbie Keith was sympathetic when the Tasmanian called to explain that Jazz wouldn't be at work, and where he'd be taking her. "Let me know how you go. If it works I reckon I'll try it!" said the General Manager, his own weariness clear in his voice.

The other two Australians readily agreed to join them at the doctor's rooms and were duly collected en route.

At Jazz' insistence all three accompanied her in to meet Doc Wullie.

The doctor turned out to be a genial fellow. Christened Alastair MacAl-lister but knowing that sounded daft, he'd willingly adopted a suitable nickname when he moved to Sron Dubh a few years earlier.

He examined Jazz carefully, checked her vital signs and, most importantly, listened to her sympathetically. Very sympathetically.

"There's verra few in these parts that arnae sufferin' as ye are, lass, maself
included. Tha's no' tae make light of yer condition – far from it. Ye seem
tae be worse afflicted than most I've encountered. Ye're healthy enough,
which is just as well, or by noo ye'd be a verra sick young woman."

He wrote a prescription for potent sleeping pills. "Ye'll no' get these in
the shop next door. They're long oot of stock. I'm afraid ye'll have tae go
into Bowmore tae find them. If ye'd like, I can gie ye a jab tae help ye get
some rest while yer friends go tae the pharmacy."

"I'd like that a lot," admitted the engineer.

"We can take the car into town if you'd like to stay with her, Wilko," offered Elizabeth.

The Tasmanian nodded mutely, numb with concern for the woman he was
realising he loved.

John B. had a curious expression on his face as he said, "Doc, you were in
the church yesterday morning. I know this seems like an irrelevant question, but I feel like I can trust you. What do you think of the Reverend
Dotterel?"

The doctor looked up in surprise, and thought for a moment. "A verra
intense man. Verra old-fashioned, which suits some in the village much
more than others. Always had a very 'anti' sort o' message. Anti-fornica-
tion, anti-idolatry, anti-witchcraft."

"And that goes down well around here?"

"It didnae used tae," Doc Wullie admitted with a shrug. "The numbers at
yon kirk had dwindled right doon. Then last few months, there's been a
big surge. Like the old time religion's suddenly come intae fashion. The
Snug closed. Public toilets, playground swings, slides and such are all
chained up on Sundays."

Stewart nodded. "Would that be about the time people started getting bad
dreams?" he asked mildly.

Doc Wullie looked at him slightly open-mouthed, eventually saying, "Aye, it might be. I hadnae…"

Whatever he was going to say next was cut off by his receptionist, Nursie Mary, flinging the door open with a cry of "Doc! Emergency!"

The doctor sprang from his chair and was half way to the door when a teary Kevin Macalpine strode in, carrying cradled in his arms his unconscious son.

MacAllister and Stewart cleared the way to and on the examination table for the boy to be laid down.

The father spoke through his sobs, "Jock McKeever found him lyin' huddled by the wall o' his paddock, oot on the edge o' the village. I've been frettin' masel' all night, nae sleepin', wonderin' where he was! I know he sometimes stays oot a bit late wi' his chums, but niver all night… I drove around a few times tae look fer him, but I niver thought tae look all the way oot there. If only I had…"

"Please sit down, Mr. Macalpine," said Elizabeth, ushering the man to her chair. "You've got him now, and brought him straight here, that's what's important."

With Nursie Mary checking pulse and breathing, John B. carefully helped remove the boot and wool sock that the doctor was cutting away from the shattered ankle.

The other three looked at each other helplessly.

Doc Wullie spoke over his shoulder to the frantic father. "Ye're son's a lucky lad, believe it or no', Mr. Macalpine. Shock and exposure ha' left him in a bad way. Just lucky the shelter o' the wall and a good thick long coat gave him wee bit o' protection. As tae what's happened tae his foot, we'll have tae ask him when he wakes up. I'd rather that wasnae fer a while. If his signs are alright, Mary?" The nurse/receptionist nodded. "I've a sedative already prepared I'll gie him tae keep him as comfortable as possible. I'm sorry, Miss Parrish – I'll set another yin for ye shortly."

"It's okay. I can wait – just help Kev," Jazz answered earnestly, winning a grateful glance from the elder Kevin.

"Mary, get on the phone and see how soon we can get the lad on a Care flight tae Glasga. He'll need a hospital and a good surgeon tae repair this. Kevin, are ye up tae goin' wi' him…?"

"No man better try tae stop me!" answered the distillery handyman with feeling.

Just as Nursie Mary picked up the telephone and began to dial, the front door flew open again.

A thin little woman rushed in, shepherding her even thinner son.

"Help us! Help us!" she wailed. "Ma Wee Chrissy's gone blind!"

It was no exaggeration. The boy stumbled and cursed as he collided heavily with the little table in the waiting room. His mother was too agitated to be an effective guide for him.

"Wha's happened, Mrs. McCandless?" cried Nursie Mary, telephone number only half dialed.

Having somehow made it to the sanctuary of the clinic, the poor woman could only babble incoherently. It was Wee Chrissy who managed to pull himself together.

"Are we here? Is this the clinic – is Doc Wullie there?"

"Aye lad – be wi' ye in a minute! Somebody help them tae sit doon!" The doctor couldn't help but hear the commotion.

Elizabeth rushed into the reception area to assist Wee Chrissy and his mother, gesturing to Nursie Mary to finish the phone call.

MacAllister gave young Kev his injection, carefully but with more haste than he'd have liked, relying on his unexpected purple-shirted assistant to keep the boy's arm still.

"We'll wait outside," said Jazz, taking Wilko's arm. "You have to take care of Wee Chrissy."

At her son's name Mrs. McCandless wailed again. Another sedative, a milder one, would be needed, Doc Wullie realised.

Elizabeth carefully guided mother and son into the doctor's room, and at a gesture from MacAllister, led Macalpine out while a curtain was drawn around his sleeping son.

"Would ye stay and reassure Mrs. McCandless while I examine the lad, please lass?" the doctor asked Elizabeth.

"Can Mum… wait outside, please?" asked the boy uncomfortably.

"Of course, if ye'd prefer," agreed Doc Wullie. "Mary can fix her some-thin' tae help her settle."

"I'll help her outside, Doc," offered John B.

Wee Chrissy's head rose sharply and he looked around the room – well, tried to.

"I ken tha' voice! Tha's the guy in the purple shirt! Och, can ye stay, please, mister?"

The wizard looked at the doctor, who shrugged and although puzzled, nodded in reply.

"Sure mate," said Stewart reassuringly.

With Nursie Mary enduring a frustrating time getting useful information from the airport, it was Elizabeth who again led Mrs. McCandless out. The poor woman was in such a state that she was too worn out to disagree as the brunette gently took her arm and led her back to the waiting room.

"Let me deal with that call, eh?" Q suggested kindly to the harried nurse. "I'm used to bureaucratic nonsense. The doctor wants this lady to get a mild sedative."

Mary willingly handed over the receiver and vacated the desk.

With an arm wrapped around Jazz' shoulders Wilko shook his head. He was wondering, not for the first time, what sort of a mess he'd walked into. Then he looked at the woman he held and told himself emphatically that she was worth it.

Doc Wullie was shining a small torch and peering into Wee Chrissy's eyes. The boy scarcely flinched. He explained the sensation as being like a dim and distant light through thick fog.

It was how he'd woken up, he explained. He'd had a bad dream, opened his eyes and thought his room must have been full of smoke. Gently examining his skull, the doctor asked if he'd hit his head recently. What had he been doing in the evening before going to bed?

Wee Chrissy's voice dropped. This was why he'd wanted his mother out of the room. He explained in honest detail what had happened at the churchyard, including their flight when Mills had given chase.

"It's him ye were warnin' us aboot, wasnae it, Mr. Purple? I'm sorry – we all should ha' listened tae ye."

Stewart couldn't help grinning at his new nickname, but his voice was serious as he said, "You can call me John B., Wee Chrissy. That's my name. And yeah, Mills is the… man I had in mind." Clearly there were other words he'd considered using. "Was Kev with you, mate?"

"I dinna want tae get anyb'dy intae trouble…"

"The only one in trouble is going to be that mongrel Mills," promised Stewart, earning a raised eyebrow but silence from the doctor.

"Um, aye, he was there." There was a moment's pause as the implication of the question dawned on the lad, probably the quickest-witted of the little gang.

The combination had established the three natural leaders of the group – Wee Chrissy's wits, Kev's size (for all his gentle nature) and Scuzzy Wullie's attitude.

"Is Kev alright?" he asked in a quiet voice.

"He will be lad, dinna worry," soothed Doc Wullie. "His foot's been busted up right an' proper, an he's had a bad night oot in the weather, but I'm sendin' him over tae the hospital in Glasga tae be taken care of." The doctor tugged at a stray strand of hair. "I'm thinkin' tha' might be the best place for ye, too, if ye're willing. I cannae see owt that's obviously wrong wi' ye, and they'll have equipment I've no seen since I were a student."

The boy squirmed in an agony of indecision. "Aye, I ken I should go, Doc – but Ma cannae take time off tae go wi' me. She needs the money frae her job tae pay the rent an' feed the bairns."

The arrival of twin daughters had been the final straw for George Mc-Candless, a wastrel of a man who'd abandoned his wife and children for the heady life of a homeless man on the streets of Edinburgh five years earlier.

"Ye know Kev's Pa, don't ye?" The boy nodded. "I'm sure he'll be willin' tae keep an eye on ye. He'll be travellin' wi' his son."

"Ma'll fret, but she's got the wee yins tae take care o'. Willis is in lookin' after them while I'm here, but she wouldnae leave them wi' her fer long."

Doc Wullie clasped the young man's shoulder. "Ye're a bright lad, Chris McCandless, and an aye brave one at that."

The boy smiled a little, but shuddered. "I didnae feel it last night, Doc. Tha' dream in the classroom was bad enough. I'm sure it was Scuzzy Wullie I saw, ye ken…?"

"Aye, I know the dream you mean, mate," the wizard replied. Chrissy wasn't surprised. He'd have believed anything of this man with the strange accent.

"That wasnae the *really* bad yin, though. I got back tae sleep after tha' yin, horrible as it was. Twas the later yin – ye ken how when ye're a wain, ye're Ma always tells ye not tae look intae the sun? It was like I was standin' right up beside it, wi' someb'dy holdin' ma head so I couldnae turn away. Then I woke up, an', well, here I am…"

Stewart and MacAllister looked at each other but said nothing.

The doctor gently said, "I'll do all I can, laddie, and I'm sure ma colleagues on the big island will do likewise. Do ye want somethin' tae help ye sleep?"

"Sleep? No' bloody likely!"

Both the doctor and the Australian each laid a reassuring hand on Wee Chrissy – a shoulder apiece, but it was the wizard who spoke.

"I don't blame you, mate. But how about something to help you rest? Less of a worry for your Ma if she knows that Doc's doing something to try to help, especially if you're gonna fly off to the big city."

 The boy nodded slowly. "Aye, ye're right Mis… Johnbee. Okay, Doc, gimme a wee jab, eh? An' tell Ma I'll be off tae Glasga. Maybe they can fix me. Hey? An' if no', well – I'm nae dead yet, am I?"

 Doc Wullie nodded, and set about making the boy comfortable.

 Elizabeth badgered the poor unfortunate at the airport into contacting the appropriate carrier on another phone line while she held, then added Wee Chrissy to the Macalpine's booking. Nursie Mary had looked on in awe as the Australian simply demanded what she wanted and refused to back down until it was delivered.

 "She's good at it, isn't she?" observed Wilko, who'd seen the brunette in full flight before.

 And finally, Doc Wullie was able to help Jazz. The events of the morning had only added to her distress so the injection was welcome. With all possible speed she was conveyed to the front seat of Anastasia and taken back to the cottage to rest.

 Wilko pulled up a chair to sit beside her bed. Clearly he wasn't going anywhere.

 After doing all he could to make his friends comfortable John B. quietly asked the Tasmanian, "Could we take the keys to the Rover, please mate? I'd like to leave you two in peace. Take Q for a bit of a drive, y'know?"

 With an understanding nod Wilko handed over the keys. "Look after her," he said, and then clarified, "I mean the car. I know you'll take care of Elizabeth."

.o0o.

27 A HOLY PLACE

Much of the drive up the A846 was spent discussing what had happened to the boys. Wee Chrissy's admission of what they'd done seemed compelling evidence that the Reverend Dotterel had a significant hand in what had befallen them. Nothing that would stand up in court: even if Mills' actions could be proven he'd probably never 'rat' on the preacher, and how could a man be tried for other people's dreams?

But that was an act of spite. Petty, impulsive revenge. What was behind the dreams that had been going on for months?

They were driving to Finlaggan. There was family history for Elizabeth to investigate, she hoped. And John B. could still clearly recall the words: "heir tae the legacy of Saint Findlugan". What had the preacher meant?

As they drove into the Finlaggan site they passed another standing stone, like a sentinel watching over a precious treasure – an image that proceeded to sit in the wizard's brain like a stray piece of gristle wedged between two back teeth.

Finlaggan turned out to have an excellent Visitors' Centre. They had a look around, but then John B. looked out through one of the glass walls. He called Q over and pointed towards the horizon.

"Clouds are gathering, sweetheart. I think we should seize the moment to look outside, and be ready to zip back here if we have to," he said.

She looked at him with an eyebrow raised. "Zip? Really?"

"Well, *you* might, darling…"

A modern wooden walkway led out onto the larger of the two *crannochs* – man made islands constructed probably in Neolithic times as defensible positions. This was Eilean Mor, which had been the home and administrative hub of the Lord of the Isles.

Determined preservation works in the past few decades had rescued the ruins of a handful of buildings from total collapse. At the eastern end of the little island lay the remains of the chapel, perched on a limestone outcrop that was probably the oldest, most prominent part of the island.

It was around this outcrop that Eilean Mor had built up by a combination of alluvial deposit and human endeavour. This had been the chapel dedicated to the saint whose name the site now bore, although as Cecil had indicated, it had almost certainly been constructed on the site of a much older monastery built of wood and thatch. Among the relics of walls and foundations lay a flat tombstone, now protected by a Perspex panel. The stone was much weathered since its placement in the very early 16th century, but still recognizable was the carving of a fighting man, dressed in his *aketon* – the quilted garment worn as a light form of armour, or in combination with chain mail.

West of the chapel were the sparse remnants of Great Hall of the Lords of the Isles where feasts and social gatherings had been held and music played. There was actually less left of the Great Hall than of the food preparation area that had serviced it.

Near the southernmost tip of the island stood what was left of what had been the Lords' residence. From there they could see where once there'd been a causeway stretching for fifty metres or so across to the small *crannoch* where the Lord of the Isles sat with his chiefs and thanes around a stone table.

The small island was called Eilean Na Comhairle – the Island of the Council. A little of the remains of the Council Chamber could be seen, together with traces of the massive limestone walls of the ancient castle thought to predate that structure.

At some point in the distant past, perhaps 5000 years earlier, a thick drystone walled building had surmounted the entire man-made island. A fort maybe? One of the imposing, mysterious towers called *brochs* that were features of ancient Scotland? With only fragments of the wall now fringing the south and west of the island it was impossible to tell.

It was clear that the wizard was frustrated at not being able to get over onto the Council Island. He paced back and forward along the shoreline, gazing out at it.

After watching him for a little while, Q shook her head and decided to leave him in peace. She walked away and sat on a convenient stone by the carved warrior in the chapel ruins. She pulled a couple of Australian coins from her bag and flipped them under the Perspex, as many other visitors before her had clearly done.

"There's some bad stuff being done here in the name of your faith, mate. I don't know if you were the sort of bloke who'd object or support it, but I reckon you've got a good face. Any help you can offer – well, that'd be welcomed. Thanks."

It felt a little strange talking to a piece of stone. She wasn't much into 'spirituality', old fashioned or New Age, but time spent around John B. Stewart was giving Elizabeth cause to think along lines that her mind hadn't travelled much before.

She took out the guidebook they'd bought at the Visitors' Centre and started to read.

Tired of fruitless pacing John B. sat on a lump of stone that was all that remained of a wall and looked out over the loch. Focus. Focus and think. Try to be aware, he told himself. Breathing slowly he slipped into a meditation he'd learned from his Hawaiian friend Harlan. Eventually he got up and walked back to Elizabeth.

Frowning he said, "It's not here."

"What isn't? What was that all about?"

"The more I use this magic, the more I'm starting to get an idea of what it can do. That still doesn't mean I can control it though, more's the pity. I was trying to - I dunno, tap into something. But whatever we're looking for is long gone."

Elizabeth gestured at the ruined buildings that surrounded them and said, "Babe, *everything* is long gone from here."

"Mm. I've a feeling this is longer gone than most. Whatever it is. Come on, the weather's closing in again. This wee island would be no place to spend a storm."

 Walking hand in hand they went back to the Visitors' Centre, and fortified by coffee spent another hour or so examining and reading every display.

 They learned a lot, but couldn't be sure how much, if any of it was relevant.

.oOo.

28 TWO HEADS ARE BADDER THAN ONE

It wasn't often that Victoria dined with her father any more. She was happy to visit, but preferred to spend her nights in Bowmore. It made it easier to get an early start in the office, she told him.

This was true, but they also both realised that too close a proximity could mean 'tangling' their powers. For the woman, especially, this wasn't desirable. She was more than willing to support and assist her father, but she had her own agenda to pursue.

On this particular rainy Monday night though, with their perceived indignities still running hot, parent and child had shared vegetable soup and fed each other's rancour. Whilst there was a certain degree of satisfaction with the punishment dealt out to the ringleaders of the little gang of boys, there was still a simmering resentment that such defiance was even possible.

The 'lesson' that had been taught needed to be reinforced. Authority had to emphasized, and emphasized as the will of the Almighty. And the dire consequences of failing to respect that authority had to be seared onto the minds of everyone in the community.

After dinner they discussed a topic that had troubled them in the past, and was now exercising their minds even more powerfully: namely, that there were some people who seemed able to resist their influence. They might receive the dreams, but yet remained defiant.

A combined effort was called for. They'd been acting independently, supportive of each other and aware that each other's efforts were enhanced by their own, but tonight would be different.

The classroom was beyond warm, it was hot. There was a fireplace in the corner of the room. Of course, it had always been there. But the fire was blazing too brightly to look at, but too brightly to look away from either.

Up and down the rows of desks stalked the schoolmistress, her featureless face reflecting the glare of the flames to make her more than ever a figure to strike awe.

As she strode amongst the class her voice was an insistent jackhammer.

"Obey! Respect the Church and obey Its teachings. Obey me. That is the only way tae escape your terrible fate. Damnation for eternity, punishment in the here and now. Damnation for eternity, punishment in the here and now. Obey! Obey!"

The teacher's voice repeated those sentences like a litany, over and over again.

She stopped between two desks and reached to grab a collar in each hand, hauling two boys to their feet.

"Master Craig, ye and your little dark friend here have defied me, have ye not?"

The pale skinned boy was considerably the larger of the two, but was childishly small beside the teacher. The young Macadam hung from her hand like a doll. Both boys shook their heads in mute protest. Without releasing her grip on their collars she propelled them to the front of the class – the small dark boy's toes scarcely scrabbling on the floorboards.

With steady deliberate strides she approached the roaring fire, holding the struggling boys out in front of her. They writhed and moaned, desperately trying to cover their faces.

"There is no escape from the fires of Hell. There is no escape from my authority. There is no…"

Suddenly the small dark boy was gone. He'd simply disappeared, leaving her hand clutching empty air. The schoolmistress recoiled in shock. Even the fire seemed to shrink back in surprise.

The classroom and the fire winked out of existence.

The candle flame on Gordon's desk guttered and went out. The Reverend stared at it open mouthed. Sitting in a leather chair beside her father Victoria wore an expression as much of outrage as of shock.

Such defiance should simply not be possible.

.oOo.

29 LONG SHADOWS OF THE PAST

Doc Wullie's sedatives appeared to be helping, Wilko noted with some satisfaction. If she'd dreamed during the night she had no recollection of it, and she'd shown no sign of distress at the time. The Tasmanian had spent much of the night watching her.

He yawned over the first coffee of the morning, "Are you sure you want to go to work? The Doc's happy for you to spend a couple of days catching up on lost sleep."

Jazz smiled, warmed by his concern. "Thanks for the thought, hon, but I want to show poor old Robbie as much support as I can. If I run out of steam I can always call you to come pick me up."

"Of course you can. But if you run out of steam, wouldn't you be out of a job?"

She looked at him in bafflement for a moment. Her head was still fuzzy from the drugs. Then the penny dropped and she laughed. "You've been hanging around John B. too much, mate!"

"Probably. Speaking of John, I didn't get to talk much to him and Elizabeth when they brought the car back yesterday. Even when I took them home I… well, I wasn't much company. After I drop you at the distillery I'll go round and see how they got on at that place up north."

Sitting in the Hines' parlour later in the morning Elizabeth recounted to Wilko some of her discoveries about the history of the island, and by extension of her family.

"Nothing of much use in solving the 'dream' issue, though," she said sadly.

She and the wizard had already resolved not to mention Stewart's 'sixth sense' of something missing. The Tasmanian was doggedly skeptical. He called it practical.

It was in such spirit that Wilko suggested a visit to the Bromleighs to talk about what they'd learned. The old couple seemed the best source of local knowledge they'd encountered.

To their collective relief they got an effusive welcome from April, and a restrained but warm greeting from Auld Wullie. Over a cup of tea and a plate of ginger biscuits Elizabeth and John B. gave their impressions of Finlaggan.

As they spoke Auld Wullie closely watched his purple-shirted visitor. Watching the old man as unobtrusively as possible, Elizabeth almost fancied she could hear the wheels turning in his head. 'We've triggered something,' she thought.

Sure enough, moments later Bromleigh walked over to rest a hand on Stewart's shoulder. "Would ye be up tae a visit wi' a friend o' mine? I'll drive us there."

"I'd had it in mind tae visit Effie, ye ken, an' I don't like tae walk so far when yon damp weather's affectin' me knees," said April, who may or may not have been being contrary.

After only a small nudge from Elizabeth, Wilko offered, "Um, we could give you a lift to your sister's…"

"Och, could ye? Aye, laddie, that'd be kind o' ye. I'm sure Effie'd be glad o' the company."

The quick glance that Auld Wullie gave Stewart cast some doubt on that statement, but John B. restrained a chuckle.

The wizard and the old distiller needed no time to ready themselves, and were in the 1951 Rover 75 and away in a very few minutes.

April took rather longer to prepare herself. There was a perfectly good pot of tea to be finished, for one thing. It was another twenty minutes or so before the more recent incarnation of the Rover 75 drew away from outside the cottage.

Notwithstanding Auld Wullie's unspoken reservations, the middle sister proved to be quite comfortable with receiving guests, especially ones who'd already eaten.

Effie was a keen traveller of the world, but unfortunately that travel had been confined to her little cottage for many years. Television documentaries and a bookshelf burgeoning with well-thumbed travelogues had filled the void since long before Husht Wullie Lindsay had passed away quietly in his favourite chair after a good meal. April had mentioned in the car on their way over that he'd never been known to say much even before he married Effie.

Visitors from the far side of the planet were a welcome treat, although it wasn't immediately apparent. April had by far the most outgoing nature of the three.

At one point there was mention in passing of a conversation that had happened while the four friends were all having dinner at April's.

"Oh aye?" said Effie. "I wouldnae mind a wee conversation wi' you all maself. I dinna get many visitors."

"Well, that's yer ain fault, Effie. If ye'd offer folk so much as a cup an' a slice…"

"I'm just a poor old widow…" began the protest that the youngest sister knew too well.

Elizabeth yet again stepped into the diplomatic breach. "I'm sure we can bring something along if we're invited, Effie. April has told us there are nice cakes to be had at the dress shop, of all places."

"Mm. Dottie McKenzie isnae a bad cook. In ma younger days o' course I… well, I cannae stand in the kitchen fer long enough noo and that's all there is tae it. So aye, I'd be verra glad tae have ye all tae tea. Thursday, perhaps – after yer wee lassie's finished work?" she suggested, addressing Wilko.

"Er – sure, that sounds great. Thanks very much."

Under Effie's gimlet gaze he couldn't even look to Elizabeth for confirmation, but was relieved when the brunette said, "Yes, Thursday afternoon will work nicely, thank you Effie."

Q realised that there may be more, or at least different, information to be had from Effie without the presence of her younger sister.

It seemed that April was shrewd enough to realise that too. "Och, I'll no' be able tae join ye, I'm afraid, Effie. There's a meetin' o' the new tap dancin' group I've promised tae attend."

Elizabeth and Wilko exchanged glances. The image conjured for both of them did not rest easy on the mind's eye.

"I've said I'll bring along some CDs an' sheet music fer the young yins," April explained. The Australians smiled and nodded as their imaginations cleared. "They're the same ones as we use in ma Jazzercise class."

'Oh dear, let's not think of the spandex,' was the telepathic exchange reflected in their eyes.

"Noo, what were we talkin' aboot? Och, aye. How yon brass besom Victoria Dotterel thinks she can get elected tae Parliament," continued April. "I was talking tae Ina McCaffrey about it…"

"Mrs. Speakaminute? It's a miracle ye got tae speak *to* her and not just have her speak *at* you. She doesnae draw breath! I think the woman must inhale through her ears!" It struck Elizabeth just how much like Rose her sister Effie could sound.

"Aye, well, she doesnae listen through them, but she hears right enough," agreed the youngest sister. "She said that Nell Crowdie was told by Annie Buchan, wha's married tae Bookie Wullie tha' runs the SP, tha' the Reverend's lass is odds on tae win the seat."

"Hmph. They might no' be sae keen tae vote fer her if they knew the lassie's family history," was Effie's scornful assessment.

That caught Elizabeth's attention. "What was Mrs. Dotterel like? Jazz told us Ishbell McNeill's version of the story."

"The English lassie told ye? Hmm…" Effie looked thoughtful.

Her sister was quick to reply, "I wouldnae gie two bob fer Ishbell Mc-Neill's opinion! She was a sad woman, Jeanette Dotterel. A harsh man tae be married tae, an' the loss o' a child…"

"Mrs. McNeill mentioned the accident, but didn't want to talk about it, or the late Mrs. Dotterel," said Wilko.

April looked surprised. "Late? She wasnae deid when she left the island! I dinna ken wha' happened tae her afterward but she was well enough alive when she got away frae the dark hand o' her husband."

"Sorry!" exclaimed Wilko. "From the way she spoke… I should know better than to assume, with the lovely Mrs. McNeill."

Elizabeth nodded sympathetically. "I made the same assumption. I suspect in Ishbell's view 'divorced' and 'dead' mean much the same."

"Aye lass," agreed April. "Her mind's sae narrow flies have tae walk on it in single file."

Effie was in her own little reverie. "Accident, she says. Hmph."

Her sister chided her. "O' course it was an accident. Poor wee Jenny fell off the cliff. Doctor Cruikshank was an honest auld duffer, an' tha's wha' he said at the time."

"Aye, so I remember. But I remember what I saw, too," she said in an undertone. Effie went quiet.

Elizabeth's gentle questioning got brief, barely polite evasive answers. April's prodding got even terser responses. The old woman had wrapped herself in a dark mood now. Whatever she remembered, clearly she wasn't going to share it today.

*

"How do we know our host will be home when we arrive?"

"I called ahead," replied Auld Wullie, briefly brandishing a mobile phone he took from a vest pocket.

 John B. looked surprised. It wasn't a piece of technology he'd expected the old bloke to be carrying. He realised he was imposing his own self-confessed Luddite attitude – he'd only just reluctantly acquired his own mobile at Q's insistence.

"Ye should always look tae use anythin' new tha' can be helpful tae ye," Bromleigh advised.

 Stewart patted the timber dashboard. "This darling is hardly new, my friend."

"Makin' the most o' the new dinna mean ye have tae abandon what already works. The idea is just tae use wha'ever's best fer the job at hand. And aye, 'best' can sometimes mean wha'ever ye're most comfortable wi', so long as it gets the right result."

 The wizard didn't have a lot of time to mull over this advice as he looked out at the seascape they were passing. The old Rover was soon parked by a tangle of scrub at the top of an embankment that sloped away towards the bay. A steepening slope gave way to a sharp drop into a tiny cove.

 A narrow path through the bushes led down to a cottage – barely more than a hut, which clung to the hillside like a barnacle. Auld Wullie knocked on the solid wooden door that looked like the most robust part of the whole structure.

"Come in, lads!" called the cheery voice of Arsaidh MacAdam.

 There was an armchair and a couch squeezed into a small sitting room, off from which hung a galley kitchen and, behind a closed door, what John B. correctly presumed to be a bedroom. The Black Elf got out of his chair to shake hands with his guests.

"Not at work, mate? Has Craig's caseload finally eased off?" asked Stewart.

The dark man's smile slipped.

"Did ye sleep last night?" he asked.

"Not much," the Australian admitted. "Tossed and turned for hours, finally dropped off properly sometime after five."

MacAdam and Bromleigh exchanged looks.

"There was another dream, wasn't there?"

MacAdam didn't specifically answer. Instead he said, "When I went tae Craig's office this mornin' he announced he was nae longer interested in pursuin' matters pertainin' tae donations tae the Dotterel family. Ma services were nae longer required."

"Wow! He's fired you?"

"He's not himself," observed the Sith Dubh quietly.

Auld Wullie sat on the couch and gestured for the Australian to sit beside him. "Ye called us here tae talk aboot somethin', Arsaidh. Wha's on yer mind?"

Settling in his chair, MacAdam fixed his gaze on Stewart. "Wha' d'ye know o' the history o' Islay an' it's surrounds?" he asked.

"More than I did a week ago. Historical Society lecture, a fair bit of reading, a visit to Finlaggan, lengthy chats with Auld Wullie's wife and her sisters…"

"Aye, enough there tae stand ye in good stead," agreed the small man. "And what d'ye know o' the history o' the Christian Scriptures?"

John B. blinked. That one had come out of left field. He thought back to his studies of history and recited such details as he could recall. The

208

translation into the English of its day commissioned by King James in the early 1600s. The Council of Florence in the 1440s that delivered the official Church opinion on what was canon. The Vulgate of the late 4th Century that was the first 'official' Latin Bible. Oh yes, the Council of Trent in 1546 that issued the decree making the decision of a century earlier, and the Vulgate itself, into absolute articles of faith. Anyone who said otherwise was declared 'anathema'. More recently, the various 'Dead Sea Scrolls' that have turned up over the years, containing fragments of Scripture known and unknown.

The Elf nodded. "Ye're well ahead o' many, lad. Noo, consider this: wha' King James' collection o' scholars were translatin', and long earlier wha' Jerome was translatin' intae Latin in 384 were texts in Greek, Hebrew, Aramaic – even some older Latin texts. Even by poor auld Jerome's time there'd been over three hundred years o' men giein' their opinions aboot a lot o' different gospels an' letters an writin's – wha' was valid, wha' was spurious, wha' was sacred, wha' was heretical, all based on their ain opinions."

"And their own agendas, political or philosophical or whatever," said Stewart.

"Well said, lad. Men like Eusebius o' Caesarea, fifty years afore Jerome, an' others before him. We only ken o' a few o' them noo, but there must ha' been a muckle o' them, all tryin' tae advance the cause o' their own branch o' the kirk."

"It's not like we've got the original source documents – just translations of translations of translations. Each being done by hand, probably by one or two blokes who were mostly working on their own. Chinese whispers," was the Australian's spoken thought.

"Wi' who kens wha' added or subtracted along the way."

"That's true too, Arsaidh," agreed Stewart. "Now you mention it I do remember reading more than one analysis that was pretty certain that books like Matthew's Gospel showed signs of really being written by more than one author. Certain phrasing, words used, inconsistencies – that sort of thing."

"Tis interestin' ye mention Matthew. D'ye ken the Book o' Kells?"

"I know *of* it. I haven't read it, as such."

"A curious thing, the difference one word can make. There's a verse that in Jerome's translation comes across tae English as *I came no' tae send peace, but a sword.* The Kells manuscript has the word *gaudium* which is "joy", no' *gladium* - "sword". So the line translates as *I came no' only tae send peace, but joy.* Changes the whole tone, aye?"

 As a child John B. had read a lot of Scripture in the orphanage that had been his home for a while. He rifled through the mental filing cabinet, and eventually said, "Matthew Chapter 10. It's where Jesus gives his twelve apostles their 'mission', right?"

"Correct. Noo, who's tae say if the wee mannie workin' on the Book o' Kells in the year 800 was workin' off the same text as Jerome or somethin' else? Could even be muckle older. Ye ken? Noo – hold tha' thought. In the 500s Findlugan's reckoned tae ha' established a wee monastery on the isle that used tae bear his name."

"Eilean Mor at Finlaggan," said Stewart to confirm his recollection.

"Aye. In the first few hundred years after Christ, I dinna think there was a kirk, abbey or monastery that didnae' have some sacred relic tae call their own. Saint Paul must hae had twenty-seven fingers an' twice as many toes, the number o' his bones scattered across Europe. But some were reputed tae possess things a mickle less grisly, like rare auld manuscripts."

 John B. smiled. He could see where this was going, up to a point at least. "An early edition of the Bible was Findlugan's treasure?" he suggested.

"A wee piece o' it. A verra, verra early fragment o' the book o' Matthew."

 Recognising the doubtful look on the Australian's face Arsaidh explained that one of his antecedents – "a man o' great faith an' greater courage" – had been at the old monastery at the time when the character of the island was shifting from a religious centre to an administrative base in the 10th

Century. Fearing that the treasure was becoming more highly regarded for its secular prestige and financial value than its sacred significance, he had helped spirit it away to the small monastery on Texa. The handful of occupants of that rocky outcrop treasured their isolation, deeply immersed in the contemplation of their faith.

Four hundred years later, the Lord of the Isles built Dunyvaig Castle on a small cape overlooking the isle of Texa. As befitting a point on this most prestigious of sea routes, at a time when control of those routes was the key to international power, the island became home to a new, grander chapel. But when the old structure was razed its secret treasure was again moved to a tiny, secluded hermitage where it would be kept from profane and greedy hands.

For over a thousand years, MacAdam said, 'his people' had guarded this holy relic – the earliest version of Christ's instructions to his disciples.

"Matthew Chapter 10. That's a coincidence," said John B., in the voice of a man who'd stopped believing in coincidences.

Depending on what its contents were revealed to be, such a document could validate or destroy over a millennium of religious tradition. Possession of it could bring power, prestige, and a great deal of money.

"Such an item could do a great deal mair harm than good," remarked Auld Wullie quietly.

He'd said nothing throughout Arsaidh's explanation, but his tone of voice and the expression on his face bespoke a deep concern.

The Elf continued. "He's no' talkin' aboot it publicly, ye ken, but the Reverend Dotterel claims tae have had a vision – a visitation fra' Saint Findlugan himsel', wi' Saint Matthew standin' at his shoulder, holdin' up both hands wi' the ten fingers spread."

"Sounds like Matt was telling him to cease and desist!" was John B.'s interpretation.

MacAdam grinned at that. "He told his daughter tha' it was a sign an' tha' he was called tae be one o' the Lord's chosen few. He got it intae his head that the saints were bestowin' upon him both responsibility an' a great gift – all he has tae do is find it. The lass spoke tae Lachlan Maclean aboot the law surroundin' 'valuable antiquities', an' Maclean spoke tae me aboot 'local religious history' as he put it."

"But they don't know what to look for, or where to look?"

"Nae, they dinna have a clue, Mr. Stewart. And I'm verra happy tae keep it that way. Auld Wullie, d'ye ken the auld still out south o' Eilean Bhride? Aye, o' course ye do. There's a wee nook, the mirror image o' the yin that the still sits in. Ye'll ken the stones tae shift when ye' find them. Gentlemen, I fear I may ha'… drawn mair attention tae masel' than I'd ha' liked. That's why I'm tellin' ye all this. I've nae kin left, but I ken ye both are tae be trusted."

Both his visitors gave almost identical small bows of acknowledgement and thanks, a coincidence that neither appeared to notice.

Auld Wullie seemed curious about only one thing. "The dream, Arsaidh – how was it that ye - ?"

The Black Elf cut him off. "A wee trick ma' family's known for a verra long time. I dinna think the Dotterels can touch me in their own way…"

John B. was starting to have a good idea what 'their own way' entailed.

"…I do think though tha' I can expect some sort o' pressure from Lachlan Maclean."

"And/or the charming Mr. Mills," growled John B. who then gave a wry laugh.

"What amuses ye?" asked MacAdam.

"Thinking of the Dotterels, and the end of Matthew 10. *I come to set a man at variance against his father, and the daughter against her moth-er…*"

.o0o.

30 GRAVE EVENTS

Auld Wullie and John B. drove back to the Bromleigh's cottage mostly in silence. There seemed little to say. Stewart had resolved to try to keep an eye out for MacAdam's safety, but the dark little man seemed sanguine about his prospects. His family 'mission' had been passed on and that seemed enough for his contentment.

It seemed too that Auld Wullie was content to be the repository of that knowledge. He'd made no attempt to explain the Sith's directions. Stewart knew that Eilean Bhride – Bridget's Island – was one of the deserted places dotting the bay, but even if he could identify it on a map, he had no idea about the location of a small cave with an old still, or its 'mirror image', presumably on another nameless rocky outcrop nearby. 'If he wants me to know, he'll tell me in his own time', mused the wizard.

April and the other two Australians had returned from Effie's by the time the old Rover rolled down the narrow driveway, past its 21st Century counterpart parked out on the street.

Neither party mentioned much about their respective meetings. It was as though everyone had come away with a sense of unease, and was waiting for time alone with their nearest and dearest to talk it out. Conversation was polite, and farewells were warm and genuine, but it wasn't long before the Australians were waving their goodbyes from Anastasia.

John B. had offered to make dinner for the group and serve it in the little parlour of their lodgings. The excellent butcher they'd noticed in Bowmore was the obvious source for some good local meat, so after collecting a drowsy but cheerful Jazz from the distillery, Wilko headed up the A846.

Once again the sky was darkening as they drove. Winter was closing in, and it looked like being a wet one.

As they left the butcher, happily supplied with a bag of fine looking lamb cutlets, John B.'s gaze happened up the hill that overlooked the little town.

"Does anyone fancy a little sight-seeing before the weather turns nasty?"
he asked.

After general assent he led the group up the hill to the round white church
that stood sentinel over Bowmore, explaining as he went, "According to
tradition it was built circular so that the Devil wouldn't have a corner to
hide in. It's a nice story, and I wonder if it's a rationalization of something
much older. Some of the oldest stone structures in Scotland are round
towers called *brochs*. They go back to the Iron Age. Maybe there was an
old tradition of something like that on the site when the church was built."

Unfortunately for their curiosity, when they reached the summit and got
to the building, a small sign on the door said that the Church was closed
until Sunday. They settled for a short look at the cemetery that fringed
the white walls of the church. The couples walked arm in arm, enjoying
the company and paying nodding respect to the departed folks whose last
resting places they passed.

They were at the back of the church, not visible from the streets of Bowmore, when an unpleasantly familiar voice came from behind them.

"How bleedin' lovely ta find ya all again, I don't reckon." DS Mills stood
in the shadow of the church, the gun in his hand aimed squarely at Elizabeth. "Talk about luck, eh? 'Ere am I 'avin' a nice quiet visit to town,
when I sees this silver car I recognise. Then along you lot wander and I
figured I'd follow ya, and 'ere we are. Perfect place to find some dead
bodies, eh? And no witnesses to even know I was 'ere."

Any attempt to move by any of them and it was obvious that Mills would
shoot. He was going to shoot anyway, it seemed. He was just enjoying
prolonging their anticipation.

"You're surrounded by witnesses, Mills. You're in the dead centre of
town."

"Eh? That's down there…" Mills stopped himself from glancing away
and taking his eyes off his prey.

Smiling implacably John B. gestured at the surrounding headstones.

"A grave misunderstanding," he said, drawing a groan from Wilko who couldn't believe he could make puns at gunpoint. "I really don't like the way you're staring at us. I wish you'd take a gander at something else."

"Hah! Not likely! I…"

Suddenly the sky went dark and a cacophony of honking filled the air. An enormous flock of geese flew over the church – thousands of them, momentarily blocking out the sun. Nobody could blame Mills for looking up in surprise – three of his four intended victims did the same.

The exception was John B. who seized the moment to fiercely kick Mills' hand and send the gun flying. It hit the church wall and ricocheted over Wilko's head, spinning behind a gravestone.

"Run, you lot!" snapped the wizard. They did, Wilko snatching up the gun as he went. Instead of following, as they'd expected, Stewart stepped in front of Mills to block his pursuit.

The Englishman was still wringing his hand, but snarled at the shaggy man in his way.

"I'll bloody kill you, I will," he snarled.

"Yeah, you keep saying that. But here I am. Believe it or not mate, not everyone's as bloodthirsty as you. I really don't want to kill you – I just wish you wouldn't follow us."

"Fat chance of that!"

Mills lunged, grabbing Stewart in a rugby tackle. The Australian surprised him by not resisting going to the ground, but then rolled quickly. The back of Mills' head smacked into one of the tombstones and he went limp.

John B. freed himself and stood. He examined the name on the grave.

"Thank you, Rita," he said with a bow. "That must be why they're called headstones, eh DS?" he quipped.

The groan in response told him the thug wasn't quite unconscious so he knelt and spoke quietly. "Don't mess with me, Mills. And don't threaten my friends. You reckon you're tough, but I can match you. I might not use guns but I use magic."

"Urgh? Magic? Whadya mean…?" The Englishman's voice was a croak.

"Yes DS. I'm a wizard. But I guess magic goes over your head. Just like those geese just did. You should lie there and have a little rest. Oh, and this is for a young bloke I reckon you know."

With careful aim Stewart jumped heavily on Mills' ankle, after which he patted his adversary on the shoulder and walked away. He walked straight into the arms of Elizabeth who'd turned back as soon as she'd realised he wasn't running with them. She'd seen, if not heard, the whole exchange.

"You should finish him off. Wilko's still got the gun."

"And be no better than him? No, sweetheart, that's not me."

Q looked at him and blushed. "You're right. I'm sorry babe – my temper got the better of me. He's such a… a…"

"Whatever he is, I'm not. And neither are you, my love. Come on, let's get out of here. Did the others head for Anastasia?"

The woman in his arms nodded and said, "Wilko's having to half-carry Jazz. I don't think Mills mixes well with the drugs she's on."

"He doesn't mix well with anything, or anyone."

They quickly made their way back towards the Rover. Minutes later, as they drove away from Bowmore, Wilko flung the pistol from the car window into a soggy patch of peat bog they were passing. The ugly snub-nosed weapon landed in an old cutting and sank into the wet black mass at the bottom of the ditch.

.oOo.

31 THE LEGENDARY REVENGE OF THE SITH DUBH

The year was 1598. John MacDonald and his clansmen were pursuing the hated Macleans along the slopes that formed the western bank of Loch Gruinart in the north of Islay.

The Macleans hadn't been particularly hated until quite recently. But James VI, King of Scotland, had seen fit to grant 'possession' of Islay to Sir Lachlan Maclean of Duart. The politics of the Scottish court were a mystery to most of the MacDonalds. They were farmers and fishermen and when necessary, fighters.

When the arrogant Sir Lachlan had arrived with four hundred of his clansmen, claiming 'his new estate', the resident MacDonalds had seen it as nothing short of invasion.

Maclean had been confident in his force of arms, considering the Ileachs a disorganized rabble. A shadowy little dark man, apparently known locally as the Sith Dubh, had approached the new Lord with an offer of brokering a peaceful settlement between the clans. He had been dispatched with kicks and curses, but not before having the location of the MacDonald stronghold beaten out of him.

Boldly the Macleans had marched to overrun the upstart locals, laying siege if it was required. It had been a considerable shock to discover that they'd blundered out into the middle of swampy flats, where a misstep could sink a man into the mire.

Then the MacDonalds had appeared – local men with local knowledge. They knew where to run, where to stand, where to fight.

It had been a slaughter. Broken in body and spirit, the proud Maclean force had quickly disintegrated and fled, as best they could.

Now around thirty survivors were scrambling along the shore ahead of John and his companions. Sir Lachlan may have been amongst them –

few of the MacDonalds would recognise the man and it was said that he'd thrown off his trappings of rank to disguise himself as he fled. Perhaps they had a boat moored in the deeper waters off Ardnave Point, three miles or so ahead. Perhaps they were aiming for the sanctuary of the monastery on Nave Island.

It seemed indeed that sanctuary was the aim of the fleeing men, for now they'd come across the little chapel called Cill Naoimh that overlooked the middle of the loch.

John was well back in the numbers of pursuing men so he couldn't bear witness to all that occurred. By the shouts and cries of "Sanctuary!" he knew that the Macleans had barricaded themselves inside the church. Someone said later that the fleeing invaders had murdered the priest as they burst into their sacred refuge – that may have been a hastily concocted excuse or it may have been the true reason for the rage that swept over the leading MacDonalds.

The rage that led them to set alight the church. For only a short while did the MacDonald clansmen stand and watch the blaze. The cries of "Sanctuary!" had so quickly been lost in the screams of the dying. None escaped.

There was no victory cry, no song of triumph or exultation from the Ileachs. They turned, shouldered their weapons and began the walk back to their farms and their crofts. The screams and cries dwindled as the smoke bloomed up into the heavens.

If a vengeful Sith Dubh sat somewhere nearby to watch the violent end of the Macleans, no one knew for certain. But it would pass into legend that he did, and that it was the Elf's bewitchment that led Sir Lachlan to his doom. For the MacDonalds that day, it didn't matter. What mattered was that their land – their homes, were secure. John wiped the sweat from his face. It was tainted with the smell of smoke – the scent of burnt wood and of burnt flesh.

John B. sat up in his bed, his eyes snapped open. Rain was falling outside so there wasn't enough light to see his beloved Q in the opposite bed, but he could hear her quiet rhythmic breathing as she slept.

Already the details were disappearing. Trying to capture his thoughts as he woke was like trying to hold on to an armful of smoke. But one thing he knew: what he'd witnessed had been history. This was not something anyone had planted in his brain.

Certainly not one of the Dotterels, anyway.

.oOo.

32 CONDITIONS CLEARING, CHANCE OF STORM LATER

It wasn't a morning that Reverend Gordon Dotterel enjoyed. Most
days he enjoyed strolling through the village buying a small quantity of
provisions – he was a man of simple tastes and modest appetite, and he
was pleased to receive a good proportion of his needs as donations from
respectful parishioners.

This particular morning though he'd found his cupboard bare of some
basic items like tea and sugar. Distracted over the past few days, he'd not
noticed his supplies dwindling. Victoria had evidently used the last of
them the night before and neglected to mention it.

Mary McMurtrie (the Reverend determinedly avoided the companionable
nicknames the villagers used) was suitably respectful, but not deferential.
She had a business to run to keep herself fed and clothed, and her margins
weren't big enough for her to be giving stock away to anyone, even a man
of the cloth.

The passing of the plate on Sunday had seen rather less income than
usual. Attendance was down, but there also seemed to be a little less generosity than expected from those who had attended. The groceries were
still easily afforded, but counting out the coins was a sharp reminder of his
irritation.

Then, after leaving the *General Store* just as he crossed the street the skies
had opened and he was caught in the sudden downpour. He'd had to dash
over to the cover of the awning of the *Curry House*. Any frisson of satisfaction he may have had from the Closed sign in the window was dashed
when the next two people to shelter huddled against the same shopfront
were the infuriating Australian in the purple shirt and the woman who he
consorted with.

John B. and Elizabeth had been walking off an excellent early breakfast
of home-smoked kippers that Rhona had prepared for them before kindly
dropping them in the village, and similarly caught out in the sudden cold

rain. They had each other for warmth and comfort though. Gordon had only the fire of his righteousness, which this morning warmed only his temper, not his bones.

 And now the wretch had the temerity to engage him in casual conversation!

"No, sir, Sunday evening's congregation was not more of a 'full house' as ye put it! As I'm quite sure ye are already aware!"

"How could I be? I wasn't there. I'm sorry your numbers were down. A temporary thing – a hiccup, surely."

 And the woman stood there saying nothing, smiling politely, *just* to be infuriating.

 John B.'s voice bespoke casual interest. "You spoke quite a bit about John's *Revelation* on Sunday morning. I was wondering what your thoughts are on the *Revelation of St. Peter*?"

"That… that is not part o' the canon o' the kirk," spluttered Dotterel, caught completely off guard.

"Well no, it's not. But there are other non-canonical works that are at least cited by serious Biblical scholars. Tobit, Matthias, Ecclesiasticus. And of course, there are alternative Gospels, and variants on the ones we commonly know."

 Both of the Australians wore bland smiles, but their eyes were fixed on the man in black, gauging his reaction. Elizabeth had only the sketchiest knowledge of what Stewart was talking about, but knew enough to appreciate that he was pushing buttons.

 And it was working. Dotterel was caught between irritation at the man's presumption, surprise at his evident knowledge, bafflement at the line of conversation and intrigue as to whether this was coincidental or contrived.

 He managed to compose himself and huff, "We accept the Holy Word as divinely inspired. We must further accept that those who determined the canon were similarly guided by the Will of God."

The wizard nodded thoughtfully. "Mm. That's another article of faith, I suppose. Thinking of gospels, Matthew 10:35 pops into my head – '*I came to set the daughter against her mother.*' What happened to your wife, Reverend?"

The sudden swerve in the direction of discussion caught Gordon in its momentum. He snapped an answer without thinking.

"The doctors called it a 'breakdown' but it was a punishment from God for her weakness!"

"I'm sure you were a big help," said Elizabeth, her face calm but her voice a masterful blend of concern and contempt.

"Seek not to condemn me! It was God's will that she flee this place!" replied the preacher angrily.

"Where did she go?" the brunette persisted.

"I neither know nor care!"

"And your other daughter?" asked John B. quietly. "Was her death God's will too?"

Dotterel paused. For a moment, conflicting emotions danced in his eyes, but brimstone quickly asserted itself.

"Of course! A terrible accident, but her loss made Victoria and I stronger."

"Fire tempers steel, you reckon? Well, I'm sorry for your loss, Reverend." Turning to Elizabeth the wizard said, "Come on, sweetheart, I think the rain's easing off. Excuse us, Reverend, we've got places to be and people to see."

With a salute so sincere as to be galling, the man in purple took the arm of the brunette and strolled away. The preacher was sure that if he followed them out into the drizzle that persisted, the rainwater would turn to steam on contact with his brow.

When the rain failed to dissipate completely after several more minutes the grumbling clergyman strode back to his little manse beside the kirk, the rain only adding to his mood as black as his clothing.

He'd changed into a dry set of identical garments, lit a fire in the grate and allowed himself the luxury of drowsing in his armchair in the hope it might settle his mind. It didn't. When a knock at the door signaled the arrival of DS Mills a few hours later, Dotterel was still very much a bear with a sore head.

Mills hobbled in, damp and scowling from his own stubborn headache that was a legacy of Rita's tombstone. The Englishman had been rightly accused on numerous occasions of having a thick skull – in this instance it had been to his benefit.

He explained his hobble by showing the Reverend how he routinely wore Army boots under his baggy trousers, and proudly said how that had protected his ankle. When Dotterel looked at him blankly he rewound his story and told a heavily edited version of the incident in the Bowmore cemetery.

Partially this was due to a memory hazed by the blow to the head, but Mills did also recollect that he'd had no direction to actually murder the four. What's more, he was concerned that the Reverend may not approve of violence on hallowed ground, even if it wasn't his own hallowed ground.

Admitting that he couldn't recall details after being "attacked from behind, all coward-like", DS mentioned that the shaggy fellow in purple had said that he was a magician.

Dotterel had been only half listening to his minder, but the last remark caught his attention. To Mills it had only been "a bit of a weird thing to say", but to Gordon it rang out. An explanation for that morning's exchange perhaps, but most assuredly a challenge. It provided a clue as to how a scruffy, undistinguished and, in the Reverend's view, uncharismatic man could seem to be influencing the carefully cultivated flock.

"Make some tea, DS," the Reverend instructed. "I want tae think about how we may go about breaking the hold this 'magician' seems tae have on my village."

*

While the preacher had been steaming in front of his fire, Elizabeth and John B. had continued their stroll to the Bromleighs' cottage. They'd barely come through the door when April announced her intention to visit her sister Rose. The "young yins" were, of course, invited to accompany her.

As the rain was still falling Auld Wullie had volunteered to take the three around to Rose's in the Cyclops. The Australians were already soaked but appreciated the offer, especially when they'd each been swaddled in one of April's woolen blankets.

Auld Wullie hadn't accompanied them in to see his sister-in-law, saying that he had "a few things tae attend tae". Whatever the 'things' were, they didn't require the presence of John B. – "nae just yet" he added cryptically.

As they entered Stewart reached down with his right hand and flexed his fingers as if scratching the head of a welcoming collie. April smiled at the memory of being greeted at the door by Gem back when Black Wullie Ellison had been alive.

Quickly unwrapped from their blankets, John B. and Elizabeth were set to dry rapidly in front of Rose's kerosene heater. Rose was unconcerned about her brother-in-law's departure.

"Ask nae questions, get told nae lies," she counseled.

"Just how old *is* Auld Wullie?" asked Elizabeth.

Both women looked thoughtful.

224

"D'ye ken… I'm really no sure," admitted Rose.

Even April looked vaguely mystified at the question. "Everybody already knew him as Auld Wullie when he swept me off ma feet."

"Must have been a big broom he was sweepin' with – ye were built like a hoos even back then," her sister replied casually.

"That was Effie! I was a wee slip of a lass!"

"Aye well, we know yuir memory's nowt tae speak of. Fancy no knowin' yuir own husband's age. There must have been a birth date written on the marriage register, ye ken," said Rose.

April waved dismissively. "Och, that's a government form. Ye could make up any old number tae put on tha'. I'm sure you have over the years."

Rose tilted her head defiantly. "I have not. I've always been proud of ma age."

That won a wry smile from April as she replied, "Ye know that Effie would say ye've got a lot tae be proud of."

The two sisters looked hard at each other for a moment, then both broke into a laugh.

"Aye," agreed Rose. "She would, at that."

It was a light hearted day, and the weather reflected that with the rain clearing across the afternoon. The sudden and unexpected end to the most recent classroom dream had lifted a little of the air of oppression in the village – not much, but any improvement was welcome.

The feeling of having scored points against Reverend Dotterel lifted the Australians' spirits to the extent that after leaving Rose's they collected the makings of a picnic. When Jazz finished work at the distillery (where Wilko had also spent the day, ostensibly doing odd jobs to help offset the

staff shortage but really keeping a watchful eye on the pretty blonde engineer) the four climbed into Anastasia and drove up the coast to Claggan
Bay.

 It was a beach of pebbles rather than sand, but it was peaceful and picturesque. They settled comfortably on a grassy verge fringing the beach.
Watching seals near the shore, they laughed and chatted as the light faded.

 Jazz was still not at her best, but Doc Wullie's medication was helping her
to sleep more soundly at night. As the last of the wine was finished, they
were all looking forward to a peaceful night.

 Which just goes to show that John B. Stewart's magical powers didn't
extend to seeing the future.

.o0o.

33 THE PLAY'S THE THING

As much as the picnic was enjoyed, Jazz had to admit it wore her out. She got Wilko to drop her off at the cottage even before taking Elizabeth and John B. back to the guesthouse.

She really did want to still be awake for her little guy when he got back, but even without taking another of Doc Wullie's sedatives she could feel her eyelids slamming shut. Must have been that last tumbler of white wine.

A persistent drizzle was falling on Stratford-Upon-Avon. A storm flickered in the distance.

It was a quiet afternoon's trade in the White Horse. *That was fine by young Jacinta, though she knew her father would be happier with more coin coming over his counter. At least she could catch up on chores like cleaning the fire grate while keeping an eye on the few customers.*

The three old sisters huddled together at one table were no trouble. She knew from past experience that their mugs of beer would be made to last a goodly while as the women nattered and argued amongst themselves.

The other tableful of customers required more attention. Oh, they were harmless enough – polite even, some of them, the four chaps from the Theatre. They were regular customers whenever their chief creative came home from the City for a sojourn of writing.

The serving girl overheard snatches of conversation indicating that the City house in which he lodged was a riot of argument between father and daughter over her marriage to "that wastrel Stephen", and it was impossible for him to work through the continuous din. But with no pressure to perform there they could indulge their thirst. Best not to leave an empty tankard in front of any of them for long.

The grate clear and an ale provided for Mr. Mellifont who drank at a faster rate than his three companions, Jacinta was able to set about wiping soot and grime from the painting on the wall. More than two hundred

*years old, she knew, and still in good condition – a source of pride
and pleasure for her father. And to her too, she realised as she carefully
removed a smudge from a celestial face. Were there truly such things as
angels? It was what she'd been taught, and she could only hope it was
right.*

*Jacinta discreetly worked close enough to the actors' table to overhear
some of their conversation. She was a bright young woman, but after the
basics of her childhood most of her education came from what she could
glean from the* White Horse*'s clientele. Luckily for her, some of them were
clever and not too proud to share (even unwittingly).*

*They were discussing the new king. Not surprising – many people were,
unsure of what to expect from this peculiar figure from the north. He was
apparently altogether unlike good Queen Bess, in much more than just
gender. But she wondered if all the rumours could be true, or even any of
them.*

*"They're all savages up there! Well known fact," expounded Mr. Melli-
font. "That's why the Romans built that wall, you know."*

*"That was a very long time ago, Horace," said one of his companions
quietly.*

*"Indeed Jack," agreed the homecoming Stratford native with a smile.
"But if we are to ensure the survival of our company we must win the
favour of this particular Scotsman of our own time. And I have some
thoughts…"*

"You inevitably do, Will," enthused their fourth – Evan Cherry by name.

*Cherry made Jacinta a little uncomfortable. Should a young man be quite
so… pretty? Apparently he often played the role of a woman on stage.
That didn't surprise her.*

*The writer Will ignored the flattery he'd heard too often to be meaningful
any more. From a satchel at his feet he extracted a few loose pages and
brandished them.*

"Our new monarch is a writer himself," he said. "King James has written a treatise on witchcraft in his native country –"

"See! I told you they were savages!"

Will ignored Mellifont's interruption. "A few pages – er… fell from a folio in a private collection and found their way into my possession. I thought we might open the play with some of James' own words. He reports some incantations that are quite interesting."

Jack looked at Will through narrowed eyes. "Do you know what these spells are meant to invoke?" he asked.

Will looked slightly sheepish as he replied, "Ah… no. Alas, I fear that information may have been on the next page."

"What does it matter?" laughed Mellifont. "Do you fear invoking a curse? You surely don't believe in witchcraft, Jack Butler!"

"There are more things in heaven and earth than are dreamt of in your philosophy, Horace Mellifont," said Jack.

Will smiled, making a mental note, as he often did when he heard a line that would suit a new script, or one of the frequent revisions of an old one. "Whether Jack or you or I believe is not important," he said. "It is our audience who matter, both our patrons from court and the humble folk whose coppers put bread on our table and ale in our tankards. Here – young Jacinta!"

The girl scurried to the table. "Yes, sir?" she said.

"You can refill my ale please, lass, but first tell me – do you believe in magic?"

She turned her deferential gaze up from the floor and looked Will in the eye. "I don't know that I 'believe' in it, sir, but I reckon the world's a poorer place if there's no such thing."

"Good girl!" the writer replied with a laugh as the landlord's daughter took his tankard. "Now, gentlemen, let us set about giving some credence to our new ruler."

"A historical piece?" suggested Cherry.

"Much of the history of the Scottish throne is one of conflict with England. Not the message we want to deliver, I think," mused Will. "Jack, you've some knowledge of Scottish history. Any thoughts?"

Butler sipped at his ale while he pondered. "There was a King Malcolm who was raised in the Northumbrian court after his father was overthrown by his cousin Macbeth. Won the throne back with the aid of the English army. That was six hundred years ago, though."

"Far enough back to be a mystery to all but the most serious scholars, then," said Will with a nod.

Jack looked unconvinced. "Malcolm Canmore – Malcolm the Bighead – was an unattractive character. Sooner or later he betrayed everyone who ever supported him. Much like his father, which is why Macbeth had fought him in the first place."

"But he took the throne with English support, you say. That's enough to work with. The rest can be embroidered."

"Never let the truth get in the way of a good story, eh Shakespeare?" boomed Horace Mellifont.

One of the old women across the room glanced over her shoulder, giving the bombastic fellow a withering look that may even have quietened him if he'd noticed it.

"Speaking of truth, Will, I should point out that King James' line has no connection with Malcolm. It was another 300 years before the Scottish throne was claimed by the family that eventually begat James VI."

"Embroidery, dear Jack, embroidery. Find me some detail that our new

king will recognise about his ancestry and I'll weave it into the story. And don't worry about big-headed Malcolm. We'll make – what was his name? Macbeth. We'll paint him such a dark villain all the honour will be in the opposing. And by extension we can endorse our new majesty before his new subjects, thereby earning his gratitude."

"And his patronage," added Cherry keenly. "The play's the thing in which we'll catch the kindness of the king!"

"Something like that," agreed the writer.

As Jacinta brought Will his ale, and took orders for more from Mellifont and Cherry ('Why could they not have ordered them before?' she thought to herself) Jack was asking, "What of the witchcraft connection? I know of no suggestion that any of the Scottish monarchs were inclined towards hexing their enemies. A curse cried out in battle, perhaps, but nothing of a sinister magical bent."

"Make this Macbeth's wife a witch. She uses her sorcerous powers to get him the throne," suggested Mellifont.

Shakespeare looked uncertain. "Hmm... what do you think of that idea, lass? What's your womanly perspective on Horace's notion?"

"I think that if a woman were to have such powers she should apply them to her own benefit, not to be attendant to a man who may or may not reward her labours," she answered boldly. This writer wanted an honest answer – he'd get one!

"Well thought lass, thank you," said the writer.

Jacinta bobbed a curtsey and went to pour the drinks as two of the men smiled or laughed, appreciating her bluntness.

"Let us not taint the throne too directly with the scent of witchcraft, I think. James has studied the subject, but that doesn't mean he approves of it," said Shakespeare. "Make it an influence..."

"A malign influence," said Evan earnestly, crossing himself.

"A malign influence, yes, but not a direct one. Something subtle, manipulative…" continued Will thoughtfully. "But who might make such mischief? This witch – what sort of character could plausibly play games with destiny?"

"Legend does tell of the power of three in matters of magic," said Butler as he stared into the depths of his tankard.

"What sort of characters, then?"

The others fell quiet, allowing Shakespeare his reverie. They'd seen him work often enough before.

The serving girl brought their drinks, and then went to check on the old women. The sisters waved away the suggestion of more beer.

As if the offer had been a signal the oldest of them drained the dregs from her mug and struggled to her feet. She shrugged off the support of her two siblings as they all shuffled to the door of the White Horse.

"When shall we three meet again?" asked one – by a slight margin the youngest of the trio.

The eldest crone peered out into the gloomy weather and bitterly replied, "In thunder, lightning or in rain, no doubt."

Grumbling, the three sisters made their way out into the drizzle. Will Shakespeare's eyes twinkled.

Jazz's eyes opened with a start. Wilko snored creatively but peacefully beside her. Where had *that* come from?

.oOo.

34 BURNING DOWN THE HOUSE

It was a still clear night. A little past midnight John B. and Elizabeth decided to go out for a stroll.

The picnic had been fun, and then Wilko had dropped them back at the Hines' guesthouse. Watching television in their cozy room for a little while had given way to what they smilingly called 'mutual self-indulgence' (although in fact they were each more focused on the other's pleasure than their own – always a recipe for a good relationship). Unsatisfactory drowsing afterwards had prompted the thought that, as the sky was so clear, it'd be nice to go look at the stars.

Rhona had earlier left the key to her little car in the front parlour "just in case they needed tae go fer a wee spin at any time". As appealing as the waterfront of Port Ellen could be, on impulse the pair decided to drive up to the village. Perhaps late at night, with them in good spirits, it might reveal a charm they'd not yet really felt.

The car parked under one of the streetlamps, with an arm around each other's waist they strolled the streets of Sron Dubh. No wandering pack of boys tonight. With the three 'ringleaders' variously incapacitated, the rest of the little gang had no heart for nocturnal roamings.

There were no vehicles on the road, either, although as they walked they did hear the sound of one engine not far away. Had they been alert they may have recognised it from the night of the ceilidh in Bowmore.

Every so often they would stop and turn into each other's embrace for a few moments of passionate closeness. It was in the middle of one such interlude that Q suddenly pulled away, wrinkling her nose.

"It's not you, babe," she reassured John B. "I just got a strong whiff of… petrol?"

The wizard sniffed the air. "Uh-huh… I reckon you're right. That and… smoke!"

They followed their noses at a run, realising almost immediately that they were heading towards the distillery.

It was the tenement building that was burning.

A figure in black stood watching the fire from the hill above and behind the building, a safe distance away and unseen in the darkness.

The flames are rising through the timbers. You can feel the heat on your skin, and the sign 'Sron Dubh Distillery' is all that is visible through the swirling smoke. This is the fault of the distillery. This is the inevitable outcome of allowing this sinful place to fester in the village. The screams of the people inside – your own screams – they are your own fault. You allowed this. You encouraged this.

At the sound of the screams the Australian couple accelerated their running. The doors of the furthest two houses were opening as they got to the building but the two closest stayed shut, with smoke curling out from around them.

John B. didn't break stride. He hit the nearest door shoulder first, smashing it off its hinges. Following the sound of screams he bounded up the stairs, with Elizabeth close behind. A figure was reeling down the hallway. Stewart grabbed the man and pushed him into Q's arms. She steered him back down the staircase, trying to maintain a narrow line between the hot wall and the burning handrail.

At the door of a small bedroom John B. peered through the smoke. He dropped to hands and knees and scuttled to the figure he'd made out in the corner of the room. It was a woman huddled over two small children, coughing as she desperately tried to protect them. The wizard caught the kids up in one arm, wrapped the other around the mother, and at a crouch shuffled them all out into the hall. Propelling the woman in front of him he tucked a child under each arm and followed Q's rapidly narrowing path to safety.

With the parents and children being tended to by their neighbours, Stewart headed to the last house in the row. The door was unlocked, but as he opened it the rush of night air caused a mass of flames and smoke to belch out. The Australian threw himself sideways to avoid the worst of it, then plunged in through the fire. He dived into a somersault across the floor as he hit the front room to crush out the flames he'd felt flickering from the t-shirt on his back. He winced at the impact on the bruise, still raw.

There was a terrible crash as part of the staircase collapsed. Looking up, John B. saw the silhouette of a woman swaying at the top of where the steps had been, the fire behind her throwing weird shadows on the smoke that filled the tenement. He just had time to lunge forward with his arms out as she toppled forward.

Stewart cursed as he had to plough his way through the burning debris of the staircase to catch the falling figure. He relied on his momentum to carry him through the flames, the woman's body landing neatly in his outstretched arms as he passed below.

He staggered, and hugged the unconscious form to his chest. He went to prop his shoulder against a wall, but the heat almost set his sleeve alight. The paint was blistering and the wall itself was smoking. Eyes streaming, he tried to aim for where he thought he'd come in. All he could make out was a wall of flame. He shrugged and charged.

Waiting fretfully outside the blazing building, Elizabeth heard the sound of falling timbers. The sight of the door frame catching alight and starting to collapse was too much for her. She dashed in through the opening just in time to see John B., head down and hunched over someone cradled in his arms, collide with a blazing coffee table. The would-be rescuer and his charge hit the floor and rolled.

Elizabeth grabbed two handfuls of the scorched purple t-shirt and hauled Stewart to his feet. He still clung to the woman he'd caught. The brunette didn't release her grip. She propelled her beloved towards the remains of the door, following at a run. They burst through to the outside just before the jamb crashed down. Seconds after that, the ceiling of the ground floor did the same, sending up a great billow of smoke, flames and sparks.

You will stay asleep. You will see this. You will experience this. You will learn from this! The flames and smoke persist, but the screams have diminished. That's because they're dead. You know they're dead! They've died because they deserved... Who? Two shapes in the smoke – one purple, one sea green. They... save? No! They do not save! They are not the way to salvation! They cannot... Look! See the flames – feel the heat! These are the consequences of sin and disobedience! Fear them! Know Hell! Hear the screaming! Listen to the... the... silence...?

Collapsed on the grassy slope, Elizabeth drew in ragged breaths. In the light of the blaze she could see the rise and fall of John B.'s chest as he lay on his back, smoke-filled eyes still squeezed shut and streaming. She could also see who it was that he'd carried out of the last building – the distillery's office manager, Moraig McConnell.

Others had arrived to help now, most still wiping sleep from their eyes. Doc Wullie was amongst them. He'd checked on the family, and now turned his attention to Moraig. Satisfied that her vital signs were okay, he knelt by her rescuer. He squeezed water from a plastic bottle across the Australian's scorched and smoke-stained face. With Elizabeth's help he removed the ruined purple t-shirt.

"It's a good thing this is a decent thick fabric," observed the doctor. "There are a couple o' superficial burns on your arms an' shoulders an' back but nowt o' lastin' damage. A nasty bruise aboot yuir kidney ye might ha' done well tae tell me of when ye saw me last, ye ken."

"Others?" John B. managed to croak as he reached for the bottle that had mostly cleared his vision, and squeezed some of the welcome cooling water down his throat.

Doc Wullie gently took back the water, not wanting him to overdo the fluid in one go. "Much as yerself. Some minor burns and smoke inhalation. Shock in a couple o' cases." There was a roar as a large section of the tenement's roof collapsed. The building wouldn't last much longer. "A small miracle ye were both here when ye were, an' that everybody's gotten oot alive."

Elizabeth stroked Stewart's singed hair. He'd lost quite a few of his shaggy curls and a good proportion of the beard that had just started to be worthy of the name. Some of her own hair had burned too, she realised, but she also knew that it could have been far, far worse.

She smiled at the doctor. "Magic," she said.

.oOo.

35 STIRRING THE EMBERS

There was a meeting called the following morning at the distillery. The remaining on-site staff – all eight of them plus what was left of the management team (i.e. Robbie Keith and Jazz) were surprised to be joined by Auld Wullie Bromleigh and the normally reclusive Hamish Hine. The three Australian visitors were there too, along with the three peat cutters.

Robbie had arranged it to try to lift morale, or if he judged the mood to be beyond that, to suspend operations indefinitely. The General Manager felt especially ill-suited to the task that morning. Even as everyone was gathering, his Office Manager Moraig was being airlifted to Glasgow, still suffering the effects of smoke inhalation. He'd been summoned to report to the Board of Directors again.

Sleeping in a hotel in Bowmore, he hadn't even seen the blaze in a dream – the news had come via a frantic phone call from one of the first escapees in the early hours of the morning. He was relieved that there were no serious injuries or fatalities, but concerned that this might be a death blow to the spirits of the last of his personnel.

As a motivational speaker, however, Robbie Keith was as effective as a cardboard fry pan. After his fourth or fifth "Um, well… what next…" had petered off into an awkward and self-conscious silence Hamish took a step forward out of the little group.

"Mister Keith," he began, "I dinna ken if ye're aware, but I used tae occupy your very office many years ago. Long before the current owners, and long before any o' ye good folks worked here. Savin' yerself, Auld Wullie – I recall ye comin' by tae help on more than one occasion. Ma point is that this distillery has been through a lot over the years. By rights we thought it'd close many times over but it hasnae. Sometimes it was a new boss, or new owners, or the economy turned aboot, or somebody had a bright idea aboot a change tae the product…" (That was accompanied by a sidelong glance at Bromleigh, who gave an acknowledging nod in response.) "But always – *always* – the people here have kept going. This village was built around the distillery, an while it might no' employ the

numbers it used tae, it's still at the beatin' heart o' this wee community."
The Sron Dubh locals stood a little taller.

Keith smiled awkwardly. "I appreciate that thought, Mr. Hine, and yes, I
have seen your name on the Honour Roll upstairs. My concern is that we
have enough people left to remain productive. We're not as automated as
some of the big mainland distilleries that can produce ten times our volume with a staff of four plus a couple of managers…"

"Aye, an' their whisky tastes like it were spat oot o' a machine, too," muttered Lanky Wullie.

Auld Wullie folded his arms and looked around the group. "None o' ye
that work here are sae daft that ye cannae do mair than yer own job, are
ye? Wi' a bit o' help an' guidance ye can keep the stills goin', an' the rest
o' the important parts o' the process."

"Yes, up to a point, if everyone's willing. There are limits of course…"
Robbie wanted to be positive but his own discouragement was clear.

It was John B. who strode up to stand alongside the General Manager,
and turn to face everyone. "This is not insurmountable. Nobody was
killed. The building was insured, wasn't it? You can rebuild. Moraig will
be okay. Robbie, reassure the directors. Do *not* give up!" He opened his
arms to the assembly. "There are enough of you left to carry on, going
on Auld Wullie's advice. Okay, don't start a new batch if you haven't got
the resources to do it properly. Maybe the bottling of what's already in
the casks has to slow down or stop for a bit. A nuisance, but it won't kill
the business – a little more time on the wood will never hurt. What you
can do is make sure that what's on the floor now isn't wasted. Look to the
vats, look to the stills. Don't let these bastards *win*."

Gordon Macintosh grinned. "I don't know aboot Duncan, but I wouldnae
mind comin' in frae the peat fer a bit tae help wi' the actual makin' o' the
whisky."

"Aye – count me in!" agreed his brother.

"I don't have the experience you folks have, but I've a pair of willing hands and I'll bloody try anything that needs doing!" promised Jazz.

"Same here. As long as someone tells me what I'm doing, I'll have a go!" Wilko realised he wasn't going to let her bear any load without him if he could help it.

The handful of other men and women who worked at various elements of the distillery's operations enthusiastically indicated their willingness to continue. The Australian had challenged them – they might not have been sure of who the bastards were that they weren't going to let win, but they'd all decided that they were up for the fight.

Robbie Keith looked around, a little embarrassed, a little bemused, and more than a little moved.

"Right," he said, "I'm off to meet with the directors and tell them that while we have some problems to resolve, the team here will do what's necessary. Sron Dubh has standards to maintain. Mr. Hine, Mr. Bromleigh, I'm delighted to have your experience to draw upon. The rest of you – all of you – what can I say but 'thank you'? I'll be back."

In a quiet aside to John B. he whispered, "I've never felt less like Arnold Schwarzenegger!"

As Robbie Keith headed back to his office to finish packing his briefcase Hamish and Auld Wullie set about organizing the small workforce. The two veterans were smooth and efficient. Experienced as they were, they were also smart enough to draw on the knowledge of the younger, newer members of the team.

Auld Wullie called John B. and Elizabeth to him.

"I ken it was a busy night for the two o' ye. Ye're no' best served by spendin' the day here, I think. I think… I think ye should drop in on Effie's cottage. There'll be somethin' there o' help tae ye."

The Australians looked puzzled, but John B. especially was learning to take Bromleigh at his word.

"We've been invited around for tea anyway," Elizabeth recalled. "If we get something appropriate from the cakes at the dress shop I'm sure she won't mind our arriving a bit early."

Auld Wullie and John B. shared a grin at the optimism, and the shrewd choice of bribe. The wizard and his beloved said brief farewells to the others and went to depart for the walk up to Effie's cottage.

"I wonder what he meant by 'something to help' – a restorative version of one of his brews maybe?" said Elizabeth.

"I suppose so, pretty lady," the wizard replied thoughtfully. He realised that the old distiller sometimes spoke, and thought, on more than one level.

A few minutes later Robbie emerged from his office. Auld Wullie tapped Wilko on the shoulder.

"Would ye mind deliverin' Mister Keith tae the airport?"

"Eh? Oh, sure," replied the Tasmanian. "I guess I am the most expendable person here." There was neither rancour nor false modesty in his voice. He was practical enough to realise that unlike all the others he had no experience in any facet of the whisky industry. He rarely even drank the stuff. So the old Scotsman's request made sense.

Bromleigh nodded. "And when ye're done, ye might drop by Effie Lindsay's. I've reminded yer pals tae drop in on her. Best ye see they're alright."

Wilko looked puzzled. "Effie's not dangerous, is she? I mean, I know she can be a bit cantankerous…."

Auld Wullie smiled. "That wasnae what I meant."

The Australian gave a small slightly guilty start as the penny dropped. He'd heard from some of the others about the fire he'd managed to sleep through, and the heroic efforts of his two travelling companions. He really was a very sound sleeper, he realised, notwithstanding the jibes he heard from everyone (except Jazz) about the sounds of his slumber.

For his part, Robbie appreciated the lift. He might have left his own car at the airfield as he usually did, but had to admit that with his nerves in their current state, he was happier to not drive.

As they travelled Keith asked some questions about Stewart. Why *was* his consultant engineer, a woman whose intelligence he'd come to deeply admire (an observation duly noted and approved of by Wilko), so sure the scruffy Aussie would be able to resolve the strange problems that were besetting the business? The whole village, in fact, he admitted.

Wilko gave carefully considered responses. He knew John B.'s experience in the Public Service. He knew his old friend had studied extensively – more extensively than first thought he'd recently discovered. He did have a knack for being around and apparently sorting out weird situations. What sort of weird? Er… strange weather conditions. Dangerous people. What sort of dangerous people? Er… tricky one. Best not to be too specific about the deranged American colonel, or the three Russians.

"Well, there was this – I suppose you'd call her a terrorist, in Hawaii. Had a mad idea about blowing up a volcano."

"And your friend stopped her?"

"Um… well, yeah. Yeah, he did."

Robbie looked impressed. "That's encouraging! How?"

"Ah… oh! Look, we've arrived!"

The distillery manager was distracted enough not to pursue his questions, much to Wilko's relief. The Tasmanian was resolutely cynical about anything and everything 'supernatural' but months of close-up experience of uncanny events – good and bad – around John B. were taxing his imagination. How *was* his old friend such a focal point for improbability and coincidence?

He shook Robbie Keith's hand and wished him well as the manager headed off to catch his flight. The drive to Effie Lindsay's cottage was spent in the sort of quiet contemplation he seldom slipped into, and rarely enjoyed.

*

The atmosphere in Craig's office was unpleasantly quiet. Craig himself sat at his desk saying little, performing mechanical tasks with a defeated air.

Lachlan Maclean was in his usual corner, stewing in his own dissatisfaction. He'd expected the lawyer to have crumbled completely. Given up, and given the business over to him. Despite his training in both disciplines his own preference was for accountancy over law, but he could hire someone straight out of University, cheap, to take care of such legal matters as cropped up on Islay. He really didn't grasp the size of Aaron Craig's business on the mainland.

But the big man was still there, disengaged but functioning, and showing no sign of handing on the business. Maclean had complained bitterly to Victoria, and received no sympathy.

"I'm content to have Craig around," she'd said. "And docile. He's still a canny lawyer, and that may yet prove useful to me."

"I can be just as useful! More so! I already am!"

The platinum blonde had shown an insincere smile, as she might have given a potential voter's new puppy. "Of course you have your uses, Lachlan. I'm just aware of your limitations. More so than you, I ken."

She was practicing her 'politician' speaking style, carefully modulating her accent to not sound too 'local'. Maclean knew that when she did this it meant she was taking him even less seriously than usual.

"Be fair, Victoria. I have a valuable network here. Ma family has been on this island far longer than Aaron Craig's. And very much longer than yours, I must point out."

Her condescending smile didn't waver. "You know, Lachlan, or you should by now, that my interest in the past is directly proportional to how valuable it is to my future. And as we both are aware, your family's history on Islay did not get off to a very distinguished beginning."

"That's legend, not history! That damned Sith Dubh…"

"Which reminds me – Arsaidh MacAdam has become a serious vexation to ma father, and thus to me. He has a document of some… significance, we believe. Mills could perhaps force an answer from him, but I doubt he has the intelligence to know if he's being lied to."

Maclean smirked in agreement.

Dotterel continued. "You, Lachlan, can be trusted to ask meaningful questions, and make a considered assessment of the answers you're given. Ma father wants Mills tae pay a call on one of those mad old biddies in the village, thinking she has some insight into what we seek. Even if she does, I doubt that DS is the man to learn anything from her. No, I think the two of you may be more effective in tandem, and I think the so-called Elf to be a more valuable source of information."

The aspiring politician proceeded to spend some little time giving Maclean instructions. She provided an idea, though no detail, of an 'item of great value' that she thought MacAdam either possessed or knew the whereabouts of. She knew the accountant was loyal to her, although not as stupidly slavish as Mills had become to her father, but also recognised that in his own way he was ambitious. He was a useful resource, but he shouldn't be allowed to get ideas above himself either.

In truth, there was little risk of that. Lachlan Maclean was from an old fashioned aristocratic line - a man who knew his place. He would treat 'inferiors' with thinly disguised contempt (except when they could be useful) but knew exactly who to be deferential to. Frustrated as he might be, there was no chance he'd cross her. Those frustrations would just have to be taken out on someone else. The Sith Dubh.

He sat at his desk, waiting for Mills to arrive. His mood only darkened.

*

Playing the hostess came as naturally to Effie Lindsay as tai chi to a march hare, but she deserved credit for trying. The rich fruit-and-whisky cake that Elizabeth brought certainly helped. It was a nice adjunct to the plate of oatcakes spread with blackberry jam that Effie provided.

Over tea and sweets the small talk didn't last long. Effie had things she wanted to discuss.

"What do ye know o' yer wee English friend?" she asked.

"Jazz? Um… she's from Stratford, she's an engineer, she travels around the world a lot, she's fun when she's not exhausted…" said John B., who'd known her longer than Elizabeth.

"Her family I mean. What d'ye ken o' her kinfolk?"

The Australians looked at each other, puzzled. They related as much as they could recall of what the Englishwoman had revealed of herself in Rose's cottage. It seemed fair to assume Jazz wouldn't mind what had been shared with one sister also being told to another.

As the story was recounted Effie nodded, as if in confirmation. When Elizabeth finished, the old woman sat with furrowed brow, considering what to say next. She looked long and hard into the eyes of her two guests before making up her mind to speak.

"When I first saw the lassie I thought she was familiar. She's the spittin' image o' her mother. Afore she got hersel' awa' tae England, Jeannie Parrish was known here as Jeannie Dotterel."

Jaws didn't quite drop, but the news was more than a surprise.

In a quiet voice Elizabeth asked, "Do you think the Reverend's really her father?"

"Och, I doubt it. She doesnae seem tae have his taint aboot her. Mind ye, neither did the other sister."

"The one that fell off the cliff?" the brunette asked. John B. was quiet, evidently deep in thought.

"Fell, ma foot!"

"You don't think it was an accident?"

"I *know* it wasnae. I *see* things, ye ken. I saw the two wee lassies go up ontae the cliff top together. I turned ma heid fer a moment, when I looked back the red-haired lass, Jeanette, was gone. The wee blonde vixen was holdin' a michty big rock, that she proceeded tae toss over the edge. O' course, when the body was found Victoria was as shocked as a'body. Oh no, *she* hadnae been on the cliff. She couldnae say why poor Jeanette would ha' gone up there on her own – she wasnae her sister's keeper."

Stewart looked grim. "The fall, or at least the landing, would have disguised any mark of a blow. What? Animal cunning at 12, 14? Because her sister was younger? Prettier?"

The look on Effie's face matched that of the wizard. "She's no' one tae share, yon besom. O' course, the irony is the power o' three is so much the stronger. Poor Jeannie had the Sight, but I think didnae ken how tae use it. Her three daughters together might ha' been… interestin', what wi' the Reverend's own past. Mind ye, Victoria's probably never foond oot she'd got another sister. Perhaps best she doesnae, eh?"

"I think you're right," said the wizard slowly. "Should Jazz know, d'you think? With a different father – would she have the same power? The Sight?"

Elizabeth looked doubtful. "Can't say that she's struck me as particularly magical."

"She clouds Wilko's mind sometimes, and I think she might have done the same with Harlan. I don't know that it's deliberate or conscious though," said Stewart, a smile indicating that he was joking.

"It doesnae have tae be," said Effie seriously.

They were all silent for several moments before John B. spoke again.

"Instinct tells me that Jazz doesn't need to know this little bit of her family history. Not right now. She's lived quite happily with little thought of her Mum for this long, I don't think we need to disturb that yet. It might explain why the dreams have been particularly intense for her, though."

"And what about you, babe? How did you come to be getting them on the other side of the world?"

John B. shrugged off his beloved's question. "The magic, I guess. Which reminds me – Effie, you made some reference to Reverend Dotterel's own past. I remember April saying he was descended from some sort of Hindu holy man."

In reply Effie waved towards one of her crowded bookshelves, indicating a volume that was tilted forward to be readily found. It was a rather dense old textbook on comparative religions. Clearly the widow Lindsay read very widely.

The old woman busied herself with repairing the hem of a cardigan while Elizabeth read over John B.'s shoulder as he scanned the book, particularly the section on Hindu mysticism. One particular paragraph stood out.

> A *Mantrik* is someone who specializes in practicing mantra. In India the word mantrik is synonymous with magician in different languages. Generally a mantrik is supposed to derive his powers from the use of charms, mantras, spells and other methods, chanting to please a god or evil spirit for his own benefit. Mantras are sacred chantings containing magical and mystical words.
> A Mantrik is known for his use of sorcery and magic and can be called upon for the casting of spells and magic, divination, astrology and all aspects of sorcery. Mantriks are normally associated with the darker side of magic and its relevant practices.

"Could it be knowledge passed down from generation to generation, do you think, babe? It doesn't sit well with the religion he spruiks," said the brunette.

"Or maybe it's a genetic thing – an ability that isn't actually attached to a particular religion," the wizard replied.

Suddenly Effie looked up from her sewing. Distracted, she poked herself with her needle. "Och, I've stuck me ain thumb!" She stared towards the village. "There's evil comin' this way," she said ominously.

.o0o.

36 TILTING AT MILLS

There was a loud violent pounding at the front door of the cottage.

"I'll get it," offered Elizabeth.

"Whatever they're sellin', I'm no' buying," said Effie firmly, winning a smile from her guests.

When the door was opened slightly Mills pushed his way in past the brunette, then stopped suddenly in the entrance hall, blinking in surprise at the unexpected figure who'd unintentionally let him in.

"What are you doin' here? Ah – who cares?" he growled and strode into the sitting room.

After seeing Elizabeth even Mills wasn't surprised to find her purple-shirted boyfriend in the room with Effie Lindsay.

"Hello DS. I'd say 'fancy meeting you here' but truthfully, I wouldn't fancy meeting you anywhere," said Stewart with an annoyingly cheerful smile.

Before the Englishman could respond Effie addressed him sternly. "I hope ye're no' expectin' the likes o' a cup o' tea, young man. I'm a poor old widow, an I cannae afford tae cater fer unexpected guests who arrive unannounced."

Disconcerted by her response the thug had to work his jaw a few times before words came out. "I don't want a bloody cup of tea! I…"

"Manners, young man! Ye'll no come intae ma hoose unbidden an' then swear at me! Ye'll keep a civil tongue in yer bloody heid. Noo, what is it ye're wantin'?"

Elizabeth had followed him into the room and taken up a position standing beside Effie. She and the wizard flanked their hostess like sentinels, clearly ready in case the enforcer made any move towards her.

Fists clenched, the burly man drew himself up to full height. Eyes fixed on the old woman, he launched into the speech that had been prepared for him. "The Reverend Dotterel sends his respects, Mrs. Lindsay, an' asks if you can give 'im some information. Please."

The last word came out with all the difficulty of coughing up a tennis ball. Expressions didn't change. Both women continued to look stern, and the shaggy magician still wore the infuriating happy smile. Mills was sure the bugger was laughing at him, if not out loud, but couldn't think of why. He resisted an impulse to check his fly.

The middle sister made a sound very like a *harrumph*. "I wouldnae give yon man the time o' day, far less…"

"Hang on, Mrs. Lindsay," interrupted John B. "It might be interesting to find out what information the good Reverend is after."

She turned and looked up at the wizard. Picking up on his smile, she replied, "Aye, it might at that." Turning back to Mills she said, "All right – oot wi' it then. What does the auld misery want fra' me?"

DS had to bite down hard on his reaction to the disrespect to his mentor. He composed himself, and delivered just as he'd been instructed. "The Reverend understands that you're a well read woman what knows a great deal about the history of the area." He paused, unsure about the presence of the two Australians. Should they be hearing this? He had no instructions about that possibility. Ah, well – he could deal with them if they caused trouble. He was going to deal with them when he got the chance anyway- they'd gotten lucky before, that was all. Nobody had spoken while he thought, so he continued.

"It 'as come to the Reverend's attention that an interestin' old mannerscrip may 'ave found its way ta Sron Dubh at some point in the past, an' he wonders if you might 'ave any knowledge of it."

"What sort of manuscript?" asked Elizabeth, pointedly correcting his pronunciation.

Glaring at her, the Englishman replied, "Sumfin' of a religious persuasion, per'aps, I'm told."

"Och, I've got a muckle o' books like that, lad," Effie said with a vague wave towards her library. "Ye'll have tae be more specific."

Mills was at a loss. He'd been told to ask for information, and use his own judgement about searching the place. But he wasn't sure of quite what he was looking for, and the prospect of working through a collection of books was more daunting than another run-in with these bloody Australians. He clung to the little he knew.

"Sumfin' old an' valuable." It was inconceivable to him that a book could be truly valuable – there had to be something more to be found.

Effie forced her face into a thin smile. "If I possessed somethin' old and valuable d'ye think I'd be hunkered doon in a wee cottage, livin' on the pension? Dinna be daft, man."

"Don't call me daft! 'Is Reverence reckons you might know sumfin' useful, so I'm tryin' ta be nice. But I don't mind bein' not nice either, understand? Just gimme a straight answer."

The old woman somehow maintained the smile, though it clearly wasn't coming easily. "Young man, how can I gie ye any sort o' answer when ye dinna know the question? Ye've asked aboot a manuscript, I've shown ye where ma books are. Ye mentioned religion, I can point ye tae those books if ye've a mind tae look. Ye talk aboot old an' valuable. I've told ye ma thoughts on 'valuable', an' I dinna ken how 'old' ye mean."

With something between a grumble and a growl, Mills made a show of examining the crowded bookshelves. He looked as out of place as a penguin in a tropical jungle. None of the others offered any assistance.

Very shortly after Mills' arrival Wilko had turned up at the cottage. Seeing the big black vehicle parked at the top of the rise he frowned. Across his mind ran a very clear memory of a shiny black four wheel drive bearing down on the lovely Jazz after the ceilidh in Bowmore. The Tasmanian

had a very good idea who the driver had been. Jaw clenched, he parked
Anastasia in a nearby laneway where she was unlikely to be noticed.

 He approached Effie's cottage, but stopped before he got to the door. He
didn't trust his temper, knew he was no fighter, and didn't want to create
a situation where John B. would get into another brawl with the brawny
Englishman, this time on his behalf. His old friend had come out ahead
in the first two rounds, but may not be third time lucky. Angry as he was,
Wilko really didn't like violence. There were no loud noises coming from
the cottage – better to walk away for a bit rather than inflame whatever the
situation was that was happening inside.

 The Tasmanian strode up the hill and examined the vehicle. There was a
wallet on the front seat. On impulse he tried the door, and was surprised
to find it unlocked. To satisfy his curiosity, or really, to confirm his suspi-
cions, he opened the wallet.

 It contained a driver's licence in the name of Duff Samson Mills. A suspi-
cion confirmed and a riddle answered. Little wonder he chose to be called
DS. With an uncharacteristic snarl Wilko tossed the wallet back onto the
seat. He bumped the gearstick and realised that the vehicle hadn't been
left in gear when parked. Again acting on impulse, he released the handbrake.

 Quietly closing the door, he nonchalantly leaned on the bonnet of the car.
Not too heavily – he was hard-wired to be law-abiding despite his righteous anger. Furthermore he wasn't a big man, and the vehicle was heavy.

"Hang aboot – I'll gie ye a hand."

 The unexpected voice nearly made Wilko jump clear over the bonnet.
He hadn't seen Scuzzy Wullie tramping up the hill. The scruffy teenager
had followed Mills' wagon at a very cautious distance (not least because
he was on foot, but he'd spotted the black brute going up the hill). Scuzz
may have lost his arrogant self-confidence, but he knew what Mills had
done to his mate Kev and nursed vague notions of revenge.

 Carving something appropriate into the shiny black paintwork had been
his initial idea, but the little foreign bloke was clearly onto something even

better. He stood beside Wilko with his back to the wagon, planted his feet firmly, and shoved.

Without conscious thought the Australian put more weight into his own effort. Suddenly the vehicle wasn't there any more, leaving the two of them momentarily staggering as it trundled backwards down the hill. It picked up only a little speed as it rolled. There wasn't time for it to do more. The road curved. The four wheel drive didn't. It dropped over the edge of the road, and the edge of the steep incline that a little further along became the precipitous cliffs at the point of Sron Dubh. There was surprisingly little noise from the vehicle landing first on its tailgate then flipping onto its roof before sliding down for the bonnet to crumple against the trunk of a solid old tree.

Scuzzy Wullie grinned broadly and quietly said, "Oops!" He gave Wilko a friendly pat on the arm, said "Nice workin' wi' ye, pal!" and ran off back towards the village feeling much lighter of heart.

The Tasmanian didn't quite share that response, but he realised he didn't feel remotely guilty, either. Best not to linger too visibly though, he realised. He returned to Anastasia and drove away unhurriedly. A little trip to Port Ellen and back ought to be enough for him to arrive innocently after Duff Samson Mills had left the cottage. A good plan, it worked out neatly (which was unusual for Wilko's 'good plans').

Mills had enjoyed as much success in scouring the bookshelves as his three watchers had expected. To be fair to the Englishman, Dotterel had given him little to work with, perhaps not least because the Reverend himself didn't have a clear idea of what to look for. The widow Lindsay was regarded as one of the village's best sources of knowledge of 'the old days' (along with her sisters) and he considered her the least belligerent of the three siblings. Which just proved how little he knew of them – each was as proudly intractable as the others. The idea of 'pressuring' informa- tion from any of them was simply misguided, as DS was discovering.

Elizabeth gave the bodyguard a benign smile and said mildly, "I do think your friend the Reverend could have made your job easier if he'd actually told you what to look for. Don't you think it was a little unfair of him, babe?"

"Oh aye," agreed John B., slipping into local parlance again.

With only a cursory glance up from the sewing she'd resumed Effie added, "Well if ye've no' found what ye were after, I cannae help ye. Ye'll be
on yer way then."

It was as clear a dismissal as possible – even Mills understood, and he
was sufficiently uncomfortable not to argue. The Englishman was a bib-
liophobe, although he wouldn't have recognised the fact himself. He'd
been a slow reader at school, and one teacher in particular had given him a
very hard time about it.

That had gone on to have a number of effects: it fostered the young Mills'
aggressive, bullying nature as a direct response to feeling humiliated by
the teacher; it left him with a deep-seated aversion to books so that now
his reading was confined mostly to war comics and simple religious tracts
(he liked the ones that had cartoons in them – there was one with pictures
of Hell in it that he especially enjoyed); and it made him especially sus-
ceptible to being influenced by dreams about classroom discipline.

The enforcer stood in the middle of the room. In truth, he was more than
happy to leave, but didn't want to feel that he'd been pushed.

"You will remember to tell the Reverend how co-operative Mrs. Lindsay
has been, won't you? It's just a shame he didn't feel he could explain to
you what to look for," said Elizabeth sweetly. She was now wearing the
same damned innocent smile as her shaggy boyfriend.

The old woman wasn't. "Ye found yer way in, now ye can find yer way
out," she snapped.

Without a word, Mills strode to the door. Just as he exited, he lashed out
a petulant foot and kicked over a small table. Both the vase and the flow-
ers in it were plastic, so he didn't even have the satisfaction of hearing a
smash when they hit the floor as he walked out.

As John B. calmly closed the door and picked up the table and its orna-
ments, Elizabeth could no longer contain the giggle she'd been suppress-
ing.

"I almost feel sorry for him," she said.

"He's so dense he absorbs light," agreed the wizard. "But don't waste your sympathy. There are plenty of folks in the world that aren't very clever, but most of them don't become vicious thugs."

"Mickle o' mind an' mean o' spirit," was Effie's sour observation.

 The subject of discussion was standing out on the street where he'd left his four wheel drive, looking bewildered.

"Black Beauty?" he said aloud, sure that this was where he'd parked. He looked around, bereft of ideas. Some instinct made him walk downhill, and he soon spotted the tracks in the verge where the wagon had failed to take the curve. He looked over the edge, and saw the battered remains of what was now a truly off road vehicle.

'I must've left the handbrake off,' he thought to himself. It never occurred to him that anyone might have done this deliberately. He gave other people grief – they didn't try to mess with him. Well, except for that bloody Aussie in the purple shirt, but he'd been with him in the cottage the whole time.

 Cursing, DS started to trudge back to the village to report to the Reverend. Black Beauty wasn't going anywhere – he'd retrieve his wallet on the way, and later figure out what to do about the wreck. Lost in his musings he didn't even notice the silver Rover pass him as it headed out of Sron Dubh.

 Wilko didn't stay long at Effie's cottage. Four visitors, one of them uninvited and unwelcome, were rather more than the widow normally received in one day. She was the most solitary of the sisters. Mark Twain once claimed to love humanity, it was people he couldn't stand. Effie Lindsay was less charitable in her views.

 The Australian trio thanked her for her hospitality – she had made an effort and did seem to genuinely appreciate the visit of John B. and Elizabeth. That was true. Like her sisters, Effie's real passion was learning, and these two certainly did stir up what that Belgian character the Christie woman wrote of called 'the little grey cells'.

*

By the time Mills reached the Reverend's home, his temper was starting to boil again. He wasn't sure how, or who, but someone must have been responsible for the loss of Black Beauty. He always preferred to blame others rather than accept something may have been his own fault.

Victoria Dotterel was with her father when DS arrived to explain his lack of success at the widow's cottage. Unlike the cautiously diplomatic Reverend, she was scarcely disguising her amusement as the burly minder paced about the parlour like a big lion in a small cage.

"Whoever it bloody was, I'll tear their bloody 'ead off! I'll bloody teach 'em they can't mess wiv the biggest ignoramus in town!"

As his daughter barely contained a snicker, the elder Dotterel sighed and gently said, "Er, DS – you do realise that an ignoramus isn't a type of dinosaur?"

"Them big monsters on Jurastic Park? No?" He stopped pacing and stood baffled and blinking.

"No, son. It… well, it means 'idiot'."

Mills looked like he was chewing a golf ball sized wad of gum, his jaw worked so hard without sound coming out. He fair charged from the room, clearly intent on doing violence to someone, somewhere.

"He's been calling himself that for a couple of weeks, and of course no-body's dared say anything. Oh, it's just been too delightful for words!" laughed the white haired woman.

Dotterel turned to his daughter. "You might have told him sooner."

She shrugged. "I suppose so, but it was funny to watch."

"That's not a very Christian attitude, dear," he said, but his indulgent smile belied any criticism of Victoria. "Go after him, please. See if his anger can be directed somewhere that's useful to us. This might be a good time tae send him to confront MacAdam with your friend Lachlan."

"Deal with that wretched Black Elf once and for all," snarled the woman.

"If needs be. I'd nursed a slim hope that the widow Lindsay might have offered some help, but I see now that it's time tae take firmer action."

 The aspiring politician smiled and nodded. She was quite in favour of that idea. Carefully changing her expression to one of earnest concern, she went out after the infuriated Englishman.

 He was ready to be dangerous – even more so than usual. All that was needed was to steer him. That wouldn't be difficult.

.o0o.

37 UP, DOWN AND GONE

The three Australians had just arrived back at the distillery to find Auld Wullie Bromleigh waiting for them in the car park.

"John B.! I'm glad ye're here. I would ha' called ye otherwise. I need ye tae come wi' me," he said gesturing towards his old Rover.

The wizard looked at his equally baffled companions.

"Sounds urgent, babe. You go – I'll see you back at the house. Won't I, Mr. Bromleigh?" Elizabeth added pointedly.

"Och aye, aye – in a wee while. Noo we must awa'," said the old man in uncharacteristic agitation.

Stewart gave Q a quick kiss. "Take care, JB," she whispered.

Wasting no time, the two men climbed into the Cyclops and took off out of the car park.

"The old thing's got a fair turn of speed when necessary," observed Wilko.

Elizabeth looked concerned. "Both the car *and* the driver. It's the 'necessary' bit that worries me."

To John B.'s surprise their destination turned out to be a small mooring on the outskirts of the village. A little skiff was tied up at the miniature dock. Auld Wullie had said nothing during the brief drive, and his passenger had respected the silence, but as they clambered into the craft the Australian felt compelled to seek answers.

In clipped sentences as they rowed the old man explained that he'd missed a call on his mobile from Arsaidh MacAdam. The message left by the Black Elf indicated it was urgent, but when Bromleigh had tried to return the call only a few minutes later the phone wasn't answered.

"And the reason we're going by boat?"

"If the wee man's gone oot in his *currach* it's likely his phone wouldnae work. This way we'll know straight away if it's yet moored below his hoos – michty hard tae see from above."

Stewart nodded in understanding. He remembered the topography of MacAdam's home, clinging limpet-like to the cliff side.

The *currach* was tied up in the little cove that Arsaidh's home overlooked. That meant there was some other reason for the Sith Dubh not answering Auld Wullie's calls. The two men looked up the cliff.

"Ye'll have tae climb," observed the old distiller.

A clear and unpleasant memory of a cliff climb in Hawaii jumped sharply into John B.'s mind. He'd been lucky to survive that, and still bore scars on his feet from the experience. Still, this was less of a distance, and looked somewhat easier. The bottom of a rope ladder dangled tantalizing-ly several metres above.

With a shrug he set off, picking hand and footholds that may have been natural or may have been cut so long ago their edges had lost any sign of human manufacture. He realised that the climb down would be more chal-lenging, with the 'steps' not visible as they were on the ascent. Growing more confident, he persisted with climbing the rock face itself even after he'd reached the bottom of the rope ladder, and very shortly found himself standing on a ledge. MacAdam's home was a few more metres above.

John B. noticed a length of metal poking out from a narrow horizontal cleft in the rock. It turned out to be a long gaff pole, a strangely angled hook at one end. What looked like two elderly iron railroad spikes pro-truded from the stone under the cleft. Weathered to the same colour as the dark rock, they were effectively camouflaged.

The wizard smiled. The Black Elf certainly protected his privacy. With a jolt of concern for the dark man, Stewart set about clambering up the rope ladder to the seaward side of the hut. The rope was old and creaked alarmingly under the Australian's weight – he was considerably heavier than the man who usually availed himself of it.

With considerable relief he arrived at a small flat area, fringed with shrubs. This was Arsaidh's equivalent of a back yard, or perhaps his back porch overlooking the cove and sea that was his real 'back yard'.

The seaward door was closed. John B. knocked, and called Arsaidh's name. No reply. He opened the door, unsurprised to find it had no lock.

A few paces into the hut were enough to reveal what the wizard already suspected. The Black Elf appeared to be sitting comfortably in his wicker chair, his clasped hands resting in his lap. The small man's chin was on his chest as if he were asleep, but there was no rise and fall of that chest.

Stewart checked for a pulse, and held a glass in front of the dark face looking for any sign of a breath. Gently he opened one of MacAdam's eyes. Blank. Lifeless.

On the small table beside the wicker chair was the mobile phone that hadn't been answered. John B. picked it up to pocket the device. Auld Wullie would know what to do with it. As he did he realised that there was an envelope under the phone – an envelope marked "Mister Stewart" in small neat handwriting.

Inside the envelope he found a letter, in the same formal hand. Thoughtlessly dropping the envelope, he stood and read.

> *"Dear Mister Stewart.*
> *My thanks for your kindness, and efforts to help me. They are not, and will not be forgotten.*
> *I am old and not as strong as I was. I know that continuing to fight at this time is beyond me, and so I will be on my way. I require neither grieving nor revenge.*
> *I am the last of my line here, but we will not soon be forgotten, and the emptiness that consumes Maclean at the forfeiture of his clan's power is shall be a great comfort to me.*
> *As to she whom he serves, she is as beyond my power as I am*

Stewart looked again at the small still figure in the wicker chair. The letter made little sense to him, although he had the feeling that it should. He remembered the Sith Dubh's earlier comment: "The events of legend have happened, but not yet to me."

He heard the sound of shale skittering against the door of the hut. Someone was making their way down the treacherous path from the road above. Probably Maclean, or Mills, or both.

His assumption was correct. The Dotterels' two stand-over men had just arrived in the accountant's bright yellow Volvo, having bickered their way from the village. Victoria had called Maclean in Bowmore and instructed him to collect Mills from her father's house. The strategy she'd discussed with him earlier was to be put into action. MacAdam was to be forced to reveal what he knew about an ancient document of great religious significance – an object of great value, as she described it, without giving away too much detail. Lachlan was to use his brain, DS allowed to give free rein to his brawn and already explosive temper.

The wizard folded the letter and slipped it into a pocket of his jeans alongside the phone, forgetting about the envelope on the floor. He gave the earthly shell of Arsaidh MacAdam the Dark Elf a respectful small bow and then hurried out the back door.

About three metres down the rope ladder, he stepped off onto the small ledge. He grabbed the long gaff pole. Reaching up with the pole he managed to unhook the top of the ladder and draw it down. Best to not leave a means of being followed. Clearly this was the means Arsaidh had used for his own security. Hearing the sound of MacAdam's door being kicked in – that would be Mills, he thought, not even checking to find it was unlocked - he attached the ladder to the iron spikes and continued his descent.

Auld Wullie sat in the skiff, drawing on his pipe. As John B. had dropped the ladder Bromleigh had caught its tail and pulled it into the little boat. He offered a gnarled hand to help the younger man's balance as he reached the last rungs and stepped aboard. The two men gripped the rope sides and yanked hard. As they'd hoped, the old rope above, adequate for the light weight of the Sith Dubh, snapped and the ladder tumbled down.

Bromleigh's long even strokes propelled the skiff away around the point quickly, well before it occurred to either Maclean or Mills to look out the square cut holes that passed for windows over the water.

"All done?" asked Auld Wullie.

"Arsaidh's not with us any more. He left me a note. Said you'd know what to do 'on his behalf'. That make sense to you?"

"A mickle, no' a lot. Enough. All things have their time – all things and all men. But I've long suspected tha' may mean something a bit different for the Sith Dubh an' his ilk, just as it does for the likes o' us."

Stewart waited for some further explanation but none was forthcoming. The phrase 'the likes o' us' in particular sat in his mind like a small frog in a whisky glass, defying understanding of why it was there.

Meanwhile Mills and Maclean had found the Black Elf's lifeless form sitting in his chair. Mills frisked the body, unconcerned about roughly handling the corpse. At the same time Maclean began a rapid but futile search of the hut for anything of value. DS trod on the envelope marked 'Mr. Stewart'. He heard the paper crinkle, picked it up and pocketed it with a growl.

Neither finding anything resembling the 'treasure' they'd been sent for, the two men went out onto the small flat area at the back of the hut.

The accountant smirked and said, "It's a pity he's already deid, hey DS? You might have been a chance in a fight wi' him. Victoria tells me you've been coming up a little *short* yourself in your last few rounds!"

"Don't you bloody laugh at me!" barked Mills and slapped a backhanded blow across the other man's face.

Lachlan Maclean reeled backwards, and plummeted headfirst down into the little cove Stewart and Bromleigh had so recently vacated.

Mills peered down and saw the figure of his erstwhile partner bob to the surface and float face down.

"Bugger. Didn't mean for that to 'appen," muttered DS. "I'll have to tell the Reverend the Sith Dubh managed it some'ow. Magic or somesuch."

He strode back through the hut and scrambled back up the slope to the Volvo. The fact that the keys were still in Maclean's pocket was only a temporary inconvenience to a man of Mills' experience. He drove off, grumbling to himself. He wasn't having a good day. It never occurred to him that Maclean's and MacAdam's had been worse.

.o0o.

38 COMES A TIME

There was a deep and thoughtful silence inside the Cyclops as she was driven away from the skiff's mooring. Auld Wullie had read Arsaidh's final note after the pair had come ashore. If he had a clear understanding of what the Sith Dubh had meant, he didn't share it with John B.

The wizard wasn't sure if the old distiller was being deliberately obtuse, or if he genuinely thought that the Australian understood the message. He was however aware of a great solemnity about Bromleigh, and didn't push any questions.

Instead of going to the Hines' guesthouse they went straight to see April. John B. was made comfortable in the front room, then Auld Wullie ushered his wife into the kitchen. Whatever was said there was said in hushed tones that didn't carry – the quietest conversation Stewart had known April to have.

If there was any mistiness in either pair of eyes when the old couple emerged, John B. determinedly didn't notice. April bore whatever her husband had said to her with stoic calm. The wizard had a sense that news she'd long expected had finally been delivered.

"Would ye be so kind as tae drive me doon tae ma wee boat, an' then bring the car back tae April please, John B.?" Auld Wullie asked quietly.

"Of course. I'll – er… I'll wait for you in the car," the Australian replied, reaching out to accept the key.

He spent only a very few minutes drumming pensive fingers on the wooden dashboard before the old master distiller arrived and wordlessly settled onto the passenger side of the leather bench seat.

It didn't take long until the Cyclops pulled up beside the little dock.

John B. turned to squarely face the man beside him, who now looked something beyond merely old. "I'll not be coming back to pick you up, will I?"

"Nae. I'll nae be back this time, ye ken. I've work tae do oot there," Bromleigh said, pointing out towards the tiny offshore islands. "An' awa'… somewhere north I think. Then west. I'm no' the Navigator, alas."

The navigator, not *a* navigator – the distinction nestled in a corner of John B.'s mind, together with a recollection of a man in Hawaii who'd been called by exactly that title.

"There's work to be done here too, you know," the wizard observed.

"Aye, I ken that right enough, but noo it isnae ma job tae interfere in these things. That's yuir responsibility."

Just for a moment John B. was struck by another recollection, this time of a conversation in Alice Springs with an old black healer.

"Alright. I won't pretend to understand. Should I know more about what Arsaidh MacAdam wrote to me?"

Auld Wullie looked uncertain, but only for a moment. "If ye dinna know noo… well, perhaps in time. When ye need tae. But here an' noo, yuir place is on this island. Take this," he said, handing over a small blue bottle he drew from a pocket of his fawn vest.

Thinking it a final shared dram, Stewart went to uncork the bottle. Bromleigh quickly grabbed his hand. "Wheesht, mon! Dinna drink it! Ye'll ken what it's for when the time comes!"

John B. sighed. He was aware of a great deal of pressure of expectation, and of some significant gaps in the knowledge he was expected to have. He slid the bottle into a pocket of his jeans.

Auld Wullie looked back towards the village. He quietly said, "Perhaps ma work is nearing an end at last – unlike yers, ma friend, I'm sorry. I'm muckle sure I'll be back some day, one way or another. Of all the distillations, all the spirits in the world, this yin is closest tae ma heart."

'Whisky, or April?' wondered Stewart.

The two men shook hands as the old man opened the car door. "Look oot fer the lassies, aye? Mine an' yers."

"Aye. I will. Godspeed, my friend."

"Fare well, John B."

*

As Mills drove into Sron Dubh it dawned on him that being seen driving Lachlan Maclean's car was probably not a good idea. It was widely known that the accountant owned the car. There were very few Volvos seen on the island, and none other with the same dazzling sunflower colour. All in all, hard to miss, and someone would probably soon ask awkward questions about its (late) owner.

He was nearing the distillery when that thought crossed his mind. Convenient. He swung the Volvo into the car park. Ah – ideal! There was the silver Rover that he knew those bloody Australians were getting around in. He brought the bright yellow car to a stop right behind Anastasia, jumped out and went to work.

The Rover 75 was designed to be a difficult vehicle to steal. But while DS Mills was not the most intellectually gifted man on Islay, there were certain talents he'd learned to excel at. Car theft was one of them. Even so, the task took him a little time. Almost but not quite enough for him to be caught.

Jazz had finished work and was just walking out of the main building, followed by Wilko and Elizabeth, when Anastasia raced by.

At least the engineer managed to exclaim, "Hey!" as the silver car passed. Wilko's mouth opened and closed but no sound came out. It was never a good look for him. Stepping out first, Jazz had recognised the driver while the others only saw the back of the departing vehicle.

"It was that bugger Mills! He's nicked my bloody car!" she shouted. The three stood watching helplessly as the rented Rover disappeared from view.

Casting about for ideas of what to do next, they looked around the car park. Wilko knew not to expect to see the black four wheel drive. He'd kept to himself the story of its demise – hindsight had left him none too proud of his actions, even as provoked as they'd been. Now the car Jazz was responsible for had been stolen, evidently as a replacement. It was almost enough to make him believe in karma, not that he would admit to it. Too much like believing in magic!

But Jazz did recognise the bright yellow Volvo parked right behind where Anastasia had been. Storming over to it she snapped, "This is Maclean's car! He must be here somewhere too. I didn't see him with Mills… Hey – it's not locked. I reckon I could… wait a minute… that's odd."

"What is?" asked Elizabeth, arriving at her friend's side. Wilko was approaching more cautiously. He had a bad feeling about this.

The engineer pointed to some wiring hanging untidily from under the dashboard.

"I was going to have a go at hotwiring it and going after that bugger Mills, but it looks like someone's already beaten me to it," she said.

The Tasmanian, hearing this, first looked thoughtful and then concerned. "Mills isn't clever but I reckon he's got a gutter rat's capacity for self-protection. There's no sign of Lachlan Maclean – I reckon DS has pinched this car first, then decided to do a swap. Taking him up on it's not a good idea. Not only because it's car theft, but if Mills has abandoned this one there must be a good, or rather a bad reason."

The brunette nodded. "I can't fault your logic."

With wrinkled lip Jazz conceded, "Unfortunately, neither can I, honey. I guess my next move better be to report the bloody theft, and hope there's someone on the island who'll do something about it."

Reluctantly she walked away from the yellow car. Wilko took her hand.

"We'll think of something," he said.

"You better believe it," agreed Elizabeth, putting a supportive hand on the Englishwoman's shoulder. "And you can bet JB will have something to say about it, too."

Jazz smiled her gratitude. "Maybe he can wish it back to me, eh?"

The Tasmanian bit his tongue.

Hamish Hine was just walking out of the distillery. On hearing the news, he proved to be more than happy to offer the companions a lift home. The short journey contained much dire commentary on DS Mills' character, lineage, and the fate he undoubtedly deserved.

With Jazz and Wilko already delivered to their cottage, Hamish and Elizabeth arrived at the guesthouse just as John B. was getting out of the Cyclops. April had insisted the Australian use the car to get himself home. With a start his girlfriend realised he was getting out of the driver's side of the car. That was odd.

His grim expression and purposeful stride toward the door was startling, too. Clearly he hadn't noticed his beloved and their host. Elizabeth found herself not miffed, but worried.

Once they were all inside and Stewart had related the events of the day she understood his distraction, and knew her worry was justified. When she in turn recounted the theft of Anastasia it was the wizard's turn to look worried.

He didn't know about Maclean's unintended but unlamented death at Mills' hands. Nor did he or Q know about what had happened to 'Black Beauty'.

"It could just be that Mills has slipped his leash and he's in business for himself. I'm absolutely sure it was him I heard breaking into Arsaidh's place. But really, I suspect that sanctimonious bloody 'man of God' has wound him up and sent him out," said John B. bitterly.

"Either him or his bitter and twisted daughter," suggested Elizabeth.

Rhona said nothing to defend either her local clergyman or her likely soon-to-be elected representative. Her chief concern was for her husband's health. The prospect of getting actively involved in the distillery again had livened him up – was it really only that morning he'd set out to volunteer his aid? But this news, and the tense manner of their two guests, were clearly distressing him.

She rubbed her husband's shoulders gently. "Ye should awa' up tae yer bed an' have a wee lie doon, ma pet. Pour yersel' a dram, an' I'll bring ye up a cup o' tea an' a slice."

With a nod, and a weary wave to their guests, Hamish rose from his chair and shuffled to the stairs.

"This is a dark time for oor wee village, an' I fear ye find yuirselves right at the heart o' it. I dinna quite grasp the how or why o' it but I ken ye've set yersel' tae help. I cannae offer mair than a cup o' tea an' ma prayers, but ye've aye got them," the landlady told the Australians softly but earnestly.

"Gratefully received, thank you Rhona," replied Stewart. He turned to his beloved. "A cup of tea and a few deep breaths before we go and see Wilko and Jazz, okay? Something tells me we'll need them before the evening's done."

Lips drawn tight, Elizabeth nodded. A dangerous light flashed in her green eyes.

*

The first element of Mills' report to Gordon and Victoria had been to break the news of Arsaidh MacAdam's death. This drew only irritation from the elder Dotterel. No sense of the pious concern for the small man's soul that might have been expected from a clergyman. Only annoyance that no useful information had been extracted before his passing, and that nothing had been found in the search of his hut.

Describing the fruitless search prompted the Englishman to explain how Lachlan Maclean had gone out the back door of the hut to check outside.

There'd been a scream, Mills said. When he'd rushed out to see what had happened the accountant was gone, with only a greasy mark on the ground to indicate where he'd presumably slipped and fallen to his death.

"Wouldn't surprise me if that bloody elf 'ad set some sort of trap," he said, adding colour to his lie.

If he'd feared that Victoria would be distressed by the loss of her staunchest supporter, such a concern proved groundless. Like her father she was much more irked than grieving. Finding another book-keeper who was quite so malleable would be inconvenient, but certainly not impossible.

Maclean had been an irregular member of the congregation at best, so the Reverend was no more upset than his daughter.

DS continued his tale, explaining that he'd had the clever idea of not leaving Maclean's car near the Elf's hut (so it couldn't be connected to the small man's death), but parking it in the distillery car park. That bloody place was still obviously working, he said disapprovingly.

It was that observation that generated the biggest reaction from the Dotterels. Gordon had intended that the closure of the distillery would be the jewel in the crown of his domination of the moral and spiritual community of Sron Dubh.

"Your hold is slipping, father dear," Victoria said with a note of smugness.

"I… I… I cannot…" He wanted to say that he couldn't agree with his daughter's assessment, but a combination of indignation and a deep-seated inner fear that she was right stopped the words leaving his throat.

"It's that bloody Aussie, I reckon. The one in purple. Fings 'aven't been going right since 'e bloody well arrived," Mills observed sourly, trying to support his mentor.

The Reverend's brow creased. The shaggy outsider had certainly made an impression. And his claims of 'magic'… Magic. Influence. Hmm…

"I think ye may have a point, DS," conceded Gordon after a thoughtful pause. "But I think he is also receiving significant – *support* from within wer own community. An' I think the time has come tae pluck some verra particular weeds from the garden that we tend. MacAdam's defiance has reaped its deserved reward. The same fate must noo descend upon others who ha' set themsel's against my righteous path! They three sisters…"

"The old women? Ye don't think the crones are any threat do ye?" asked Victoria mockingly.

"No' a threat," answered her father with a scowl. "But their intransigence is like a lightning rod that others in the congregation may see deflecting holy wrath. I cannae be havin' this any longer. This night, DS, ye and I shall go oot and deal wi' them directly. The Lord shall guide wer hands and the Godless shall be smited!"

Victoria leaned back in her chair. This was the most animated she'd seen her father outside the pulpit, where she knew his rhetoric and histrionics were carefully calculated. Things were coming to a head, it seemed. Let the old man strike out as he wished. She'd keep a discreet step back from that in case anything went wrong – who knew what Mills was capable of? She would protect her own interests, in her own way.

Dotterel Senior laid his hand on his English acolyte's shoulder and said, "Tonight, ma friend, tonight we shall go oot and gather together these enemies of wer holy path, an' together they shall be struck doon fer all tae see. Victoria, I will have need o' ye in searin' the images o' their example intae the minds o' ma flock such that their example will never be forgotten. We will remain in contact, aye?"

The woman nodded. She knew the 'contact' he meant – a psychic link the two could share when it came to manifesting the power they both possessed. It was a link she knew nobody else was aware existed, nor would have understood if they did. She could assist her father in ridding himself of his 'vexations' without risk to herself or her reputation. Satisfactory. Perhaps even fun.

"Noo, leave me be fer a while, the pair o' ye. I would spend some time in prayer an' meditation. Gather ma strength fer the mighty task tae come," said the Reverend ominously.

 Mills answering smile was unpleasant. He had things of his own to gath-er.

.o0o.

39 THREATS AND CONSEQUENCES

When John B. broke the news of Auld Wullie's departure to Jazz and Wilko their reactions were a mix of shock and concern. It prompted the wizard to realise how little he'd been shocked himself. As much as the old man had seemed to somehow recognise him, Stewart had 'got' Bromleigh in a way that no one else except April did.

To the others, the master distiller's behaviour seemed strange, callous, or even an indication of dementia. To the wizard it was very sad, especially for April, but in a strange way inevitable. He couldn't quite explain that, but he'd found some comfort in the reaction of the woman who'd shortly be calling herself 'the widow Bromleigh'.

A quiet tear or two had been shed but she'd squared her shoulders and said, "Aye, I knew this'd come tae pass. Nowt for it but tae get on, is there John B.? Thank ye fer… well, fer bein' here. Ye've let Auld Wullie do wha' he must."

Jazz and the three Australians had chosen to have their conversation while strolling in the evening air, so as to avoid any eavesdropping by Ishbell. The landlady hadn't said or done anything particularly intrusive or unpleasant for a few days, but she was a looming presence – watching, listening, and most often glowering.

"Like a stranger at a wedding," Elizabeth had observed. "Or a funeral."

All four were rugged against the cold wind that was steadily building. Even John B. had accepted a jacket from Rhona – a tweed coat that 'didnae fit Hamish noo' (and probably hadn't for several years) in colours of heather. Other than his new silk shirt it was probably the nattiest item of clothing the others had ever seen him wear.

"Jeez, it's like the coast of Tasmania - there's teeth in this wind," said Wilko as Jazz snuggled into him.

"And a storm in it too, I think," suggested John B. who walked in a similarly insulatory embrace with Q. "This seems to be a place for them."

They'd been ambling at a leisurely pace, but Jazz slowed even more, evidently deep in thought. She stopped, so the others stopped with her.

"I think… I think we should go visit April," she said hesitantly.

"Pay our respects, sympathies, that sort of thing? Probably a good idea," said Wilko.

The engineer shook her head. "It's more than that, hon. I've got a feeling, and not a good one. About April, *and* her sisters."

The English girl and the wizard in purple exchanged a long thoughtful look. He had the same apprehension. Elizabeth saw the look in both pairs of eyes. With what she knew of her lover's magic, and what she'd learned of the blonde's origins, if they were worried, then she was worried. At her suggestion, they retraced their steps, climbed into the old Rover Cyclops, and with John B. at the wheel headed for the Bromleighs' 'wee hoose'.

They found April dressed ready to go out, as though she'd been expecting them. Red cardigan over a pinkish flannelette shirt and generous fleecy track suit pants – also bright pillar-box red, she finished her ensemble with 'good sensible boots' over woolen socks. Any storm would have to work hard to penetrate that lot.

Although unable to offer any further substance to their misgivings, she grimly agreed with John B. and Jazz.

"We've toil an' trouble in wer path tonight, I fear," she said.

April slid herself onto the front passenger seat of the Cyclops as she had done so often before. If the presence of John B. at the wheel instead of Auld Wullie had any emotional impact on her, she didn't betray it. The other three fitted comfortably in the back of the car, Wilko contentedly in the middle.

The next destination, at April's prompting, was Effie's place. They found her sitting out on her porch, gazing out towards the small islands. Was she watching where her brother-in-law had gone? How far did the Sight extend? A brief touch of her younger sister's hand and a respectful nod were the only expressions of sympathy that the others observed.

"Definitely a storm brewin' I ken," Effie said without glancing at the sky. Somewhere overhead a gull cried out. The middle sister nodded to herself, "Aye. 'Tis time, 'tis time."

Drawing her pale blue cardigan tightly about herself, she gathered up her two black walking sticks and hobbled towards the car. Like April, she wore track suit pants (pastel blue) and brogues over woolly socks. Effie thought flannelette was "unladylike" though, and under her cardigan wore a dark blue knitted top with a lacy collar.

No words of where they were going had been exchanged. Clearly there didn't need to be. Q sat between April and John B. on the front bench seat so that Effie could take up her usual place behind the driver. Wilko was silently impressed at how roomy the old car was proving to be – he was pleasantly but not uncomfortably squeezed together with Jazz.

It wasn't a long drive to Rose's place, just long enough for the middle sister to break the silence by grumbling, "I hope she'll no be difficult. Ye ken she's always been the contrary yin."

To which the younger sister replied, "Ye've been heard tae argue on mair than one occasion."

"Och, never withoot good cause. No' like Rose. Or ye, when the mood takes ye. Stubborn, ye are, April Bromleigh."

"I'm no' stubborn! I'm just... determined."

Further discussion of that point halted when the Cyclops pulled up outside Rose's cottage. All six of them made their way inside, the Australians and Jazz helping the two sisters as unobtrusively as possible.

Calling Rose's lounge room 'crowded' would be a serious understatement. Rose occupied her usual chair, dressed like her sisters in a collection of warm clothes, this time in shades of green. After a few moments of silent stand-off over the other comfortable chair Effie was about to concede to April as an unspoken gesture of sympathy. At the first tilting of her sister's head the youngest of the three dropped herself onto the couch. The webbing under the cushions groaned audibly.

"I ken how yer knees trouble ye, Effie. An' yer hips – ye're best off in the chair, eh?" she said. The youngest sister was only marginally less arthritic, and it would take considerable assistance from John B. and Wilko to get her back out of the low slung couch, but Effie accepted the armchair without further demur.

Elizabeth fitted neatly on the other end of the couch. Jazz and Wilko occupied the chairs they'd brought in from the kitchen, and John B. sat cross-legged on the floor, one hand unconsciously stroking a space where Gem would lay her head.

Once the creaks and groans of settling in were done, it was the wizard who opened the discussion. "Ladies and gentleman, I'm afraid we're at a point where things are about to get nasty. Or perhaps I should say, 'nastier'. I've a very strong feeling that Gordon Dotterel has been up to something for a while, but for whatever reason, he's now going to strike out more directly."

"Well, the reason's obvious, laddie," said April matter-of-factly. "He's bein' challenged. An' aboot bloody time somebody stood up tae him. We've all been agin him, but since ye've come tae the village there's folk startin' tae question the old gowk what hasnae before. He dinna like it, ye ken."

Effie shook her head dolefully and said, "Och, I knew ye were trouble when Auld Wullie was all over ye when ye met."

That took John B. by surprise. "All over me? He said four words."

"That's three more than most would get from ma man," April admitted.

Rose grunted disdainfully. "And two more than Effie's had for years. Still, it's more than her Husht Wullie used tae give tae most people."

"Ma Wullie always had words for me!" objected the middle sister.

Her older sister didn't change expression. "Aye, there's plenty o' folks ha' words for you, Effie Lindsay…"

Stewart, realising he had to break up the characteristic bickering, exclaimed, "Stop it, the three of you! It beats me how three women so like each other can be so lousy at getting on."

"Ooh, I'm nothing like *them*!" said three indignant voices in perfect unison. They glared back and forth at each other.

John B. continued. "We need the three of you to work together. I'm not sure how that happens, or what happens when it does, but I do know Auld Wullie had a lot of respect for what you could do when you co-operate."

That brought a silence from the sisters – part embarrassment, part respect, part thoughtfulness.

Rose nodded, speaking quietly for all of them as the eldest. "Aye. Right enough."

Silence reigned for some time, everyone in the room evidently deep in their own thoughts. The three old women kept glancing between themselves, as if conducting a telepathic conversation. Perhaps on some level that was what was happening. Frequent glances went toward the shaggy man in the purple t-shirt. For his part, John B. appeared to stare at a point in the middle distance, one hand reaching up to hold Q's, the other resting either on the floor or on Gem's back, depending on your perception.

Finally, it was Rose who spoke. "Aye, 'tis tonight when all o' this hurly-burly's tae be done, and a battle lost an' won. It'll no' be here, but. Lassies, we're best awa' ye ken," she said to her sisters.

"Where, then?" asked Effie.

April stroked a pensive chin. "Auld Wullie would go off up intae the hills…" she mused.

A very clear image came into John B.'s head. "I know the place. There's a cave up by a standing stone. Well hidden, dry, and I think probably big enough for all to be safe in, if a wee bit snug. The Still Cave."

"Aye, I'm no' surprised," said April. "I've no' been there but I kenned it existed, right enough."

"Wilko, can you take the ladies in the Rover please? It'll be squeezy, I'm sorry, but you'll manage. I'll give you directions of how to get there and how to get in."

The Tasmanian looked blank. "How do you know…?"

"Auld Wullie showed me. At the time I wondered why – now I reckon I know." Another memory struck him. "There's a wildcat you might find up there – don't trouble with him. I think he's on our side."

Wilko looked skeptical but knew he'd be outnumbered in an argument.

Stewart continued. "I'll go looking for the Reverend, although I suspect I won't have to look very hard. I reckon he'll be looking for us. Or at least he'll have Mills out after us. I can deal with him."

"We can, babe. *We* can. The car will be a bit more comfortable with one less person in it." Elizabeth was clearly not intending to be anywhere other than at John B.'s side, and no one in the group was foolish enough to argue.

As she hauled herself up from her chair Rose said, "Ye dinna have tae go lookin' on foot." She reached into a bowl on the sideboard, and tossed a key to John B. "Ye can ride a motorcycle by the look o' ye."

Stewart grinned as he got to his feet. "Aye, I've been known to." Memories of riding a World War 2 vintage Ariel around Central Australia had brought the grin.

"Oot in the shed there's an auld bike an' sidecar Black Wullie an' I used tae get aboot in."

"Ye've no' still got tha' auld thing?" exclaimed Effie in surprise.

"Why would I no'? There's nowt wrong wi' it. I turn the motor over every noo an' then just tae make sure o' that."

Rose had long shared the late Black Wullie's interest in things mechanical – his name had come as much from the near-constant grease and oil stains on face and hands as his jet black hair. In fact they'd first met over the engine of a recalcitrant Vauxhall she'd been driving.

"Ye cannae be ridin' it, surely?" asked April, astonished at the thought (as were the others whose imaginations conjured up the unlikely image).

"Och, o' course no'. Twas Black Wullie wha' allus drove, but I kenned it were a handy thing tae keep, just in case," Rose explained.

"And so it's turned out," said Elizabeth quickly, hoping to prevent any more argument between the siblings.

The other sisters were helped to their feet. Rose indicated where blankets and cushions were stored, and a pair of large torches. A similar torch was in the Rover, April advised.

With surprising speed given their infirmity the sisters made their way out to the car. Rose and Effie occupied the back seat. Jazz had considered sitting between them as a diplomatic barrier, but she clearly fitted more easily between Wilko and April. The Cyclops had a column shift, so there was no awkward gearstick for her to straddle, and she could snuggle close beside her boyfriend.

Leaning through the driver's window, John B. went over the directions once more.

"It's okay John B., we've got it. Don't worry – we'll get everyone there safe," assured Jazz as she squeezed the driver's knee. "We better get going before this weather makes up its mind to go bad. You guys take care of yourself, and give that bloody preacher one for me, eh?"

With a final nod of agreement, Wilko got the old Cyclops rolling. John B. and Elizabeth waved farewell and turned to walk down past the side of the cottage towards the wooden shed.

Unbeknownst to the two Australians, just as they passed the front of the cottage they were spotted by the occupants of an approaching station wagon. It was Gordon Dotterel's car, with Mills a restless bundle of tension in the passenger seat. The Reverend stopped the vehicle in front of the cottage, where their quarry couldn't see them.

The clergyman gripped the steering wheel tightly, knuckles whitening as his mind raced. A plan was suddenly taking shape in his mind. He'd paid a couple of fruitless visits to the Ellison abode before, and had a good idea of where the man he now considered his nemesis was going.

"DS, I want ye to follow that old car that just took off. That will be the old women, trying to flee the Lord's wrath. See that they don't succeed, and I dinna mind how ye accomplish that," he said meaningfully as both men got out of the wagon.

The Englishman's smile was full of malicious anticipation. He may have liked one more chance to get square with the guy in the purple shirt, but he'd willingly settle for taking his anger out on others. That would hurt that bloody 'magician' anyway, even if he did manage to survive whatever his Reverence had planned for him.

Before Mills departed, Dotterel on impulse reached into the back of the wagon. He took out a jerry can full of petrol he habitually carried in case of emergency. Trusting in divine assistance was one thing, but it was important to be prepared, as another man of moral certainty once said.

By the time the station wagon moved off, John B. and Elizabeth were inside the old shed. It took both of them to haul the heavy canvas off the bike – Rose had evidently been lifting one corner just to regularly turn the engine over.

The wizard whistled in appreciation. Despite the canvas a good layer of dust had built up, apart from around the areas where Rose had been carrying out her routine.

"I was expecting something English, but this is an Indian Chief – the pride of Massachusetts. Built just after the War, by the look of her. What a beauty…"

Q shrugged. A bike was a bike, although this one probably did look pretty snazzy when clean – the sidecar sported nice chrome trim (speed lines they were called) that would show up nicely against the black.

As she helped fold the canvas she said, "Just as long as it helps us find the preacher man, babe."

"Oh, it's alright. I've found ye!" came a triumphant voice from behind them.

They barely had time to turn their heads before the shed door was slammed shut and bolted.

The little wooden structure was perfect for the Reverend's sudden scheme. It was small and would burn quickly. He threw petrol from the jerry can over the door and as much other exposed timber as he could see, carelessly slopping some on his pants, shoes and the ground as well.

John B. and Elizabeth had dashed for the door as soon as it slammed. It wasn't as flimsy as it looked. The wood shook but didn't break as the wizard's shoulder crashed in to it.

"There shall be no escaping the justice o' the Lord!" Dotterel shouted.

"JB! I smell petrol!" Q whispered urgently.

"Yeah, I noticed. Not surprised," her lover replied in a similar undertone. He raised his voice to shout to the preacher outside. "I wish your fiery plan would fail!"

Even as the words left John B.'s lips, the first spatterings of rain started to fall. Startled, Dotterel looked up. Could he really…? No! This was no more than a coincidental drizzle. No storm yet. Not heavy enough to stop the shed from burning and the flames consuming his enemies. And besides, the matches he carried were waterproof! The circumstance was enough to inflame his desperation though.

"Heathen!" the Reverend shouted. "Thou shalt nae defy me! Thou shalt burn, and my flock shall see thy death!"

 He started to mutter a chant as he stared at the locked building, searing the image into the minds of everyone in Sron Dubh who'd ever suffered any of his dreams of hellfire. His power amplified by that of his daughter, it didn't matter whether his targets were asleep or not – the image sprang up sharply behind their eyes.

 It was almost enough for Wilko to swerve off the road. Jazz was in no position to help him, but April was unaffected and was able to reach over and keep a firm hand on the steering wheel.

"Hold on, laddie," she said grimly. "I ken we're nearly there – you work the pedals an' I'll keep us on the road!"

 The unconventional driving arrangement worked for the brief time that was necessary, even through the woods and along the rough narrow track, although clipping the occasional tree or bush. They'd soon arrived at the point that Auld Wullie had taken John B. to, and that the wizard had then described.

 Awkwardly the five clambered out of the Rover, each dealing with their own infirmity – the sisters' painful arthritic limbs, Jazz and Wilko struggling to see past the images that were superimposed on their brains. Images of a locked barn door, and the threat of impending fire. Making the best speed they could, they struggled up the hillside. Light rain made the grass slippery – the sisters' walking sticks did sterling service as hiking aids. As the gloom gathered Wilko hoped that Stewart's explanation of 'lining up' the stones in the paddock would make sense by torchlight. It was hard enough to see!

In Rose's shed John B. had found a sledgehammer. He swung it at the door. The blow succeeded in smashing a hole in the timber, but not a large one. Worse, though – the head flew off the aged implement and landed outside, hitting the damp ground at the Reverend's feet with a squelch.

Dotterel jumped at the flying hammerhead, but when it landed harmlessly he began to laugh. It wasn't an altogether sane laugh.

"Do ye see? Do ye see? Your magic cannae harm me! I am protected by the Almighty!"

The Australians watched through the new hole in the door as he struck at his own chest. Glaring at them he controlled his voice, and in the stentorious tones he'd so often used from the pulpit said, "I have known this since birth. It is my heritage, my power and my responsibility. My given name is not Gordon Dotterel – it is Gordeep. 'God's light' I was named and so I am!"

John B. slapped his own forehead and exclaimed, "Oh spare me! Another one!"

Q looked sideways at him. "Another what?"

"Ever since I got that whack on the head," Stewart explained, "I keep running into nutjobs who want to be gods, or think they already are."

"No!" shouted Dotterel, hearing the conversation through the hole in the shed door. "I am a servant of God! I serve with holy fire!"

Stewart shook his head. "Funny – I said this same thing to your hard case daughter a little while ago. I don't know about your God, but mine's a god of love." Q squeezed his hand as he continued. "You are one more egocentric ratbag with some kind of power who gets his kicks out of using it over other people."

Dotterel glared at the shed with eyes wide. His 'transmission' of the scene was breaking up as his concentration on that task was compromised. Back at the manse Victoria sneered. She could feel her father's agitation but either couldn't or wouldn't help him.

The Reverend railed at John B. "And are you so different? You and your 'magic' you claim to have? Your witchcraft? A means to control others!"

Stewart stared, meeting the preacher's gaze through the door, and after a pause slowly answered, "No. No, I really don't think so. That's *really* not what I'm about. I might not know exactly what's the story with this talent I've got, but I do know I've got more respect for people than that."

Snarling in a tone that DS Mills would have approved of, Dotterel took two paces toward the shed, taking a match from the waterproof box and preparing to strike it.

Suddenly he appeared to trip over something unseen - his own feet perhaps. Landing awkwardly on his knees the preacher felt a sharp pain in his wrist. He thought he must have sprained it somehow, despite his hand not hitting the ground.

Through the hole in the door John B. could see the outline of a collie in the drizzle – Gem was biting the hand holding the matches. The matchbox fell from Dotterel's grasp and landed on the wet ground.

Elizabeth had found a crowbar among Black Wullie's old tools. She pushed past Stewart, saying, "You get the bike going, babe – I'll get the door!"

She found the right spot and the right leverage to pry the door enough to rip the bolt off.

Still on his knees the Reverend Dotterel looked up and screamed in impotent rage as the motorcycle roared past him. He raised an arm to shake his fist when the breath caught in his throat. He was momentarily aware of a terrible pain in his chest, and then he toppled forward, the unused match still squeezed between thumb and forefinger. The steadily increasing rain drenched his body, soaking the spilled petrol.

Gordeep Dotterel didn't end in fire – not in this world, anyway.

*

Trailing well behind, Mills had seen the old Rover turn off but took a little time to locate the trail in the woods. It was only by luck he was able

to find the rough track his quarry had taken. The awkward 'co-operative driving' of Wilko and April had led to them clipping a tree as they'd
turned. The lights of the station wagon caught the crushed bracken and
the newly exposed wood where the solid old Cyclops had torn off some
bark.

"Reckon 'is Reverence must be lookin' after me," chuckled Mills as he
turned down the track.

It wasn't long before he found the Cyclops parked in the little clearing.
He jumped from the wagon and looked around, cursing the gloom and the
rain. 'Should have brought a torch,' he thought.

The obvious direction was up, he realised, so took off up the gentle slope.
His big Army boots slipped on the wet ground, causing some sharp twing-
es in the ankle that was considerably sorer than he'd let on.

The Englishman was hobbling by the time he reached the crest, but the
pain was forgotten when he saw the light of torches in the paddock below.

Half running, half skidding he descended to the paddock. There was a
fearsome *yowl* from somewhere nearby as he ran.

The five fugitives stopped sharply and looked around. It was the first
sound other than their own passage that they'd heard.

"That were a wildcat!" said Rose.

Wilko's eyes darted anxiously. "John said there was one around here, and
that we shouldn't disturb it."

"Aye, they're *kelpies* best no' disturbed!" agreed April emphatically.

With their own movement ceased, they suddenly heard the sound of running, heavily booted feet. Jazz swung a torch in the direction of the noise.

Mills stopped suddenly. The light had prevented him colliding with the
edge of one of the standing stones. He'd been dimly aware of its mass,

but not the actual shape. 'I'm bein' looked after again – thanks Rev!' he thought.

He raised a pistol at the girl holding the torch. Bracing his back against the monolith, he waved the gun, making it clear he was covering the whole group.

Grinning evilly Mills said, "I'm glad I brung an automatic. Plenty of bullets for the whole bloody lot of ya."

Remembering the weapons he'd thrown in the sea and the peat bog, Wilko glared and asked, "How many of those bloody things have you got?"

"Hah! I'm a collector, I am."

"Pity you didn't just stick with stamps," said Jazz drily.

There was another loud feline cry. Mills' glance flicked towards where it had come from. Wide eyes, close to the ground, reflected torchlight. The gunman fired in their direction – there was a glimpse of a striped furry form leaping away.

"Hah – you're a lot less agile than that bloody fing anyway," barked DS, returning his attention to his real targets.

The three sisters had shuffled together and were standing shoulder to shoulder, saying nothing but glaring at Mills with a collective gaze that could have melted steel.

Jazz and Wilko stepped in front of the old women defensively.

"You get to die first," said the Englishman happily, selecting the girl as his first target.

Before he could squeeze the trigger the wildcat screeched again and dived out of the darkness, claws raking at his leg. Mills swore and batted at the beast with his gun hand. It leapt away safely, leaving blood to well from the man's calf and seep into his already rain-soaked trouser leg.

"Bloody animal! I'll deal with you after this lot!" he roared.

At the same moment Rose was quietly remarking, "Tha's three times yon stripey cat has howled."

Her sisters nodded in unison.

Jazz wasn't about to stand there and be shot. As she tensed herself for a desperate spring at the gunman Mills brought the automatic up in her direction. Just as Wilko started to lunge there was a terrific crack of thunder.

A bolt of lightning struck the standing stone. There was a blinding flash and a fearful noise. Mills was flung to the ground. Stunned, he didn't even realise that the stone had sheared in two with the impact. The top half of the ancient monument seemed to jump, and crashed down onto Reverend Dotterel's most faithful follower.

The hand still clutching the gun was all that was left to be seen.

"Noo there's a thing ye dinna see every day," said Effie mildly.

April made a *tsk-tsk* sound. "Great pity aboot yon stone," she observed.

"One o' the stones in the Ring o' Brognar in the Orkneys was struck the same way, ye ken. The Wounded Stone, it's called. I read aboot it," explained Rose, as if informing a tour group.

The Tasmanian was considerably less sanguine. He was trying very hard not to be sick. Jazz put an arm round his shoulders and turned him into an embrace.

"Thank you for trying to jump in front of me, honey," she said softly into his ear. With her kiss his stomach settled.

From somewhere in the dark sharp ears might detect a contented purr from a brindled throat.

"I think we might get oot o' this weather, eh?" suggested April. "Do ye ken how tae get intae this cave o' Auld Wullie's?"

Shaking himself, Wilko recalled John B.'s instructions.

As the rock 'door' swung open, all five were surprised at how large the 'Still Cave' was. It had evidently been used as a meeting place of sorts, with ledge seats cut into the stone walls. Presumably folk had gathered to sample the products of the succession of stills over the years. The most recent contraption was visible in a corner. Empty though, as if Auld Wullie had known he wouldn't be needing it again.

"We'd better wait here till the storm passes," said Wilko quietly.

Bemused but watchful, he was holding tight to Jazz. The tension was catching up with her. At moments she'd vibrate like a harp string in his arms.

The cushions and blankets were arranged to make everyone as comfortable as possible.

Well swaddled, Rose said grimly, "This is nae over ye ken, but oor part in it's done."

Effie sighed in agreement. "It'll be a long wait till morning." It was an observation, not a complaint.

The youngest sister shrugged and replied, "Och, we'll ken when tis time, right enough."

All three grey heads promptly bowed onto ample chests. Within moments it seemed the sisters were either in a trance or sleeping. It was hard for Wilko and Jazz to tell.

Satisfied that the 'door' was securely closed against the weather or any other marauders the Tasmanian turned off the torch. The woman he loved nestled in against him.

Gazing out towards the paddock and the fractured stone, Wilko softly said, "Thanks, cat." It was as close to a mystical moment as he'd let himself get.

.oOo.

In the manse, Victoria's sneer had been replaced by a look of anger. She'd found some amusement in her father's frustration but had expected that, with her assistance, he would prevail and the irritating Australian's fiery death would be in and on the minds of the local population.

She'd maintained her 'link' with him only up to the point when the motorcycle had roared past him, so hadn't shared in the moment of his demise. Perhaps though she'd shared in some of the unraveling of his mental state, because what she did next could hardly be called rational.

Eyes closed, a murmured chant on her lips, she reached out to the people of Sron Dubh. It wasn't a call, it was a command. A loud insistent instruction in the authoritative voice that had haunted their dreams.

"Come tae the cliff top! Come tae the point of Sron Dubh! Come now!" she repeated over and over.

The order burned into the brains of the villagers, asleep or awake. Her always considerable power, fuelled further by rage, was irresistible. Across the village folk rolled or struggled or fell from their beds. Others turned away from whatever they'd been doing, eyes glazed.

Like a small phalanx of zombies they walked at as brisk a pace as they were able out of their homes and cottages. The population converged on the slope leading to the top of the dark point that gave the village its name. Some had thrown coats on from habit, or autopilot, others were still in their sleepwear. All were so deep in Victoria's thrall that they were heedless of the rain and flashes of lightning.

Across the village there was only a handful of people unaffected by the hypnotic call. One such was Rhona Hine, who'd spent hours fretting. She'd alternately look out the window to the spot where her guests had been parked, and at the bed where Hamish tossed restlessly in his sleep.

When Victoria's mental command came it fell on Rhona's mind like rain on a tin roof. The landlady was far too focused to be affected, especially when she saw her husband starting to struggle out of bed.

"Here, pet – ye dinna want tae be oot on a night like this," she said as she put a tumbler of whisky into his hand. Instinct more ingrained than the authority from his dreams made him raise the glass to his mouth and sip at the 'water of life'.

Unprotesting, Hamish allowed himself to be led to the kitchen table. As he sat, half aware of savouring the single malt, Rhona quickly grilled some potato scones and served them.

She pulled up a chair and sat beside the love of her life. The food and whisky were effective distractions, but it was really her own presence that held Hamish safely from Dotterel's malign influence. Rhona may not have had the Sight, but she had a pretty good imagination. Whatever was going on outside, she was determined that neither she nor Hamish would be involved.

She was sure that their houseguests, John B. and Elizabeth, would be in the thick of it. That thought comforted her. There was something about that couple that inspired confidence, even in the face of nameless ominous threat.

*

John B.'s intention had been to go to the Still Cave. But as he steered the big old bike in that direction he found himself swerving and braking to avoid people walking across the road in front of him.

In their trance the locals were making no move to avoid any traffic, going around obstacles like automatons. The wizard slowed down dramatically. Just as well – Lush Wullie Barclay strode onto the road and almost landed on top of Q in the sidecar: not a situation she would have appreciated.

Stewart brought the Indian to a stop at the side of the road.

"There's no reaction from any of them. It's like they're sleepwalking," said Elizabeth.

"Aye, and we know how dangerous sleep can be around here," agreed John B.

The brunette looked back over her shoulder. "Do you think we should go back and deal with the Reverend once and for all?" she asked, unaware of Dotterel's fatal heart attack.

Stewart shook his head, raindrops flicking from his shaggy curls. He'd accepted a rough trim to make the areas singed in the tenement fire less obvious, but there was still plenty of hair.

"Looks like everyone's heading in the same direction. I reckon we'd better do likewise. Whatever the big attraction is, it's where I think we need to be, pretty lady."

Q pushed a lock of wet hair off her face. The rain wasn't heavy but in the open sidecar it was enough to be annoying.

"The preacher's daughter?" she asked as Lanky Wullie McPhee marched past. A flash of lightning illuminated his bony frame, incongruously clad in striped shorts and a string vest.

The wizard nodded, and got the Indian rolling slowly again. He was content to follow behind the procession rather than plough through it. There was a loud clap of thunder – unbeknownst to the two Australians it attended the bolt of lightning that struck not far away, ending the threat of DS Mills.

Suddenly John B. accelerated. It had dawned on him where they were headed for. Was Victoria Dotterel twisted enough to lead everyone over the cliff like lemmings? In the sidecar, Elizabeth whistled softly in appreciation at her lover's deft steering of the machine through the gathering crowd. Picking up on Stewart's urgency, the realization of their evident destination struck her, too.

As they neared the cliff top it became impossible to safely maneuver the big bike and sidecar through the milling villagers who made no move to get out of their way. The wizard stopped the Chief at the side of the road and jammed the key into a pocket of his jeans, feeling it clink against the glass of the little bottle he still carried.

The couple started to run, overtaking the villagers who moved at as brisk a walk as their bodies were capable of. Some were familiar, some less so. They spotted Scuzzy Wullie, Postie Mary, several familiar faces from the distillery, and Nursie Mary, blindly heading towards the doctor who'd chanced to be among the first at the cliff. There was Ms. Chisholm, red hair plastered down by the drizzle, marching near Giddy Mary. For once the girl wasn't being hectored, although she wasn't aware of it.

As they neared the top they passed an expensive German sedan. Victoria had wasted no time positioning herself in readiness for her flock of sheep.

The aspiring politician stood at the top of the point, comfortably wrapped in a waterproof white fur-lined coat while 'her people' assembled in their soaking nightwear. She was illuminated by the flame of a hurricane lamp she'd set on top of the small memorial cairn that commemorated all those lost at sea off Sron Dubh over many years.

The sleepwalkers weren't going over the cliff. Not yet. They were standing in a shambolic mob, the front of which was a little away from the cairn. The later arrivals simply stopped and stood when they reached the back of the 'congregation'. John B. and Elizabeth pushed their way to the front. It wasn't difficult – nobody offered any resistance. Indeed, they didn't appear to even be noticed. All eyes were on the lamp and the white figure beside it.

Victoria held up an imperious hand as the Australians approached.

"Stop where you are, you two!"

The man in purple obeyed, and grabbed his lover's arm to halt her. The platinum haired woman was unpredictable. Her hold on these people was such that just physically grabbing her would very likely achieve nothing. Nothing good, anyway.

"I figured this would draw you here. You may have succeeded in defying my father. He's…" she paused, probing for her 'link' to the Reverend. If the realization of his death disconcerted her she gave no sign of it. "He was old and weak. I am not, and I will stand for no such defiance."

"Really? What do you propose to do about it?" demanded Elizabeth.

Victoria ignored the brunette and stared at John B. as she answered, "I know your type – I know what makes you tick. You fancy yourself a hero, trying to 'save' these people you scarcely even know."

Stewart tilted his head sideways. "No. Actually I've never thought of myself as a hero. I'm just a simple bloke, who simply doesn't like to see power being abused by anyone."

"Hah! I know you're more than that. Not quite sure what, but I do know your weakness. You won't let anyone suffer on your behalf. But here and now, I tell you they will. Call it a final vengeance for my father. Maybe he couldn't kill you by fire, but I can order you to *throw yourself off this cliff*!"

Stewart stared at her. "You're joking. You must know your spell or whatever it is doesn't work on me…"

"Indeed. Apparently not. But it works on all of these, and I'll simply command them to do my bidding, one by one, until you do. Ishbell Mac-Neill! *Do as you're told!* Walk. Towards the lamp. Off that edge."

Eyes glazed, the landlady stepped forward. Her misfortune was simply to be the closest person to the cliff and thus most convenient for Victoria to exercise her power over. The big hob-nailed boots crunched on the black stones. Skinny Mary didn't react at all as the closest thing she had to a best friend walked away. Gazing straight ahead, Mrs. MacNeill strode over the edge and plummeted to the rocks below.

She didn't utter a word as she walked or as she fell or as she died. Neither did any of the other villagers who stood in the way of any effort John B. or Q might have made to grab the doomed woman. A few, like Doc Wullie, might have twitched or flinched slightly, but not a hand was raised.

"I can send them all after her."

Both the Australians lunged toward the white-clothed figure.

"Hold them!" Victoria commanded. The nearest villagers seized the pair, grabbing limbs and clothes, restraining them by their dead weight.

Dotterel's mouth curled in a satisfied smile. "These people will remember nothing more than I tell them. It'll be like you were never here. Their lives will return to what passes for normal for them. Once I'm in Parliament I'll have a platform – a media presence – to expand my influence. Oh, I don't need to control everyone in the country, but I can and will control enough to rise to whatever level of authority I desire."

"And you desire a lot, I'm sure!" snarled Elizabeth as she wriggled in the grasp of a half-dozen pairs of hands.

"Actually, you're right," admitted Victoria, as casually as if being interviewed by a chat show host. "I think the term is 'striding the world stage'. I think that's worthy of me."

The references to the Reverend in the past tense had sunk into the wizard's awareness. He was surprised, and even a little regretful. Standing very still, John B. growled, "You're a lot more ambitious than your father. All he wanted was a faithful flock. You want the whole wool industry."

"My father was a fool!"

Stewart shook his head. "No he's not. Wasn't. Arrogant, yes. Misguided, I reckon so, and I was determined to stop him messing with people's heads. But I think he genuinely believed in his faith. There's nothing stupid about that. You just use the authority you think it gives you…"

The daughter sneered. "Oh, faith is so last century! He never understood the potential of the power our family has. I do, though."

"What about your sister? Did she? I wish your past would come back to haunt you," said John B. as evenly as he could.

Elizabeth looked over to him and said, "No good appealing to her conscience, babe. I don't think she's got one."

At last, Victoria turned her gaze away from Stewart as if reluctantly acknowledging the existence of the green-eyed woman. The cold smile broadened.

"Seeing you held so nicely I realise – you don't have to jump. You might as well be pushed. *Cast them over the cliff!*" she cried.

The villagers holding the Australians started to surge towards the precipice. Q and John B. struggled and writhed in the collective grasp, being shoved as much as carried toward their doom.

John B. managed to squirm an arm free. Instinctively he pulled Auld Wullie's bottle from his pocket and flung it like a dart at Victoria Dotterel. She flinched slightly as the little blue missile bounced off her white coat.

The glass smashed on the memorial cairn and the contents splashed onto the hurricane lamp. The villagers propelling the two Australians stopped in their tracks. Everyone on the cliff top was staring at the cairn.

A weird light seemed to rise up from the lantern, curling like red smoke. It took on a vague shape. Something like a figure appeared on the cliff edge, from the right angle, a young woman with long red hair.

Eyes wide, Victoria stumbled backwards, desperate to keep away from the hazy form. She just had time to say "Je…" before stepping back off the cliff.

Did the spectral figure push her? Or was it just her appearance that sent Victoria over the edge? John B. neither knew nor cared. He grabbed Q's wrist and pulled her away from the precipice they'd both been far too close to for comfort.

The spectral red-haired figure had vanished as suddenly as she'd appeared. The villagers around them were starting to blink and shake their heads. Those deepest in trance still stood blank-eyed, but others were clearly waking. Just as clearly, they had no idea of where they were, or why. It also became clear that they had no memory of what had just happened, including the deaths of Ishbell MacNeill and Victoria Dotterel.

But there was a sense of relief. Even among the confusion, the cold, and in many cases the embarrassment at their inappropriate attire, there was a feeling of a weight having been lifted. For now though, few amongst the villagers were prepared to meet each other's gaze as they headed for home as quickly as possible.

Soon, John B. and Q were the last ones left by the cairn. Arms around each other, they watched the last of the bemused little crowd disappear into the darkness.

"I'm glad that's over," they both said in unison, then looked at each other in surprise.

"Snap!" said Q with a giggle of relief.

"Great minds think alike," John B. answered before drawing her close for a lingering kiss.

He then carefully picked up the blue glass fragments that were scattered on and beside the cairn, and cast them into the sea.

"What do you reckon Auld Wullie put in there, JB?"

The wizard shrugged. "Wouldn't care to guess, pretty lady. Auld Wullie Bromleigh was a man good with all kinds of spirits."

As he removed the hurricane lamp he idly patted the top of the cairn. Eventually two more names would be added to the plaque on its side. Perhaps the sudden death of father and spiritual mentor respectively had driven them both to suicide. Who knew? The few who cared reminded themselves that the Lord works in mysterious ways.

.oOo.

41 FINAL RITES

There had been some sore and muddled heads on the Sunday morning after the ceilidh. A week later most of the population of Sron Dubh felt like their skulls were wrapped in cotton wool.

Many slept until midday or beyond. That happened across Islay, in fact. It was the first deep, peaceful sleep that some people had enjoyed for a very long time.

Lanky Wullie slept until lunchtime, without having had so much as a dram before retiring. Craig slept even later, waking refreshed and happy, but startled to find it was three in the afternoon.

Even Scuzzy Wullie slept soundly and eventually woke feeling strangely at peace with the world.

In Bowmore, Gordon and Duncan Macintosh were among the many Ileachs who started the day vaguely disoriented. As the day progressed though, they felt refreshed and invigorated. By mid-week there would be a full and productive workforce back at the Sron Dubh distillery. Robbie Keith's bosses never quite understood what had happened – neither did he – but the business and his career were both back on track.

The detailed plans that Jazz had completed were more than enough for a small team of fitters and plumbers to install a system that would make even the chilliest corners of the workplace much warmer and more comfortable. Nobody was surprised that the English engineer didn't want to stay more than a couple of weeks to supervise the commencement of the work. Many were disappointed, but not surprised.

Aaron Craig likewise was soon his old self, and set about unraveling the knots and undoing the damage that the Dotterels and Lachlan Maclean had done, aided and abetted by his new Administrative Assistant, Giddy Mary.

Some damage would never be undone. Wee Chrissy would never regain his sight. He found work in Glasgow in a call centre, becoming the breadwinner for his family while he learned Braille and worked his way up to management. Kevin Macalpine Junior would ever after walk with a limp, although he did take up a job alongside his father and inspired by Jazz' designs eventually went on to study engineering. Seribreyong Phunket Goom's wife did come to the village and take over the *Curry House*, but as welcome as she was made in the community she felt the loss of her husband for a very long time.

The bodies of both Dotterels, Mills, and Ishbell MacNeill were found, and their deaths labeled as mysterious tragic accidents (although their memorial services were far less well attended than any of them would have hoped).

Despite all that had gone on in preceding days (and weeks and months) and especially the night before, a sizeable congregation turned up at the kirk on Sunday evening. Rhona was there, accompanied by a remarkably hale and hearty Hamish.

So too was John B., dressed up in his carefully cleaned silk shirt. Elizabeth, Wilko and Jazz had accompanied him, moved by a mixture of curiosity, concern and support for people they'd quickly come to regard as friends.

The three sisters weren't with them.

Skinny Mary had the key and in the absence of any instructions otherwise, let everyone in.

For a few minutes everyone sat in their pews, looking vaguely bewildered. Then Rhona opened a song book and launched into *Morning Has Broken* – a hymn long before it became a folk singer's staple. The rest of the assembly joined in with gusto.

At the end of the singing Doc Wullie walked to the front of the room. He consciously stood in front of, not behind, the stone pulpit and spoke from the heart. He spoke of forgiveness, and love, and faith. No mention of fear or retribution.

"Does anybody else have owt they'd like tae say?" the doctor asked when he'd finished.

Elizabeth nudged John B. quietly and whispered, "Go on. You could…"

"Not my place to," he replied softly.

She squeezed his hand. "I think it is."

Meanwhile, Skinny Mary stood and nervously coughed. When she spoke, her voice was surprisingly clear. There was still some timidity, but there was something more underneath.

"Ah… Thank ye, Doc Wullie. It's… it's been a long time since there was lay preaching in Sron Dubh. Too long, maybe. Maybe it *is* time we looked to wer own hearts for guidance, and to the Scriptures of course – but not to the instructions of others. Not without clear thought, and prayer. I'd like… could I… speak next week?"

Alastair McAllister smiled. "Aye Mary, I think that'd be grand."

"Y'see Q? They don't need a leader, and even if they did, it's not me."

Rhona gave them a quick "Shh!" before leading a closing hymn – *Amazing Grace*.

As the song ended and the congregation shuffled, preparing to leave, the unfamiliar voice of Hamish Hine rang out. "Should we no' close in prayer?"

Everyone stopped. Many eyes closed and heads bowed.

The old distillery manager continued. "Oh Lord, we all have much tae be thankful for. Each in his or her own heart knows what most for themselves. I know ma own most precious gift. We've come through darkness. No' for the first time evil deeds ha' been done in Your name. We'll miss those we've lost, aye, and are grateful for those Ye sent tae help us in whatever manner. Noo we ask that Ye give us all the strength and the wisdom tae go on, and be better. Thank Ye, Lord. Amen."

Soon after, Wilko and Jazz were strolling hand in hand back towards their cottage. John B. and Elizabeth were seeing Rhona and Hamish home, intending to join their travelling companions afterwards for drinks and a meal of whatever could be pulled together from the kitchen. Toasted cheese seemed the likeliest prospect.

Wilko said, "Y'know, other than the odd wedding and funeral, that's the first church service I've been to since I was a kid. Not quite how I remember them."

Jazz was holding his hand. "Yeah, I remember a lot more pomp and cer emony. That was nice, but." She smiled at him. "We helped make that happen, mate. Us and the sisters and I think especially Elizabeth and John B."

"I suppose so. I dunno about magic, but stuff does happen around him. Weird stuff. But it does seem to work out. No way I'm telling him that, of course!"

"Of course! He'd never believe it if you did – probably think you'd been kidnapped by aliens or hypnotized or something." She stopped and pulled Wilko close. "Don't change," she said and kissed him.

*

After the service John B. returned the bike to Rose, Elizabeth following at the wheel of Rhona's car.

As he handed over the keys after putting the Indian back in the shed and replacing the canvas, the eldest of the sisters quietly said, "I'm aye proud of ye, *draoidh* and *fechter* both."

"Credit to you and yours too, you know," the wizard replied, moved by the old woman's comment. "You're a formidable team when you all want to be."

"Och aye – April and Effie have got good fine hearts an' minds, the both of them. Ye're never tae tell them I said so, mind!"

"I wouldnae dream o' it!" John B. replied with a laugh and a long hug.

Q joined in the good will, sharing her own affectionate embrace with Rose before walking hand in hand back to the car with the wizard.

*

As executor of Ishbell's estate, Craig was happy for the tenants in her guest cottage to stay on rent free. Having both experienced attempting to sleep in close proximity to Wilko's snoring, Elizabeth and John B. surprised the Hines by willingly staying on their 'cozy wee room'. The Tasmanian, while he'd never openly admit to the noise he made, was sufficiently self-aware to not be offended. Besides, having the small cottage to themselves was something to be treasured in their fledgling relationship.

Anastasia was recovered from outside the manse, and was put to good use by the Australians as they explored Islay while Jazz finished her work.

One night in the *Lost Goose* Jazz got a call on her mobile. Looking at the incoming number with a furrowed brow she retreated to a quiet corner and answered it.

The three Australians watched in concern, particularly Wilko. Only when the engineer started to smile broadly did they all relax.

The blonde came back to the bar with an evident spring in her step. "That job in Africa – I've gone and bloody got it!" she announced cheerfully.

"No graft or corruption involved?" asked Stewart cheekily.

Jazz' answering grin was just as mischievous. "Actually, yeah there was. But not mine! They're hiring me to repair the damage caused by the last bugger who bribed their way into the position."

The news made for a festive evening, although as the night wore on Wilko grew quieter.

Eventually, holding his girlfriend's hand he said quietly, "I'm realising how much I'm going to miss you."

"Why not come with me?"

300

The Tasmanian looked astonished. "To Africa? And do what? Get eaten?" he exclaimed.

Jazz ignored his tactlessness, correctly ascribing it to his distress. Instead she replied teasingly, "Maybe. I think you're a bit tasty."

John B. shrugged and said, "Go figure." Looking at his own beloved he added, "But then, there's clearly a lot I don't understand about women's taste."

With a playful squeeze of his leg Q replied, "Oh, we don't understand it either. But we're too nice to say so."

Soon after, the girls had gone off to the Ladies' together in the way that females seem to often do to the perplexity of males.

Wilko let the smile he'd maintained slip. Staring at his glass he said sadly to his old friend, "I'm just a poor little public servant, who's already taken too much leave. I don't have a high-flying job like Jazz, or a huge inheritance like you lucked onto."

Stewart gave a small nod of acknowledgement. The 'inheritance' was the story he used to explain the legacy of the Russian scientist whose work and death Wilko had seen but never really understood.

The smaller man continued. "I can't afford to keep jetting all over the world like you guys, and I'm not going to accept charity."

"I wouldn't insult you by offering it, mate, but I do wish circumstances would allow you to reconsider going with Jazz."

"Don't try your magic stuff on me, you know I don't believe in it," Wilko said resignedly.

Quietly the wizard replied, "Yeah, but I do."

The girls returned, and Wilko worked hard at cheering himself up. If they were going to be apart again for however long, he'd better enjoy the time they *did* have together.

Two days later the foursome were visiting the little village of Bridgend. Over a light lunch in the elegant pub dining room Elizabeth broke the news that she and John B. were about to head east to explore other parts of Scotland. She explained that the history bug had bitten her. Without going into detail she said that she wanted to learn more about the country's past and more particularly her own.

"Your family's Scottish, then? I suppose I should have guessed, with a name like McKew, eh?" smiled Jazz.

Elizabeth returned the smile. "I don't know much detail, but I aim to find out," she said between mouthfuls of pheasant pate.

"I'm just going along for the ride," said Stewart, who was looking forward to being absolutely anywhere with his green-eyed 'pretty lady'.

The next day Wilko and John B. at last managed to fit in a round of golf on the Machrie course. The Tasmanian won by a lengthy margin, which surprised neither of them. It had simply been a good day out. Elizabeth had spent a last day shopping and happily pottering around Bowmore while Jazz had been at work.

Before a final dinner at the *Harbourside* John B. and Elizabeth had paid a round of last visits to particular people. April Bromleigh had been the final name on their little list.

Coming to terms with Auld Wullie's absence, she was a little more sub-dued than when they'd all first met but still embraced them with warmth.

"I've a wee something for ye both tae remember Islay by," she said.

The brunette laughed and replied, "I don't think we're ever likely to for-get this place."

The old woman's eyes twinkled as she handed a paper bag to the wizard. "Aye, I dinna doubt ye're right there!"

Stewart withdrew the contents of the bag, his face split by a huge grin. It was a length of plaid – a rich tartan of purple and black.

302

April was happy with his reaction. "It's called 'Heritage Tartan'. Postie Mary managed tae get it sent over. I'm nae seamstress but I'm sure ye'll find somebody as ye go that can turn it intae summat ye like. Noo, ma bonnie lassie, we couldnae find a plaid that would quite go wi' yer eyes, but I hope ye like this."

She handed over a little white box that the Australian girl opened carefully. The green eyes widened in delight as she took out a silver brooch. It was round, with classical Celtic knot work carved around a large central stone. The stone was a translucent green-yellow.

"Yon's a cairngorm. I got it frae the Lapidary Club, an' Postie Mary helped tae set it. No' actually a jewel as such, ye ken, but there's no many aboot any more…"

"April, it's beautiful! Thank you!"

"Aye, well… these are frae the three o' us. The pair o' ye… well, ye've made a difference ye ken. So really, they're wee tokens frae the whole o' Sron Dubh. We can all be getting' on wi' things noo, thanks tae ye."

John B. took the old woman's hand. "It couldn't have happened without the three of you. You, especially – you've lost more than most…"

April's smile was a little wistful as she interrupted, "Nae lost, laddie. Nae lost. I've some braw memories tae sustain me for a while yet. And as tae after that, well, who's tae know, eh?"

The three fell into a group hug. It was a moment when more words would be superfluous.

*

The last hiccup came the next day at the little Islay airport. The plane that was to take Stewart and McKew over to Glasgow was having some small mechanical issue that took some fixing, but nobody seemed sure how long.

To kill some time, Wilko and Elizabeth both availed themselves of the airport's internet booths to catch up on world events. Jazz and John B.

companionably worked together on a magazine crossword.

In a little while the problem was resolved. Final hugs were exchanged, along with solemn undertakings to keep each other advised on where they were and what they were up to.

After a last wave to the departing pair, Wilko and Jazz turned to stroll out of the airport.

"Oops – hang on – I'd better log out," said the Tasmanian, returning to the computer terminal.

Suddenly Wilko gasped and sat heavily in the chair, momentarily lapsing into his goldfish impression.

"What's wrong, honey?" asked Jazz in alarm.

"Not wrong – just… wow!"

The engineer looked over his shoulder. On screen was an Australian stock market report. The Tasmanian indicated one particular line.

"Do you remember when we were all in Central Australia?" he asked.

"Of course, you dill. That's where we met, hey?"

"Yeah, yeah, of course, sorry… A bit distracted. Well, on the way back south we stumbled across a little opal mining operation that was just starting up. On a bit of a whim I bought a few hundred shares, thinking they might be a decent little investment. Later I figured that I wasn't thinking straight after everything that had happened. But now…"

Jazz grinned. "Turns out they were a decent investment after all?"

Wilko nodded and swallowed. "I bought those opal shares for a bit under $1 each when the company was starting up! They're up over $100 now – the company's signed some contract with the Japanese! They've added two decimal places to their price while I wasn't watching!"

"Two words for you honey. Sell. Now."

Still nodding, Wilko started to quickly send the appropriate instructions across the net.

"It's John's magic, isn't it?" said Jazz.

"Don't you dare tell him that! But whatever it is, I guess I'm not complaining."

"I should bloody hope not, mate. When you're done with that, we can see about getting you on the same flight as me. Assuming you're interested."

Wilko looked up at the pretty blonde standing beside him. "Yes," he said simply.

"Bloody excellent! Thank you!" She squeezed his shoulder. "You can call whoever back in Oz from the cottage after."

"After what?"

Jazz just looked at him and smiled.

*

In the sky above the west coast of Scotland, Q turned to the purple-shirted figure beside her. He'd been gazing into the middle distance for some time.

"You're a bit quiet, babe. What's wrong?" she asked.

John B. sighed and admitted, "Sorry, pretty lady. I don't mean to be a downer. I'm a bit worried about what the Reverend was saying. Maybe I am controlling people, without even realizing it. I mean, I don't understand how this magic works. What if…"

Elizabeth grabbed his hand and held it as she said sharply, "You listen to me! I don't know how it works either. It confuses me and frankly it scares me sometimes. But what I do know is you're a better man than that."

She drew the wizard close to her and kissed him. "Anyway," she said some moments later, "You don't really think you can control me, do you?"

John B. smiled as he looked into her eyes. "Wouldn't dream of it."

.oXXo.

-DEIREADH-

The *Dubious Magic* Books:

THE WIZARD OF WARAMANGA

THE CARVINGS OF COBBEMARMOO

THE MAD MACHINES OF MUNDARA

THE WARRIORS OF WIWO'OLE

Visit ***www.renoirwords.com***
or
www.patreon.com/Renoir

Next: Warriors have traversed the sea passage between the Shetland Islands and Norway from the Vikings to World War 2 and beyond. On both shores there's been death and intrigue. John B. and his beloved Q discover that hasn't changed. What they find is murder, mysticism and an unexpected old mate.

THE SAILS OF SVALGSAY
The Sixth Book of Dubious Magic